Hard Candy Saga

Hard Candy Saga

Amaleka McCall

www.urbanbooks.net

Urban Books, LLC
97 N18th Street
Wyandanch, NY 11798

ISBN 13: 978-1-62286-783-7
ISBN 10: 1-62286-783-1

First Trade Paperback Printing July 2016
Printed in the United States of America

10 9 8 7 6 5 4 3 2 1

Distributed by Kensington Publishing Corp.
Submit Orders to:
Customer Service
400 Hahn Road
Westminster, MD 21157-4627
Phone: 1-800-733-3000
Fax: 1-800-659-2436

*If you know both yourself and your enemy, you can
win a hundred battles without a single loss.*

The Art of War—Sun Tzu

*To know your enemy,
you must become your enemy.*

—Sun Tzu, *The Art of War*

Chapter 1

A raucous laughter erupted through the house. The strange men's voices were muffled through the homemade ski masks they wore.

"Hold ya head up, nigga!" one of the men instructed, taking delight in his victim's pain.

Easy did as told. His neck, snapping left and right as they took turns hitting him, was throbbing with an unbearable shooting pain. Another blow to the face caused something to crack at the base of his skull. It felt like a fire had erupted in his brain. The pain rendered him speechless with shock.

"You a tough guy? You ain't gon' try to scream, beg, ask for mercy or nothing?" one of the masked intruders belted out.

Easy felt the butt of a handgun connect with his skull. His pride wouldn't allow him to budge. He was cut from a different cloth. From a rough childhood, he had clawed his way to the top of the drug game. His reputation in the streets preceded him, and he wasn't going to show weakness now.

"A'ight, nigga, if you so tough, get up and save your family, motherfucker!" one of the masked men taunted, his breath hot on Easy's nose and lips.

Easy continued to let his head hang, his blood dripping on the expensive Oriental rug that covered his living room floor.

"You gon' die a pussy even if you don't say shit. We gon' teach you a lesson, since you think you're invincible in the streets," said the main instigator amongst the intruders. He wanted Easy to beg for his life.

Easy's body swayed from the incessant blows, but he still didn't lift his head or give the men the satisfaction of knowing they were hurting him. The high-pitched screams of his youngest daughter, however, penetrated his resolve.

"Daddy!" Brianna wailed from some distant place. "Daddy, help me!" she screamed again, this time her voice more high-pitched and frantic.

Easy opened his battered eyelids, turning his head painfully toward the sound of his youngest daughter's voice, which grew louder as the intruders dragged her by her hair to Easy's location.

"I want my daddy!" Brianna belted out again.

Brianna's voice caused a sharp pain in Easy's chest. Out of his severely swollen eyes, Easy could see his baby girl squirming and fighting, blood all over her face. His breathing became labored as a surge of hot adrenaline suddenly coursed through his veins.

It was the first time Easy felt nervous since the entire ordeal had begun. He had conditioned himself to believe that he would die in the game, so this end wasn't totally unexpected. But he'd never thought that his enemies would come after his family like this, especially when everybody in the streets knew his creed was "no women and children."

"Now, nigga, I think you gon' change ya fuckin' mind. I want you to whimper, beg, cry, like the pussy you are!" one of the men said.

Easy closed his eyes in anguish. He didn't want to see them kill his baby girl. At that moment, he envisioned himself killing all of the intruders slowly, torturing them mercilessly.

"You gonna beg or what?" another man asked him.

These men were hard-pressed to get Easy to beg, but it wasn't happening.

"Eric, please! Give them whatever they want. Please," Easy's wife, Corine, begged.

When the men had finished raping and beating Corine, they brought her to Easy's side, bound with nautical rope that had cut into her soft skin and left rope burns.

Easy had been unable to look at his wife until now. The only man to ever have her sexually, it hurt him to even imagine another man touching her, much less having sex with her. Easy was being emasculated before his family.

Corine let out another bloodcurdling plea. "Eric, please! I'm begging you!"

Easy didn't budge. He refused to open his mouth. It wasn't pride or selfishness; this moment was like living an art-of-war principle for him. The one rule he was going to live and die by was never to give in to the enemy when they would kill him, anyway. That would be like giving them double satisfaction.

"Eric!!!" Corine screamed, attempting to break through his calm reserve, but her pleas fell on deaf ears.

The intruder who had been taking the lead said, "A'ight, the tough-guy gangster is not going to fold on his own, so we'll fold for him."

"Take off her clothes," the man demanded.

The men were ramping up their act in a desperate attempt to get a rise out of Easy. When he heard the man's words, he began fidgeting against the layers and layers of duct tape and rope that held him captive. His knees burned from the kneeling position he was in. Easy felt as powerless as the first time he had been beaten by his caretakers as a child.

"Daddy!!" Brianna let out another throaty gurgle, her ponytail swinging as she tried to get away from her captors.

The first man slapped Brianna with so much force, she hit the floor like a rag doll.

Easy watched as one of the three men stood over her and began unzipping his pants. He bit down into his jaw, drawing his own blood. The metallic taste filled his mouth and made him thirst for revenge. Easy could feel vomit creeping up his esophagus, his blood boiling in his veins, but he did not utter a word.

"You still playing hard-ass? Well, I'm about to show you real hard-ass," the same intruder said. "Do it," he ordered, and the other two intruders forced Brianna's small legs open. The main man climbed between them and used his manhood as a weapon. The little girl let out an ear-shattering scream from the pain.

Easy rocked back and forth now, his fist clenched so tight, he was sure the bones in his knuckles would burst through the skin.

"Yeah, you ain't so tough now, Eric—I mean Easy," the rapist huffed as he banged into the little girl's flesh.

Easy finally recognized the man's voice. His heart began to pound, knowing who was perpetrating this heinous act on his daughter.

"Junior?" Easy rasped, blood dripping into his mouth and eyes.

"What, nigga? You calling out my fuckin' name?" Junior said as he continued to rape Easy's youngest child.

"Oh shit! Man, how the fuck did he know it was you?!" one of the other men asked nervously.

"Fuck him! You shoulda never crossed me, Easy," Junior said evilly.

"You're a dead man," Easy said, his voice muffled.

"No, you the dead man, bitch nigga!" another one of the intruders said, leveling his weapon at the back of Easy's head.

Candice sat up, and her heart racing. Sweat had drenched her sheets and her pajamas. She touched her face and realized she had been crying in her sleep. Using her hands, she wiped away her tears and took a deep breath.

She flopped back down on her pillow, realizing the nightmare was over. "This is getting ridiculous now," she whispered to herself as she tried to shake the horrible images from her mind. The dreams had now become a regular occurrence in her life.

Although she wasn't in the house when her entire family was massacred in cold blood, she was the one to find her mother, father, older brothers, and little sister. Candice had deduced that the killers had viciously raped and sodomized her mother and her eight-year-old sister. They had also brutally tortured and killed her father.

"I miss you, Daddy," Candice whispered. Then she looked over at the pillow next to her and relaxed a little. "Y'all still here, boyfriends? Always down to ride to the bloody end," she whispered, speaking to the two semi-automatic handguns—a .40-caliber Glock and a .357 SIG Sauer that she lay next to at all times.

She immediately thought of Tupac's lyrics and smiled. "All I need in this life of sin is me and my *boyfriends*, me and my *boyfriends*," Candice mouthed, changing the lyrics a little bit. She laughed at how she'd butchered the song. It still wasn't nearly as bad as what Jay-Z had done with Pac's song when he had done a remake, as an ode to Beyoncé.

The joke didn't last long enough to erase Candice's pain. She covered her eyes with her forearm. She wanted to feel better about today—the four-year anniversary of her family's murders.

Although she had a beautiful luxury apartment, high-end furniture, and flat-screen televisions in every room, she was lonely. Candice found that material things only made her feel better temporarily. Nothing could be a fix for the loss of her family. In fact, she often wondered what life would be like if her family was still alive. She envisioned her father hugging her and her baby sister as he showered them with gifts, his smooth Hershey's chocolate–colored face plastered with a smile. "Here, sweet Candy Cane," he would say. "This is for you from the only man who will ever love you."

Now eighteen, Candice wondered if her father, a revered figure on the streets of Brooklyn, would've threatened whichever boy she brought home to escort her to her high school prom. She knew for sure her two older brothers, Eric Jr. and Errol, would have been very protective of her. Candice was a tomboy, playing sports with her brothers and challenging them on a regular basis. She also wondered about her little sister, Brianna, who would've been twelve today. Candice could see her sister's moon-shaped face and tried to imagine what she would look like on her twelfth birthday. On her twelfth, Candice had gotten a Tiffany diamond pendant and necklace with the matching bracelet. Her father had also thrown her the biggest party that year.

A smile formed as she pictured her mother's face, the color of butterscotch, smooth and milky. Candice didn't always get along with her mother, but she knew her mother loved her just the same. If she was more girly, she was sure her mother would've been easier to get along with.

Candice could still hear her mother's voice fussing with her about coming home late from basketball practice. *"Candice, why are you so late? You think the sun rises and sets around you? Eric, you have to do something about that girl! We are not going to keep waiting for her to eat dinner and to get things started in this house."*

Candice's father, of course, would jump to her defense. *"Corine, you leave my little Candy Cane alone."*

The day her family was murdered, Candice was rushing home from basketball practice. As she exited the A train station at a feverish pace, her basketball shorts whisked back and forth in the wind, and sweat made her white tee stick to her athletic chest and abs. She whizzed past the usual corner and stoop hangouts in the neighborhood.

Candice just knew her mother was at home beefing over her chronic tardiness. It was Brianna's eighth birthday party, and the family had gathered to celebrate. Though it was still the middle of the week, a large party for family friends was planned for the upcoming Saturday.

Candice slowed her sprint to a walk as she neared home. She could only imagine the spread her mother would have laid out. A grand birthday cake that looked more like a wedding cake, with purple and white frosting that would surely be the center of attraction. (Purple was Brianna's favorite color.) There would probably be enough food to feed the entire United States military. The Hardaways never spared any expenses when it came to their children's birthdays.

Candice had been told several times to be home on time. In fact, her father had told her that he would have one of his workers pick her up from the gym, but she protested, saying, "Daddy, I'm old enough to get home by myself. Getting picked up is for lames."

Candice hated being treated like a little kid. She was fourteen and needed to be a little independent. Her dad didn't agree with her taking public transportation, but she was the one person who could have her way with him. She was her dad's first daughter, and his heart definitely belonged to her.

When she got to her brownstone, she realized her keys were in the pocket of her jeans, which were inside her gym bag.

Candice placed her bag down on the stoop and fished around in her gym bag until she located the keys. As she was about to insert the key in the door, she noticed something that looked like blood on the doorknob, but she couldn't be sure. Confused, she used her shirt to try to wipe the substance off, twisting her shirt over the knob to clean it, and the door clicked open.

Candice knew her father would have a fit if he found out any of them had left the door unlocked. They all knew what their father, known in the streets as "Easy," did for a living, and so did the entire city of New York. With Easy's line of work came danger and high paranoia, so he'd always preached to them about locking doors, making sure the home security system was on, and being cognizant of their surroundings.

Candice pushed the door open cautiously and walked into the grand foyer, where she noticed a trail of bloody sneaker prints. She dropped her gym bag and covered her nose with her sleeve. The smell of raw meat gone bad made her gag. Swallowing hard, her heart began pounding as she moved forward slowly. Although there was loud music blaring around the house, she thought the house was eerily desolate.

"Daddy?" Candice called out as she continued to creep forward. Her legs felt like butter melting against the hot sun, and an eerie, unsettling feeling took over her stomach. "Daddy! Mommy!" she called out as the hysteria began to build.

She reached the huge wooden sliding doors that led to their living room. "Daddy!" Candice cried out in a shaky soprano voice when she noticed blood seeping under the door. A tingling sensation came over her body as she reached out and slid the doors open. An unknown force seemed to be propelling her forward, but her mind screamed, *Danger!*

Candice's eyes popped and her mouth fell open at the shocking sight before her. Open, vacant eyes, dead and unforgiving, stared back at her. Urine ran involuntarily down her legs.

***

Candice began to cry again. Her fists were balled so tight, it caused the veins in her hands to pulse fiercely against her skin. The hot tears leaked from her eyes and pooled in her ears. These tears, four years later, made her even angrier than she was the day she'd discovered their bodies.

She pulled herself up out of bed and stalked over to her dresser. She lifted the family portrait off the mahogany wood and ran her fingers over each face, sucking in the sobs now. She would've given anything in the world to have her family back. After finding them all dead, she wasn't even able to attend their funerals. That was too risky.

Whoever killed her family thought that they had taken out every member. The news had reported that the entire family, including all of the children, had been massacred, so no one knew there was one Hardaway still alive. Candice didn't just lose her family, but her identity as well, as she was forced to begin a new life.

Candice used the pad of her thumb to dust off the glass that covered the photograph. Gently placing it back on the dresser, she looked into the mirror. Her eyes were dull and sad, but familiar. They were her father's eyes. She swallowed hard. She contemplated observing this miserable anniversary by staying in bed all day long, sulking and crying, but she knew that wasn't an option. She had a mission to carry out.

She walked over to the far left of her bedroom, where she had set up a mini office, complete with a computer, a small file cabinet, a safe, and a printer that doubled as a fax and scanner. Although she didn't need to really work or go to school in the traditional sense, she had set up her bedroom like a college dormitory.

Before she sat down to check her e-mails, she looked up at the cork bulletin board that hung above the computer desk. Smirking, Candice examined all of the grainy pictures she had thumbtacked to the gauzy cushion. She looked each man in the eye and studied his features, as she had done so many times before.

Her heart thundered with excitement. "One by one, day by day, I'm coming for y'all. Y'all motherfuckers ain't never met candy harder than this piece. Hope y'all niggas got a serious sweet tooth."

Chapter 2

Candice jiggled her key in the familiar old rusted door lock. "Why the hell doesn't he get this shit fixed already?" She grunted in frustration. "Unless he got this shit booby-trapped again." Finally the lock clicked. "Damn! About time." Candice sighed and rushed through the door. She was glad she had kept her keys to Uncle Rock's apartment after she turned eighteen and moved out.

Everything was in its usual place. The sun streaming through Uncle Rock's old-fashioned metal blinds accentuated the dust particles on his dilapidated furniture. She shook her head. "He must really miss my ass," she whispered. When she lived there, she dusted and kept the place clean.

"Uncle Rock!" Candice called out. She didn't get an answer. "Uncle Rock, you here?" she called again. There was no sign of her uncle, except for the herbal tea packet on the table, which indicated he'd had his liquid breakfast.

She heard a noise coming from the small bathroom to her left. Placing her face up against the raggedy wooden door, she shouted, "Uncle Rock, you all right?"

No answer.

Candice knew something was wrong. She rattled the door-knob, but the door was locked. Candice's uncle was a master locksmith and booby trapper, so getting inside could prove very difficult.

Candice was worried sick about her uncle Rock. She knew he wasn't well but wasn't sure what exactly was wrong with him. Lately he had changed. He didn't exercise anymore. She remembered a time when Uncle Rock would ask her to load his back down with the heaviest books in his library so he could do push-ups with them on his back. An impossible feat it seemed, but he would execute it effortlessly. Not anymore.

Uncle Rock was a very private man, who didn't complain when he was in pain; in fact, he rarely complained about anything.

Candice decided to wait for him to come out of the bathroom on his own time, so she resigned herself to the threadbare sofa that sat in the middle of the nearly empty living room. She placed her fist up against her cheek in sheer boredom because there wasn't even a television in the apartment. Now that she thought back, she didn't know how she had ever survived as a teenager living there with no electronic entertainment. Maybe that was why as soon as she got her own place, she purchased every gadget imaginable, including flat-screen TVs, Blu-ray DVD players, and iPods. You name it, she had it.

The one thing Uncle Rock did own was shelves and shelves of books. When Candice first began living with him, she was so bored, she read every book in his library, including *The Art of War* and *The Anarchist Cookbook*. Looking around the room, she remembered her first night at Uncle Rock's house, four years ago today.

Faced with the massacred bodies of her family members, Candice bent over and retched up the contents of her stomach onto the floor. A fine sheen of sweat covered her entire body, and her legs and hands shook fiercely. She wiped her mouth with the back of her hands and stumbled toward the front door and down the outside steps.

Terrified, Candice fled her house and ran down her block. When she got to the corner, she was out of breath, so she leaned up against the base of a silver lamppost to get her bearings. She whirled her head around in several directions. Although there was no one behind her or even looking at her, she felt like she was being chased. Her mind was flooded with wild thoughts, especially, *What if my family's killers are looking for me right now?* She didn't know where to go or what to do.

Candice's father had always taught her and her siblings to be wary of the police, so she never even considered calling 9-1-1. But then she remembered something her father told her one day, after she'd heard him arguing with one of his workers named Junior.

"Daddy, what's wrong?" she had asked her father as he paced the floor, clearly fuming mad. She wasn't used to seeing him so upset and angry.

Inhaling deeply, he walked over to her and stroked her head. Candice could tell he was fighting to keep his composure, since he didn't like to display anger in front of his children.

He bent down and got on eye level with her and said gently, rustling his hands in her hair, "If anything ever happens to me or your mother, you and your brothers and sister run straight to Uncle Rock. He is the only man I trust with your life, Candy Cane, even if your mother thinks you're hard like a boy." Then he picked her up and hugged her tightly.

Candice could tell he was in a better mood already. "Daddy," she said breathlessly as he held her tight in his arms.

"Yes, Candy Cane?"

"I can't breathe."

Candice faked like she was suffocating, and they both busted out laughing.

With the memory of that day flooding her mind, Candice fled to the one person her father had trusted with her life.

Gasping and sweaty, she banged on the door three times before Joseph "Rock" Barton finally pulled back the door to his tiny apartment. Candice's chest was heaving and she was covered in sweat. Not only had she practically run the entire distance on foot, but it had taken her a while to remember the specific neighborhood and house where he lived.

Candice knew she looked half-crazed, her eyes stretched wide and wild, her body trembling with suppressed emotions. She looked up at Uncle Rock and opened her mouth, but no words would come out. She then jumped into his arms, which caught him completely off guard. If he wasn't the master of balance and coordination, the jolt would have sent both of them tumbling to the ground.

Shocked and at a loss for words, he stiffly held on to Candice's trembling form. Of course, Rock recognized Candice as the eldest daughter of his longtime friend and business associate, Eric "Easy" Hardaway. Candice was sobbing into his neck, while her long legs dangled from Rock's rigid arms.

At fourteen, Candice was tall for her age, and she loved to play basketball. This much Rock knew about her, since he was a regular at the Hardaway home. Easy had always made him feel like a part of the family, even instructing his kids to address him as Uncle Rock, which he found deeply amusing.

Uncle Rock stood rigidly, holding Candice as she cried. This was the closest human contact he'd had in fifteen years, aside from the handshakes and shoulder bumps he shared with Easy whenever they met to discuss business. Candice finally moved her wet face from Uncle Rock's neck and spoke through her tears. Rock's ears were ringing, and his stomach muscles clenched anxiously. He knew he wouldn't like what was about to follow.

"Daddy told me . . . that if . . . if anything ever . . . ever happened to him and Mommy that I am supposed to come to you," she managed to blurt through gasps of breath.

Rock flexed his jaw so hard, his temples throbbed from the pressure.

But instead of continuing the explanation, Candice burst into more racking sobs.

Rock walked over to his raggedy couch and placed her down on it. Then he sat across from her in his favorite recliner, a beat-up, old-fashioned La-Z-Boy that looked as if it had been to Vietnam with him when he was in the Marines. The chair had holes everywhere, and the cushioning was spilling out in spots.

Rock looked around at the shabby décor, old moth-eaten curtains, scratched and chipped wood furniture, mismatched table chairs and worn-out couch and chair full of holes. For the first time, he felt slightly embarrassed about his home. He never had visitors, except for Easy, so he never paid much attention to such things.

"Candy, what happened to your daddy?" he finally asked, his voice cracking. He didn't talk much, but when he did, it took a while for his vocal cords to work.

Candice looked over at him with her swollen eyes. "They are all dead! Somebody killed them. There was a lot of blood. All of them! Bri-Bri was naked and real beat-up. Mommy was tied up, and Errol had a cut on his neck. The birthday cake was still on the table, and Daddy's head was busted open in the back. Eric Junior's head was like, like almost missing. He was right by the door. There was a gun. And, and they all had tape and rope on their arms and legs!"

Rock listened intently, his face stoic, but his blood rushing hot in his veins, as Candice wailed, incoherent at times, describing the scene she'd come across. He was having an Incredible Hulk moment and felt like he'd just explode out of his clothes and turn into a monster. Her description of the scene was making him physically sick. Rock couldn't help but think that what had happened was partly his fault, a residual effect of a hit he had recently carried out for Easy, killing one of Easy's top workers, and an overwhelming sense of guilt transformed his mood.

He placed his head in his hands and squeezed his balding head. He felt off-kilter, like the room was spinning off its axis. Easy was his only friend and family. Rock was grinding his back teeth and didn't even realize it. Feeling angry enough to kill someone with his bare hands, he gripped the edges of the recliner to prevent himself from bolting out of the chair.

"Can I please stay here with you?" Candice pleaded. "I don't have nobody else."

The question reverberated in Rock's ears like a loud explosion. He knew he wasn't equipped to take care of a fourteen-year-old girl. His lifestyle, his home, and his profession were not at all conducive to child rearing.

Rock stared at the helpless teenager, speechless. A self-proclaimed loner, he hated noise and relished quiet. He didn't speak much and often stayed up all night long studying his craft and doing research on his marks. All he had in his home was a bed, recliner, couch, chairs, bookcase, refrigerator, stove, and very little food. He was a dedicated professional and spent nearly all of his time preparing for his hits.

Yet, something deep inside his chest stirred him to life. He wanted to be there for her, but he knew he had long since closed his heart to love or affection, which she clearly needed right now.

"Uncle Rock, did you hear me?" Candice asked softly. She could tell he was uncomfortable with the situation, but something in his eyes told her he would keep her safe.

***

"You're here early," Uncle Rock's voice boomed behind Candice.

She jumped, startled out of her daydream, and turned toward his voice, and a sense of panic set in when she looked at him. He looked unbelievably thinner and older than the last time she'd seen him, two weeks ago.

She furrowed her eyebrows with worry. "Uncle Rock, are you okay?" she asked, noticing that he dabbed at his mouth with a rolled-up white towel. "I wish you would tell me what's wrong. Since I moved out, you seem like you're sick. Please tell me what's wrong," she pleaded, the corners of her mouth pulled down in dismay.

Rock walked over to his raggedy La-Z-Boy recliner and flopped down. He clutched the towel like Linus would his security blanket.

"Are you going to work today? Because, on a day like this, I think you should take off. It's not like you need that job, anyway." Rock was an expert at changing the subject to avoid questions about his health.

Candice rolled her eyes in frustration. "Yeah, I'm going in. I just came by to check on you. I wish you would tell me what's wrong. You've been losing weight, and you haven't been working out. We haven't even been to the gun range in weeks," she said, pressing the issue, concern lacing her words.

"I'm a big boy. You need to stay focused on taking that test and getting your diploma."

Although Easy had left a trunk full of money behind in Rock's care, which he had given to Candice when she turned seventeen, Rock still wanted her to get her high school equivalency diploma. He had spent years homeschooling Candice during the day after she had moved in with him. At the time, he believed that it was the only way to protect her. In Rock's assessment, the killers assumed they had killed the entire Hardaway family, so Candice couldn't risk going back to school.

Rock had made all of the funeral arrangements, since Easy didn't have relatives and Corine's had disowned her after her marriage. However, he'd made sure that Candice had a very private service prior to the public viewings and burials. Rock was amazed at how many of Easy's own enemies had come to the services just to make sure he was really dead.

Candice sucked her teeth and stood up. She knew Uncle Rock meant well, but she wasn't interested in taking the GED test. There was only one thing she was interested in these days.

"I gotta go," she said. "I just came by to let you know that I'm okay with today. I know I usually fall apart on this day, but for some reason today I feel fine about it. I'm going to work."

Candice had tried to convince Rock that she was working as a bartender during the evenings and studying for her GED during the day. But Rock knew better. He eyed her up and down seriously. He knew when she was lying and telling the truth. Rock knew exactly what had her preoccupied, and it definitely wasn't a job or a test.

Over the years he'd studied Candice like she was one of his marks, watching her body language and listening for hidden meanings behind her words. Over the last four years, he had come to know her like she was his own child. He had actually started to feel like she was his daughter.

Rock knew when Candice was hurting or happy. He was there for her when she got her first period and when she had nightmares about the murders. More importantly, he helped teach her the necessary skills for surviving in the streets.

At first Rock tried to hide his profession from Candice, but she was too sharp. Candice watched Uncle Rock leave on some days, dressed in all black with his long, black military bag thrown over his shoulder. She would take those rare opportunities to search his bookshelf and his nightstand drawers. Uncle Rock always had addresses written on small slips of paper, and each time he returned, he'd burn the papers in an ashtray. He also owned a large box filled with brand-new black leather gloves. Candice noticed he would get a new pair from the box each time. She even recalled her father instructing him to "make that nigga ghost."

One day after Uncle Rock had prepared Candice a sandwich with chips and a soda, her favorite meal, she pushed away from the table as he was preparing to leave and confronted him. "Uncle Rock, I know you kill people for a living," she blurted out matter-of-factly. "I want to learn how to do it, you know, so I can get back at the guys who killed my family."

Rock, caught off guard, dropped his black bag on the floor and swiped his black knitted hat off his head. Nostrils flared, he stormed into his bedroom and slammed the door.

Candice stood in the middle of the floor at a loss for words. She had never seen Uncle Rock react so strongly to anything she had said. She began to cry. She knew she had overstepped some unknown boundary. She thought for sure he would kick her out, and her family's murderers would then find her.

Candice pleaded with him through the door to come out. She apologized over and over again, until she finally fell asleep on the floor in front of his bedroom door.

When Uncle Rock finally emerged, he picked her up from the floor and put her in her bed. He sat and stared at her for hours, contemplating how to handle her request. The next day, as soon as Candice had awaken, Uncle Rock sat her down and gave her a stern lecture. He told her he was not a killer or hit man, but a "cleaner." He explained that cleaners simply rid the world of despicable people who make the world unsafe, while hit men killed for their own selfish gain.

That made sense to Candice, who had listened intently. Then she begged Rock to teach her everything he knew about being a cleaner.

Reluctantly, Rock went about training Candice, little by little, showing her the real way to hold a gun and how to use her sights. He also warned her against using the "sideways cowboy style" that hood niggas liked so much, where they ended up always missing their intended targets and shooting innocent bystanders. He also taught her the two-handed, thumb-over-thumb hold and worked with her for hours on her grip.

"Squeeze with your support hand and relax your strong hand," he told her, after explaining the different role each hand played.

Candice found that this method was quite effective at keeping the weapon from flying up out of her small hands whenever she shot.

Uncle Rock made her stand with the gun in her hands in the proper hold and with her arms extended for long periods of time.

"This is so you never get tired in a gunfight," he explained. "You need to be able to shoot until the threat is eliminated."

He also tested Candice on the nomenclature of several types of weapons, including the MP5. Rock took Candice to a gun range in New Jersey and trained her until all of her shots were center of mass on the targets. He even taught her about different types of cover, showing her how to blade her body behind something as skinny as a pole and become nearly invisible to a distant target.

Candice had the most fun when Uncle Rock showed her how to shoot from a prone position and from a fetal position with the gun between her knees. Hitting a target center of mass while lying down on her side and stomach was exciting.

"See, as long as you use your sights and have the proper trigger pull, you can hit anything from any position," Uncle Rock told her.

Uncle Rock spent an entire week using himself as a crash test dummy as he taught Candice how to make a person catatonic with pressure points on the body, like the jugular notch and brachial stun. When she placed her index and middle fingers into his jugular notch and applied pressure, she forced his large body to his knees.

Gasping for breath afterwards, Uncle Rock told her she was a natural. He'd even tested her on the arteries she needed to hit "to make someone bleed out in less than ten seconds." Candice had remembered the term *femoral artery* by equating the word *femoral* with *female*, she being a female that now knew how to kill someone in ten seconds.

Rock didn't know if it was his overwhelming sense of loyalty to Easy or guilt that made him take care of Candice and guard her with his own life. Today he watched his protégée prance toward his apartment door as she prepared to leave. She'd grown into a beautiful young lady, a far cry from the rail-thin tomboy that had shown up on his doorstep.

Rock had protested initially when she first told him she planned to move out. He knew deep down inside that one day she'd grow up and leave his home. He also knew of her intentions on the streets. Rock had failed to take revenge on the people responsible for the massacre of the Hardaway family. At the time, he felt he was too emotional after the murders to exact revenge, but he'd also been very preoccupied with caring for Candice. He refused to carry out hits while his emotions were running wild. Being emotional while working could cost him his life. Rock's philosophy was that emotions weakened one's natural instincts.

In the end, all of the suspects ended up literally getting away with murder. Rock knew who they were and their street affiliations. The streets were always talking. He had even taken pictures of them and done a history workup on them, complete with addresses and criminal histories, and had stored the information in a secure hiding spot from Candice. Or so he thought.

Rock watched Candice as she walked out of the door. He started coughing fiercely as soon as she left. He coughed until he began to gag. He looked down at the towel he held to his mouth and stared at the Rorschach inkblot pattern of bright red blood. He didn't know how much longer he'd be able to hide his illness from Candice, whose face he could see in his mind's eye.

He closed his eyes and felt nostalgic about how far he'd come and how much he had grown to love the little girl who had shown up at his door so many years ago.

Rock had been drafted into the United States Marines when he was just seventeen years old. He never protested the draft because he'd grown up extremely poor. When the United States first went to war with Vietnam, he'd heard on the streets that the soldiers were being paid high salaries and provided with great benefits, so he didn't bother to dodge the draft like some of the guys he knew from his neighborhood. When he left for the war, his mother never shed a tear for him. He had been a great burden to her, another mouth to feed. He'd been sent to Vietnam a boy and returned a man.

Rock joined the Marine Corps Forces Special Operations Command and became a trained Scout Sniper. He had served the United States proudly until he was assigned to a POW (prisoner of war) rescue mission. Rock was to be the countersniper assigned to assist the Force Recon officers, a group of elite reconnaissance Marines who carried out deep reconnaissance operations.

When he and the other highly trained Marines arrived in the remote village in Vietnam, they had instructions and intelligence information necessary to find the American POWs. But all of those plans went out of the window when they arrived and found nothing but women and children in the camp. Some of the Recon Marines, believing that the women were hiding and covering up for the Vietnamese soldiers, began beating and torturing some of the women and children, cutting them with knives and pouring salt on their wounds, and removing fingernails and toenails. Of course, these methods didn't work. The intel was bad from the very beginning, and the Vietnamese civilians suffered enormously because of it.

Rock witnessed a Marine attempt to rape and sodomize a five-year-old Vietnamese girl. The white Marine had been behaving erratically throughout the entire mission. He would laugh at nothing in particular, and he liked to collect bones from dead bodies they'd pass in the jungle. The Marine grabbed the little girl, kicking and screaming, from her mother's arms. He used a hunting knife to cut away her clothes. Then he threw her tiny naked body down on the ground and dropped to his knees in front of her, as her mother let out bloodcurdling screams from behind.

"Shut the fuck up!" He cracked the mother in the face with the butt of his gun.

Some of the Marines watched, while others turned away.

Rock's heart throbbed against his chest bone as the Marine attempted to mount the girl. He quickly took action, by grabbing him by his neck and dragging him away from the little Vietnamese girl.

Some of the white Marines yelled at Rock.

"What the fuck you doing, Barton? You nigger!"

Rock ignored them. He took the Marine by the scruff of his neck and proceeded to bang his head face-first into a huge tree trunk, rendering him unconscious instantly. The Marine's face split open like a watermelon.

But Rock was possessed. He continued to bang the Marine's head on the tree. When he fell to the ground, he started to kick him all over his body.

Rock ended up beating his fellow Marine to death and shooting two others who tried to stop him. Rock went on the run in the Vietnamese jungle for two weeks after that, surviving on sheer instincts and highly classified countersniper training he'd received from the military.

When American soldiers finally found him, they treated him worse than some of the Vietnamese prisoners being held by the Americans. He was beaten and tortured. Rock was dishonorably discharged from the Marine Corps and held in a military prison for a court-martial.

However, it wasn't long before the CIA heard of his superior abilities to move alone in the jungles of Vietnam. And they offered Rock a deal he could not refuse. Rock became a covert operations officer for the CIA in lieu of being court-martialed and sent to prison for the murder of his fellow soldiers. Serving as a CIA covert ops officer was ultimately where Rock learned how to make himself invisible and to make people disappear. The government had trained him to be a first-class "cleaner."

When Rock finally returned to the United States after the war, he chose to live a demure, circumspect life. He ended up in his hometown of Brooklyn, New York, where he rented a small apartment and began his very low-key life. Rock would leave his apartment once a day to purchase food and staples he needed for that day, frequenting the same store each day, a small bodega two blocks up from his apartment, which was where he'd first met Eric "Easy" Hardaway. Rock always felt that their meeting was predestined.

It was a hot summer night, and Rock had already turned in for the day. He'd gone on his morning store run and purchased some of his usual food items, like green tea, whole wheat bread, and skim milk. On that particular day, after the sun had gone down, Rock started feeling slightly ill. Rock was never one to get sick and could count on one hand the number of times he'd had so much as a common cold. But, that day, he had an incessant pounding in his head and a very high fever. He'd tossed and turned for hours before deciding he needed to get some pain relief.

When he got to the bodega, he noticed several guys hanging around talking and several skeletal-looking men and women passing the guys every couple of minutes. Rock wasn't stupid. It was clear to him that there was drug dealing going on. He wasn't judgmental about anyone's hustle. Some of the guys noticed Rock, and a few of them made comments.

"Look at old dude walking around like the grim fuckin' reaper," one of the young guys commented about his all-black clothes and his size, garnering laughs from the others.

"I see that big-ass nigga e'ery day, and he always look scary as hell. That m'fucka taller than Shaq," another one of the guys joked.

"I don't care how big that bitch-ass nigga is. His ass better be scared of this," the first guy said, lifting his shirt to display a firearm in the front waistband of his pants.

Rock continued to walk into the store. All of his life people had commented on his size—six feet nine inches tall and a good two hundred and sixty pounds. Rock's skin was like onyx, and his eyes were perfectly round, like big dark brown marbles. His hands were so big, he could palm a basketball and get his fingers around the top and bottom of the ball.

Rock took notice of all of the men and made mental notes of their most prominent features. He locked eyes with one of the young guys who didn't make any comments about his appearance. Rock noticed that the guy was quiet, stood alone, and did his hand-to-hand sales very discreetly. Rock could tell this young dude didn't want fame and glory, unlike the other loudmouth punks on the corner. Something about the quiet kid bothered him.

Rock entered the store and stood at the counter buying his BC Powder for the pounding pain in his head. As the clerk rang up his purchase, Rock kept his eye on the corner boys. Rock shook his head left and right, the pain nearly blinding him. But he continued to watch the quiet boy, sensing that something was very wrong. Finally, Rock waved it off, silently scolding himself for being paranoid. He decided to go home and mind his business.

As he was preparing to leave the store, he noticed that the quiet kid had suddenly started arguing with a girl. The skinny, poorly dressed girl looked like she was on some serious drugs. Her clothes hung off her bony body, and dirt was visible on her pants and the front of her shirt. And her hair was a wild bird's nest atop her head.

Rock could see her wagging a skeletal finger at the quiet boy, who was up in her face by now. He stopped for a minute and watched the exchange, but he couldn't hear the words.

The quiet kid, a scowl on his face, suddenly grabbed the horrible-looking girl around her neck and picked her up off her feet. She was dangling like a choked chicken.

The other boys on the corner laughed, jumping up and down, egging the quiet boy on.

Then, out of the corner of his left eye, Rock noticed a strange man in a swinging black trench coat rush up from the corner behind the quiet kid. Rock was immediately on alert. A trench coat in the sticky August heat was a definite red flag.

The quiet corner boy dropped the girl back to her feet and gave her a kick in her ass, and she scrambled up off the ground, still screaming and arguing with him.

The stranger in the trench coat seemed to pick up his stride.

Rock noticed the gun that the man had secreted up against his leg. All of a sudden, Rock was on the move. He dropped the BC Powder on the floor and rushed out of the bodega. He took five huge strides and was standing behind the quiet kid as the trench coat stranger got right up on him.

The trench coat stranger with the gun was caught off guard by Rock's interference, but he still attempted to raise his weapon hand. He never got the chance, though.

Rock grabbed the man's wrist and clamped down on his "God's notch," and the bones in the man's wrist immediately crumbled under Rock's grasp. The man cried out in pain as the gun fell to the ground.

When the guys on the corner noticed the commotion, they all began to scatter.

"Oh shit! A gun!" one of them yelled.

Rock realized his first impression of the so-called tough guys on the corner was right. They were pussies.

The girl who was engaged in the argument with the quiet corner boy immediately stopped screaming and rushed to the aid of her man, who was rolling around on the ground in severe pain. "Baby, you okay?" she cried out.

Rock picked up the man's gun, dropped the magazine out of it, dismantled the slide, and threw the bottom half of the gun at him.

"Oh shit! That bitch tried to set me up!" the quiet corner boy screamed, his heart racing as he realized what had just happened.

Rock nodded in agreement.

"Fuck! Thank God you were here. That nigga woulda shot me right in the back of my fuckin' head," the quiet boy said to Rock.

Rock nodded again, but still no words.

"I'ma fuckin' kill him!" the boy screamed.

Rock put his hand up to the boy's chest to stop him. "Not here. Not now," he said calmly.

The boy backed down. Something about Rock's words, the way he said them, had calmed him. "I'm Eric," he said, introducing himself, "but everybody calls me Easy."

"Rock." He shook Easy's hand firmly.

"Yo, man, how can I repay you for that shit?" Easy asked as he eyed the girl and the guy scurrying away.

"No need." Rock handed Easy the magazine full of .40-caliber rounds and the slide of his would-be assassin's gun.

"Nah, there has got to be something. Some money, some food, clothes, something," Easy said.

"Just go inside and get my BC Powder. I have the worst headache," Rock said.

Easy scrambled to do as Rock asked, and their friendship was sealed after that day.

Rock had never given Easy a price for saving his life, but as Easy moved up in the game, he continued to look out for Rock. Every day when Rock went to the store, Easy would pay for his groceries, and they'd walk and talk.

Soon, Easy graduated in the game from corner boy to boss, but he continued to frequent the neighborhood just to visit Rock. He and Rock had gone from walking and talking, to riding in whatever luxury car he had on a particular day. Easy and Rock would have long, serious talks about life.

Rock grew to trust Easy, which wasn't an uncomplicated undertaking. Easy also grew to trust Rock. In fact, Rock was the one person Easy trusted with his life. Easy trusted Rock so much, he shared his childhood with him, specifically his being born into the game. Literally.

Easy's mother was one of the first female drug dealers in Brooklyn. His father had turned her on to the game, and they were an unstoppable duo, until jealous rival dealers executed them both. Easy grew up with his grandmother, who he believed died of a broken heart shortly after his mother's murder. Then he moved in with an aunt, who treated him like shit and let her husband beat Easy at will. Though Easy didn't have an easy life, he was convinced that he knew how to hold his own in the streets.

Rock wasn't impressed. Easy still had a lot to learn. In turn, Rock revealed to Easy his talents as a professional cleaner for the CIA.

Easy was impressed. Sometimes he would joke with Rock and say stuff like, "Get the fuck outta here, Rock! That's some shit out of the movies."

Then came the day when Easy's life hung in the balance once again. A rival hustler had threatened his life and murdered one of Easy's workers, to drive home the point. This time, Easy hired Rock to take care of his problem. The job was done so well, the police never found the man or any trace of him, despite the number of missing persons posters hanging in the neighborhood. Rock had made him ghost and had quickly become Easy's personal hired cleaner.

Easy used Rock to carry out his most high-profile hits, but no one on the streets knew about Rock, who was like a ghost himself. He'd appear when Easy needed him, and disappear just as quickly. He could wipe out a person's entire identity, but he did have one rule that he never broke—no women and no children. That became Easy's street creed as well. Rock didn't mind carrying out Easy's hits because, unlike the government, for which he carried out hits on people simply because they had information that made the government look bad, Easy killed only people who tried to harm him or his family.

When Easy met Corine, he went to Rock for advice about whether or not he should trust her. Corine, the daughter of a retired NYPD homicide detective, had been forbidden to see Easy. Easy desperately needed Rock's advice, but Rock, unable to speak about women or love with Easy, clammed up and cut his visit with Easy short when the subject of Corine came up. And Easy didn't push the issue.

It was a sensitive topic for Rock. The one woman he'd loved had gotten pregnant by another man by the time he returned from the war. At least that was what she told Rock when he returned home to find her with a son. Rock was devastated. The entire time he was at war, she had been his motivation to return home.

Afterward, Rock gave up on the concept of love and marriage, and anything associated with it, and decided to never let another woman into his heart. Aside from occasional sex to satisfy his basic needs, he never deluded himself with notions of love again.

Rock didn't attend the wedding, nor did Corine's parents, who had disowned her for associating with street trash. When Easy began having children, Rock's heart began to soften a bit. He would attend the christenings, birthday parties, and any other special occasions, and slowly but surely, the Hardaway family became like his own.

Rock coughed up more blood as he doubled over in pain. Each day, the burning and pain seemed to intensify. He was starting to wonder if he should have started the chemotherapy. Rock wasn't a strong believer in modern medicine, and his time with the government had made him paranoid. He knew all about doctors experimenting on perfectly healthy people, especially poor people with little or no medical coverage. Even after his diagnosis, Rock believed that the government had placed the cancer in his body as a way to, over time, eliminate him. He held a lot of government secrets and was also one of the few highly trained operatives that could probably take down an entire army platoon alone.

A nagging thought in the back of his mind was causing him to second-guess his decision to refuse treatment. The thought of leaving Candice behind all alone was unbearable. The doctors had already told him that if he didn't get chemotherapy and radiation treatment immediately, he would not make it another two months. Rock had a difficult decision to make, especially now that he knew Candice was venturing into very dangerous territory.

Chapter 3

Candice took the last bobby pin out of her doobie and threw it on the dresser.

Candice bopped to Usher's lyrics as she sauntered over to her full-length mirror and checked her face, hair, clothes and, most importantly, her assets—tits and ass—for good measure. "Candy, you's a fierce bitch when you wanna be," she said out loud to herself as she looked over her shoulder at her almost heart-shaped backside which made her leggings look like they'd been painted on. On most days Candice wore jeans or sweats. Although she'd grown into a beautiful young lady, she preferred to be tomboy-comfortable rather than sexy. Candice thought her looks were merely average on a regular day, but her smooth skin, full lips, long, slim legs, and flat stomach had garnered her more than a little bit of attention on the streets. And attention was exactly what she was seeking tonight. She wanted to be noticed and ultimately accepted by the most important players in the game.

Candice had taken the first lesson she'd learned from Uncle Rock to heart—always know your mark's first and last move before you make your move; never rush to judgment until you know absolutely everything about the mark. She smiled just thinking about how she'd goaded Rock into teaching her all of his skills. He had been a little miffed that she'd found out what he did for a living, but she would not give up until he started teaching her about weapons, defensive tactics, and how to go ghost.

In true astute pupil fashion, Candice heeded Uncle Rock's words, and had been doing her homework for a few weeks now, this time on human marks. She was confident that she had gone unnoticed while she did her research. She had their routines down pat in her mind. Now the time had come for her to throw the bait.

***

When Candice arrived at Club Skyye in midtown Manhattan, the first thing she did was drive her midnight blue Audi A5 slowly past the long line outside. Her windows down, she noticed heads turning as dudes and chicks on the line realized it was a girl driving the high-priced car. Candice felt powerful for just a fleeting moment. It immediately reminded her of how people in the streets used to react when her father walked into any public place. Easy would command a crowd's attention no matter where he went.

Just as she pulled up to the club's valet station, her cell phone rang. She picked up, knowing who was on the other end. "Speak."

"Candy! Was that you that just rode by here in a fuckin' smokin' hot Audi A Five?" the voice on the other end screeched with excitement.

Candice started laughing. She was right about the caller's identity. It was Shana, her new friend. "Yeah, that was me. I'm on my way to meet you." Candice felt giddy inside. Achieving the first feat in her plan wasn't that complicated. In fact, it seemed more like fate than effort that led Candice to Shana.

Candice was on her daily research mission, driving one of Uncle Rock's old beaters—a 1978 Oldsmobile Cutlass—as she followed her first mark, Broady. She was using one of the several cars Uncle Rock used when trailing his marks. She was late getting to her usual surveillance spot outside of Broady's house, so she did not see him getting into his car but made it just in time to catch him pulling out. Candice followed the car, and when it pulled into the big car wash on Pennsylvania Avenue where all the high-level hustlers went to have their shit shined up, she did, too.

The door to the Escalade swung open, and a beautiful raven-haired female emerged.

Candice felt deflated but decided to stick around, get her car washed, and watch the girl. She followed the girl inside the long glass tube where patrons lined up to watch their vehicles go through the brushless wash. The girl was a few people ahead of Candice and was talking very loudly on her cell phone. Candice could hear the girl complaining about some nigga.

When the girl went to pay in the store, Candice followed. Then fate intervened.

"Oh my God! Girl, I have to call you back!" the girl shrieked as she frantically fished around in her purse. "I fuckin' forgot my wallet in my other bag! I cannot believe this shit! I have no fuckin' money on me!" she cried to the counter clerk.

The clerk was unfazed and looked at the girl like she had heard this story a million times before.

The girl whirled around in a panic.

"The car was already washed. You need to pay," the clerk said dryly.

"What the hell am I supposed to do? I was arguing with my boyfriend and forgot my wallet at home. I swear I will come back and pay!" The girl placed both of her hands up to either side of her head.

"I will be forced to call the police if you do not pay," the clerk said in her heavy Indian accent.

Candice's heart quickened in her chest. She made a snap decision and stepped up to the counter. "I'll pay for hers," she said, placing enough cash on the counter for both cars. Candice knew Uncle Rock would've chastised her for revealing her identity to someone close to one of her marks.

The frantic girl looked at Candice with big, round doe eyes. "Oh my goodness! Thank you so much! I have money, trust me. I walked out with a new bag and forgot my wallet right there on my leather sofa. I live in a big house. You see the car I drive. I have money. This is a Gucci bag, not a knockoff. I have plenty of money. I'm not a slouch. My man has money too. I can definitely pay you back. I swear, I'm not broke. Oh my goodness! I cannot believe I forgot my wallet. What if it was a real emergency? What if you weren't here? I'm so embarrassed." The girl moved her hands nervously as she rambled on and on, the heat of embarrassment evident on her face.

"It's okay," Candice said. "I believe you have money. We all have these kinds of days."

"Well, I'm gonna pay you back. I swear! My name is Shana. Here, take my number down. I will meet you right after we leave here and give you your money back." Shana made Candice jot down the numbers she was calling out.

"It's all good. I'm Candy. Here is my number as well." Candice recited her cell number, and Shana punched the numbers into her cell phone.

Tonight, Candice sauntered down the crowded Manhattan block to meet up with Shana. If she'd planned correctly, she would be meeting some real important pawns in her game tonight. Candice had made the decision that she didn't want to be like Uncle Rock, secretive and furtive, when she took her revenge. She wanted her marks to know who she was, wanted them to look into her eyes before she took them out. Risky or not, she was hell-bent on revealing herself and letting them know just why they were getting theirs.

Candice noticed Shana waving and smiling from up the block.

Shana bounced anxiously like a starstruck fan spotting her favorite celebrity. "Hurry up, girl! I can't wait to get inside! Broady's friend that I was telling you about is anxious to meet you. I'm so excited that you're here!" Shana squealed, flashing her cosmetically perfect smile.

I'm anxious to meet his ass, too. Candice smirked to herself as she got closer. "I'm here. I'm sure he can wait."

The one thing Candice couldn't stand about Shana was all of the excited talking and high-pitched shrieking. After all, she'd lived with a recluse for the past four years.

She plastered a fake smile to her face and made herself grin and bear Shana's overly bubbly personality.

Candice surveyed the crowd outside of the club and, as she'd been taught, made mental notes to herself about faces and features. She could feel more than one set of eyes on her, but she didn't feel the least bit uncomfortable. She knew she could probably beat half the men out there in a fight, and the entire club in a gun battle.

"Owwww!" Shana screamed as Candice finally got close enough for Shana to examine her closely.

Candice smiled, still slightly annoyed by her boisterous friend.

"Bitch, you is doin' it up in those fuckin' leggings, that shirt, and those hot-ass pumps! And that clutch is fire. Bitch, you gettin' it in t'night!"

Candice blushed. She wasn't used to having girlfriends or the playful derogatory name-calling and banter that came with them.

"Stop it! You're the one looking hot as ever. That dress is poppin', and those stilettos are the shit! I know they cost at least a grip!" Candice said, returning the compliment.

Shana smiled and nodded her head in the affirmative. She wanted to impress Candice; that much was clear.

Candice's compliment was genuine. The flowered silk kimono-style dress with big pink, royal blue, and yellow flowers on it flattered Shana's caramel skin. Shana was a pretty "around-the-way" kind of girl. Candice could tell that fast money had changed her from a hood rat to a hood superstar. She was rocking a new weave, different from the one she wore the last time Candice saw her. This time it was a straw set number with very fine, tight curls that bounced around her face. Shana seemed to change hairstyles like she changed her drawers—every day it was something new. In true haute couture style, Shana wore a large colorful tropical flower tucked into the side of her hair. Shana was short, so the heels she always wore made her look taller. Her legs were thick, and her ass sat up, round and firm. Her average face was graced with a perfectly round black mole on her right cheek, lending her an exotic look.

Shana grabbed Candice's arm and dragged her toward the club's doors.

"Where we goin'? You don't see this line?" Candice asked, feigning confusion. She knew damn well they didn't have to stand in the line. She just hoped like hell they didn't ask for her ID. Candice had a driver's license, thanks to Uncle Rock teaching her how to drive by the time she was sixteen, but she wasn't twenty-one yet.

"Candy, do I look like I stand in lines? I told you before, my man and his brother owns this place. I was only outside looking for you," she explained.

Of course, Candice already knew this. She played stupid as Shana practically dragged her to the door. The big bouncer at the door nodded and stepped aside when he saw Shana. It was like Rihanna and Alicia Keys had showed up all at once.

Shana bragged, "See what I mean?"

Candice had to admit to herself, it felt good to get that type of treatment. She wondered if her father had basked in the deference he received from others.

Shana said a few hellos and gave a few hugs to various club goers as she maneuvered her way through the crowded club with Candice beside her. Shana screamed to Candice over the music, "I told Broady all about you. He is looking forward to meeting the chick that saved his baby from embarrassment at the fuckin' hood car wash and who also has me hanging out, keeping me out of his hair these days."

Candice nodded. *I already know Broady. This meeting is just a formality.*

Shana continued rambling loudly in Candice's ears. "I also told his friend Razor about you, too. I told him you was too cute and that you had bomb legs. I wish I had your legs. Girl, those are killers. Do you work out? I know that's a stupid question."

Candice had to focus to keep up with Shana's rapid blabbering. She didn't know if she even wanted to meet a dude who called himself Razor, much less date him. But she knew there was little she wouldn't do for her cause.

Candice noticed that Shana was leading her toward the roped-off VIP section of the club. *Typical hood shit.* The one thing she'd found out while doing her research was that Broady and his crew were typical ghetto-ass hustlers. Everything they wore was big, gaudy, and attention-grabbing—the obligatory multicolored diamond Jesus pieces dangling from long chains that hit them in the center of their chests; huge, chunky diamond studs that resembled miniature ice cubes in their ears—and, of course, all of their cars could be seen five blocks away sitting on the biggest rims, with the brightest trims and darkest tints. In other words, all bling and no brains, their flashy lifestyle only making them huge magnets for stickup kids and cops.

Everything Broady and his crew did was outlandish. One day Candice had watched from her hidden perch as Broady embarrassed one of his little teenage workers right on a street corner by making the boy take off all of his jewelry, sneakers, and fitted cap and hand it over to him. A crowd formed as Broady screamed in the boy's face and humiliated him.

So, although it was just another typical night at Club Skyye, nothing was ever typical with Broady. He had the VIP section roped off with thick white velvet ropes, clearly armed bouncers standing guard in front of the VIP entrance, and half-dressed groupies posted up outside, desperate to get inside. A bunch of street dudes posted up around the club, keeping an envious eye on the VIP section.

"Watch me make these wannabe groupie, hood rat-ass bitches mad right now! They all wanna be me so badly!" Shana screamed into Candice's ear.

Candice had already figured out that Shana, although a pretty girl, had low self-esteem and was the type that constantly had to prove to others that Broady was hers. But Candice knew the real deal, having witnessed him with more than one chick on several occasions when Shana was out of the picture.

"What's up, Black!" Shana smiled at a tall, dark-skinned VIP bouncer, cutting her eyes at the groupies.

The bouncer smiled back and stepped aside so Shana and Candice could enter. Candice noticed the bouncers checking out Shana's ass and taking no notice of her. *Fake-ass security. They don't even know my ass is armed.* She smirked as she stepped by the big-for-nothing bouncers.

When Candice and Shana walked beyond the velvet ropes, the first person they encountered was Broady. Candice knew he was a big dude, but seeing him from a distance was nothing like standing in front of him. She had to crane her neck just to look up at him. *This nigga is a monster.*

"Where the fuck you been at?" Broady barked at Shana. His reaction startled Candice, but Shana didn't seem fazed by his hostility.

"I told you I was outside waiting on my friend Candy. This is her." Shana opened her arms as if presenting Broady with a prize.

Broady eyed Candice up and down, squinting his eyes to get a better look. "Your face looks familiar. Where you from?" he asked, raising his eyebrows as he stared her down.

A sudden hot flash came over Candice's body, and she felt something akin to nervousness flit through her stomach. She had waited for this day for a long time and didn't want anything to mess up her plans.

"Not from around here," she replied with an attitude.

Broady eyed her up and down, a lazy grin on his face.

Candice could tell that all of the expensive bottles of Ace of Spades had worked on him. She held his gaze, shooting daggers at him with her eyes.

The moment felt surreal to her, almost like looking into the face of the devil. Candice could feel her heart thumping in her throat. She bit down into her molars to keep herself from screaming. It was really him, in the flesh. Her nose flared; she tapped her foot.

According to the hood, this was the man who had bragged about emptying a 10-round magazine into the back of Easy's head. Candice didn't know exactly who had actually shot the weapon that ended her father's life, but she knew Broady was heavily involved.

"I know you not from my hood, because I know everybody around my way. But, like I said, you look like somebody I might know. Something about your face is real familiar, baby girl, that's all," Broady said, his voice slurring.

Candice lowered her eyes into slits and gritted. "I'm not your 'baby girl,' and you sure as hell don't know me." She instantly regretted the words after they had slipped from her mouth. Candice could feel her emotions taking a hold of her. She had to get it together, or she'd be in trouble. The sudden tension was as thick as the haze of weed smoke that hung in the club.

"You got a live wire for a tongue, huh? You better watch your tone. I may think I know you, but judging from how breezy you talkin', you certainly must not know me." Broady lifted his drink to his mouth.

Shana started laughing nervously, sensing that shit was getting critical. "Broady, you don't know her. You always think somebody is familiar-looking. Stop the madness. We came to have fun. No more drama from ya ass," Shana said, dragging Candice by the arm toward an empty table.

"Girl, I'm so sorry about that. That nigga can't hold his liquor for shit, and he always think he know some damn body from somewhere."

"I'm fine. I'm a big girl. I can hold my own." Candice folded her arms across her chest. She wasn't fine at all. She wanted to drop her bag and pull out her Glock and take Broady's fucking head off right then and there.

"Well, look . . . take a drink. All of the shit up in here, no matter how expensive, is free. I'm gonna go get Razor, so you can at least meet him. I mean that *is* the whole reason you came out tonight, right?" Shana said, eyeing Candice suspiciously.

Candice just nodded. She was lost in thought. She saw Shana get up, walk over to a group of dudes, and come back with one.

"Candy, this is Razor. Razor, Candy," Shana called out over the music.

Candice stood up and gave a halfhearted smile and extended her hand for a shake. The man she had been introduced to did the same. She gave him the once-over. *Way too short, way too ugly, gold teeth, and a long pinky fingernail.* Candice cringed. This man could do nothing for her by way of attraction.

She sat back down, and Razor sat across from her at the table. She considered him for a moment. He might not prove entirely useless. Perhaps he might know some details of how Broady killed her father.

"Candy, are you as sweet as you look?" Razor licked his lips like he was about to indulge in a succulent meal.

Candice didn't hear the question, because she couldn't stop looking in Broady's direction.

"Yo, w'sup with your friend?" Razor asked Shana.

Candice was sure Shana would intervene to divert Razor's attention. She could hear them talking, but she wasn't listening. Right now, she had one mark on her mind, and she wasn't about to let him out of her sight.

Broady Carson stood a hulking six feet seven inches tall by the time he was fifteen years old. His dream was to go to the NBA, but like with so many of his counterparts on the streets, it never materialized. The streets had called him early, as conditions at home with a single mother and absentee father deteriorated.

Broady's older brother, Davon, who everybody called Junior, had always tried to protect his big little brother from a life in the streets. When Junior was hustling and trying to make a name for himself in Brooklyn, he'd chastise Broady for staying out late, and he would try to encourage him to go to school and get a basketball scholarship.

But Broady worshipped his older brother and always wanted to be just like him. He started hanging out on the street corners with his friends who were already hustling, and in the local gambling spot run by a dude called Shamrock. In fact, it was in Shamrock's gambling hole that Broady got caught up in an event that ultimately changed the course of his life.

It was a cold winter night, and Broady ran top speed all the way home. He was drenched with sweat under his North Face bubble goose jacket, fear danced in his eyes, and his heart was like a jackhammer in his chest. When he reached his building, he took the stairs two at a time and burst through the door of the project apartment he shared with his mother and brother.

He ran straight for Junior's room, which he had already been forbidden from entering. "Where the fuck is it?" he huffed under his breath, his chest heaving up and down as he rummaged through his brother's belongings, tossing Junior's numerous shoe boxes around. "Got it!" he said triumphantly as he finally found what he was looking for—a silver Beretta special.

Broady had seen Junior stuff the weapon in his front waistband many a day. He also knew that Junior used a different weapon when he was on his monthly trips out of town.

"Now, bitch! You wanna try to play somebody? Like a nigga can't get his hands on his own ratchet. Well, we gon' see who the boss now." Broady gritted as he unzipped his goose, lifted his sweater, and tucked the weapon securely in the front of his pants, just as he had seen his brother do in the past.

"Who is that out there? Junior, is that you?" Betty called out just as Broady rushed out of Junior's room.

Broady sucked his teeth. He always knew his mother didn't give a damn about anybody but Junior. She didn't care if Broady fell off the face of the earth, as long as she could have her favorite son, Junior. Nothing Broady did, even playing basketball, could satisfy Betty. Consequently, most of the responsibility for Broady's care fell on Junior.

Broady ignored his mother's calls and walked calmly down the small hallway of their apartment to the front door. He took the project stairwell down, holding on to the cinder block walls so he could skip down the stairs two at a time.

Outside, the cold air stung the inside of his nose and made tears leak from the sides of his eyes. Broady was huffing and puffing, causing a steady stream of frosty breath to escape his lips. "You a dead bitch-ass nigga now," he said out loud to himself. He had already made up his mind about what he was going to do. There was no backing down or turning back now.

Broady continued the pep talk with himself until he reached his destination. He banged on the raggedy wooden door three times.

"Who?" a man's voice boomed from the other side of the wood.

"Junior!" Broady called out, lying about his identity. Broady figured that after the earlier dust up at the spot, they wouldn't let him back in. He also knew his brother was well respected in the streets of Brooklyn, so saying he was Junior could get him into many places.

When the door swung open, Broady placed the end of the pistol in the man's face.

"Whoa, cowboy! What the fuck is you doin'?" Shamrock said, putting his hands up like he was being arrested.

"Where is that nigga, June Bug?" Broady huffed, his hands shaking fiercely.

"He back there still playin'," Shamrock murmured nervously. Shamrock had gotten his nickname because he was no bigger than a leprechaun. Standing five feet tall on a good day, he was no match for a hulking, young cat like Broady. "C'mon, man, you ain't gotta do this shit here," he pleaded.

Broady grabbed Shamrock's arm and dragged him along with him to the back of the small basement. The local illegal gambling spot was usually always packed, but it was three o'clock in the morning, and most of the dudes who spent their days there had already lost their money and dragged their sorry asses home. But June Bug just so happened to be playing his last hand of ghetto poker.

"Everybody, stand the fuck up!" Broady screeched, placing his gun against Shamrock's head.

Shamrock pleaded with them with his eyes. One false move and he knew his brains would be all over the floor.

"Young'un, what the fuck is you doin'? Your brother know you here?" an older man at the poker table asked.

June Bug stood stock-still. He instantly regretted slapping Broady earlier in the day and taking his money back from him at gunpoint. June Bug was a notorious sore loser, so when Broady beat him in a game of cee-lo, he took it back by force. June Bug swallowed hard because he knew he was Broady's intended target. His gun was strapped to his ankle, so he knew he couldn't reach it without being noticed. Any sudden movements from him and his ass was as good as dead.

"Nobody fuckin' move!" Broady screamed.

The room went still. The only sound came from the small black-and-white TV that sat on top of a milk crate in the corner.

"Everybody empty y'all fuckin' pockets on the table now!" Broady barked.

At first, nobody moved.

"Oh, y'all think this is a joke?" Broady crinkled his face into a scowl and let off a shot into Shamrock's left foot.

Shamrock shrieked, his body buckling to the floor and blood soaking through his sneaker. Suddenly, all of the gamblers were emptying their night's take onto the table with quickness.

"Yo, Broady, man, we can discuss this shit," Pops said.

With his gun still trained on them, Broady walked around the table and grabbed up as much of the money as he could handle with one hand. He was sure he got his money back and then some.

"You slapped me in my fuckin' face like I was your bitch, right? You pussy!" Broady growled, getting close to June Bug.

June Bug opened his mouth to answer, but before the words could leave his mouth, Broady raised his gun hand high and cracked June Bug in the mouth with the butt of the gun.

"Oh shit!" June Bug howled as blood and two teeth shot from his mouth. He doubled over, holding his mouth, dark red blood seeping through his fingers.

"Now who's the bitch?" Broady placed his finger on the trigger and pulled it before he could even give it a second thought. He wanted to prove a point that night, consequences be damned.

June Bug's head exploded like a pumpkin being thrown off of a tall building and smashing to the ground, making one of the men vomit instantly.

Broady had gray brain matter all over the front of his coat. He didn't know what to do next. He contemplated killing everybody in the room so he wouldn't leave any witnesses, but he was already spooked. He whipped around like a paranoid nut and then bolted from the basement onto the street. Broady knew he needed to call his brother, because he didn't know what to do next. Junior would take care of it; he always knew what to do.

"Candy, your ass been acting funny all night! Let me find out you's a quiet drunk and shit. You ain't hardly say shit to Razor all night. Girl, that is Broady's best friend in the whole world and his second in charge. I wouldn't hook you up with none of his other little flunkies. You better stop playin' and treat a nigga right," Shana rambled on, eyeing Candice like she was disappointed in her or something.

"I'm good. I don't get drunk, first of all. What did you want me to do? Jump up and down and hang off of Razor's neck? I mean, he seems nice and everything."

Shana perked up when Candice gave Razor a halfhearted compliment, figuring that was a start. Shana had a very important stake in Candice and Razor hooking up, and she wasn't giving up that easily. If she could hook Candice up with Razor, it would make her life easier because she would be able to use Candice to be around Broady more often.

"Well, come to breakfast with us. We always go out after we leave here. Sometimes the fuckin' party even spills over to our place, even though I hate that shit," Shana said, her words beginning to slur. Shana had had a lot to drink tonight.

Candice looked over at Broady and Razor and their entire crew. They were drinking, laughing, and being rowdy as usual. They really disgusted her.

Candice was about to decline Shana's invitation when she spotted a man who appeared to be gliding on air. He walked like Barack Obama, and people seemed to move out of his way as he walked by with his six henchmen in tow. Candice was blinded by his jewels, even from a distance. Her toes balled up in her shoes, and she clenched her fists so tightly, her knuckles paled. He looked much different than the picture she had of him on her corkboard. He seemed older and had grown a mustache and goatee, just like her father had worn for years. Candice wondered how much he had changed since he had committed the heinous crimes against her family.

Suddenly her ears burst with the sound of her father's voice. *"Junior, don't you ever fuckin' question any of my executive decisions. I'm the boss. Remember that shit. If you don't want to be excommunicated and shut out of this hustle, you better do what the fuck I said to do."*

When Shana noticed Candice looking past her in a daze, she turned around in her seat. "Oh shit! Here the fuck we go," Shana said, turning back around quickly and taking another glass of poison to the head. Shana was acting as if she'd seen a monster.

"What's the matter?" Candice asked, her eyebrows furrowed. She knew who the man was and his so-called street reputation, but she wanted to understand why Shana seemed so spooked by his presence.

"Girl, that nigga that just walked in the club like he is fuckin' King Midas is Junior. He is Broady's brother and a royal pain in the ass. He is the boss of all of this shit. But when he's around, Broady acts different. Like real stupid and violent.

It's like he be tryin' to impress Junior or something." Shana's voice trailed off like she was reminiscing on something painful.

Candice continued to take in an eyeful of Junior and the man that made a move every time Junior moved. She needed to observe as much as possible, just like Uncle Rock had taught her to observe everything about her mark—even small things, like a twitch, limp, or left-handed versus right-handed.

"When you say 'the boss,' what do you mean?" Candice asked innocently.

"Well, I'm not supposed to talk about Broady's business, but for some reason even though I just met you, I trust you, Candy." Shana lowered her eyes and her voice. She leaned in closer and whispered, "I don't really have too many friends, you know, because of Broady. Anyway, Junior is a drug boss, like a kingpin." Her eyes darted around to make sure no one else could overhear her. "I heard he killed a bunch of niggas to get to the top and shit. He is ruthless, but he is very rich."

Just as Shana finished her sentence, they both jumped, startled by a small commotion at Broady's table. Junior was slapping hands and hugging Broady. Then several members of Junior's entourage did the same with Broady's crew members. Candice couldn't hear what Junior was saying over the music, but she made a mental note that the two brothers had a close relationship.

"See what I mean? Now I'm gonna get the fuckin' wrath of Broady showing off, trying to impress his big brother tonight. Junior don't want nobody to get close to Broady but him. I'm telling you, Candy, that nigga Junior is pure evil and fuckin' crazy." Shana took another glass to the head.

Candice silently agreed. Shana's statement was ironic. One time Candice's father had said that same thing about her brother Eric Junior. Eric, always angry and unusually aggressive, had been the Hardaway family's biggest secret. When he got old enough for Easy to start grooming him to take over, he would often get himself into trouble because of his temper. He was a great disappointment to his father and a constant source of frustration. Later in life, he'd been diagnosed as manic-depressive.

Maybe the moniker Junior *guarantees one to be fuckin'
evil,* Candice thought.

Candice and Shana watched as Junior went around the table smacking fives and chest bumping with Broady's friends.
She noticed them furtively passing small knots of cash under
the table and one of Junior's guys picking up the money. It
was definitely clear who was the boss around there. Candice
knew right away she was in the right place and had the right
dudes. The information she had taken from Uncle Rock's safe
was correct—all of the major players did appear to congregate
in this one place.

"C'mon, we leavin'," Broady barked at Shana, hovering over
her like a giant ogre.

Shana gave Candice a look of desperation that said, "Please
come with me." She stood up to leave with Broady.

Just as they were about to step away, Junior and the man
at his side the entire night approached. "Shana, you ain't
gon' introduce me to your friend?" Junior asked, smiling at
Candice.

Junior looked different than the pictures Candice had of
him. His complexion was much lighter than his mug shot
photo. Junior and his brother were definitely like day and
night, in terms of complexion. Junior had definitely aged
over the past four years, the salt-and-pepper specks in his
mustache and goatee indicating that much. He was also taller
than Candice had imagined him to be, but he wasn't nearly as
massive as Broady.

The bigger they are, the harder they fall. Candice did
not respond to Junior's comment, and an awkward silence
ensued.

"W'sup, Junior? How are you? Me? Oh, I'm doing just
peachy. Thank you for asking." Shana rolled her eyes. Her
disdain for Junior was clear. She was usually very good at
hiding her feelings, but the drinks she had thrown back during
the night had given her a strong dose of liquid courage.

Candice smirked, secretly pleased with her friend's brash-
ness.

"Damn, baby brother! You ain't got this bitch in check
yet? I guess I haven't taught you well enough," Junior said
to Broady.

It was like a master giving an attack dog a command. Junior had put the battery in Broady's back for sure, and Broady took off like the little pink Energizer Bunny. Before Candice could even react, he lifted his huge Sasquatch hand and backhand slapped Shana across her face.

Shana was caught off guard, and her body went tumbling backward as blood squirted from her nose. She hit the floor dead on her ass because she was unable to prepare for or break her fall. Shana's tailbone throbbed.

Candice was in shock. All of the dudes surrounding them were caught off guard as well.

"Yo, man, why the fuck you hittin' on a girl?" Junior's right-hand man growled at Broady.

Junior didn't say a word. He just looked on with a stupid-looking grin on his face.

Candice jumped up and grabbed her bag. Instinctively, she began reaching for her gun but remembered quickly that she was outgunned twenty to one. "What the fuck are you doin'?" she screamed in a somewhat delayed reaction as she rushed over to help her friend off the floor.

"I'm minding my fuckin' business and leaving yours alone," Broady hissed.

Junior watched Candice closely.

"Damn, baby girl! If I didn't know any better, I'd think you was a cop, the way you came to that bitch's aid," Junior said to Candice.

Candice turned to face him, her head spinning around like the possessed girl in *The Exorcist*. "Far from a cop, actually. And I ain't gotta be a cop to know that a nigga that hits on a girl to impress his brother is a bitchass!"

Junior and his crew began laughing. They obviously loved Candice's cocky attitude. She was definitely different than the girls they were used to hanging around with, who fawned all over them. Candice had a confident air about her, almost like one of the fellas in Junior's crew.

Candice turned her back on Junior and attended her friend.

"Girl, I'm fine," Shana mumbled as her nose leaked blood.

"No, you're not fine. What the hell was that all about?"

"I told you that is how he gets when Junior is around. I'm going to be all right. Why don't you just head home, Candy? This ain't really the place for a nice girl like you." Shana was embarrassed that Candice had seen Broady behave in his normal asshole way. Shana had taken many a beating from Broady, but lately he had begun to do it in public, sometimes without even provocation.

"I'm not going to leave you in this place and in this condition if you think you won't be all right," Candice said firmly.

Although Candice had initiated their friendship because Shana was a means to an end, she was starting to care about the annoying ghetto girl. Shana was a sweet, harmless, fast-talking bubblehead that had an asshole for a boyfriend. She was a victim of sorts that needed protection from the likes of Junior and Broady.

During one of their early brunch meetings, Shana had told Candice all about how her mother had been a drug mule and went to jail when she was just seven years old. Shana then went to live with her maternal grandmother, but after she died, Shana was basically knocked around in foster care until she met Broady.

Essentially, Shana went from the frying pan into the fire when she got into a relationship with that man. Broady became her caretaker, lover, friend, her everything. Shana really didn't have anyone else. For that reason, when Broady said jump, Shana asked how high.

Candice could totally relate. Of course, she wasn't fully honest about her childhood with Shana, telling her that her parents had died in an accident. At least, it wasn't a total lie. She pulled on Shana's arm and steered her toward the ladies' room.

Shana wasn't too mortified about her bloody face, since there was only a scattering of people left in the club.

Broady yelled at their backs, "Hurry the fuck up!"

Candice gritted her teeth to keep from saying something she'd regret later.

Once inside the bathroom Shana tried to brush it all off. "It's really nothing, girl. I'm so used to this same routine. Liquor, plus his ego, plus that fuckin' brother of his. Really, Candy,

I'm fine," Shana rambled as she cleaned up her face with the hard industrial paper towels. She wet the paper and blotted at her nose. Her cheek was starting to show green right through her makeup.

Candice watched as Shana limped over to the hand drier, pressed the large silver button, turned around, and lifted the end of her dress in an attempt to dry the huge wet spot on the back of it. She'd fallen right into a puddle of somebody's spilled drink. Shana continued to make conversation, while Candice looked on in disbelief.

"He usually keeps his cool in front of people most of the time. I don't know . . . maybe he had too much to drink. I really was nasty to Junior, and I should've just been nice. Like I said, though, it's all right, Candy. I know I sound like I'm making excuses. I'm just trying to explain. I just want peace. I . . . I'm . . . just . . . Look at you, looking at me like I'm crazy." Shana ended her succession of words with a high-pitched laugh that bordered on hysteria.

Candice could see right through Shana's act. "It's never all right for a man to hit you, Shana. But I'm not one to judge anybody's choice in men. Broady is going to get his."

Candice immediately regretted the words after they left her lips. Uncle Rock had always told her, "Words are like eggs dropped from great heights. You can't ever put the pieces back together after they hit home."

Shana, preoccupied with fixing her appearance, didn't seem to notice or care about Candice's offhand comment. "You ready, Candy?" she asked, smoothing down her dress when she felt it was dry enough.

"If you are," Candice replied, yanking on the door and holding it so Shana could leave first.

Shana rushed out of the bathroom so fast, Candice could barely keep up with her. Trying to catch up, she walked headfirst into someone. Startled, she jumped back to put some distance between them. "Oh, excuse . . ." Candice looked up into the face of a stranger. "Sorry, I didn't see you."

"Excuse me, too. Is she all right?" The man motioned his head in Shana's direction.

Candice recognized him as the man who'd been at Junior's side all night. She immediately put a scowl on her face. Why didn't his ass do something besides talk, when Broady had slapped the shit out of Shana? She had heard him referred to as Junior's "lieutenant" throughout the night. In her assessment, anybody who was a friend of Junior's was an enemy of hers.

"Nah, I don't think you would be all right if somebody six times your size slapped the shit out of you in a club filled with people." Candice pursed her lips.

"I feel you, ma. I know that li'l dude, Broady, be fuckin' up. I'ma talk to him," the man said.

Candice softened the look on her face once she realized he wasn't half bad-looking. In fact, he was damn near fine. Her cheeks immediately flamed over at the thought. He was about six feet two inches tall with an athletic build and had the most beautiful chocolate-colored skin Candice had seen, aside from her father's, of course. The man's head was shaved clean, and he had a long, prominent chin. His most striking feature, however, was his eyes, which were chestnut brown and showed up much lighter against his smooth, dark complexion.

"Anyway, ma, I'm Tuck. I don't think we've met before," he said, extending his hand for a shake.

Candice had to snap herself away from staring at his perfect white teeth. He either had a great orthodontist or he had purchased them.

"Candy. Nope. We haven't met," she said dryly, keeping her hands at her sides. She felt a little fluttering in her stomach that made her want to run in place or move her body. Or maybe even run away from him. She shifted her weight from one foot to the other. This indescribable feeling was a new sensation for Candice—uncomfortable in a good way, but extremely dangerous, given her current mission.

"It's real nice to meet you, Candy," Tuck said, putting his hand down to his side when he realized she wasn't going to shake it. "Look, I don't ever agree with that hitting-on-a-woman bullshit. Broady is a little asshole that wants to be a man so bad like his brother. That was some bullshit."

"Yeah, well, birds of a feather . . . " Candice walked away from him in a huff. She wanted to turn back and look at him so badly, but her pride and ego would not allow it. She couldn't help but wonder if he was watching her. *You're on a mission. You ain't here to look at no dudes. Getcha mind right, Candy.*

Love for a man wasn't something Uncle Rock had taught her. In fact, he had warned her against falling in love. "Falling in love is a waste of time," Uncle Rock had cautioned her on numerous occasions. "It never lasts."

But Candice couldn't help thinking about the tiny possibility of falling in love. When she was sixteen, she would stay in Uncle Rock's bathroom for hours practicing kisses on her hand, making a pair of makeshift lips with the edges of her thumb and index finger. As she grew older, she began to explore the erogenous zones of her body with her hands. Uncle Rock would always ask her what was taking her so long in there, and she would reply, "I was memorizing my pressure points."

Candice planned to tell Shana that she was done with Broady, Junior, and the entire scene at Club Skyye. She was going to let Shana know that she was leaving and that Shana was more than welcome to accompany her. But when she saw Shana by Broady's side and pretending that all was well, she just shook her head from left to right. *This poor girl.*

"Yo, apologize to my fuckin' brother," Broady growled at Shana, who stood by his side, shifting her weight from one foot to the other, looking like she had to urinate urgently.

Pitiful. The whole scene infuriated Candice and she had to will herself to keep her cool. She thought she'd come to Shana's rescue, but Shana didn't want to even help herself.

"I apologize, Junior. I was just joking," Shana said, in a real soft baby voice.

Candice squinted her eyes into evil slits, and her nostrils opened and closed with every breath she took. Now she wanted to slap Shana herself for being so meek and stupid.

"Candy, this is Junior. Junior, this is Candy." Shana introduced her as though they hadn't even met earlier in the evening. If it was a formal introduction they wanted, Shana was aiming to please.

As Junior extended his hand toward Candice, she twisted her lips into a scowl, keeping her hands at her sides.

"Shana, I just came to tell you that I was leaving. Call me when you can," Candice said, holding eye contact with Junior, then Shana.

"Oh, okay. That's fine, Candy," Shana said, avoiding eye contact.

"Damn! These bitches get more and more breezy the older I get. I guess it's hard to find a quiet, obedient motherfucker to lay on her back and bring up the rear," Junior remarked as he was set to turn away. "It was nice to meet you, anyway. What's your name, again? Lollipop or something like that?" Junior looked into Candice's eyes like he had seen them a thousand times before.

Candice inhaled deeply, willing the hot sensation of anger welling in her chest to dissipate. She finally broke her gaze with Junior and sashayed away from the group without another word, her heart thumping wildly in her chest and the fine hairs standing up on her neck. She wanted to pull out her gun and make Junior's head explode. Candice's emotions were taking over, and she had to get out fast. She was breaking a cardinal rule in Uncle Rock's training manual—keep a cool head, no matter what the provocation.

"Candy! Hold up!" Razor called after her.

Fuming mad, Candice picked up her pace, with Razor close on her heels. He just didn't know who he was messing with.

Chapter 4

Rock was huffing and puffing by the time he made it up the stairs to his apartment door. His lungs were on fire as he coughed uncontrollably. He stood with his back against the hallway door, letting his bags fall to the floor. Rock was frustrated and exhausted. Droplets of blood oozed from his mouth and formed a teardrop pattern on his shirt.

Rock's hands shook as he fumbled with his keys. He was wishing he had fixed the old rusty lock on his door because, at times like this, he hated fighting with it. When the lock finally gave, he spilled into his apartment and lay in a heap on the floor for at least fifteen minutes. He was feeling worse with each passing day and had definitely overdone it this time. With each rise and fall of his chest, he thought for sure he saw flashes of the devil.

Not the type to let illness defeat him, he bit down into his jaw and pulled himself up off the floor, determined to go through with his daily routine.

He finally managed to get to his small Formica-top kitchen table. He'd had it for so long, the flowers embedded in the material appeared to be masked by a smoke screen. Rock dropped his bags onto the table and flopped down into one of the mismatched chairs. He popped the little plastic top on his cup of green tea and opened up his *Daily News*. No matter how much his chest and stomach burned, he needed his daily cup of green tea.

Barely able to grasp the small paper cup, Rock held the small cup of tea to his mouth and took the first sip. He winced. He smoothed out the newspaper and read the first bold headline. Pain shot through his body like a bolt of lightning. A mouthful of tea and blood splattered all over the table.

***

Candice's phone ringing startled her out of her sleep. She bolted upright, thinking something must be wrong with Uncle Rock. He was the only one who would call her this early in the morning.

"Hello," she huffed into the phone, her voice sounding like a frog was lodged deep in her throat.

"Candy! Wake up!" Shana screamed in Candice's ear.

Candice was surprised to hear her friend's voice on the line. "I'm up. I'm up," she reassured her friend, wishing she would just get to the point.

"Girl! Razor been missing for three days!" Shana screeched, her voice shaking.

Candice sat upright in her bed. "What? What do you mean, 'missing'?"

"Candy! Nobody ain't seen Razor since he ran after you at the club! Oh my goodness! Broady is going crazy around here. I can't even stay in the same room with this nigga right now, it's so bad. Candy, they're saying somebody might've kidnapped Razor ass."

"Damn! That's fucked up. Who would want to do that?" Candice asked calmly. Her stomach cramped as soon as she asked the question. Suddenly, she was on her feet, feeling the need to pace, a coping mechanism she'd acquired over the years to deal with rushes of emotions.

"They found his truck on the side of a road out in New Jersey. Girl, niggas in the streets are saying that he might be dead. It's not like Razor to even miss a day—much less three days—calling Broady or coming around to make money."

Candice didn't really know what to say to comfort Shana. "Why would somebody want to kidnap him? Did he owe somebody money? Did Broady do something to somebody?" Candice asked, pacing the room. She closed her eyes and tried to picture Razor's face the night he'd followed her out of the club.

"Girl, they finally put a thing about it in the paper. Just because his baby mother is making such a big deal about it."

"Damn! It's in the newspaper?" Candice immediately thought about Uncle Rock and his daily morning newspaper review. Her heart thumped a little bit. She wondered what he would be thinking if he read about Razor in the paper, if he'd even realize who Razor was.

"I still can't see why somebody would want to kidnap a grown-ass man," Candice said, wanting to hear Shana's assessment of the situation.

"Well, Broady is convinced it's some uptown dudes that want to move in on his spots in Brooklyn. Broady had beef with some of them from back in the day. I heard Broady saying something about he recently got into something with these dudes. I think Junior and Broady will surely prepare for war if Razor don't turn up soon. I'm telling you, this is not going to be a good look. If they don't find Razor safe and sound, it's about to be war out here, Candy."

Candice was quiet on the other end of the phone. The fact of the matter was, Corey "Razor" Jackson was missing, and she was one of the last people to see him alive and in the flesh.

Junior Carson paced up and down his living room floor, rubbing his neatly trimmed goatee with his left hand. All of his workers, including his brother, were silent. They didn't dare interrupt him when he was thinking or pacing, or both. Junior finally turned toward his brown leather sectional, where all of his workers sat uncomfortably quiet and looking at their feet.

"I leave for one fuckin' week and y'all niggas go buck wild, partying e'ery day, flashing big money, beatin' niggas up on the streets and embarrassing them. I mean, I can't fuckin' step out for a minute without shit getting out of hand." Junior slammed his hands down on the oak bar that sat on the far left of his living room, near the sliding glass doors, making a few of his workers jump.

"Now what the fuck are we supposed to do? Y'all sayin' y'all think it's niggas from uptown that got Razor, but why? Why would Phil and those cats even reach all the way down to Razor's level if they were tryin' to make a point?" Junior's words were stiff and bitter as he looked each man in the face. His crew's assessment of Razor's disappearance just didn't sit right with him.

Broady jumped up and screamed, "It was those niggas! Hands down! Who the fuck else would do some shit like that? Brooklyn niggas know better!"

What he failed to say was that just last week he and Razor had encountered Phil's girlfriend in a club uptown. When Broady tried to push up on her and she refused him, Razor stepped in and tossed a drink in her face. Broady mushed the girl's head so hard, it really constituted a slap, and she almost hit the floor. Broady was sure that she had reported the events of that night to Phil soon afterward, explaining his suspicion that Razor's disappearance was related.

Junior eyed Broady with menace in his gaze, giving him the unspoken signal to sit his ass back down.

Broady stood his ground, his face curled into a scowl and his fists clenched. There was nothing Junior could say to comfort him.

Razor had been Broady's friend since he was five years old. All of the times Junior had beaten Broady up as a child and their mother let Junior get away with it, Razor was the one who comforted Broady and let him hide out at his house.

Now that Broady was older, wiser, and bigger than Junior, he was growing sick of his brother's domineering ways. Broady had at least seven inches and one hundred pounds on his older brother. He'd always resented the favoritism his mother showed Junior, but at the same time, he felt like he owed Junior his life and freedom. Junior was the one who had paid off all the dudes in Shamrock's spot so they wouldn't testify as witnesses against Broady in June Bug's murder, sparing Broady a serious prison bid.

But Junior was also the one who had turned Broady on to the streets after his basketball dreams went up in smoke. "You need to learn how to earn your own keep," Junior had told him one day soon after the incident at Shamrock's. Junior had already decided that Broady's future in basketball was over, so he turned Broady on to the only other way he knew how to make money.

Broady was growing a bit wary of living in his brother's shadow, but he also understood that Junior had taken over an empire. He realized, too, if he played his cards right, he could be the next in line to take over the family business.

As Broady became immersed in learning the business, he began to see his brother as a hypocrite and a fake. Junior had completely stolen Easy's street style and identity. Easy didn't like his workers to be flashy and loud, but Junior was very flashy and loud. Easy had chastised Junior several times, but it had all finally come to a head when Easy gave Junior a direct order that he blatantly disobeyed. Easy was furious, and he quickly shut Junior down, taking away all of his spots and sending him back on the corner to do hand-to-hand sales. Junior was furious beyond words and soon after began plotting his revenge.

Now Junior was walking like Easy, talking like Easy, and adopting Easy's same low-profile style. But Broady knew who his brother really was, and he was nothing like Easy. In Broady's assessment, Junior wasn't nearly smart enough to run the empire that Easy had grown. Broady knew he was just as good a candidate as his brother. If nothing else, his sheer size and determination would garner him the respect and admiration needed to take over operations in Brooklyn.

"I'm telling you right now this shit ain't over. I know it was those cats, and I'm ready to bust my gat at those niggas. War or no war."

Junior finally walked over to his brother and looked up into his face. Broady could see the fire in his eyes reflected in his brother's.

"Bruh, you don't want war with me. Sit down and we gon' talk about this." Junior gritted, roughly placing his hand on Broady's huge shoulder and forcing him back down into the sofa.

Broady relented for the time being.

"I don't want nobody to make a move until I have a chance to call a meeting with Phil. I need to find out what the deal is. Right now having all y'all niggas sitting in here tryin'a figure out if and how a nigga came up missing is costing me cake. Everybody get the fuck back to work, except you, Tuck."

All of Junior's workers stood up and began filing out of the room. Broady sat slouched in his chair, mean-mugging his brother. Junior was sitting at the end of his couch with his feet up, like a grand pasha. Their eyes locked on each other, and the room seemed to crackle with energy.

The same way you got that seat by overtaking niggas' shit is the same way I'm gonna get it, too. For the first time in his life, Broady contemplated doing physical harm to his older brother, for his indifference toward Razor's possible death.

"Yo, Tuck, I need you to get in contact with Phil's main dude. I'ma have to talk to these niggas and see what's really good. I gotta run damage control. Probably something these hothead-ass niggas done did." Junior sucked his teeth and huffed in disgust.

Tuck sat on a bar stool next to the couch and took it all in, while Broady was still glowering at Junior.

Junior said to Broady, "Son, why don't you go home and fuck your bitch or something? You look like you need some ass." He grabbed his remote and clicked on his sixty-inch flat-screen television.

Avon Tucker sat in a darkly tinted Lexus LS 400 with a black hoodie on his head and dark shades covering his eyes, even though it was well after midnight in Brooklyn. He looked out his windshield at the desolate surroundings. He was parked under the Brooklyn Bridge on a street that had only one streetlight, which just so happened to be out. A rat that resembled a baby otter wobbled by and stopped to sift for food in the various piles of trash that littered the concrete.

Avon held his burner on his lap, his left hand gripping the handle. Every ten seconds he glanced into his rearview mirror, then left and right, scanning his surroundings as he had been taught. *Better safe than sorry.*

After a few minutes, he picked up his "other" cell phone and dialed the phone number again. It rang. Avon's heart jerked in his chest.

"Hello," a female voice huffed into the phone.

Avon just listened.

"Hello?" the female said again, more urgently this time.

Avon quickly disconnected the call. He closed his eyes and bumped his head back and forth on the car's headrest. That had been the fifth call he'd made in the past thirty minutes. He knew she would be asleep, but he couldn't help himself. He pictured her smooth skin being touched by another man, her caramel legs intertwined with a man's thick, hairy leg. His imagination was running wild now. He thought if he called and listened to the background he'd be able to tell if his wife was still all his. He didn't know why he wouldn't just speak to her, ask her if she was cheating on him while he was away. Or just tell her he loved and missed her like crazy. But he couldn't do that. Not right now. It was still way too dangerous.

The truth was, he didn't know who he was right now. He certainly wasn't the same man who'd gotten married in an intimate ceremony on a Caribbean beach four years earlier.

Hearing gravel crunch behind his car, Avon sighed and let his shoulders go slack as he spotted the car he was waiting for in his rearview. He watched the man climb out of his old black Impala with its blacked-out tints and rush toward the Lexus like he was being chased.

After looking around like a paranoid schizophrenic, the man quickly flung open the car door and slumped into Avon's passenger seat. Everything had gone smoothly.

Avon removed his shades and looked over at the blue-eyed, blond-haired man sitting in his passenger seat.

They both looked each other over, noting how much they both had changed over the past few months.

The man cracked a smile and broke the awkward silence. "So, Tucker, how the fuck do you let one of our main targets go missing?"

Avon gripped his gun tighter and clenched his jaw. "Listen, don't get in my fuckin' car and start barking and asking me bullshit accusatory questions. Nobody knows what the fuck happened to Razor—"

"You mean Corey Jackson, don't you?"

"Whatever you want to call him, man. Razor went missing unexpectedly. It was out of nowhere. I was with them one day, partying, the usual shit, and then *Boom!* He was gone." Avon snapped his fingers.

Avon had been working with Brad Brubaker for four years now and knew how to handle him. They'd both been through hell and back together. The men were, after all was said and done, friends.

"I'm sorry. I wasn't trying to be all up your ass, but you know his disappearance has had headquarters asking questions about your operation," Brad explained.

"You know what? Fuck headquarters! I'm the one under-cover every day, risking my life out here. I'm living with these motherfuckers, rubbing elbows with them, wearing a wire against my balls! So don't tell me what headquarters thinks or is gonna say."

Avon swiped the hoodie off of his head and rubbed his bald head with his free hand, gripping his weapon with the other. Razor was one of his major targets. He knew that Broady was looking to go to war over Razor's disappearance, which had him very distressed. He couldn't afford for that to happen. It would completely fuck up his career.

"Don't shoot the messenger. This shit just stinks. If the local yokels get involved and start getting their own 'Keystone' narcos into this, it could fuck up all these months of work."

Avon knew Brad was absolutely right. He was painfully aware that any little bump in the road caused the bigwigs at the Drug Enforcement Administration, his current employer, to get their drawers in a bunch. He'd been there, done that. He knew what it was like working for the government, where the bureaucrats accentuated anything negative and played down the positive. Politics ran most government agencies, and that was just a fact of life Avon had to accept.

"Tell those suits up in the glass offices to calm the fuck down and just give me a chance. I'm this fuckin' close to finding out who the connect is that Junior took over after Easy Hardaway was murdered." Avon came close to putting the tips of his index finger and thumb together, trying to make his point.

"This missing person's case is just a bump in the road. I doubt if anybody else will come up missing."

Avon was asking for more time, but he wasn't sure if it was so he could do more work or just so he could stay under longer. This undercover persona and lifestyle were all he knew right now. He didn't feel like he'd ever live a normal life again. Junior and his crew had become like his second family. He had days where he totally lost sight of his mission and lived completely as Tuck—his undercover street persona. He hadn't spoken to his wife in a month of Sundays, which he justified by telling himself it was too dangerous to make contact. And so he continued to live the life of Tuck—a single, drug-dealing lieutenant in Junior Carson's illegal army.

"I can buy you some time, but not much. This kind of shit can't happen, Tucker." Brad prepared to exit the vehicle. They were already over the fifteen minutes alloted to their undercover/case agent meeting.

"A'ight, Brubaker, I got it," Avon said, exasperated. He was anxious to leave.

"Oh yeah, I saw Elaina and the kids. They're doing well. She says you haven't called. You might want to get in touch your wife." Brad gave him a serious look.

"Thanks. You go find a woman and invite me to your wedding. Until then, let me handle my situation with my wife and kids. You keep your bosses at bay so I can make this fuckin' case. After our fuckup, we both need this to work out. I think you'd agree with me there."

Standing up now, Brad stuck his head back into the car door for a quick minute. "By the way, just in case you forgot, your name is Avon Tucker, not just Tuck. You are an undercover DEA agent. You don't really work for Junior Carson. You have a wife and two kids that love you. So those girls you have hanging off your neck every night that you may even be fucking, they're all part of this act. This Lexus, that diamond necklace, and the money in your pocket belong to the federal government."

Avon squinted his eyes into little dashes and gazed at Brad with contempt. Brad's words stung him like an angry swarm of yellow jackets.

"Just thought I'd remind you." Brad slammed the door.

***

When Avon Tucker was ten years old, the New York City chief of police had handed him a folded American flag amid a flood of flashing camera lights. Avon felt a stomach-sickening mix of emotions, grief and pride among them, of course. He reached his small arms out and accepted the triangular folded material and pressed it up against his small chest. The flag had just come off his father's mahogany casket.

Avon remembered the sun burning his eyes as he tried to look up at his mother's wet face. Her body was shaking with sobs as a chunky older woman belted out a soul-stirring rendition of "Amazing Grace."

Holding his flag with one arm, Avon reached out and grabbed his mother's hand. A wet, crumpled piece of tissue clutched in her palm prevented the skin-to-skin contact he craved. Nonetheless, he would take what he could get at that moment. He squeezed her hand tightly and closed his eyes, wanting to see his father one more time.

When Avon had received the news of what happened, he couldn't even cry. It didn't seem real to him.

As the gunshots echoed into the air, Avon could still hear the words his mother had spoken to him the night before: "Avon, you're the man of the house now." It was a role Avon Tucker accepted with pride.

Months after his father's funeral, when all of the media coverage of the "Undercover Narcotics Detective Shot Dead in a Buy-and-Bust" had died down and extended family and friends finally stopped visiting and returned to their normal lives, Avon and his family got less donations and fewer calls from his father's police peers and the public at large. Eventually, the money ran out.

Avon's mother had always been a stay-at-home mom, his father insisting that he be the only breadwinner. After his death, with only ten years of service, his father's pension was barely enough to provide for Avon, his mother, and two sisters.

To keep his family above the poverty line, Avon started working odd jobs at fourteen years old. After many stints in summer school, he finally graduated high school. Avon enrolled at John Jay College of Criminal Justice only to collect from the Children of Fallen Officers College Fund and the surplus tuition assistance from Pell and TAP.

Although he had never done well in high school, college had somehow seemed a lot easier to him. Perhaps the fact that he found his courses interesting was what made the difference. Avon completed his bachelor's degree in criminal justice in three and a half years. Though he chose to study criminal justice, he had been vehemently against entering the law enforcement field. His father's death in the line of duty had vanquished any such aspiration in that area. Yet, a lingering curiosity prevented him from completely dismissing the idea.

As he prepared for graduation, Avon desperately needed to find a job. There would be no more PELL and TAP checks to help pay the mounting bills at home. So it seemed like fate when he just happened to be passing through the large auditorium-style room where a job fair was being held. He had taken the route as a shortcut to his career advisor's office.

As he rushed through the exhibitor tables, he was waylaid by an African American recruiter from the Drug Enforcement Administration. "Hey, young brother, let me talk to you for a minute," the recruiter called out.

"Nah, not interested," Avon grumbled and brushed past the man. The name of the agency alone was a big turnoff.

Avon made it to his career advisor's office with seconds to spare. He slung his backpack on the floor and slumped down in the chair in front of Ms. Bender's desk. His advisor was a skinny old white woman who smelled like mothballs and looked like the crypt keeper from *Tales from the Crypt*.

She looked over Avon with her icy blue eyes and unfolded her wrinkled, liver-spotted hands. "Well, Mr. Tucker, I have reviewed your records. There are not many options for a student with barely a two-point-five GPA and a major in criminal justice. The private industry bigwigs recruit from us, but they only want the magna and summa cum laude graduates."

Avon rolled his eyes in disgust. He'd always believed that college was one big-ass hustle, anyway.

"There is always the military or some police force somewhere." Ms. Bender laid her hands flat on top of his file like she was offering it its last rites.

Avon rolled his eyes and hoisted his bag up off the floor in a flustered huff, affronted that Ms. Bender would even suggest a police force, especially since his father's picture hung in memoriam in John Jay's main building, along with those of hundreds of other fallen officers. Avon wanted to slap the shit out of the old woman, but instead he stomped out of the office without looking back.

He left with a heavy mind, recounting his mother's words from earlier that morning. "The house is in threat of foreclosure." Preoccupied with thoughts of his future, he nearly ran headfirst into the same DEA recruiter.

"Hey, my brother, just stop by for a half a minute. Trust me, this career ain't like regular police work. You're not going to be walking a beat and running down crackheads. It's one of the only government careers where you can make six figures in five short years," the recruiter spouted.

Avon turned his full attention to the eager recruiter. The man had said the magic words.

When Avon returned home that day, he told his mother of his intention to join the DEA as a special agent. She was visibly shaken and upset and pleaded with him to reconsider. And Avon explained to her that it wouldn't be like the narcotics unit where his father worked.

But that wasn't entirely the truth. Avon had omitted to tell his mother that he would be going undercover, conducting buy-and-busts, and rubbing elbows with dangerous drug dealers, to spare her the worry.

Avon completed his training and graduated, for the first time in his life, at the top of his class. His career began rather successfully. He was living the life, cracking drug cases like a pro. Within his first two years as an agent, he had won several prestigious awards and was viewed in his field office as a "golden boy."

Avon's career took a turn for the worse, however, when, during a drug raid on the home of a well-known drug dealer, he accidentally shot a fifteen-year-old boy. Unfortunately, the DEA's confidential informant had provided the wrong address.

When Avon's unit rammed the door of the home and entered tactically, there was a lot of screaming and running. As they worked to clear the house, he and Brad Brubaker searched the back rooms to make sure everyone was accounted for. In one of the bedrooms, Avon could hear someone breathing hard in the closet.

Brubaker put his fingers to his lips to indicate silence, and the two approached the closet on deft feet. Brubaker pulled back the closet door for Avon to clear, and a young boy jumped out with a black crowbar raised in his hand.

Avon, in knee-jerk reaction, overreacted and let off a single shot. The boy died later that day at the hospital. There was a huge public fallout. Everyone in the city wanted Avon's head on a platter; firing him wasn't going to be enough. Avon was ultimately vindicated of any wrongdoing because he was able to articulate his perceived threat—the boy could've just as easily had a gun—but his name was forever tarnished by the incident.

To restore his good name, Avon volunteered to go under-cover into the dangerous world of Junior Carson's crew. Avon needed to bring Junior and his connect down. He couldn't afford for this case to slip through his fingers or for anything or anyone to get in his way. It wasn't just his reputation on the line; it was his job as well.

Chapter 5

Shana slid into the opposite side of the restaurant's booth where Candice already sat nursing a tall glass of raspberry lemonade.

Candice immediately looked at Shana with a suspicious eye. *Dark shades indoors. Hmm!*

"W'sup, girl?" Shana huffed, her breath causing her nose to flare in and out.

"Why you so out of breath?"

"I was rushing here from the car. I didn't want to keep you waiting. I know how people hate to wait." Shana's breathing slowed down as she began to relax.

"People or Broady?"

"Whoever," Shana snapped back.

"Anyway, how've you been in the past two weeks?" Candice asked, looking directly at Shana's shades.

"Girl, shit is still fucked up around the way. And at my house, forget it. If you thought Broady was acting up when Razor went missing, try thinking about how this nigga is acting after the detectives went to Razor baby mother's crib and told her they found his mutilated body." Shana's right leg shook under the table as she brought Candice up to date.

Candice suddenly started coughing. Some of her lemonade had gone down the wrong side of her esophagus and just so happened to be right on cue with Shana's revelation.

"Damn, girl! You a'ight?" Shana asked, leaning forward with concern.

"Yeah, I'm good. Went down the wrong pipe," Candice gasped, patting her chest.

"Like I was saying," Shana started again, her eyes round as marbles as she looked around the restaurant, then leaned in closer to whisper, "They found Razor dead off on the New Jersey Turnpike near Exit Seven A, close to Great Adventure. Over there, where they have all those bushes and shit. Someplace nobody woulda never thought to look." Shana's eyes darted around the restaurant.

Candice wanted so badly to tell Shana that details about bushes and highway exits were unnecessary and to just get the hell on with the story, but she nodded encouragingly, hoping that would do the trick.

"I heard Broady saying that whoever killed Razor had cut off the nigga hands and feet and most of his teeth was pulled the fuck out. It was only by DNA tests that they identified him. Good thing the last time Razor got locked up they had just started that taking DNA samples shit in jail. Can you believe some crazy, deranged bastard would do something like that?" Shana prattled on.

Candice softened her facial expression and feigned sympathy. "That is a gotdamn shame. And he had a kid? These niggas are ruthless over drug territory," she commented, shaking her head.

"I'm telling you, this shit here has got Broady buggin'," Shana said, relaxing back into the tight leather cushion of the booth.

"That's why you got on those shades, huh?"

Shana's body stiffened, and her leg stopped vibrating underneath the table. She folded her arms across her chest. "Look, Candy, I know you think I'm stupid for sticking around with Broady, but you wouldn't understand. He has a bad temper, yes, and when it's bad, it's bad with us. But, on the same token, when it's good, it's good. A girl like me that comes from nothing, I gotta take what I can get." Shana lowered her eyes. She could feel the heat of embarrassment rising up her chest and settling on her cheeks.

Candice immediately felt bad for making Shana feel small. The girl had few options in her life, and Candice shouldn't have been so hard on her.

"I may not fully understand everything, Shana, but you should never let a man make you think that a little bit of good can make up for a lot of bad. Nothing he says or does can make up for the black eyes and bruises. If you don't get out of there soon, your life itself may be at risk."

Shana was struck silent by the reality slap she'd just received. She knew Candice was right. Silence fell between them like a lead anvil dropped in the center of the table.

Shana lifted her shades from the bridge of her nose to swipe at the tears falling from her eyes, and Candice caught a quick glimpse of the part purple, part black-and-blue rimming around the bottom of Shana's eye.

Candice wiggled her toes uncomfortably in her shoes and flexed her jaw. She would make sure that, when she was ready, she would have a special dose of evil for Broady's ass.

"I'm sorry for crying, Candy," Shana said, breaking the awkward silence. "We're supposed to be here to kick it, not run rehearsal for some *Dr. Phil* episode." She inhaled deeply and then exhaled. "Okay, I feel better. Enough about my life," she announced in her usually bubbly, high-pitched baby voice, a half smile on her lips.

"So you were telling me about the Razor situation," Candice reminded her.

"Oh yeah. So, anyway, whoever killed him wanted him to suffer. The medical examiner people said all that cutting shit was done to him before he was dead. Girl, can you imagine somebody taking your fuckin' teeth outta your mouth one by one while you just sit there alive and screaming? Candy, they woulda had to use a gotdamn pliers and force those teeth out. Can you picture all the blood from them cutting through his wrists to get his hands cut off? He could've bled to death, but the killers ain't give him a chance. The real cause of death was bullets to the back of the head." Shana placed her hand over her mouth as if she was holding back vomit, just thinking about it.

Candice took a long gulp from her lemonade, feeling nauseous as well.

"The funeral is supposed to be this Friday. Of course, Broady and I will be hosting the after-funeral food and shit at our house. Razor's family is type broke, and his baby mother ain't got shit but whatever Razor was giving her. This shit is going to definitely be off the fuckin' chain."

"I bet it is," Candice commented, ideas whizzing through her mind like cars at the Indy 500.

Tuck and Junior sat across from Phil and Dray, their uptown equivalents in the drug game. Phil lifted his glass of Cîroc and Coke and sipped the liquid relief. He'd heard Junior out, but now it was his turn. Slamming his glass down, Phil looked at Junior quizzically.

"Really, bee? Do you hear yourself? Y'all motherfuckers got it fucked up. You think a nigga like me"—Phil placed an open palm on his chest and hit himself gently—"at my level, would actually kidnap your mans and fuck him over like that?"

"I'm sayin', son, we just don't know who else would go in on a nigga like that for no-ass reason at all."

Phil cocked his huge, misshapen rock head to the side and furrowed his eyebrows, trying to figure out what exactly he was being accused of. He leaned all the way back in his chair, as if he didn't even want to be in the same breathing space as Junior.

Phil's right-hand man intervened before things got out of hand. "C'mon, Junior, man, we ain't on it like that, bee. We ain't got no fuckin' beef over territory. That shit don't even sound right. I'm sayin', your brother damn near slapped Phil's wife in the fuckin' face, and as bad as we wanted to get at that nigga, we let that shit ride off the strength of the peace shit we been on after we split up Easy's pie. We coulda brought that shit to that nigga straight up. You know fuckin' with a nigga's family, especially his woman, hands down, is a sure way to die out here in these streets." Dray punched the palm of his left hand with his right fist to emphasize his point. "We laid low on it and didn't get on some ol' bullshit. Feel me? This was weeks ago. Why the fuck would we start buggin' out of nowhere now?" Spittle flew from Dray's mouth like sparks of fire while he made his point. "Trust, we definitely ain't no delayed-reaction-type niggas. Feel me?"

Junior's face paled, and his lips curled downwards. He thought his ears were deceiving him. He shifted in his chair and furtively balled his fists under the table. Dray's words felt like a powerful slap in his face. His right eye immediately started twitching, and a huge green vein emerged through his high-yellow skin and throbbed fiercely at his temple.

Tuck interjected when he noticed Junior was at a real loss for words, "Wait. Whatchu mean?" This little nugget of information made Tuck's heart rate speed up just as much as Junior's.

"Oh, what? Y'all niggas gon' try da act like y'all ain't know about that shit?" Dray asked, his eyebrows arched high with surprise.

Junior wanted to just push his chair back from the small card table and storm out of Phil's makeshift office, but he still had to pass through Phil's barbershop to get out of the building, so the embarrassment would've been even more evident if he tried to run from the situation.

Junior had little choice but to be honest now. He cleared the lump that sat at the back of his throat. "I was out of town. I don't think my brother mentioned it to me."

"Yeah, that nigga Broady and his little posse of fake-ass thugs was up here partying with some knucklehead uptown niggas that we don't even fuck with. Ba'y bro' was way the fuck out of his league up here, kno' mean, bee? My wife told me he tried to holla at her." Phil's voice rose an octave. "Grabbed up on her and shit."

"I'm sayin', how she know it was Broady?" Junior interjected in a last-ditch effort to clear his brother's name.

"C'mon, bee. Ain't too many people that don't know Broady. Plus, my lady recognized him from that function of yours we attended last summer in the Hamptons. And she don't never forget a face. I'm sayin', who wouldn't recognize that big, loud, rowdy-ass nigga?" Phil said, making a point to slip his insult in, putting Junior on the defensive. "Like I was sayin', bee. He touched up on her and shit, and when she refused him, he put his hands in her face and mushed her real hard. One of them threw a drink on her and shit too. My peoples around the way told me the hit almost knocked her to the ground. That's how my shawty described it to me too. When she bucked on that nigga, his dude—the one you sayin' is dead now—got all up in her grill. She was outmanned by two faggot-ass niggas in my book. When she told me, I started to buck on a nigga, kno' mean, but out of respect for you, the little peace shit we been on since Easy got murked, I let it ride." Phil's baritone voice was booming.

Junior knew Phil wasn't lying to him.

"Trust, I wanted to send you that nigga in a body bag, Junior, but I got respect for you and this game. War ain't on my agenda." Phil was breaking eye contact with Junior, letting him know the meeting was over.

Junior had come there with the intention of shutting Phil down, but Phil put him in his place.

"A'ight, man. Don't take it no way. I'm good with your word that you ain't reach out and touch Razor. I'ma talk to my brother too." Junior stood up from the table.

As if given a stage cue, all of the men stood up too. Tuck reached out and fist-bumped Dray, then Phil.

Junior reluctantly did the same. He hated to feel powerless in any situation. His insides roiled. He couldn't wait to lay hands on his baby brother.

"Yeah, man. Just talk to your li'l dude Broady and shit." Phil placed his hand on Junior's shoulder.

Junior felt like Phil was trying to school him in the game, and didn't like it one bit.

As they exited Phil's little office space and started through the barbershop, a tall, lanky boy bounded toward them, interrupting their fast stride.

"Whoa, whoa, little nigga! Slow down," Phil said, putting his hands in front of him.

The boy stopped but impatiently bounced on the balls of his feet, appearing to be in a feverish rush. "Phil, can I have two hun'ed dollars? I got a hun'ed myself . . . and those new Pradas came out today."

"Mello, you are twelve. What the hell you need with three-hun'ed-dollar sneakers?" Phil asked, laughing because he knew he was about to dig deep and give his little brother whatever he asked for.

As mad as he was, Junior smiled at the conversation. He could remember when Broady was younger and begging him for money for new Jordans or the latest gaming system. Junior always hooked his brother up because he knew his mother wouldn't do it. He felt a pang of jealousy at Phil's relationship with his little brother. He missed the days when

Broady was a teenage boy interested in only girls, basketball, and clothes. He realized he had turned his brother into a monster by allowing him to get involved in the game.

"A'ight, son. Sorry again about the misunderstanding. Handle your business with li'l man right here," Junior said to Phil, smiling at Phil's little brother.

"Thanks, bee." Phil chuckled. "You know how it is. These li'l niggas gotta always be stylin'."

Junior nodded.

Phil said to Junior, "And listen . . . don't even worry about the misunderstanding and shit. I'll even send flowers to that nigga Razor's funeral."

With that, Junior crossed the threshold of the barbershop and headed toward his whip.

"Stay up," Tuck commented as he exited the barbershop behind Junior. Tuck's mind whizzed like a motherfucker now. If Phil didn't order Razor's murder, who did?

Rock sat at the table with all of his armorer's tools laid out in order of smallest to largest. Sweat caused his reading glasses to slide down the bridge of his nose. He carefully picked up one small steel piece, held it close to his eyes, examined the end of it, and fitted it with another piece of steel that he held like a fragile piece of crystal.

Rock was careful and deliberate, like an artist or sculptor working on his next great piece of work. He had been at the table for several hours already. His back ached, and he had endured at least three coughing attacks. Nothing could interrupt his concentration when he was working like this. Not even his burning insides.

A few more pieces and he'd be done. He picked up a spongy piece of cloth and rubbed the metal until it shined.

When Rock's masterpiece was finished, he lifted it with the palms open, like a pastor would hold a baby being offered to God during a blessing. He rubbed his hands up and down the metal prize and whistled at its beauty.

The mere act of sucking in air to whistle caused him to immediately start coughing. Rock cursed in frustration. He hated the coughing and feeling-weak shit. For the last few weeks, Rock had been dosing up on the medicine from his doctor and had noticed a slight improvement in his condition, with little to no blood coming up when he coughed.

Rock placed his latest creation in the cushiony case, which he'd also handcrafted. He immediately thought about Candice. She was probably the only person in his life that would appreciate the powerful beauty that lay before him. Which reminded him, he needed to see her.

As he went to stand up, the buzzing of his cell phone startled him. He hated that thing. Candice had all but twisted his arm to purchase a cell phone, which he still didn't know how to use entirely. Aside from a singular, straight-dialed phone call, Rock couldn't make the pesky TracFone device do much else.

He let the phone go to voice mail as he hastily folded up the nubuck blanket his tools rested on. He had somewhere he needed to be, and now that he was assured the company of his new work of art, he wasn't too concerned with his weakened physical state.

Rock slid on his customary black skullcap and grabbed a pair of black gloves out of his box of gloves. Hefting the black, hard-shelled plastic case off the table, he headed out the door. Rock hoped things would go smoothly. He certainly wasn't much in the mood for bullshit these days.

Broady stood beside his parked car and let his eyes rove the parking lot of the deserted gas station.

Broady was feeling the effects of the Kush he'd smoked on his drive over. Naturally paranoid, and with heightened senses, he kept his eyes peeled on his surroundings. There wasn't a soul in sight. He checked his Breitling and sucked his bottom lip. "This motherfucker late," he said to himself in a harsh whisper.

He usually didn't get out of his car when he was making these sorts of transactions alone, but his legs ached from the long-ass drive.

Frustrated with waiting, Broady bent into the car and grabbed the prepaid cell phone he'd purchased just for this meeting and dialed the number. When he heard the line pick up, he curled his face into a scowl and began yelling.

"Nigga, you late! I don't do business like this! This is why I don't get recommendations from so-called thug niggas. You lucky I didn't say fuck it and fuck you!" Broady boomed, throwing his usual tantrum.

Within a few minutes of his rant, Broady started to ease his tone and relax the death grip he had on the small cellular phone. Broady was big on ass-kissing, and the person on the other end was obviously doing a good job at it.

"A'ight, you ain't got to apologize again, man," Broady said calmly. "Just get the fuck here. I wouldn't even be fuckin' with this if I didn't need a clean ratchet right now."

Broady leaned his head against the frame of the car and closed his eyes contentedly.

His peace was quickly shattered when an old beater eased into the parking lot. He swallowed hard. This wasn't the vehicle or the driver he was expecting.

Chapter 6

Avon rushed into his apartment and unlocked his safe. He snatched up his undercover cell phone and dialed Brad Brubaker's phone number. He only had limited time before Razor's funeral services began, and he was expected back. Avon needed to set up a meet with Brubaker stat to let him know about the new developments regarding Razor's death. He had been alarmed to learn that it hadn't been the rival drug dealers that mutilated and murdered Razor. Given these developments, he felt he needed to have a surveillance team standing by.

Avon rubbed his chin and wiped sweat from his brow as he anxiously waited for Brubaker to pick up the phone. The other end of the line just rang and eventually went to voice mail. "This motherfucker!" Avon spat, slamming the cell phone down, causing the battery to jump out of the back of the device. "Fuckin' bastard! You don't know what the fuck I want!" Avon growled out loud, as if his words would somehow telepathically reach Brubaker's ears. He could have been lying in the gutter, his cover could have been blown and his life in danger, and Brubaker wasn't answering his calls.

Avon suddenly got an overwhelming, paranoid urge to call his house. He hesitated midway through dialing the phone number, not sure if he wanted to hear who would answer on the other end. He felt a stabbing pang of resentment. "Fuck all of them!" he growled, deciding against calling his home today.

Avon tossed his undercover cell phone into his nightstand drawer, along with his wire. He reached down and picked up his long platinum and diamond chain with its big diamond-encrusted cross and slid it over his head. The sparkly piece of jewelry showed up against his all-black outfit like a splash of paint on a white canvas. Avon was now officially back to being Tuck. He smiled as he headed to his fallen comrade's funeral, to be with the only family he had right now.

***

Candice looked down at her watch impatiently. It wasn't like Uncle Rock to be late for a meeting. She'd promised Shana she would attend Razor's wake and funeral later on that evening. I shoulda went to his house and left with him, she thought. Candice sighed, looking at her watch again. She wanted to attend Razor's funeral, just to add insult to injury. She also wanted to be there for Shana, who was an emotional wreck the last time they were together.

After another fifteen minutes, she saw Uncle Rock's old-ass car pulling into the parking lot of the Black Hawk Ridge Arsenal range. She purposely put a scowl on her face to let him know she wasn't happy with his late arrival.

Uncle Rock struggled out of the low driver's seat of his classic Cutlass.

Attitude aside, Candice walked over to help him. "You're very late," she scolded in the usual spoiled brat tone she used with Uncle Rock.

"Yeah, I know, but I had to put the finishing touches on this beauty I'm about to show you," he said, wheezing slightly.

Candice noticed that her uncle Rock was still not 100 percent, but he did look slightly better than the last time she'd seen him. Once he got all of his stuff out of the car, they began walking side by side just like old times.

"We haven't done this in a long time. I miss it," Candice confessed, softening her voice.

Candice remembered the very first time uncle Rock had taken her to the gun range.

The first time she had stepped up to the firing line at the range, she was only fifteen. The adrenaline that coursed through her veins caused her knees to knock and stomach to churn. Uncle Rock had told her to relax and focus on the task. He stepped up behind her and instructed her to pick up the first gun she'd ever held—a .40-caliber Glock 22. Candice thought it would be heavier than it actually was. The rough handle felt good against the palms of her hand.

"Grip and trigger pull are the most important aspects to shooting, Candy." Uncle Rock placed her hands in the correct position and let her dry fire the weapon. When she did it the first time, she jerked the trigger.

"You're anticipating the shot. Let every shot be a surprise," he urged, trying to ease her nervousness. Finally, when he thought she was ready, he inserted the magazine into the weapon. "It's your time to shine, Candy Cane," Uncle Rock had said like a proud father.

With his words of encouragement, Candice's first five shots were dead center of mass.

Approaching the range doors, Candice realized just how much she and Uncle Rock had drifted apart since she'd moved out of his apartment. When Uncle Rock had handed over her father's money to her, she'd gotten a bit carried away, thinking she was too grown to be around him. Guilt washed over her at her arrogance and naiveté.

"It'll be worth it. You wait and see," Uncle Rock said excitedly, breaking up her reverie. He emitted a small cough. It was the excitement, he told himself. He was feeling like he did when Candice was younger and dependent on him to take care of her. It saddened him that she was older and living her own life. He just wanted to always protect her and keep her safe.

"You okay?" she asked when she noticed Uncle Rock staring at her absentmindedly.

"Oh yeah, I'm fine. Let's go on in." Uncle Rock placed his hand at her back and propelled her forward.

His gesture reminded her that he was the closest thing to a family that she had left.

Inside the range, Candice and Uncle Rock walked through the store portion and gazed at all of the newest guns to hit the market.

"Look at this baby. I'd drop a few stacks on this beast right here," Candice commented, leaning over the glass-encased counter to ogle a chrome .50-caliber Desert Eagle with a large tritium night sight with a laser dot mounted on the slide.

"That is a nice one, but wait till you see what I put together here for you," Uncle Rock said, patting the black case he held on to with a death grip. He began coughing again.

Candice and the store clerk looked at him with concern.

Once the fit passed, Uncle Rock slid his membership card across the glass and informed the man behind the counter that they would need one lane.

"Any ear or eye protection?" the clerk asked.

"Got our own," Uncle Rock told him, a consummate professional.

Uncle Rock and Candice proceeded to a large, heavy metal door, where they were buzzed in. Uncle Rock tugged roughly on the heavy door, but it wouldn't budge.

"I got it," Candice said, giving the door one forceful yank.

Uncle Rock was slightly embarrassed at how weak he was these days. He walked with his head down as he passed through the door into a small, dusty hallway that separated the store part of the range and the actual shooting range.

In the little hallway, Candice and Uncle Rock prepped for their shooting session. They double bagged their ears by inserting bright orange foam earplugs into their ear canals and then covering them with hard ear protection. They both slid clear plastic protective eye goggles over their eyes, and Uncle Rock put on his customary black gloves.

Candice hated shooting with gloves on. For her, it made getting her rounds on target and in the five rings a bit more of a challenge. But she knew if she didn't wear the gloves, she'd get a never-ending lecture from Uncle Rock about the lead particles getting all over her hands and contaminating her skin and blood.

After getting geared up like they were going into a battle-field, Candice and Uncle Rock entered the shooting range. Several of the lanes were occupied.

Candice smirked when she saw a woman no bigger than five feet tall, wearing thigh-high boots and a miniskirt, shooting a large gun almost longer than the woman's entire arm. Candice recognized the gun as an MP5. *Guess I ain't the only bad bitch around.* Candice felt a twinge of admiration for the woman. She would never have thought to go shooting in high-ass heels and a skirt.

"Come on over here and let me show you what I got here," Uncle Rock called out loudly, screaming over the resounding gunshots coming from the adjacent shooting lanes. He had already pulled down the gun rest and placed his plastic case on it.

Candice moved in closer to see this great prize Uncle Rock had brought with him. She had to admit, she'd become a big gun buff while living with Rock, but she still didn't think anyone could get as excited about guns as her uncle.

Uncle Rock slowly unlatched the case and pulled up the top in a dramatic fashion, as if about to unveil the Hope Diamond. When the case flapped open, his eyes sparkled, and he smiled wider than Candice had ever seen. "Here she is!" he announced with a flourish.

Candice's eyebrows arched high, and she flashed her even white teeth in pure delight. "Uncle Rock! You know how long I been asking you to let me shoot your AR-fifteen!" she exclaimed, a warm feeling coming over her. Candice was bouncing on the balls of her feet. She was giddy and ready to shoot Uncle Rock's prized possession for the first time.

"Candy, you were too young back then. This weapon is for grown-ups," Uncle Rock told her, like he was handing her keys to her first car or preparing her for a first date.

"Did you bring the legs?" Candice knew the sniper equipment would just make shooting the big gun even more exciting.

"Let me show you how to shoot it first. Then we'll worry about the legs. I fixed it up just for you, Candy," he said softly.

Candice scooted over as Uncle Rock set up to show her how to shoot the weapon.

"You need to put this baby on your support side shoulder, relax, then place that support side ear on your shoulder. Candy, you gotta get your head down behind the sights or else this will jump back and hit you in the face. Grip it here, like your life depended on it," Uncle Rock said, smacking the side of the weapon to demonstrate where he wanted Candice to put her hands. "Watch and learn now," he said.

Rock quickly put down the weapon when he was suddenly overwhelmed with another coughing spasm. This time, there was blood.

"Oh my God! Uncle Rock! Are you okay?" Candice screeched, her face etched with worry.

Uncle Rock tried to speak, but it took him a minute to wipe away the blood from his mouth and catch his breath. He grunted in frustration.

Candice eyed him suspiciously. She knew that Uncle Rock hated her to ask him questions relating to his health, but this was getting out of hand. "Don't tell me not to ask any questions! Something is wrong! There is blood coming out of your mouth!" Candice bellowed, her hands shaking.

"I'm okay. Let me show you how to work this now." Rock's chest felt like hot coals were lodged in it. He swallowed hard several times to get the burning to subside. Teaching Candice how to shoot the AR-15 was very important to him.

"First, you need to tell me why blood is coming out of your mouth when you cough. Have you seen a doctor?" Candice folded her arms across her chest.

"Look, when I am ready, I will give you all of the details. This is much more important!" Uncle Rock growled, one of the very few times he'd ever raised his voice at Candice.

A bolt of panic shot up Candice's spine. Uncle Rock meant business; she had never seen him this passionate about anything. She couldn't help but think his unwavering insistence that they meet at the range today had something to do with his failing health. Candice let her shoulders go slack. There was no use in fighting Uncle Rock over this issue. But she intended to find out what was wrong with him. She promised herself she would make him go see a doctor for that cough.

"C'mon, Candy, now take this. Get your head behind those sights, get a firm grasp, and learn how to treat this baby like it's your own," Uncle Rock instructed, handing Candice the oversized weapon that was almost too big for her arms to hold.

Like my own? Is he giving this to me?

Uncle Rock had regarded his AR-15 like a child. He had never even let her lay eyes on it before today. Skeptically, she accepted Uncle Rock's prize into her trembling arms. She did as instructed, getting into the proper stance and positioning the gun properly. Closing her weak eye and keeping her dominant eye open, Candice tugged on the trigger. When the first couple of rounds exited the end of the gun in rapid fire, she looked downrange at the ripped-up target. She smirked as she pictured the holey target being Broady and Junior, or anyone else who tried to come between her and her marks. Even Junior's fine-ass sidekick, Tuck.

Candice walked into the Woodward Funeral Home and followed the signs for the services of Corey Jackson. As she stepped into the small room, Shana jumped up off the hard teakwood bench and rushed over to her, eyes wide.

"Girl, I am so fuckin' glad to see you," Shana whispered, grabbing Candice's arm and pushing her back through the doorway.

Candice followed her in confusion. "What's going on?" Candice asked in a harsh whisper. She didn't appreciate being damn near accosted by Shana.

"Candy, I'm so scared. Broady is running around here like a madman. He got guns and saying he waiting for any niggas to show up here that ain't supposed to be here. He just going crazy," Shana said, her words shaky and frantic.

"Where is Junior and Tuck?" Candice asked because she knew they could probably calm Broady down, but she also needed to keep tabs on all of them before deciding on the appropriate course of action.

"They haven't gotten here yet. I just want to leave, for real." Shana shook her head.

"You better not do shit to set Broady off. I'm here to keep you company, and I don't feel like the drama y'all be having. Let's just go inside and sit in the pews and observe."

Promising a lonely girl like Shana company always did the trick. Shana smiled, relieved that her friend had provided her a rational solution to her dilemma.

"Okay, okay. You're right, Candy. If I left, that nigga would be all on my ass when he got home."

Candice looked at Shana's obviously expensive black *Nicole Miller* fitted sheath dress and her black *Brian Atwood* pumps and shook her head. *An expensive little black dress still ain't worth the matching black eye that comes with it.* Shana still donned her dark Jackie O shades, which now seemed to suit the occasion.

As Candice and Shana slid onto one of the benches, Candice glanced toward the front of the dimly lit room, at the closed casket. An 8x10 portrait of Razor stood atop the sealed body box. *Razor's condition must have been too bad to allow for an open casket.* Candice felt the urge to inspect the picture more closely.

Shana noticed Candice staring at the photo. "You wanna walk up there and see it before it gets mad crowded in here?" Shana asked, breaking Candice's trancelike gaze.

"All right," Candice replied hesitantly. She hated funerals, funeral homes, and anything related to death. She'd had enough of it to last her a lifetime.

Candice and Shana ambled slowly toward the front of the stuffy room. The scent of embalming fluid mixed with the sickly sweet aroma from the arrangements of flowers assailed Candice's senses and threatened to make her lose her last meal.

Razor's family members were stuffed together, shoulder to shoulder, directly in front of the casket. His baby's mother clutched the sleeping baby daughter up against her chest as if she expected someone to bust in and grab the baby out of her hands. An older lady, who Candice just assumed was Razor's mother, had her face covered with a small black net, and every so often she stuck a wad of tissue under it and swiped away falling tears.

"That's his family." Shana whispered the obvious as they passed the first row of pews.

When they stopped in front of the casket, Candice examined the photograph. It was apparent that the picture had been taken some time ago. In the photograph, Razor looked studious, with a collared shirt and tie, and holding what appeared to be a small diploma case. He was smiling, with no diamond-encrusted fronts on his teeth.

A cold feeling washed over Candice, like someone had pumped ice water into her veins. She realized then that she only knew Razor, not Corey Jackson. If she had to depict the Razor in a photograph, he'd have long dreads, his lips would be visibly darker than the rest of his face from smoking so much weed, and he would be wearing some sort of expensive T-shirt with the name of a designer splashed across the front, and the obligatory chunky chain hanging in the middle of his chest.

Staring at the picture, Candice felt an overwhelming sense of sadness for Razor's family. Corey Jackson had been someone's son, father, and friend. His family was now experiencing the same grief she felt when her family was murdered in cold blood.

"You ready to go sit back down?" Shana asked, noticing how long and hard Candice was staring at the picture. She just figured that Candice had liked Razor more than she let on.

"Yeah, c'mon," Candice replied, ready to return to her seat. As she turned, she noticed a flower delivery guy placing a bouquet of red roses fashioned into a bleeding heart near Razor's casket.

"Wow! That is a beautiful flower arrangement," Shana commented, impressed. She walked over to the flowers and looked at the small envelope attached to a piece of white ribbon. "Oh my God! These flowers are from Phil. The guy . . . the one Broady said—"

"Broady said what?" a voice boomed from behind Shana and Candice.

Broady was hovering over them. Too close for Candice's comfort.

Shana's legs immediately seemed to buckle a little bit at the accusatory tone. Her heart thumped wildly, and her mind raced for an answer to his question. Thinking quickly, she surreptitiously passed the small card from the bleeding heart to Candice.

Catching on just as quickly, Candice secreted the card between her palm and the back of her black leather clutch.

"I was just telling Candy how you said that this place was gonna be packed 'cuz Razor was so cool with e'erybody," Shana fabricated on the spot.

Candice noticed that Shana spoke way more broken English when she talked to Broady. *She can't even be herself around him.*

"Yeah, mad motherfuckers gon' be up in this camp. So make sure you keep your eyes peeled for any suspicious niggas and keep me posted 'n shit," Broady grumbled. He pushed past Candice without saying a word to her.

Candice felt a spark of heat in her chest. She never knew her hate to take on such physical manifestations. *That's what you get when you dance with the Devil.*

"I'll be right back, Candy," Shana said, her tone shaky as she rushed out of the room.

Candice sat in a far corner in the back of the room. She checked her surroundings and pulled the small card from the envelope. She read the inscription:

To Broady, Junior, and the crew, Sorry for your loss. We're here if you need us. Stay up.—Phil and the uptown crew.

Candice furrowed her eyebrows, perplexed. She thought Shana had told her that Phil and the uptown crew were believed to be responsible for Razor's murder. If that was the case, why would they send such a nice card and flowers? Candice knew Broady was convinced it was Phil who had commissioned Razor's brutal murder.

Inspiration seemed to strike Candice at that moment. A wondrous plan began to take shape in her mind, but first she needed to find a card and something to write with.

Frantic, she rushed around the lobby of the funeral home trying to find these items before Shana came back to look for her. She walked over to what appeared to be the funeral director's office and knocked hesitantly. When no one answered, she let herself inside. The lobby was beginning to get filled up with people fast, and she needed to accomplish this task before anyone noticed her absence.

A tall, slender older woman approached Candice from the side, scaring her out of her wits. "Can I help you?"

Candice's heart hammered, and her eyes darted around the room for Broady or Shana. She took a deep breath and willed herself to calm down. "Uh, yes. I sent flowers, and the florist forgot my card. Would you happen to have a small piece of paper I could write my note on?"

"I can do you one better," the lady offered kindly. "I have blank floral arrangement cards in all colors. This happens all of the time. Those daggone florists are so forgetful sometimes."

"Great! I am embarrassed to let anyone see that I have to put my card on after the fact. It's starting to get crowded in there," Candice said, rushing behind the woman as she fished around for the cards in the desk drawer.

"I knew they were hiding in there somewhere. Here you go," the woman sang cheerfully. She retrieved a rubber-banded stack of small, blank cards. "What color?" the woman asked Candice.

"The light blue will do."

"Here, I'll give you two, just in case you make a mistake."

Candice took the cards, thanked the woman, and rushed through the door of the office. When she stepped into the lobby, she had tunnel vision, wanting to get back inside the room where Razor's casket lay. She scanned for Shana but didn't see her.

Candice started into the room, cards in hand, and once again, she walked smack-dab into someone, and the cards went fluttering out of her hands. "Oh shit!" Candice exclaimed, startled.

"Damn! We bump into each other again. Literally," Tuck said, his deep baritone massaging Candice's eardrums.

"Maybe you should watch where you're going," Candice huffed, her words nervous and choppy. She bent down to pick up the cards, but Tuck beat her to it.

"I got it. A lady in a dress shouldn't have to bend over." Tuck picked up the two small light blue cards and handed them to Candice.

Candice straightened back up. Hands shaking, she accepted them.

"It's real nice seeing you here," Tuck said honestly. "I thought after the night in the club, Shana wouldn't ever get you to come back around us."

"I have thicker skin than you think." Candice was trying so hard to keep up her tough-girl persona.

"That's good. I love women with tough skin." Tuck licked his lips seductively.

Candice swore she could feel her pussy pulse as she watched his moistened lips. She was stuck on stupid for a moment.

"Now, if you excuse me . . ." Tuck said, touching her shoulder to move her aside. He walked toward a group of men milling around.

Candice felt a flash of heat on her neck and cheeks. She instantly felt rejected. She wanted to be the one to end their interaction.

Candice stomped back into the corner where she and Shana had been sitting earlier. She noticed that Shana had moved up a few rows to join some of the crew's girlfriends. Candice quickly sat in a vacant chair and opened her clutch to retrieve a pen. Everybody in the room was too preoccupied with their grief to pay her any attention. She placed one of the small cards up against her thigh and scribbled down the real message she wanted Broady and Junior to get from Phil and the uptown crew.

When Razor's casket was lowered into the earth, screams erupted through the cemetery loud enough to wake the dead. Candice felt cold all over her body. She intensely disliked being in the cemetery; it reminded her that she had missed her own family's burial. She wondered if she would've screamed and jumped up and down like Razor's family.

Razor's mother hollered and spread her body atop her son's shiny death box. "Why, Lord? Why my chile?!" the woman screamed.

Candice wondered if she knew what type of life her son had been living before he died, that he had been peddling poison to his own people to make easy money.

Candice kicked at the upturned, rocky red earth with her pumps. She looked around at all of the mourners' faces and decided that she wasn't sorry for Razor or his mother. She did feel a flitting stab of grief for Razor's young daughter, however. Candice knew the love between a father and daughter. Razor's daughter would never know that feeling.

Candice felt partially responsible. Maybe if he hadn't followed her out of the club that night, he'd still be alive.

Scanning the rest of the attendees, Candice caught a glimpse of Broady dabbing at his eyes. She involuntarily smirked at the sight. She couldn't help but feel a surge of satisfaction that he was in some kind of pain.

When the burial ended, Candice trudged through the gravelly dirt and grass and started toward her car.

"Candy! Hold up!" Shana caught up with her. "You coming back to the house, right?"

"I just think I'm going to go home. It's very late. I have never been to a funeral, in the cemetery this late at night," Candice told Shana. The truth was, she had never been to a burial, period.

"Well, the one-day service was cheaper, so they decided to just do it all today. If they had waited, Broady woulda had to pay another two or three stacks. You know that nigga funny with his money. As much as he loved Razor, he did foot the entire bill for everything." Shana gazed off in the distance, a look of admiration in her eyes.

"It is almost ten o'clock. I'm beat."

"Please, Candy, come back just for a little while."

Candice refused again, but Shana practically got on her knees and begged Candice to come back to the house for the funeral repast.

Candice had a lot of things on her mind. More importantly, she didn't trust herself around Junior's right-hand man, Tuck. Candice couldn't stop running their last encounter through her mind, no matter how hard she tried to think of something else. She pictured his perfect face, those even white teeth and mesmerizing voice. She imagined herself kissing his plump lips. She had always wanted to be kissed by a man but had been too afraid when the opportunity presented itself. Uncle Rock had warned her repeatedly about the dangers of falling in love. She had avoided that fate simply by steering clear of the male species as a whole.

After a few more minutes of Shana's pleading, Candice accepted Shana's invitation, convincing herself that her friend needed her support. But, deep in her heart, she really wanted another opportunity to exchange words with Tuck.

Candice had sat outside of Broady and Shana's house many times while she conducted research on her mark. The outside of the two-story house, with its plain brick front and ugly black wrought-iron gates, told nothing of what happened on the inside.

When Candice stepped inside, her jaw dropped.

"C'mon, Candy, let me show you around," Shana said, pulling Candice farther inside the house.

Candice followed Shana through a grand foyer, complete with a small statue and exquisite marble tile. She didn't even think such a foyer could fit inside the house. The house had clearly been gutted and rebuilt based on the owner's or, more probably, Shana's direction.

Shana had accessorized the dining room with just the right amount of vases, mirrors, and candleholders. The rest of the house was just as beautiful. Candice could tell that Shana had poured a lot of money and heart into her home. Now she could see why her friend had been so reluctant to give Broady up, beatings and all. Shana was living hood-rich and better than she'd probably ever live, even if she went the traditional route and worked a full-time job.

"You have a beautiful home," Candice complimented Shana as she walked through her home. Candice's steps felt lead heavy, and she felt slightly dizzy. She had always just thought of him as a mark, a monster, someone she wanted to kill for revenge, but being inside Broady's home somehow made him more human to her.

Following on Shana's heels, Candice felt a surge of adrenaline, and her pulse quickened—a mixture of fear and power.

"Thanks. I try," Shana replied, giving Candice a half-hearted smile.

They strategically dodged bodies as they passed several different groups of people holding conversations throughout the house. Some were laughing, some were still crying, while others were just eating and drinking.

Shana finally pushed through two short white swinging doors and stepped into her gourmet kitchen. "It's kind of peaceful in here. Too many people out there for me," she said, flicking her wrists dismissively. She climbed up on one of the leather stools that sat in front of the bar-style granite counter.

Candice joined her. "Are you all right? I mean, with Broady and everything. I know you said he had been acting a little erratic," Candice said, choosing her words carefully. She had finally gotten a grip on her shaking legs and hammering heartbeat.

"So far he has just been caught up with a bunch of different dudes trying to play detective behind Razor's murder. He hasn't had time to really focus on me. I know he was very happy with the way I arranged this little thing for everybody, so maybe shit will be all good tonight. Maybe his days of laying his hands on me are over," Shana said, looking down at her feet.

"So Broady is playing detective? I mean, nobody has heard any more information from the police about suspects in Razor's murder?" Candice didn't want to sound like she was prying.

Shana's facial expression turned serious. "Candy, do you really think the fuckin' jake is looking for Razor's killer? C'mon now, girl, be for real." Shana chortled, moving her hands in front of her and snapping her neck in and out. "Let's see . . . Razor was a known drug dealer, a 'predicate felon,' and ain't never paid a cent in fuckin' taxes. Those bastard-ass DTs are probably having coffee and donuts right now, saying, 'Good riddance,'" Shana replied with an angry sigh.

Candice knew she was right. She had thought all of this through when she set out on her revenge mission. Nobody would care if Junior, Broady, or even Razor was wiped off the face of the earth, as they were all menaces to society. She couldn't help but think that was the reason no one was ever charged in her family's deaths. Did the police officially say, "Fuck finding the killers," since her father was a well-known drug kingpin? Why else would there have been no arrests for such a horrific crime? The rumor mill on the streets pointed the guilty finger at Junior and his little cronies, but Candice didn't need the police to exact her own brand of justice.

"Well, I still would like to know who'd do some shit like that to Razor," Candice said. The last time she'd seen Razor was at Club Skyye when she'd stormed out of the club in a huff. Razor had followed her outside to calm her down, but she could barely remember their conversation. She was so furious with Broady that night, all she could see was red.

"Ayo, Shana!" Broady growled.

Shana bolted upright on the stool, almost losing her balance.

Candice sat up straight as well, Broady's voice sending a prickly feeling down her spine.

"Yeah, Broady. I'm in here," Shana responded, twisting her lips. She looked at Candice and rolled her eyes. "I'll be right back." Shana sighed. She wasn't going to do anything to set Broady off, with so many people milling around the house.

Candice shook her head in disgust. *When would Shana learn that no man is worthy of such blind obedience?* She drummed her fingers on the granite countertop and gazed around the kitchen. She could see herself living in a home like this, with a gorgeous man and a few kids running around.

Candice almost laughed out loud. She didn't know why that thought had crossed her mind. It would be the Immaculate Conception indeed, considering she had never even been touched by a man. She chalked up her strange thoughts to the fact that she was feeling lonely and out of place. Marrying and having children would be one way to fix that problem. But if she heeded the words of her uncle Rock, it could also mean an uncertain future. If Candice wanted to plant roots, as Uncle Rock said, she would just have to become a tree. She inadvertently smiled at Uncle Rock's eccentricity.

"You look pretty when you're smiling and not looking so angry all the time," a male voice chimed from behind her.

Candice jumped off the stool, whirling around and clutching her bag, her boyfriends (Glock and SIG Sauer) nestled safely in her purse. She relaxed a bit when she recognized the voice belonged to Tuck.

"Nobody ain't ever teach you not to be sneaking up on somebody like that," Candice huffed, attitude in full force. She knew she shouldn't have come back to Shana's house. Her pulse raced, and her heart quickened. Just being in his presence made her feel hot, flushed, and uncomfortable.

"It must be me. I must be the reason you're so mean. Because I know I just looked in that mirror across the kitchen and saw you smiling," Tuck said, moving closer to her side.

Candice swore she felt an electric current flowing between their bodies. *Is this what it feels like to lust after someone?*

"Maybe it *is* you . . . since you like bumping into people and sneaking up on them. I don't like that." Candice didn't like the overwhelming sexual attraction she experienced each time she laid eyes on him. It was dangerous. It was pure, raw emotion—something she had been taught to suppress all of her life, professionally and personally. Candice clutched her bag tightly, her lips curled into a snarl. She was going to fight these feelings. She wouldn't go panting after this guy like some bitch in heat and do something she would regret.

"I'm sorry for whatever it is that I didn't do to you," Tuck offered.

Candice snorted and rolled her eyes.

Tuck sighed. "See, I am even willing to apologize when you know good and well I ain't do a thing to you and you *still* won't throw a dude a bone. You're something else." Tuck flashed the sexy smile that always fucked Candice's head up.

"Hmm!" Candice grunted, petulantly cocking her head to one side. She wiggled her toes in her shoes. She felt agitated and hot enough to melt, but she was damned if she was going to let him know the effect he was having on her.

"So, Candy, tell me something about yourself," Tuck said, ignoring Candice's defiant body language.

"I don't tell strangers about myself." Candice refused to make eye contact, afraid that looking into his eyes would cause a floodgate to open. *Stay focused, Candy. Stay focused. Stay focused.*

"Damn, you a tough nut to crack." Tuck pretended to wipe sweat from his forehead. "Look, how about we start from scratch? I tell you one thing about me. Then you tell me one thing about you," Tuck said, dipping his head up and down and around, trying to make eye contact with Candice.

Every time he moved his head to try to meet her gaze, she turned her head and eyes in the opposite direction.

"Last I checked, this is not *Let's Make a Deal*. I'm not a game show contestant, and I don't have to negotiate a truce with you. I don't even know you!" Candice secretly enjoyed the back-and-forth and giving him a hard time. If Tuck wanted to get to know her, he'd have to work for it. Besides, Candice knew that if he got in the way of her mission, he'd have to be dealt with swiftly, and she didn't want to get attached to anybody she considered expendable.

Tuck laughed at her tough-girl façade, seeming to enjoy the byplay. He could see right through her act. Her flaming red cheeks had already given her away. "I'm sayin', for real, though . . . you are one hard-ass Candy, ain't you?" Tuck chuckled, still trying his best to get a smile out of her.

Candice opened her mouth to respond, but a bloodcurdling scream cut through the air, forcing the words down her throat like hard marbles. "What the fuck!" she mouthed, instinctively moving toward the door. She recognized the voice behind the scream all too well.

Tuck spun around like a man possessed. More screams prompted him to pull his weapon out of his waistband and race through the kitchen doors.

Candice was hot on Tuck's heels. "Oh my goodness . . . Shana," Candice whispered breathlessly.

Tuck and Candice rushed toward the commotion against a wave of people heading for the nearest exits. No one, apparently, wanted to be a witness to anything going down.

"Junior! Stop it!" Shana screeched, her voice sharp like nails on a chalkboard, her eyes stretched wide with fear.

"Fuck!" Tuck huffed, rushing over to the tangle of bodies.

"Tuck! Help him! Get him off of him!" Shana screamed, jumping up and down.

Candice was finally able to make out the identity of the individuals in the twisted heap of arms and legs. It appeared to be a fight as old as time—Cain versus Abel.

"You ain't so fuckin' tough now, you pussy!" Junior growled, his left arm wrapped tightly around his brother's neck in a headlock that threatened to crush Broady's windpipe. In his right hand, Junior gripped a .357 Magnum and held it to his brother's temple. Broady's huge body was slumped against Junior's smaller frame, but with his air supply being choked off, his size wasn't helping him.

"You're gonna choke him to death!! Ahhhhhh! Don't shoot him!" Shana bawled hysterically as she jumped up and down, flailing her hands like a crazy person. Her face was now a cakey mess of smudged makeup, salty tears, and sweat.

"Get her the fuck out of here!" Tuck hollered at Candice.

Candice rushed over to take Shana away from the fracas, although she didn't appreciate Tuck screaming at her. "C'mon, girl," she said calmly, cutting an evil eye in Tuck's direction. She felt like she was the only sane person in the room at the moment.

Tuck knew he needed to get Broady's head out of Junior's death grip. Broady's body was already going slack, like he was being put to sleep. He tried to place his hands on Junior's arm to loosen his grip, but it only made matters worse. Junior not only tightened his grip, but he pressed his gun into Broady's head even harder.

Fuck! Tuck screamed inside of his head. "C'mon, Junior, man. It ain't worth it." He couldn't afford to grab Junior's weapon and cause an accidental discharge. That would put the last nail in his career coffin.

Meanwhile, Candice tried to persuade Shana to leave the upturned family room.

Tuck tried his most compelling argument. "Junior, man, he is your brother. I know you mad, man, but—"

"I'm not leavin' him! He's gonna kill him!" Shana squealed, her voice a high, keening pitch, her body trembling. She was running in place now and screaming for Junior to release Broady.

"I said to get her the fuck outta here!" Tuck barked again.

Candice shot him another glare. *Don't this motherfucker see I'm trying to calm her ass down first? What am I supposed to do? Pick the bitch up over my fucking shoulder?*

"Stop fuckin' screaming at me! I'm doing my best!"

Tuck quickly got the message. Now he had two angry women to deal with. Things were going from bad to worse. The situation was spinning out of control, and he had to put things back in order. If Junior killed his brother and went to jail, Tuck's case would be over.

"You slapped a nigga's wife and didn't even tell me? You goin' out of borough, startin' a fuckin' beef, and didn't even tell me? Huh, motherfucker? You can't keep it one hun'ed?" Junior barked, still applying pressure to Broady's neck.

"Cuh! Cuh! Cuh!" Broady struggled for breath. His windpipe was on fire and would surely buckle under Junior's grip.

Broady's vision was narrowing; he would soon lose consciousness if Tuck didn't act fast. Junior had been holding him in the dope fiend sleeper hold for too long.

"You embarrassed me!" Junior belted out, his words coming out in raggedy, clipped breaths. All of the liquor he had consumed during Razor's funeral services didn't help the situation either.

"Junior, man! You gon' fuck around and kill this motherfucker! He turnin' blue and shit." Tuck touched the outside of the arm wrapped around Broady's throat.

At Tuck's touch, Junior jumped. His eyes bugged out, and sweat dripping off his face, he was like a rabid dog, foaming at the mouth, and looking to take a bite out of a helpless victim. "Back the fuck up!" he hollered, moving his gun from Broady's face and pointing it at Tuck.

Tuck threw his hands up in surrender. He didn't have a choice. He thought of his father dying in the line of duty and what it did to his mother. He couldn't do that to his wife and kids.

Junior turned his attention back to his brother. He loosened his grip on Broady's neck. "You so lucky I care about my fuckin' mother and don't wanna see her have to bury your worthless ass. It's only because of her that I don't fuckin' murk you right the fuck here in ya own crib," Junior screamed, his chest rising and falling rapidly.

Broady fell forward onto his knees with a thud. His hands uncurled, and he dropped the little blue card he was holding. He gasped and wheezed, trying to get his lungs to fill back up with air. Broady couldn't stop coughing. He rolled around on the floor like he was having a seizure, his hands massaging his neck.

Shana raced over to his side, rubbing his back to soothe him. "Oh my God! Broady, are you all right?" she screeched, stooping over him. Shana glanced up and shot Junior an evil look. She really hated his ass.

"You a fuckin' punk bitch! You better stay the fuck away from me! Next time some bullshit pops off, I'ma kill you my fuckin' self and that hateful bitch standing by your side!" Junior glowered at Broady.

"It was those niggas, and you takin' they side," Broady rasped, barely audible. His lungs had finally caught enough air for him to get in a few words.

"That nigga Phil gave me his word. You got it fucked up. Phil ain't kill ya manz, but you know what? He shoulda fuckin' killed you for slapping his bitch. Your name is mud in my fuckin' book and in the streets. You dead on ya feet, nigga, so watch ya back. I might not be finished with ya punk ass just yet." Junior hawked up a wad of spit and hurled it at his baby brother. Then he pushed past Tuck and Candice and stormed toward the front door of the house.

Junior's hard-bottom dress shoes slammed against the marble floors, like gunshots ricocheting through the silent house. The noise chilled Candice right to the bone.

Tuck looked down at Broady. He noticed the little blue card on the floor but quickly dismissed it. He had bigger issues to deal with right now.

"You a'ight?" Tuck asked, walking toward Candice.

Candice furrowed her eyebrows. She had noticed his slightly puzzled gaze on the little blue card on the floor. She stared at Tuck like she didn't understand his question. As he moved closer, she began backing out of the doorway, one step at a time. Her eyes wide and wild, she looked disoriented. Maybe even in shock.

"Candy, what's wrong?" Tuck asked.

Candice wished she could bend down and pick up the card. It was too late. She spun around and rushed toward the door.

Tuck watched in confusion as she broke into a full jog. "Wait!" he screamed at her back, but it was too late. She had bolted, maybe this time for good.

Chapter 7

Avon paced inside his undercover apartment with sweat dripping down his back. He jumped at every little noise. Every car sound he heard outside caused him to rush over to his window and peek through the slats of his blinds.

He looked at his watch and sucked in a deep breath of air. The vibration of his undercover phone against the wood on his nightstand shattered his nerves. He rushed over and snatched up the device. "Where the fuck are you?" he screamed into the phone.

"Don'tchu fuckin' dare move until I get there!" he ordered.

Avon skipped down the building's steps two at a time. Once outside, he looked up and down the deserted block. There was no one in sight. The doctors and lawyers residing in the area must've all been inside their condos and expensive townhomes getting ready for another day of being responsible, upstanding, tax-paying citizens. In Avon's book, his neighbors were all boring-ass prudes who sat around having quiet cocktail parties where, the conversation was so low-key, one could fall asleep mid-sentence.

Either way, the serenity of the neighborhood was one of the reasons the DEA undercover research team had chosen the Park Slope block for Avon's new residence. Although Avon surreptitiously maintained another apartment in Brevoort Houses, where his alter ego, Tuck, resided, as far as Junior and the crew were concerned.

Avon rushed up the street, looking over his shoulder several times. Finally, at the corner, he made a left. He walked at a feverish pace until he made it to a small hole-in-the-wall, pub-style greasy spoon. After checking his surroundings, he dipped inside.

The owner of the restaurant was used to Avon holding his regular meetings there. Avon nodded to the greasy-haired man behind the counter and continued all the way to the back of the place. He squeezed into the cramped booth and exhaled. He sat opposite of Brad Brubaker. Avon's eyes hooded over and his shoulders tensed.

"You all right?" Brubaker smirked, his blue eyes rimmed and icy today.

"Don't fuckin' ask me if I'm all right! Where were you when I called you?" Avon growled in a harsh whisper, his fists clenched tightly next to his thigh as he leaned into the table.

"You know how it is. I had to fly out to D.C. and deal with those motherfuckers after Corey Jackson went missing." Brubaker was unnervingly calm, almost like he was mocking Avon. "You can thank me later for once again saving your ass and your fuckin' case."

"Fuck you! I don't need you to save my ass from those monkey suit–wearing motherfuckers. I need you to protect me on these fuckin' streets! You're my fuckin' case agent. Act like it!" Avon scowled. He felt like slapping the shit out of his smart-ass coworker. They had both fucked up in the past. But for some reason, the DEA insisted on placing the brunt of the blame on him for the incident that had changed both of their careers.

"Well, I'm here now. Let's talk," Brubaker said, softening his tone as he decided to get to the point of their emergency meeting.

"Shit is not right out here, Brad. I found out that Razor wasn't murked by rival drug dealers. He left the club running behind a girl and then just vanished. Next thing, we get word from the New Jersey locals about the body. I'm sure you heard how bad he was fucked over . . . missing fingers and shit. I think somebody is watching Junior's crew, and it ain't as simple as pitting one gang of hustlers against the other."

Brad wore a serious expression. He seemed to be concentrating. Both men were silent for a few minutes as they digested the information.

The fat waiter waddled over to their table, breaking up the moment. "What can I get you fellas?" The man huffed like he'd just run laps around the place.

"Our usual," Avon answered, rushing the man away from them.

"So the last person to see Corey Jackson alive was a girl?" Brad asked, rubbing his chin.

"Yeah. She's a friend of Broady's girlfriend, Shana. Remember? The one I told you I almost blew my cover protecting one night when he was beating her," Avon reminded Brubaker. "The night Razor went missing was the first time I had ever seen this new girl." Avon could see Candice's cute face and thick hips in his mind's eye.

"This girl, where's she from? What's her name? Did she just show up out of nowhere?"

The line of questioning took Avon aback. He felt slightly protective of Candice even though he didn't know her very well. "Why you askin' about a chick when I'm tellin' you somebody might be after these dudes?"

"Every detail counts."

"She calls herself Candy or something like that. I don't think it was like a date. Razor followed her outside, and from what the girl told Broady's chick, she and Razor spoke for a few minutes and parted ways." Avon didn't give up too many details about Candy because it would only elicit more questions from Brubaker.

"Well, she was the last person to see him alive, as you said. Maybe she set him up," Brubaker mused.

Avon rolled his eyes in disgust. Brubaker was way too jaded with life and people in general. From what Avon could tell, Candy wouldn't hurt a fly, although her mouth was certainly venomous at times. Avon thought she was too classy and sexy to be hanging around Broady's crew anyway.

"I'm just trying to help you figure this shit out," Brubaker said defensively.

"What don't you get? I'm telling you I don't feel right about this shit. Seems like there is somebody after them that we may have overlooked. Razor's death was definitely a crime of passion, considering the torture he endured."

Brubaker threw up his hands. "One low man on the totem pole goes missing and you count that as a big fuckin' conspiracy at work? What am I missing?"

"I'm in the trenches with these motherfuckers. Nobody is gonna kill somebody like Razor who doesn't fuckin' matter in the bigger scheme of things. Razor was a nobody in Junior's little chiefdom. Whoever killed him was trying to send a message! Get the fuckin' message? I need to know you got my back on this shit."

"I still think any number of people could have killed him. Maybe he picked up a prostitute that night and her pimp fucked him up. Maybe it was a robbery gone bad out there. C'mon, Tucker, think like a fuckin' cop. This guy was a fuckin' two-bit drug-dealing piece of scum."

Avon leaned into the table, ready to lay into Brubaker's ass.

"Here you go! I put some extra TLC into it tonight," the fat waiter sang, proud of his greasy creations.

Avon moved back in the booth seat and fell silent. He watched the fat man's stomach move like a bowl of Jell-O as he sat their food down on the table.

"Eat up," the fat waiter said with a yellow-tooth smile.

Brubaker attacked the meal with gusto, but Avon, upset and worried, didn't have an appetite.

Brubaker could feel the heat from Avon's eyes on him. After stuffing a couple of steak fries into his mouth, he noticed Avon's lack of appetite.

"What?" Brubaker asked resignedly.

Avon didn't respond to the prompt.

"Okay, Tucker. I heard you loud and clear. I'll set up a covert surveillance team."

Avon's face lit up partially.

"Here, take this phone." Brubaker slid a new phone across the table. "It has more than just the standard cell phone GPS chip. It has a laser locator, so we'll know where to find you at all times. Just don't put the shit in your pocket with anything magnetic, or else you'll be fucked if you get in trouble out there."

Avon furtively swiped the phone off the table and put it in his back pocket. "And don't fuckin' disappear like that again. Nothing is more important than me being out here in the trenches. Nothing!"

Brubaker nodded in agreement.

Avon grabbed a few fries off his untouched plate of food. "Make sure you tip the guy," he said as he got up to leave. "I'm sure you made some good per diem money on your trip to D.C."

Candice lay in a prone position with one eye open and one eye closed as she peered through the round scope, her legs spread, her feet lined up with each hip, just like Uncle Rock had taught her. She could hear how hard and rushed her breath sounded as it escaped her nose and mouth. Her elbows were covered with pads and rested on the hot tar of the roof.

She adjusted the scope to focus in on her target. The eye of the scope was so precise and powerful, it was like the target was standing right in front of her.

"Don't move, don't move," she whispered out loud. Keeping her body as stiff and still as she could, all Candice moved was the pad of her trigger finger. "Trigger, trigger, trigger," she chanted. Another thing she'd been taught by Uncle Rock. He'd taught her that repeating the word would keep her mind off her trigger pull and keep her from anticipating the shot.

Candice was surprised by the sound of a click. Just like she was supposed to be. Every surprise shot was always on target in her experience.

She let out a long sigh as she flipped over and lay on her back atop the black tar roof. Practicing with Uncle Rock's AR-15 sniper setup had exhausted her. Her muscles ached with tension, and she was burning hot from the sun beating she'd taken in the hours spent on the roof. Everything took practice and precision; she knew that, but she wanted to be ready. No more of her mission would be interrupted. It was time to start carrying out her plans.

After a few minutes of lying on the roof with her eyes closed, she unhooked the legs from the weapon and folded them down. Then she handled the weapon like it was a crown jewel. She placed it in the case Uncle Rock had made especially for it and then slung the leather strap of the case around her chest and let it hang down her back.

She started the stopwatch she had hanging around her neck. Then, with the craftiness of an Olympic tri-athlete, she moved her body with speed, taking the roof ladder down two and three rungs at a time. Finally, she jumped off the ladder and went back into her building.

She checked the stopwatch for her time this go-around. "Fifteen seconds. Damn, Candy! You need to make better time."

Candice was great at applying all of the things Uncle Rock had taught her over the years, but her obsession with getting her marks had made her oblivious to the obvious. A set of eyes focused on her, following her every move.

Broady sat in the small compact car that he had a hood rat chick named LaLa rent. Dark shades covered his bruised eye, but the dark circle that rimmed his neck was still visible. The gun he'd recently purchased lay on the passenger side floor, covered with Shana's leopard print Snuggie.

Broady was parked about seven cars away from Phil's barbershop. His initial plan was to wait until Phil showed up and just go Rambo and start shooting up the place with the brand-new toy he'd just laid six stacks on. But he knew better. Jail wasn't his final destination.

He watched the sun peep up behind the tall Harlem buildings. There was really nothing like a sunrise in the concrete jungle. He yawned and cracked his knuckles. He hadn't slept in two days, since his incident with Junior. His insides boiled each time he thought of Junior's betrayal, believing Phil over him. He hadn't even gotten a chance to show Junior the evidence that proved Phil had indeed murdered Razor. His anger and his habit wouldn't allow him to rest easy. Broady would deal with his Judas of a brother in good time.

"Early bird gets the mu'fuckin' worm, nigga," Broady whispered to himself. He fumbled with a note he had clutched in his hand. He read it to renew his anger for Phil.

Broady had been waiting almost six hours before Phil's sleek black S550 pulled up outside of the barbershop. It was ten o'clock in the morning and still no real hustle and bustle on the main street. Broady knew that although Phil was pulling his gates up at ten, there wouldn't be anybody strolling in before noon.

As he watched Phil climb out of the car, fish for his gate keys, and go about unlocking the iron gates, Broady had an out-of-body experience. He had murdered once and knew he could do it again. He pictured himself blowing Phil's head off and then returning to the car.

Broady's plan to push Phil inside the store, tie him up, and kill him was thwarted when another person climbed out of Phil's car. Although tall, it was clear that the boy was young. The boy was dressed in a maroon Polo shirt, a pair of fitted jeans, a maroon Yankees fitted cap and a pair of maroon and grey Prada sneakers.

Broady squinted his eyes into slits and bit down into his jaw. "Where the fuck you come from, li'l nigga?" he grumbled under his breath. He immediately hated the kid for breaking up his plan. Trying to tie up two people at once wasn't a risk Broady was willing to take. Broady seethed inside. He had sat in that little-ass car for all of those hours, and now this little boy had fucked shit up.

He watched as the young'un helped Phil pull up the gates on the barbershop. The boy was either Phil's son or brother. He couldn't be sure which. Broady could see the love for the kid in Phil's eyes and actions, his pats on the back and their shared laughter and smiles.

Broady was instantly jealous. He honed his attention in on the young boy. When Phil and the boy disappeared inside of the barbershop, Broady thought the adrenaline rushing through his veins would make his heart explode.

The boy reemerged after a few minutes to retrieve a CD from the car. He rushed back inside the barbershop with a big smile on his face.

Broady captured the boy's smiling face in his mind. He started the rental car and pulled out of the Harlem neighborhood, his anger palpable but controlled. He would write that face to his memory for use at a future date.

Rock rushed into his apartment after being out all day. He was on top of his game lately, sickness and all. He had a mission, just like Candy did, except his was to protect her from herself.

He flopped down onto his favorite raggedy recliner and unfolded the papers he had picked up from his lawyer's office. Rock's hands trembled as he read the words over and over again: *Last Will and Testament.*

Rock had never thought he'd need a will, since there was a time when he didn't have any family, through blood or affiliation. As far as he was concerned, his last will and testament could have been just one sentence that read: "Everything to Candice Hardaway." But there was someone else he needed to leave something for, not materially, but more so in the form of an explanation or maybe even an apology.

Rock had some years to make up for, but his pride and hurt heart wouldn't allow him to do it in person. He decided that in death he would be able to speak and make his peace. Time wasn't really on his side anyway, but in the meantime, while he was still alive, he had to continue carrying out his plan to keep Candice out of harm's way.

After placing the document down on his worn wood coffee table, he went to pick up his cell phone to call Candy, but a couple of rapid-fire knocks on his apartment door prevented him from completing the task.

Gently placing the cell phone down on the table, Rock stared suspiciously across the room at the door. He knew it couldn't be Candice, because she had the keys to his apartment. No one else visited him. Period. He remained quiet and waited.

There were three knocks again, this time harder and more insistent.

Rock slowly rose from his recliner and, walking as lightly as a man his size could, went into his bedroom. He retrieved his .357 Heckler & Koch and stuffed it into the back of his pants. Sweat droplets lined up like ready soldiers across his forehead, and a few drops ran down his temples. Rock felt an overwhelming urge to cough, but he stifled it.

"Barton!" A familiar voice filtered in from the other side of the door. "Open up!"

Rock's chest tightened with dread. He couldn't swallow, and he could no longer hold in his cough. Suddenly, a loud cough erupted from his chest. *They said they'd never come back. I was done with their program and set free,* he thought. His stomach muscles clenched, and the burning in his chest flared up like a newly kindled fire.

"Barton, don't make us put your business in the streets for all of your neighbors to hear. Now, open up," the voice boomed again.

Those words propelled Rock forward, his steps heavy and mechanical. Flipping and twisting locks, he finally pulled back the door, fear flitting through his heart. Rock had experienced this feeling only one other time in his life—when he'd been captured in Vietnam and offered over to the CIA.

"Barton, what's the matter? You don't look happy to see us," a tall, wrinkled white man said with a crooked Clint Eastwood grin.

Rock knew the man well. They were around the same age. Only, Rock had aged much better. He took a few steps back, stumbling as the man and his younger counterpart pressed forward, invading his personal space. Rendered powerless, Rock eyed them with unsuppressed hatred. He was willing himself not to kill them on the spot and quickly dispose of the bodies. Rock knew his plans were futile at best; the old white man most definitely had countersnipers posted outside his place. That was their style. Rock had, after all, been one of them.

"So I guess you won't be inviting us in for tea," Wrinkled Face stated, his false teeth clicking slightly against the roof of his mouth. He looked around at Rock's meager living arrangements.

"Okay, we'll just make ourselves comfortable, if you don't mind," the fake Clint Eastwood look-alike said, patting a place next to him on Rock's threadbare sofa for his partner to sit on. "So this is what became of one of our best-trained assassins, huh?" the man commented, with a smirk.

Rock's face remained stoic, his eyes hooded over, and fists clenched.

"Barton, I'll get right down to it. This is, of course, not a pleasure visit. I know we haven't spoken in eons. How long has it been? Thirty-plus years, right?" Wrinkled Face looked up at the ceiling like he was recalling their past from some far-distant place in his mind.

Rock could still hear traces of the man's British accent. He regulated his breathing and calmed himself down.

"How've you been feeling these days, Barton?" the old man continued, trying to goad Rock into talking. "We're all getting old, I suppose."

"What do you want?" Rock finally spoke, his words barely a whisper.

"We have one more job for you."

Rock's facial expression turned stony; his mood dark.

"I know after your debriefing we told you that you were free to go forever, but now there is one last thing we need from you."

Rock shook his head back and forth. The Agency had told him he was free to go. They had put him through a very painful debriefing, complete with mood and mind-altering drugs, trying to deprogram him from being a "cleaner," and Rock played along with it, enduring the ordeal. But he had never forgotten what he'd learned, as much as he wished he could at times.

"I'm free. I won't do it," Rock said firmly. He had more than paid his dues for the murders he'd committed in Vietnam.

"Oh, this is not optional. We are not asking," Wrinkled Face replied, his tone deadly.

Rock flexed his jaws back and forth.

"Barton, when we let you go, you were supposed to stay out of our business, but you couldn't. Somehow you got linked in with a couple of our most valuable street assets. We found you in the middle of one of our operations in the mid to late eighties. Ah, yes, Operation Easy In," the old man said, as if the name just popped up in his memory.

The CIA program began by distributing crack cocaine in low-income neighborhoods in New York City and Los Angeles. The distribution was to fund Reagan's Contras. Through the controlled distribution of the new and cheap spin on regular cocaine, the government was also able to set their plans in motion to rid cities of the worst ghettos, like a self-inflicted genocide.

In New York, the CIA had duped Eric "Easy" Hardaway into taking part in their distribution scheme, and in L.A. they had duped "Freeway" Ricky Ross into signing on to their scheme. The promise of a better life with riches galore had lured Easy right into the CIA's trap. When Rock learned about it through some of his old sources, he put himself in a position to protect Easy. He had tried talking Easy out of the game, but he didn't realize the only way out for Easy was through death.

"So you will do this one last thing? Or else you will go to jail for the rest of your life for the massacre of your favorite drug dealer, Eric Hardaway, and his family. We will paint the picture so vividly of how you killed them and kept one girl alive for your depraved desires," Rock's old nemesis calmly informed him.

The words flowed from the man's tight lips with ease, as if he was ordering toast and eggs for breakfast.

"You couldn't leave well enough alone, could you, Barton? Do you think she was left alive by accident? Shame on you if you did," the man said.

Rock grew angrier by the minute.

"What did you do, Barton? Feed the girl the evidence we planted so she came up with suspects? She opened up a can of worms again when she started digging. It has been four years. You should've let sleeping dogs lie, or at least controlled your protégée a little better. We will let her live if and when you complete this job."

Rock shook his head left to right. He had never told Candice anything about who had killed her father. Candice had heard about suspects on the news. Rock had locked the information he'd acquired over the years in a safe. It wasn't until long after the family's deaths that he figured out that the suspects were just fed to the media.

When Candice started showing an interest in the planted suspects—the pawns—he quickly set out to protect her, following her almost everywhere. His mission every day was to keep her safe, and he took that job very seriously.

"It was you that threw her to the wolves this time, wasn't it, Barton? What will we call our new operation? How does Operation Hard Candy sound to you? That has a nice ring to it, don't you think?" he taunted.

Rock clenched his fists behind his back. He swayed on his feet. He thought about taking his gun from his pants and killing the two devils occupying his personal space. He bit down into his jaw harder now. The metallic taste of blood made him feel animalistic.

"So, either you do this, or you go to jail for life. If you go to jail, we will see to it that the last Hardaway is taken care of. How does that sound?" Wrinkled Face was goading him.

Rock blinked rapidly, truly at a loss for words.

"I take that as a yes. Well, that is just splendid," the old man said, standing up like he'd just gotten great news.

The other man stood up as well.

"Barton, you didn't even ask me what I've been up to these days. How rude! Well, I'll just tell you. I run the same program you were in, but for all government agencies now. Even the DEA. Too bad we will never have one as good and dedicated as you. You were like a machine in your day," the Clint Eastwood look-alike said, lifting his hand and placing it on Rock's shoulder. "But even machines get old and need replacing after a while." The man laughed at his own joke.

Rock's nerve endings were on edge. His skin burned where the man touched his shoulder.

"When we leave here someone will be contacting you with information about the job. This one has to be done smoothly, or else things could go terribly wrong. I am confident in you, Barton. I'm sure you don't want to go back to where we first met," he cautioned, walking toward the door to leave.

When the door slammed behind the two devils, Uncle Rock raced over to it and secured all of the locks. He bent over and dry heaved on the hardwood floors. He felt like a wild animal, wanting to rip his prey to pieces with his bare hands and teeth. He had no choice in the matter. Candy's life was at stake, and there was no room for error. Whatever they asked him to do, he would do it, even if it meant killing someone to save Candy's life.

Chapter 8

"Yo, son, these niggas are always late. It's like they make a point of doing this shit to prove their power." Junior looked at his watch impatiently.

Avon Tucker was noncommittal. The anxiety welling up inside of him was enough to make him vomit, so he decided to just keep his mouth shut. Avon was so close to finding out who Junior bought his drugs from, it made his dick hard. That was all he needed to get the recognition and redemption he so desperately needed from the DEA. Brubaker had been putting a great deal of pressure on him lately. Now the possibility of a clean slate was dangling in front of Avon like a carrot in front of a starving horse.

Junior looked at his watch again and let out an exasperated sigh. "These motherfuckers playin' tonight, and everything in the streets is on E since we been caught up with that Razor shit."

Avon remained silent.

"Yo, Tuck. Motherfucker, I'm up in here by myself or some shit?" Junior said.

Tuck nodded his agreement.

Junior furrowed his eyebrows and stared over at the side of Tuck's face as he stared straight ahead, clearly preoccupied with other matters.

"Yo, nigga, you givin' me the silent treatment or some shit?" Junior asked, screwing his face up even more.

Avon quickly snapped out of his trance.

"Nah, I'm listening," Tuck replied, glancing over at Junior.

"You seem distant since the other night . . . you know, at my brother's crib. I ain't got to explain myself to nobody, son. You was right there and heard that nigga Phil give his word that he ain't murk Razor. This nigga Broady been out of control for a minute. I'm tired of the nigga."

Tuck was now giving him his full attention.

"I been taking care of that nigga since my moms had him. I'm thirty-five years old, and I been acting like a father to this nigga since I was ten. My moms treated that nigga like shit from birth. She decided after she had him that she hated his pops. That nigga pops used to beat my mom's ass. When he got killed at a gambling spot, it's like she just started hatin' him. Nah, more like despising him. If I wasn't around that li'l nigga, he wouldn't even eat. It's like she was depressed and blamed that nigga for her depression and shit. I was a kid, man. I couldn't see my baby brother fucked up like that. I tried to school the nigga when he started playing ball in school. Stay in school, stay in school, I drilled that nigga hard body, but it's like Broady was fuckin' determined to be like me." Junior checked his watch again.

"How did you wind up in the game?" Tuck inquired. They had nothing but time anyway.

"It was simple. Same story, different hood. Where I lived at in the eighties, shit was serious. Heroin and expensive-ass powder coke had been replaced by cheap-ass crack, and niggas was making tons of money. Once that shit made it to the hood, it was like magic for some and destruction for others. I was hungry and fucked up. My moms had been struggling after Broady's father got iced, and she lived off the system. That was it. Occasionally, she would get a boyfriend that helped out here and there. So, in essence, she either waited on men or the *man* to give her loot." Junior reflected somberly.

He made direct eye contact with Tuck to see if he had his attention now. Tuck was glued. Satisfied, Junior continued on with his rags-to-riches tale.

"I used to walk through my hood dreaming of driving those big cars and wearing the big chains and shit I used to see motherfuckers rockin'." Junior chuckled as he reminisced. "Then one day, I was being chased out of a corner store by the owner for tryin'a steal a loaf of bread for me and Broady to make sandwiches outta whatever crap we had in the crib. Shit, I used to make the best syrup and sugar sandwiches around." Junior smiled. "Anyway, that's when I ran into Eric 'Easy' Hardaway. I'm sure you heard hood legends about Easy, right?"

Tuck nodded in the affirmative. *Who hasn't heard of Easy?* Tuck only knew about Eric Hardaway from a brief he'd received before going undercover. Basically, he'd been told who killed Easy and why, but he wasn't sure how much the government's version of events could be trusted.

"Yeah, son, Easy was the man in my neighborhood, and everybody knew it. He graduated from corner boy to boss and he was on the come-up. The day I got chased by the store owner, Easy was with this older cat, kicking it in his tight-ass Maxima. Yeah, that fuckin' Maxima was the big status car of hustlers at that time. Easy's shit had the silver paneling on the side, all that. I remembered staring at Easy and the older dude through the windshield of the car and thinking I wish I could be like Easy.

"When Easy saw the store owner chasing me, he hopped out his ride and intervened. That fat Puerto Rican bodega owner backed the fuck down real quick. Easy grabbed me up and told me there wasn't no need to be stealing. He made me apologize to the store dude. Yo, that nigga Easy took me inside and bought me five bags of groceries. I mean, bread, lunch meat, rice, juices, the works. I was embarrassed at first, especially because the older dude with Easy just kept staring at me like I was a dirty thief, but Easy made me feel good, man. He never made me feel like a charity case.

"After that day, Easy gave me a job. I was thirteen years old. I started out delivering packages of weight. Then I graduated to sales. After a while, Easy let me live and have a few of my own workers. I grew up in this game. It's all I know."

"So you worked for Easy for a lot of years?" Tuck asked, although he already knew the answer.

"*Ssss!* What? Hell yeah, son. I was under Easy for eighteen-plus years when that nigga got murked. I was down for that dude from thirteen until I was thirty-one. That's a lot of loyalty right there. Easy was good to niggas to a certain extent, but he was a power tripper, ya dig? Easy Hardaway wasn't gon' let a nigga rise above him in the game, you know, one of those type niggas that always kept his thumb on ya back." Junior gritted.

Tuck could see he'd struck a nerve with Junior. "It wasn't till Easy was outta the way that you got your position at the top then?" Tuck asked innocently.

"Damn, nigga! When you ask it like that, you make it seem like I was jealous of that nigga. Or like I wanted a nigga outta the way and shit." Junior raised his eyebrows, his head cocked to the side, challenging Tuck's question.

"Nah. I'm just sayin', it seems to me like that nigga was holding you back. But I know you respected him enough to let him have his shine," Tuck said to clean up his slip.

"Exactly. I had so much respect for the nigga over the years, I woulda been happy just letting the nigga ride as the top dog. Easy gave me a tiny piece of a big pie, and I was content for a minute on that shit. I was eatin' lovely. I had my own little peoples workin' for me and shit. I was giving Easy his cut. It was all gravy for a minute.

"But Easy changed up the game. That nigga started getting fucked up in his old age, though, I'ma tell you that. Like tryin'a make his little teenage-ass son like a boss and shit," Junior explained, his tone angry. "Son, I was in my thirties. You think I wanted to be told what the fuck to do by a seventeen-year-old li'l nigga?"

"Nah, I can't imagine that." Tuck knew what it was like to take orders from somebody you didn't really respect. He had been doing it for a lot of years with the DEA.

"There was a lot of niggas on the streets not happy with Easy and his decision making. I was hearing talk that niggas wanted to get rid of him, just wipe him out completely. Not leaving no heirs to his shit, nothing. As a matter of fact, Easy's own son, who was also called Junior, wasn't happy with some of the decisions that nigga Easy was making at the time. And, yo, that nigga Eric Junior was straight seven thirty. I heard that li'l nigga used to wild out in the house, breaking shit up, trying to fuck up his mother and little sisters. Straight buggin'. They said the nigga had, um, what you call that shit, *psychicis* or some *psycho*-shit." Junior made circles with his index finger next to his head, giving the universal sign for crazy.

"You mean, psychosis?"

"Yeah, that shit you just said. He was a crazy motherfucker that needed to be on lockdown somewhere. So, now imagine how I felt with this dude Easy appointing this li'l crazy nigga as the boss of me. *Ssss*!" Junior shook his head and sucked his teeth.

"That must've been fucked all the way up," Tuck said, trying to encourage Junior to continue his stroll down memory lane. The information was certainly proving quite the eye-opener. Tuck had not been told during his undercover briefing that Easy's son had worked for him.

"Hell yeah! Then shit got worse when a nigga I was tight with, kinda like how me and you is tight right now, went missing. I'm saying that nigga Bam-Bam was my ace, my lieutenant. He had my back. Easy called me up and told me I had to murk Bam-Bam because Easy thought he was a cop. I told Easy that ain't no way this nigga was a cop. Easy insisted, and I refused. Easy didn't like it when I questioned his judgment. Easy ain't like no push-back. In his book, any little bit of pressure broke pipes. His fuckin' word was supposed to be the last fuckin' say all the time.

"I wasn't backing down on that one, so that nigga cut my pockets. He shut me the fuck down. Next thing I know, my dude Bam-Bam was missing, never to be found again," Junior said, his voice trailing off. "And I know that nigga Easy had Bam-Bam taken out." Junior had a scowl on his face, and his nostrils flared.

From the tone of his voice, Tuck could tell that Junior's deep-rooted anger was mixed with hurt and disappointment.

"And the cops never figured out what happened to your right-hand man or Easy, huh?"

"Nah, man. Whoever took out Easy also wiped out his entire family. Ain't no tellin' who killed that nigga. It coulda been any fuckin' body out there. Niggas all over Brooklyn and uptown wanted that nigga outta the way. Shit, his own son coulda done it. You know you fucked up in the game when you can't even lay your head at home without keeping one eye fuckin' open." Junior could see some similarity between his situation with Broady and Easy's predicament with his son.

Tuck was burning up inside. He wanted to question Junior further, but it was too dangerous. Junior was no dummy, and Tuck needed to protect his cover.

"Enough about me, nigga. The bottom line is, I'm in the game to stay. I'ma go out blazing like a gangsta. I will take niggas with me if they get in my way too, including that hotheaded-ass brother of mine." Junior chuckled.

Tuck laughed nervously.

"These niggas ain't coming. They musta got cold feet when I told them I was changing up the game and bringing you. I'ma have to go see my dude without you, son," Junior said, pulling his car out of the spot they'd been in for almost two hours.

Tuck's shoulders slumped. *Fuck! Fuck! Fuck!* This was going to be a major setback.

"Lift ya head up, nigga!" Broady growled, throwing another punch that connected with the boy's skull.

The boy's head snapped back so hard, a loud crack resounded through the basement.

Broady had asked the boy to do the impossible. After being tied to a chair for hours and beaten at will, there was no way he could lift up his head. He moaned as pain ripped through his skull again.

"What's ya name, li'l nigga?" Broady gritted, this time grabbing the boy's face roughly and lifting his down-turned head.

The boy's face was a bloody mess. Both of his eyes were swollen shut, and the bridge of his nose was disfigured, broken in more than one place, he imagined.

"*Car—Car—me—llo,*" the boy rasped out. His throat felt like he'd swallowed a fire-lit sword in a circus act.

Broady released his head with a shove, causing more pain to permeate the boy's cranium.

"Carmello? Who the fuck names their kid Carmello?" Broady hissed evilly, circling the boy like a bird of prey. He let out a maniacal laugh. "Y'all heard that shit? This li'l nigga is named Carmello. That shit sound gay as a motherfucker!" Broady chortled, turning to the little cronies he'd hired to abduct the boy.

The two teenaged boys laughed, scared shitless not to agree with anything Broady said.

The two boys had snatched Carmello at gunpoint after luring him to a deserted building with the promise of selling him a pair of Gucci sneakers that nobody else in Harlem owned. Given his love for fashion and his need to have the latest gear, Carmello easily took the bait.

"Carmello, you from uptown, right?" Broady asked, knowing the answer.

Carmello moved his head up and down painfully.

"A'ight then. Since you claiming that whack-ass hood, I'ma give you an uptown history test. If you pass, maybe I'll let ya little punk ass go. But if you fail, nigga, you dead." Broady gritted, spittle settling on his lips.

Carmello couldn't even respond. His eyes were shut, his mouth was bleeding profusely, his wrists burned from the duct tape, and one of his legs pulsed with a throbbing pain. He had fought Broady's little goons so hard, he'd shattered the shin on his left leg.

"Yeah, that's what I'ma do. Give you a test on some real warrior shit—pass or fail," Broady explained. The drugs coursing through his system put him in maniac mode. "You hear me, li'l nigga?" he growled, dissatisfied with the boy's lackluster response.

Carmello finally moved his head slightly to acknowledge his understanding of the situation.

"A'ight then. Now, here we go. You from uptown, and your brother is supposed to be a big-time hustler, correct?"

Broady asked the obvious, not really expecting Carmello to answer, but he nodded his swollen head in the affirmative.

"A'ight. Then that nigga shoulda been schoolin' you to the game, the history of the game, all that shit, right?"

Carmello moved his pulsing head to agree, willing to say anything to keep Broady from hitting him again.

"So, now here's where you need to play for your life," Broady announced, like a magnanimous game show host. "Question number one!" Broady clapped his hands together when he saw Carmello's head drifting to the left.

The boy jumped to attention.

"You listenin', li'l nigga?" Broady asked, grabbing the boy's head back roughly.

"Mmmm!" the boy moaned in excruciating pain.

"Good answer. Here goes your question—for life or death Who is Rich, Alpo, and Azie?" Broady asked, getting close to the boy's ear. He waited for an answer, his eyebrows arched high in fake anticipation.

Carmello whimpered, indicating that he didn't know the answer.

"Awww shit! Don't tell me your big brother ain't never schooled you about how Harlem niggas was gettin' it back in the days?"

Carmello whimpered again, fear literally choking the breath out of his lungs. He started to gag.

"Damn, nigga! I'm from BK, and even I know who Rich, Alpo, and Azie is!" Broady proclaimed, shaking his head in dismay.

Carmello couldn't speak. His heart was hammering a mile a minute.

"You mean to tell me Phil ain't teach you shit about these uptown dudes that paved the way for him? Phil been tryin'a be like them niggas for years. Damn, li'l nigga! You ain't never watch *Paid in Full,* either?" Broady asked in astonishment.

Carmello moved his head slowly from left to right, signaling he had no idea what Broady was talking about.

Broady knew Carmello was young and probably wouldn't know the answer to his question. He just needed a justification for his actions. Getting the answer incorrect was justification enough.

"Well, let me tell you a little about Rich Porter. A'ight, think of that nigga Rich like your brother Phil. See, Rich was gettin' paper up there where you from, and he had a little brother just like you. Matter of fact, I think y'all was the same age. Rich used to give his brother everything, the hottest clothes, sneakers, all that shit, just like Phil be giving you, from the looks of the shit you was rockin' and the knot you had in ya pocket. But you know what happened to Rich's little brother?" Broady asked, his voice dripping with venom.

Carmello began to moan. He obviously didn't know, but he had to be brain-dead to have not figured out how the story would end.

"A big bad monster like me kidnapped Rich's brother, cut off his finger, and sent it to Rich in the mail," Broady announced with glee.

Carmello started moaning louder and trying to shake his legs, even the broken one.

"I ain't finished yet. Then the same big bad monster cut off Rich's brother's head and left it in a McDonald's bathroom uptown!" Broady grabbed Carmello's head and yanked it back roughly, exposing his neck.

Carmello pissed and shit on himself from fright.

Candice fought with Uncle Rock's door lock once again. She'd refused to argue with him about it. She sucked her teeth in disgust. She planned to surprise him with a visit. Ever since the day at the range, she realized just how much she missed him and just how sick he might really be. She also wanted to brag to him about how she'd set up the weapon on the roof and tested out her sniper skills yesterday.

"Uncle Rock!" she called out as she stepped through the front door. The apartment was unusually stuffy and hot. Of course, it was dusty too. "Ugh!" she grunted, her face scrunched up. "Uncle Rock!" she called out again, glancing over at the bathroom door, which stood wide open. She walked farther into the apartment and peered into the bedroom. It was empty. The same for the kitchen. "Damn! I missed him." She sighed.

She decided to leave him a note to let him know she had dropped by for a visit. She looked down at the coffee table and noticed a piece of paper on it that she could use for her note. "A pen, a pen," she chanted, picking up the paper and looking around. She grabbed one from his crowded bookshelf and walked back over to the coffee table.

Bending to write on the piece of paper, she read the top line without thinking. Candice's heart seized in her chest. She became hot all over her body, and her nerve endings stood up. "What the fuck? A last will and testament?" she whispered. A sick feeling washed over her. Why would Uncle Rock have this written out? She figured it must have something to do with the cough and the blood.

Candice's mind raced, and her heart thumped painfully against her sternum. Her legs weakened, forcing her to sit down. With unsteady hands, Candice unfolded the sheet of paper and read: "I, Joseph Barton, of sound body and mind, hereby—"

"What are you doing?" Uncle Rock growled, suddenly looming above her. He had doubled back for something and found his door unlocked. He snatched the paper out of her hand before she could read any further.

Candice's eyes widened, and her mouth popped open.

"Leave! Get out!" Uncle Rock yelled, his voice an angry, booming bass. It was his only defense. He didn't know what else to say or do at that moment.

Candice scrambled off the couch with a pained look on her face. She was in a daze, her eyes wild with hurt, distrust, and fear. She couldn't even speak. Uncle Rock was a liar. It was all a lie. She took several awkward steps backward, swallowing the hard lump that had formed in her throat.

Uncle Rock stared at her, fire flashing in his eyes, his hands curled into two gorilla fists.

Candice had no choice but to turn and run out of the apartment, tears streaming down her face like a waterfall.

Uncle Rock started to give chase but decided against it. He unfurled his hands and looked down at his trembling fingers. He slapped his bald head with his hands. He squeezed his head tightly, needing to think straight. He didn't mean for it to happen like this. He needed to keep Candice far away from him right now. He knew they were watching him. Being around him would place her in grave danger.

But having her mad at him made him want to die. Pain gripped him like a vise. He slumped down to the floor, his legs giving out. Turning his head to the side, he threw up the blood that had been collecting in his mouth.

Candice raced to her car and slid into the driver's seat in a white-hot haze of fury. The tears would not stop coming. Her hands shook so badly, it took her five tries to get her key into the ignition. She kept replaying the words she'd read back in her mind. She slammed her fists against the steering wheel and screamed. *Not uncle Rock. He was all I had. He promised never to lie to me.*

It might not have been such a big deal for some people, but the bond between Candice and Uncle Rock was one that had been built on trust.

Candice couldn't think straight. Wheeling her car out of the parking spot, horns blared from behind. She was driving recklessly.

Speeding down Brooklyn's streets, Candice decided niggas had to die—and soon. She was really out for blood now. She wasn't going to let another slipup or another killer prevent her from getting to any of her marks again. She'd step up her "cleaner" game and then get the fuck out of Dodge.

Chapter 9

Avon drove down the New Jersey Turnpike, doing over one hundred miles an hour. He needed to get out of New York for a minute. He needed to think. After the big disappointment with Junior's connect not showing up, he felt like his case was slipping away from him. Avon usually warned Brubaker when he wanted a trip home. The DEA undercover team had to always account for him, so if he was leaving his assignment, he needed to let them know.

Not this time. Avon wanted to lay eyes on his wife and his kids. He felt like he needed to see them to put things back in perspective. His life as Tuck was spiraling out of control. He was losing a grasp on his case, which meant on his career and reality.

Avon had been in Brooklyn so long, looking at concrete sidewalks, crowded streets, and dilapidated buildings, the clean, quiet, tree-lined streets in the Bowie, Maryland subdivision where he had purchased a home with his wife made him feel like he was an outsider. His heart pumped uncontrollably as he drew nearer to his street. He wondered what kind of homecoming he'd receive. He knew his wife would probably scream and cry and try to scratch his eyes out for being so neglectful. He wondered if the kids would recognize him with the shaved head, a feature that belonged solely to Tuck.

Avon rounded a corner and slowed his car to ease up to the driveway. He swallowed the knot of fear lodged in the back of his throat. He didn't know why he was so nervous to be home. He was only three houses away from his home when he suddenly threw on his brakes, causing his body to lurch forward and thump back onto the seat. "It can't be," he whispered, squinting to get a better view of his driveway. He couldn't be seeing right. He could swear that was Brad Brubaker's personal car parked in front of his home.

A car behind him beeped its horn. Startled, Avon pulled his car over to a curb outside of a house down the street from his own. His house was in plain view now. It was five o'clock in the morning, too early for Brubaker to be making a goddamn check up on Avon's wife and kids. Avon's first instinct was to drive up to his house like a madman, kick in the door, and start whipping some ass, but he needed to see it with his own eyes to believe it.

He could hear Brubaker's voice in his head. *I saw Elaina and the kids. They're doing well. She says you haven't called. You might want to reach out and get in touch with your wife.* Avon's chest heaved up and down. He dug into his waistband and set his street weapon on his lap. Nobody knew he was coming home. *If I murder these traitor-ass bastards, nobody would even suspect me.* Brubaker had never set up Avon's surveillance team, as he had asked for and been promised.

"This motherfucker planned on leaving me out there for dead so he could fuck my wife." Avon gritted, his teeth gnashing together.

Before Avon could decide on a course of action, he noticed the garage door of the house going up. His heart started thumping so hard, he could feel it in his throat.

Elaina emerged dressed in a pair of skintight running shorts and a sports top. Pfeifer, the golden retriever she and Avon picked out at an animal shelter before they'd had children, came running out of the garage after her.

Avon felt a stab of pain in his chest. Being gone eight months seemed like years to Avon. He'd forgotten how beautiful his wife was. Her skin was still smooth and her hair as silky as he remembered it. Elaina started jogging in his direction, with Pfeifer leading the way.

"Shit!" Avon quickly threw himself down in the seat. He didn't want her to see him. He didn't know what he would do or say to her right then. He stayed down in the seat until she passed. He knew she wouldn't recognize the Lexus.

Elaina jogged by the car and disappeared into the running trails behind their house. This was a prime opportunity for him to enter the house, kill Brubaker, and let his wife come home to find her murdered lover in the bed—a bed she was supposed to be keeping warm until her husband returned.

But the thought of his kids sleeping soundly nearby caused him to scratch the idea entirely. He decided to wait for Brubaker to come out of the house. Then he'd blow his fucking brains out right there on the quiet residential street.

After forty-five minutes of watching the house and willing himself to stay calm, Avon spotted Elaina and the dog trotting back to the house, coming from the opposite direction. She'd run the entire five miles of the trail. Avon knew that because he used to be her running partner.

A surge of longing overcame him, but it was soon replaced with pure unadulterated anger. When his wife got to the front door of the house, Avon saw her stop dead in her tracks and smile. A few seconds later, Avon's son and daughter came bounding out of the house, dressed for school. Avon still knew the difference between their school clothes and play clothes. A hot feeling came over his entire body, a combination of hurt and extreme love for his family.

Elaina bent down and both kids hugged her neck. She was still smiling. Avon knew how much she adored her children. Inadvertently, he caught himself smiling.

His smile quickly turned into an evil grimace when Brad Brubaker walked out of his garage. Elaina bestowed him with that same smile. Avon gripped his gun tightly as he watched Brubaker kiss his wife on the lips and pick up his daughter. From where he sat, they looked like a one big happy family.

Avon racked the slide on his 9mm Glock, holding it tight in his sweaty hand. A small tornado of thoughts whipped through his mind. He could kill Elaina and Brad right there on the street, but he'd tell them just what he thought of them first.

He closed his eyes, trying to squeeze back the tears, when he saw his kids pile into Brubaker's car. Flexing his jaw in and out, Avon couldn't take it anymore. He mashed the gas pedal of the Lexus, and it lurched out of hiding. Tires squealing, he drove a few paces, taking the car haphazardly onto the sidewalk in front of his house.

Elaina and Brubaker jumped. Elaina's eyes stretched so wide, it looked as if they would pop right out of their sockets.

Brubaker swallowed a hard lump of fear that formed in the back of his throat. His face turned beet red, like a cooked lobster.

"This is what the fuck you been doing while I was in the streets, risking my fuckin' life?" Avon barked, leveling his gun at Brubaker's head.

"Avon! No!" Elaina screeched at the top of her lungs.

Pfeifer was barking ferociously and running around in circles. He didn't even recognize Avon anymore.

Brubaker put his hands up high in surrender. "Tucker, it's not what you think."

"I just saw you kiss my fuckin' wife!" Avon growled, his voice rising from the depths of his abdomen. Avon's hands were shaking, and his lips curled into a knot. He placed his gun against Brubaker's temple.

"Daddy! Stop it! Daddy!"

Avon heard his kids calling from the backseat of Brubaker's car.

The screams brought some of the neighbors from their homes. A few watched from their lawns, none daring to intervene in the family affair.

Avon's hands were shaking even more now, and sweat dripped down his forehead.

"Avon, pa-lease!" Elaina begged, tears cascading down her face. "I thought you were gone. He told me that you had left, turned on us. You never called," she cried.

"So you fuck him? You don't wait to hear from me," Avon rebutted, his voice cracking. As time stood still, Avon kept his gun pressed against Brubaker's head.

Avon heard his daughter scream out again, "Daddy! Don't shoot him!"

Avon knew this scene would traumatize his kids. His shoulders slumped slightly as he felt a sharp tug in his heart.

Focusing intently on his target, he almost didn't hear the sirens wailing in the distance. Someone had called the police.

Avon moved his gun and took a few faltering steps backwards, refusing to turn his back on Brubaker. Hastily, he jumped back into the driver's seat of the Lexus and reversed off the sidewalk, and the car came off the raised curb with a loud clang. Avon wheeled the car into drive and screeched away. He took the back exit of the subdivision, figuring the police would come through the front entrance.

As Avon drove away, he blinked back tears, his heart thumping painfully against his sternum. He had not felt a sense of hurt and loss like this since his father's death. The only thing that kept him from murdering his coworker and adulterous wife was the fact that the two traitors stood in the presence of his kids. As he navigated the car back toward I-95 North, he told himself that he wasn't done with Brad Brubaker just yet.

Although Shana was afraid of Broady on most days, right now she was too angry to feel fear. She stalked through the house in a murderous rage. *How dare this motherfucker not come home for two gotdamn days!*

Shana saw her reflection in a mirror as she passed through the hallway. She shook her head in disgust at the large, dark circles forming under her red-rimmed eyes. Running a nervous hand through her tousled hair, her chipped nails snagged in the nest of hair. *This bastard got me 'round here looking like shit, worried fuckin' sick, and he just decided he wasn't coming home? He must take me for a fuckin' fool!*

At first when Broady didn't come home, considering the fact that they had just buried his best friend, who had also gone missing and then turned up dead, Shana had good reason to suspect foul play. She had been a blubbering mess.

Between crying and pulling her hair out, she had called Broady's phone at least every two minutes. It rang each time, which told Shana that the phone was on and not turned off or disconnected. Shana had left so many voice mails for Broady that each time she called back the voice prompt "Mailbox is full" came on. When Broady finally picked up his phone and told her to mind her fucking business about where he was, Shana thought she would lose her mind on him. Although relieved to hear his voice, she cursed and screamed at him for his nonchalant attitude until he hung up on her.

To vent about Broady, Shana tried calling Candice a couple of times, but even she appeared to not be answering her phone. Shana felt dejected and distraught, but she was also seething mad.

"Wait 'til that nigga steps foot in this house," she ranted.

Over the years she had dealt with Broady's philandering. There were even times when bitches followed her home and called her cell phone just to brag about the fact that sometimes when she left the house, Broady would call them up for a quick fuck in her bed. Shana used to lose her mind over it. She would curse, cry, and scream, but Broady would always persuade her to stay on, reminding her that she really didn't have anywhere or anybody to turn to. But enough was enough. Shana told herself that between the beatings and now cheatings, she'd had about all she could take. Being around Candice had convinced her that she needed to spread her wings a bit and learn to be an independent woman. She knew if she left Broady, her homegirl would be there to support her.

Shana stopped pacing the house when she heard Broady's keys turning in the lock. A hot flash came over her body, and she whirled around with fire in her eyes. Broady came through the door, and Shana immediately lit into him. Ignoring her completely, he headed for the stairs.

Shana quickly cut him off in the dark foyer, barely able to make out his face. She didn't care if he looked angry, she was ready for this fight.

"So you fuckin' finally decide to come home after two days? Here I am thinking somebody killed ya fuckin' ass, and you was probably out with some bitch or some shit! Do you know how gotdamn worried I was, Broady? Ya brother after your head, them uptown niggas afta you, and I'm not supposed to worry?" Shana screeched, her hands flailing in front of her, and her neck dipping side to side.

Broady pushed past her. "You better get the fuck up outta my face, Shana. I'm tellin' you," Broady growled.

Shana followed him, her fury clouding her mind and giving her the necessary courage to continue. "You think you just gon' walk up in here without an explanation? Yeah, you can hit me and beat my ass, but I'm still gon' speak my fuckin' piece!"

"Bitch, I'm tellin' you to keep it fuckin' movin'," Broady said in a deceptively calm voice.

Shana was expecting him to jump on her and choke her, or slap her into obedience. Instead, he simply walked away. She followed him up the steps and into their bedroom.

"Broady! I want a fuckin' explanation!" Shana screamed, her voice cracking. Tears started running down her face from all of the built-up emotion.

Broady finally turned around toward her. "A'ight! You obviously don't know how the fuck to listen. I told you to shut the fuck up and leave me alone, but you kept right on!" Broady's voice boomed. He flipped on the ceiling light in their bedroom.

Shana's mouth dropped open. She stared at him, and he stared back at her. Her legs became weak as she opened her mouth to speak, but no words came out.

Broady approached her like a deranged lunatic. "Now you still wanna fuckin' beef?" he hissed, spit flying from his mouth. Blood was splattered all over the front of his shirt, and there were large drops of dried blood on his sneakers as well.

"What . . . what did you do?" Shana choked out in fear, stepping back slowly.

Out of nowhere, the monster advanced on her, his hands outstretched. Shana didn't have enough time to escape his quick strides.

Broady grabbed her around her neck and lifted her off her feet with one hand, her petite frame no match for his brute strength. He squeezed her neck tight.

Shana's feet swung wildly as her body fought for oxygen. Drool spilled down her lips and ran down her chin onto Broady's giant claw hands. Her bulging eyes rolled back into her head, and her entire body went limp.

Candice sucked her teeth angrily as her cell phone buzzed for the fiftieth time. She didn't bother to look at the caller ID since she already knew who it was.

"Shana! Stop fuckin' calling me. Obviously I don't wanna talk!" Candice screamed into the air, pressing the ignore button once again. Candice didn't have time for distractions. She was angry enough to shoot up an entire neighborhood right now. She certainly couldn't take a chance with any of her marks turning up missing before she had the opportunity to exact her own brand of justice. What she had read at Uncle Rock's house wasn't going to deter her from her mission. No matter what.

Candice packed her supplies and set the small black duffel bag next to the plastic case that held her AR-15. She ripped open the plastic on a brand-new pair of black leather gloves and slid one glove over her fingers. She held the gloved hand up to her face and examined the fit. Uncle Rock always told her that the gloves had to be like her second skin, with no awkwardness to impede movement. Candice dressed in all black as well. No matter what Uncle Rock had done in his past, she realized that his intentions had been good and he had taught her well.

Candice didn't have the benefit of having Uncle Rock's old beater to drive this time. She didn't care about driving her Audi, either. She wasn't worried about anybody recognizing her car.

Feeling ruthless as she climbed into her ride, she wheeled it out of the parking space and headed to Broady and Shana's house. Broady would be first. Candice thought about showing up at Shana's door, going inside, and then blowing Broady's brains out on the spot. But, she decided against it because she didn't want to put Shana through that type of trauma. She decided that she would wait for him to leave the house and follow him wherever he went that night. She was going to see to it that he didn't return home.

Candice pulled to the corner of their block but was unable to turn onto the street. A police officer came walking toward her car, giving some crazy-looking hand signals to indicate that she needed to reroute her car. The DO NOT CROSS tape was being rolled out to section off a part of the street. Lights flashed from all of the police and ambulance vehicles parked haphazardly on the street, giving an eerie glow to the night.

Candice furrowed her eyebrows. "What the fuck is going on out here?" she whispered. Her first instinct was to hightail it out of there, since she had a high-powered weapon in her trunk. But the police on the scene were too preoccupied to search her car.

Candice parked on the corner and began walking up the street to investigate the situation. A small glint of worry crossed her mind. *Maybe this has something to do with why Shana was blowing up my phone. Maybe he beat her up again. Or worse.*

She picked up her pace, inching closer to the police activity. As she got closer, she realized that Shana and Broady's house was in fact the center of attention. Full-fledged panic set in. A fine sheen of sweat broke out on her forehead, and Candice began to run, a thousand thoughts crossing her mind at once.

Though Candice worried about Shana, she was equally concerned that someone had killed Broady before she got the chance to do it herself. That would be the second of her marks to turn up dead. She remembered Shana telling her that Broady was in beef with dudes from uptown. *Shit!* What if they got him first? Candice scolded herself for not considering other such possibilities.

A uniformed officer stopped her when she got within a few feet of the house. "Ma'am, you cannot go any further," he said gruffly, placing his hand up to halt her steps.

Huffing and puffing, Candice was a mixture of nervous anxiety and physical exhaustion. "That is my sister's house," she lied outright.

"Well, you can't go in there right now," the officer chided with an attitude. "This is a crime scene, ma'am."

Candice stepped back. "Will you at least tell me if the victim is a female or male? I'm worried about my sister," she said, playing the role of a concerned family member.

"I can't give you any information. If your sister happens to be a victim, someone from the detective squad will contact you as next of kin. Your sister does have your information stored someplace, right?" The officer lifted an eyebrow. He'd heard the "that's my sister or brother" line a million times before.

Candice nodded absentmindedly. Of course, Shana had her information. Her cell phone records at least would indicate that the two of them were indeed close.

Candice took in the scene, her gaze riveted to the Emergency Service Unit parked in front of the home, as well as the FDNY ambulance. The entire scene was overwhelming. Exasperated, she turned to leave just as a storm of dark blue uniforms and trench coats rushed out of the house. Some of the EMTs were carrying a stretcher, but the police and other EMTs swarmed around the body, preventing her from seeing who was on it.

Through the static-filled police and medical personnel communication via two-way radios, Candice understood that the victim was a female with a gunshot wound. She was unconscious and had lost a lot of blood. She put her hand over her mouth. *It is Shana. Oh my God! Broady shot Shana! That motherfucker!*

"ETA to the county is approximately six minutes," an EMT reported in his call to the trauma center at Kings County Hospital.

Struck with a burst of energy, Candice raced back toward her car. She was going to follow the ambulance. She was hoping they could save Shana's life. Shana may have been just a means to an end for her initially, but she was certainly not a bad person. Unlike most people Candice knew, Shana deserved to live.

Chapter 10

Candice pulled her car onto a side street near the hospital. Still a bit shaken up by the turn of events, she exited on wobbly legs and walked toward the trunk of her car. She lifted the hard plastic spare tire cover and placed the black case and her duffel bag deep inside, near the donut spare tire. She locked the small cover with her key and then locked the trunk from the outside. She knew better than to leave her valuables unsecured in her trunk, especially given the off chance that someone could break into her car while she was inside the hospital.

Candice looked over both shoulders to make sure nobody watched her secure the items. When she was comfortable, she climbed back into the car and drove around to Clarkson Avenue, where she inched slowly down the crowded block until she found a parking space.

Candice scrambled out of the car and rushed into the emergency room entrance of Kings County Hospital. Although it was a county hospital, it had the best trauma center in Brooklyn.

"Excuse me," Candice said as she approached the reception desk.

"Take this and fill it out," the young, dark-skinned receptionist snapped without even looking up from her computer.

Candice ignored the young girl's outstretched hand and her obvious lack of customer service skills. "I'm here to see my sister. They just brought her into the trauma center."

"What is her name?" the receptionist asked dryly, still not making eye contact.

Candice was stuck on stupid. She had no idea what Shana's last name was. All of this time, she had never bothered to ask. Some friend she was.

"Hello? What is your sister's last name?"

"Shana Bellamy," a voice answered from behind.

Candice whirled around. Tuck stood just inches behind her, his expression grim. Candice didn't know how Tuck had gotten there. She wondered if it was fate that kept putting them in each other's path. Looking up at him, her body felt hot all over. She didn't know if it was the heat of her embarrassment or simple lust, but she felt like melting and throwing up at the same time.

Tuck glanced quickly at Candice before eyeing the receptionist with contempt. "Shana Bellamy was just brought in by the EMTs. Her sister needs some information right now. As you can clearly see, she is very upset," he said sternly.

The receptionist rolled her eyes and popped the gum she was gnawing on like a hungry hostage. "Hold up," she mumbled, raising a single corn-chip-shaped fingernail. She pecked on a few computer keys and looked back at Candice. "They haven't put your sister in the system yet. Follow those red doors around, and there should be a nurse or doctor that can tell you something."

"Thank you." Candice pivoted toward the red doors.

"Hold on, Candy," Tuck called after her. "I'm coming with you."

Candice didn't resist him this time. She didn't even feel the urge to be mean to him. Riding on a roller coaster of emotions right now, she didn't know what she was going to find out about Shana's condition, so Tuck's presence might not be a bad thing after all. In fact, she thought having him present might just be a welcome distraction and source of support.

When Candice and Tuck walked through the heavy metal doors that led to the trauma center, a security guard immediately stopped them.

"You can't go back there," the wizened old guard warned, moving from behind his station at the small wooden podium.

He reminded Candice of Otis, a security guard that Martin Lawrence played on his sitcom.

"My sister was brought in a few minutes ago. I need some information. The girl out front—"

"You have to sit out there like everybody else and wait for someone to come call for the family of your sister. Nobody is allowed behind these doors," the guard said, wagging his wrinkled hand at Candice.

Candice's eyes dropped. She didn't even know why she was going through all of this for a girl she barely knew. She couldn't understand her concern for Shana, when all she wanted to do was use the girl in the first place. Perhaps she cared about Shana because she knew no one else did, Shana being all alone in the world, much like Candice herself.

Tuck stepped up as Candice turned to walk away. "Wait over there, Candy," he instructed.

"Can I talk to you for minute?" Tuck said to the guard.

The guard furrowed his brows as if he was ready to shout a firm "Hell no."

Tuck didn't give him the chance. Tuck placed his palms roughly on the guard's shoulders, which prompted the old man to turn around so Candice couldn't hear their conversation. He showed the guard something and then heard the guard insist that this was all a misunderstanding.

Tuck suddenly turned with a smile on his face. "C'mon, Candy. Let's go see what we can find out." He held his hand out for her.

Candice bit her bottom lip. What the hell did he say to the guard? She hoped he hadn't flashed his gun at the guard. The last thing she wanted to do was get arrested in the hospital for being an accomplice of sorts. She would deal with Tuck later. For now, she had to focus on getting more information about Shana.

As Tuck led the way to the nurses' station, the pungent smell of disinfectant shot right up Candice's nose and sat at the back of her throat until she thought she could taste the alcohol in it. She looked around at the flurry of activity.

A plump West Indian nurse stood up behind the high counter and asked, "Who let you back here?"

"Ma'am, my girlfriend's sister was brought in. Shana Bellamy. We need information," Tuck explained to the nurse.

His girlfriend? Candice's mind reeled as she tried to concentrate on the nurse's words, spoken in a thick accent.

"This part of the hospital is for staff and patients only. You need to wait outside, and I will find out about her sister."

Before the nurse could utter another word, the air was cut with the sound of loud screams.

"Code blue! Code blue!" nurses and doctors yelled, scurrying every which way.

It seemed like everyone in the area was running to one of the small rooms. Candice's shoulders slumped. She crossed her fingers in her pocket, making a wish that Shana wasn't the intended recipient.

Tuck grabbed her arm. "C'mon, they are busy. We can't stay back here," he said softly.

Candice looked over at him with big doe eyes. She knew he was right. There was no use trying to get any more information out of the staff. They had no choice but to wait outside in the family waiting room until more was known about Shana's condition.

Inside the waiting room, several groups of people huddled together, some hugging and crying, others sleeping on each other's shoulders. The mood in the room was more than glum; it was downright depressing.

Candice found a hard plastic chair and sat down, and Tuck stood against the wall next to her.

After an hour or so, Candice noticed a doctor heading in their direction. She tapped Tuck's arm and motioned her head toward the fast-walking doctor. Her heart thumped wildly, but she relaxed back into her chair, releasing her breath in a large poof of air when the doctor called for the family of a patient named Briggs. She didn't even realize until then that she had been holding her breath.

A loud, ear-shattering scream chilled her right to the bone.

Tuck looked down at the fear mounting in Candice's eyes. "Are you all right, Candy?" he asked, placing a hand on her shoulder.

She nodded her head in the affirmative and then hugged herself tight in an attempt to stop the shivers racking her body.

"How did you find out about Shana?" Tuck asked, looking down at Candice from where he stood, his back against the wall.

"I went by her house to see her. She had been calling me for a couple of days. I didn't know anything was wrong. I mean, I knew Broady had a problem keeping his hands to himself. We

all knew that. But this? I never expected him to shoot her."
Candice wrung her fingers together to release some tension.
"How did you get here yourself?"

"I got a call from Junior sayin' he wanted me to go see
that nigga Broady. I went there to pick up some money that
was owed to Junior," Tuck lied. Junior had sent him to bring
Broady's black ass in.

"Junior's still not upset with Broady over that whole fight
the night of Razor's funeral, is he?" Candice asked, confused.

"I dunno. When I got to Broady and Shana's crib, I found
the door open and blood on the steps. I got the fuck up outta
there. I wasn't tryin'a leave my DNA or fingerprints up in that
camp. I went around the corner and hollered at nine-one-one.
I threw that fuckin' TracFone away and just laid back in the
cut. I couldn't be seen out there. I wasn't tryin'a be no witness.
I got a rap sheet and shit."

Tuck ran a hand down the side of his face. "I saw the medics
leave with her, and I knew they were bringing her to the
county. I got here before them. I ain't even call Junior yet."

"So you think Broady just finally went over the edge on
her?" Candice needed to know more details, even though she
was getting angry just thinking about it.

"With all the blood I saw on the steps, ain't no tellin' what
that nigga went and did. The jake that was out on the scene
mentioned gunshot wounds. Ain't no tellin' who did it, with
shit the way it is in the streets these days," Tuck said, hanging
his head low.

Candice closed her eyes and exhaled. She bit down into her
jaw and forced herself to remain calm. After she learned about
Shana's condition, she would find Broady. Not only was he
going to pay for allegedly participating in the massacre of her
family, he was also going to pay for what he did to Shana.

"You gon' be all right?"

"Yeah, I'ma be okay. But the cops better find Broady before
I do," Candice warned, her legs quaking with suppressed rage.

"A lot of niggas lookin' for Broady, including his own
brother. He better hope the cops find him first," Tuck said
seriously, sitting in one of the newly vacated seats next
to Candice.

***

Six hours later, Candice was startled awake by the voice of a man announcing, "Family of Bellamy!"

She jerked her head from Tuck's shoulder and jumped at the doctor's call. She wiped her face with the palms of both of her hands, trying to clear the cloud of sleep from her eyes. "That's me. I'm, um, her sister," she answered, sleep still evident in her voice.

"Okay then, Ms. Bellamy. We can go and talk," the doctor said.

Tuck stood up and grabbed Candice's arm for support. He knew from police experience that whenever the doctors wanted to take family members into the "bad news" room, shit couldn't be good.

Candice followed the doctor in silence. She allowed Tuck to hold on to her because it felt good, and she honestly wasn't sure if she could do this by herself. She finally admitted to herself that her feelings for Tuck might be a little more complicated than she had realized.

"Have a seat anywhere you'd like," the doctor offered as they entered a room with a long black conference table and swivel chairs.

Candice sat down in the first chair she saw, and Tuck took the seat to her left. Candice steeled herself for the news. Her fists were clenched so hard, her knuckles paled, and her toes were balled up inside of her shoes. Tuck reached for her hand and twined his fingers with hers.

"Ms. Bellamy, I'm afraid that your sister didn't make it," the doctor blurted out, sparing her the details. He had done it enough times to know that wasting time just prolonged the agony of the victim's family.

The doctor's blunt words came across like an explosion in Candice's ears. She blinked rapidly and stared at the doctor in disbelief, swallowing hard and shaking her head from left to right. She looked over at Tuck and then back at the doctor to confirm that she had heard correctly. Tuck's expression erased any concerns she had with her hearing.

"We tried to stop the bleeding in the brain, but it was too severe. Surgery to remove the bullet fragments from the skull is always touch-and-go. She never regained consciousness," the doctor explained.

Candice pushed away from the table and shot upright. She couldn't deal with death right now. Not at a time when she'd just walked out on her relationship with Uncle Rock. Her world seemed to be crumbling down around her. She raced down the hallway, heading toward the nearest exit.

Tuck was hot on her heels. "Candy! Wait! Let me take you home! You can't drive like this!" he yelled after her.

Candice continued at her feverish pace. She just wanted to be left alone.

As Tuck gave chase, his cell phone started vibrating in his pocket. "Shit!" He chose to ignore the call. He raced after her until they both spilled onto the street.

Candice sped to her car, refusing to stop for Tuck. Just as she hit the button to open her car door, Tuck threw himself in front of her, blocking her access. Her chest heaved up and down from the mad dash.

Tuck's chest rose and fell just as fast. "Candy, wait a minute!" he panted. "It's okay. I want to take you home. You're in no condition to drive," he reasoned, struggling to catch his breath.

Candice's lip quivered. She just wanted to get home. Shana's death had her vulnerable. "Please move," she requested in a whisper-like voice. She didn't know if she meant it, but she said it nonetheless.

"No. Let me drive you home. I will even take a cab back to pick up my car later. Let me be here for you," Tuck pleaded.

Candice was overwhelmed by feelings she had never experienced before. His face was so beautiful. She felt weakened by his simple request to help.

"Okay," she whispered, the rush of emotion too much for her to handle. Tears streamed unhindered down her cheeks. And they weren't all for Shana, a girl she hardly knew. Mostly, they were for her—for the life she had been denied.

"It's okay." Tuck grabbed her into a tight embrace as she began to sob in earnest. Tuck held on to her as if she were the last woman on earth.

Candice stood rigidly against his muscular chest. She had not been touched like this, held like this before. She wondered what it felt to be touched and carressed by a man.

In more ways than one, she wasn't prepared to deal with the overpowering sexual attraction she felt toward Tuck at this moment. As she let this stranger hold her closely, her mind became muddled and her judgment cloudy. Candice cried into Tuck's arms, ignoring everything Uncle Rock had warned her about love. She knew Uncle Rock's theories about love had been based on lies, to begin with. For the first time since she'd lost her family, she let herself be vulnerable.

Tuck grabbed Candice's car keys from her tear-soaked hands and opened her car doors, allowing her to enter from the passenger side of the vehicle. "Tell me your address," he said softly as he started the ignition.

"I don't want to go home," Candice whispered, looking at him with sad eyes.

Tuck melted a bit inside. He sucked in his breath and pulled the car out of the spot.

Tuck didn't want to degrade Candice by taking her to the apartment Junior believed he lived at in Brevoort Houses. Feeling just as weak and vulnerable as Candice, he headed for his undercover apartment. He knew it was taking a chance, but he wanted and needed to be with her tonight.

Although he was trying to be strong for her, he was also experiencing some serious trauma from his cheating wife. In fact, Brubaker was probably busy spinning a story about him to the DEA bigwigs right now.

Candice lay her head on the headrest and closed her eyes. For some reason, at that moment, she decided to trust Tuck. Just being in his presence made her feel at ease.

They rode in silence through the streets of Brooklyn, the city lights shining through the windshield and washing over their faces as they drove. Right now, they needed each other more than anyone else.

When they arrived on the Park Slope block, Tuck luckily was able to find a parking spot on the usually overcrowded street. He shook Candice awake.

She jumped up, clutching her bag close to her chest. Tuck was startled by her reaction, and he jumped too.

"Hey, hey, you okay?" he asked softly.

Candice exhaled slowly, gathering her wits. "Where are we?" she asked, looking around, her heart racing wildly. She knew better than to trust anyone, let alone a man. She couldn't believe she'd been so stupid.

"At my place," Tuck calmly replied.

Candice peered out of the window and looked up and down the block. "You live here?" she asked with furrowed brows. She had assumed he lived in one of the bad neighborhoods in Brooklyn.

"Yeah. Let's get going. You need to rest," he said, reaching out and tucking her hair behind her ear.

Candice flinched at his touch.

"I'm not going to hurt you," he reassured, his voice a soft hum. He looked straight in her eyes as he held the back of her head.

Tuck's direct gaze made Candice feel extremely nervous. She wanted to bolt from the car, but her legs felt like two lead pipes. He pulled her head toward his and gently placed his mouth on top of hers.

Candice's mind told her to resist, but her body fell into step.

When Tuck forced his tongue between her pursed lips, she resisted at first, but the hot feeling overcoming her body made her open up and accept him. Their tongues intertwined in a sensual dance. Candice kissed Tuck back like her life depended on it. What she lacked in experience, she made up for with enthusiasm.

When they moved apart, she could feel a throbbing pulse between her legs. She had never felt such an intense feeling down there before.

"You ready?" Tuck asked.

Candice wasn't sure what he was asking for, but she knew what she wanted him to mean. She nodded her head, completely at a loss for words. The pulsation between her legs was enough to drive her crazy.

"C'mon," Tuck said, opening her car door. He placed his hand on the small of her back and led her to his apartment.

When Candice and Tuck reached the door of his apartment, he opened the locks with shaky hands, his mind completely clouded by desire. He was in violation of every rule he'd ever learned as an undercover. This apartment was supposed to be off-limits to anybody who could trace it back to him.

Candice kept her eyes closed. She swallowed the lump of uncertainty and fear lodged in her throat.

Tuck quickly swept his wire and undercover cell phone into the nightstand drawer. He scanned the room to make sure nothing else could expose his real identity. He returned his attention to Candice, slowly unbuttoning her pants as she lay on the bed.

Candice was shaking all over. She started to feel some reservations about taking this any further. She was supposed to be on a mission, killing off the enemy, not sleeping with them.

She thought briefly about her uncle Rock and what he would think about her current situation. She knew he would be beside himself if he knew what she was doing.

With a small rebellious smile, Candice helped Tuck pull her pants off.

Tuck was in awe of Candice's beautiful skin and tight, athletic legs. His hot stare made her feel self-conscious and embarrassed.

Candice moved her hands to cover her most private of places.

"I want to look at you," Tuck whispered sexily as he pulled his pants and boxers off.

She moved her hands covering her neatly trimmed triangle, turning her head to the side. She couldn't look at him directly.

"Relax. I won't hurt you," Tuck said softly. He rolled on a condom and lay next to her on the bed. He could feel her body shaking. He looked at her face, stroking her hair softly. "You can trust me," he whispered.

The words just came before Tuck could even think about them. He didn't even trust himself. He couldn't tell her his real name and certainly couldn't mention that he was a married father of two. He couldn't tell her he was an undercover federal agent that was too dumb to get a handle on his emotions before he brought her to his house.

"I want you, Candy."

Tuck moved in close, the scent of his cologne wafting to the back of her throat. *I don't know what you want me to do. I've never done this before.* Candice stared expectantly at him, not knowing where to even begin. She wanted to believe that, for the first time in four years, she could trust someone other than Uncle Rock. No more tough-girl "cleaner in training." Right now, she was just a teenage girl ready to give it up for the first time.

Tuck kissed her passionately again. He moved his hot mouth from her lips and licked his way down her neck to her breasts. Grabbing each globe with his hands, he moved his tongue back and forth over each nipple until they were both rock hard. Tuck licked the pointed ridges of her areola until she lost her breath.

Diving farther down, he licked across her stomach, stopping to kiss her belly button. Candice's body was on fire. She moaned softly into the pillow, even though she wanted to scream out loud. She had never experienced such sensations in her life. Her nerve endings were supersensitive to his touch.

Tuck stopped abruptly, gazed down into her tortured face, and smiled. Using his knee to make a space for himself between her trembling legs, he coaxed her to relax. His own excitement was making him breathless. He grabbed his manhood and placed it gently against Candice's moist flesh. She jumped. Her legs were quaking against his hips. He bore down gently, assuming it was simply a case of the nerves.

"Ahh," she whimpered, grabbing a handful of the skin on his back. She felt a flash of fire between her legs.

Tuck pushed with a bit more force, using the ridge of his dick to make entry.

"*Ssss!*" Candice winced, a single teardrop escaping from the corner of her eye. The flash of fire had turned into an all-out explosion of pain.

Tuck furrowed his eyebrows, realizing only too late the significance of her body's resistance. Candice was a virgin. He suddenly felt an overpowering surge of protectiveness for her, exhilarated to know that she had chosen him to be her first. He pushed harder against her saturated labia.

"Ahhh!" Candice screamed out again, part in agony, part in ecstasy.

Tuck had broken through her barrier. Candice's tight muscles gripped his shaft like a vise. The pressure felt so good. Tuck moved deeper into her folds.

Candice held on to his back, digging her nails deeper into his skin. The burning sensation was overpowering, but so was the intense pressure against her clitoris.

Tuck moved in and out of her body carefully, her juices soaking his throbbing pole. "You feel so good," he grunted in her ear.

Candice felt goose bumps on her skin. The longer he stayed inside of her, the better it felt. She instinctively began to move her hips in sync with Tuck's. Soon their bodies moved together in perfect rhythm.

Candice felt her body getting closer to a release, the "good feeling," as she called it. The feeling she experienced only when she masturbated long enough. "Oh God!" she called out, almost at climax.

Tuck bore down deeper, putting the pressure of his hairy pubis on her swollen clit and grinding gently. It was all she could take. Candice cried out in sheer pleasure. Her head jerked up and down on the pillow as the orgasm ripped through her loins, causing her body to buck against Tuck's.

"Yeah," Tuck grunted, moving faster now.

Candice's release juices gave him more ease to move inside of her. The small pains shooting through her pussy were nothing compared to the explosion deep inside. When her body was done cumming, she felt Tuck climax as well.

Tuck gently removed his wet member from Candice, flopping down on the bed with his face up to the ceiling.

A cold feeling of guilt and shame came over Candice. She was terrified that Tuck would immediately dismiss her after their encounter. That was the lesson she'd learned from all of Uncle Rock's lectures over the years. She covered her ears with her hands, trying to block out her uncle's words. She turned onto her side with her back toward Tuck and drew her knees up into her body until she was almost in a fetal position.

"Hey," Tuck sang softly, touching her shoulder.

Candice didn't respond.

Noticing her unresponsiveness, Tuck flipped onto his side and propped himself up on one arm. "Candy, are you okay?" he asked, his voice louder and more serious now.

Candice was rocking slightly. She couldn't make the feelings go away.

Tuck realized he had taken advantage of her at a vulnerable time, but he wanted to make it clear to her that he wasn't just some dirty older man that would treat her like shit afterward. He also didn't know how to tell her he wasn't the thug drug dealer she believed him to be.

Candice was so disappointed in herself. She jumped out of the bed and began frantically searching for her clothes.

"Wait, Candy, don't go," Tuck pleaded, rising from the bed as well.

Candice already had her clothes gathered up, and she was whirling around, looking for the bathroom.

"Just stay for the rest of the night," he begged, putting his hands up to try to stop her.

Candice brushed past him roughly. She didn't want him to see her this weak. *Stupid, stupid, stupid.* She repeated the words in her head over and over again.

"It's on your left," Tuck called out at her back.

He sat down on the end of the bed in just his boxers. He placed his head in his hands and closed his eyes. It was all a mistake. It was all too much. First, his wife and Brubaker, then one of the main targets on his case might have murdered his girlfriend, and now he was falling for a girl he knew nothing about.

Tuck stayed in the same position until he heard Candice attempting to get out of the maze of locks on his door. He quickly slipped into his jeans and threw a wife-beater over his head. He was stopped dead in his stride.

"What the fuck are you doing?" he screeched, his hands raised high above his head.

Candice stood in a shooter's stance, her arms extended in front of her. She gripped her Glock 22 with the thumb-over-thumb grip, just as she'd been taught. Tears streamed down her face. The gun shook as her hands trembled.

"Candy. I'm not your enemy. I swear. I just wanted to be there for you. We can talk about this." Tuck swallowed hard.

Candice squeezed her eyes tight to fight away the tears clouding her vision. She wanted to believe him, but he was a close friend of the man who killed her father. A fact she had lost sight of a few hours earlier.

"Why did you lock me in here? Let me the fuck out of here," Candice gritted through tears.

"Let me help you open the door. I'm not trying to keep you here against your will," Tuck explained, his tone pacifying.

Candice lowered the gun slightly but kept it at the high ready, where she could return to the proper shooting position within a fraction of a second.

Tuck observed her stance, her grip, and her use of the high ready, and he immediately became suspicious. She had definitely had some professional training. He made a mental note to himself to learn from whom or where she'd acquired those skills.

He walked over to the door slowly, retrieved the keys from a small bowl, and used several keys to open the locks. He never understood why the government put those fucking lock-you-inside locks on undercover apartments anyway.

When the door was finally ready to be opened, Tuck stepped back carefully. "It's open. You're free to go."

Candice quickly stuffed her gun back into her oversized bag and rushed through the door. The door slammed behind her.

With his back against the cold steel of the door, Tuck slid down to the floor.

Candice did the same on the opposite side of the door.

Tuck sat on the floor for a few minutes. Candy was an enigma. Until the incident with the gun, he hadn't realized just how little he knew about her. He rushed into his bedroom and yanked open his nightstand drawer. He pulled out his government laptop and his system key code token.

Tuck pecked on the keys feverishly until he was logged into the system. He had already recorded Candy's plate number in his head when he had helped her into her car by the hospital. He'd done it out of instinct, rather than an actual need to know.

He punched the letters and numbers into the query screen. He drummed his fingers on the keyboard anxiously as the system worked to retrieve the information. Finally, the screen popped up. He received one hit. He double-clicked on the hit.

The name JOSEPH BARTON flashed across the screen. Tuck read the name, drawing a blank. *Maybe it's her father's car.* Certainly, no one that he knew in the drug game carried that name. Tuck pecked at a few more keys. An address came up, along with a date of birth and an entire criminal history. Things were not looking good.

"Joseph Barton, aka 'Rock,'" Tuck read aloud. He scrolled down on the screen. "DEA notes Barton's connection to Eric 'Easy' Hardaway."

There was a note in the system about surveillance tapes showing them together. *If Hardaway made a deal with the DEA, where the hell does Candy fit into all this? More importantly, why is she driving the car of a man who is connected to Junior's former dead boss, Eric Hardaway?*

Tuck needed to learn more about Easy Hardaway's biographic history. He knew his wife and kids had been murdered. But what was the connection to Candy and Barton? And more importantly, to the government?

He tried punching in Easy's full given name: ERIC DANE HARDAWAY. He was waiting for the computer to return the information when suddenly his screen started flashing a red warning banner. YOU NO LONGER HAVE ACCESS TO THIS SYSTEM, the screen flashed over and over again, the words so bright, they were almost neon.

Tuck jumped back from the computer like it was a poisonous snake. Suddenly, he felt something buzz on his desk. His cell phone was ringing. He looked at the screen and picked up the line.

"Yo, son, what's good? Yeah, I need to tell you some bad news," Tuck said, breathless like he'd been running fast. He surveyed his apartment, feeling like he was being watched. He half listened to the caller, becoming increasingly paranoid by the minute. He didn't know what to make of these latest developments.

One thing he was certain of was Brubaker and the undercover recovery team would be coming after him sooner rather than later.

Chapter 11

"In breaking news today, police have recovered the remains of a twelve-year-old Harlem boy who went missing from his school. The boy, whose name is being withheld because of his age, is the younger brother of alleged drug dealer and known gang member Phillip Beltrand. A police spokesperson for the NYPD said the day after the boy went missing, his severed finger was mailed to Beltrand's barbershop in Harlem with a small card attached. Police would not comment on what the card said or what it means.

"Police also confirmed that a day after the finger was received, the boy's decapitated head was found in a McDonald's bathroom on 125th Street. Police have commented on the eerie similarities between this case and an older case where the young brother of a known drug dealer was decapitated and his head left in a McDonald's bathroom. Police say it is too early in the investigation to determine if the two cases are related."

Junior squeezed his remote so tight, the battery cover popped off. He threw the remote across the room. It was official now. Phil's brother was dead. There was no more hope of finding him with just a missing finger. The boy was dead—tortured and dead. Junior's insides roiled. He was at war with the uptown crew now, whether he liked it or not.

Phil had contacted Junior when his brother's severed finger had arrived at the barbershop with the bloody note attached. He was livid, threatening death and destruction for Junior, Broady, and anybody else in their crew who got in the way.

When Junior got Phil to calm down a bit, Phil told him that the note had been written on a small blue card, and one side of the card said:

To y'all Brooklyn niggas. I'm sending these flowers to let y'all know how I get down. Take this one as a warning. Niggas get it how they live. - Phil.

Phil vehemently denied sending the note. He explained to Junior that he had sent a bleeding heart arrangement to Razor's funeral, but his note had merely offered his condolences.

Phil and Junior reached the conclusion together that somebody wanted the note to look like it had come from Phil. Junior silently concluded that Broady must've gotten the note from Razor's funeral.

Phil told Junior the other side of the card said:

Take this one as more than a warning. We at war, nigga. - Junior.

Again, somebody wanted the note on the flip side of the card to look like it had come from Junior, in response to Phil's "sympathy note."

Junior had given Phil his sworn word that he had not sent the note or harmed a hair on his little brother's head. The conversation got eerily quiet after that. Phil and Junior both knew who the likely culprit was. As a result, war was inevitable.

Broady was a wanted man on the streets of Harlem and Brooklyn. Whether Junior or Phil got to him first would be another matter.

Junior still wrestled with whether or not he should offer Broady his protection or simply take him out of the equation for good, a decision he would make once he located Broady.

Until the news story broke, Junior had held out hope that Phil's brother would be returned alive. He had scoured the streets for Broady. He had even sent Tuck to monitor Broady's house for a while, in case he returned.

Junior picked up his weapon off the coffee table and slid it into his waistband. He dialed Tuck's number. "Yo, did you find that nigga yet?" he asked.

"What you mean, Shana is dead? What? What the fuck, nigga! Get off this jack and come meet me!" Junior growled into the phone.

Junior knew right away that Phil had put the hit on Shana. Broady didn't have the heart to shoot her.

In the streets, when there was a war, family and bitches were the quickest way to bring a rival to his knees. Junior pinched the bridge of his nose. He didn't know how everything had unraveled so fast. It was like a bad omen had suddenly descended upon him and his entire crew. But his first priority was to find his brother. Shit was getting critical.

Brad Brubaker sat in his old beater, waiting. This time he would be the one to show up early for the meeting. Although a different type of meeting, he chose the same deserted gas station off I-95 in Delaware. He wore dark shades, a pair of raggedy jeans, and a Georgetown Hoyas T-shirt.

He looked at his watch and sighed. He picked up his cell phone and began dialing the number, but before he could finish, he noticed a car speeding into the gas station. He felt for his weapon and smiled.

The car slowed and then stopped.

Brubaker spoke loudly so his wire transmission would be picked up. "He's here," he announced. He watched the huge hulk of a man climb out of the vehicle and approach his car.

"They didn't tell me the bastard was this tall. No wonder," Brubaker whispered to himself.

The man yanked open the passenger side door and slid into the seat. He didn't acknowledge Brubaker's presence.

"I'm Brad Brubaker. Nice to finally meet you," Brubaker said, trying to ease the tension. When his greeting went unanswered, he continued nervously. "Joseph 'Rock' Barton. What do you prefer to be called? Rock, Joe, or Barton? Okay. Well, I will just call you Barton then," Brubaker said, lowering his eyes.

The name said aloud made Rock cringe. That was the name he'd been called in the Marines and while he trained with the Agency to become an assassin. Hearing his name called brought back a flood of painful memories.

Rock knew he could take this little scrawny white boy out with a flick of his wrist, but he also knew there would be drastic consequences for his actions. He wasn't going to escape the government unless he did as asked. This one last time.

"Well, here is the assignment," Brubaker said, placing a picture on Rock's lap.

Rock looked down at the photograph. He felt a sharp pain in his chest. He recognized the man in the picture. His face was etched in his mind already because, on a few occasions, he had seen the guy trying to talk to Candice. He swallowed hard.

"This guy killed a fifteen-year-old kid during a raid. We sent him undercover, thinking it would bring him some redemption. We thought we'd kill two birds with one stone and bring down the supplier for another drug dealer, named Carson. But this man went rogue. Missing meetings, acting violent, you name it, he has done it." Brubaker tried to gauge Barton's reaction.

Brubaker had been told to appeal to Rock by ensuring him that the intended target was a threat to society, but he didn't know Rock had already viewed this man as a threat to Candice as well.

"This guy here killed a kid named Corey Jackson, and we still don't have his motive," Brubaker lied without even blinking.

Rock knew that to be an outright lie. He was familiar with this game of chess and was no pawn to be played with. He knew who had killed Corey "Razor" Jackson.

"So we want his death to appear as a line of duty, you know, so nobody questions shit. Line of duty always works well. They say that's how his father died. Hate to do that to his poor mother, but this guy is armed and dangerous. You know he threatened his own wife and kids? We've got plenty of neighbors who will corroborate that," Brubaker maintained, trying hard to justify the government's actions.

Rock nodded his understanding. He was shaking from the effort it took to suppress his cough. No longer able to contain himself, he erupted into a fit of coughing.

Brubaker, well aware of Rock's condition, didn't seem too startled by the outburst. It was part of the reason he had been chosen for this job. "You all right there?" he asked, feigning concern.

Rock used a small handkerchief to wipe away the blood that had escaped his mouth. Even the medication wasn't working these days. He grunted in the affirmative.

"Here is the money. They raised the stakes this time. Seems like they want to pay you more than those hood pennies Hardaway was paying you," Brad said, tossing a tightly wrapped manila envelope onto Rock's lap.

The envelope landed on top of the picture of Rock's newest mark. Rock looked hesitantly down at the items. He slipped on his black gloves, removed the items from his lap, rubbed the door handle of Brad's car clean before exiting the vehicle. He didn't want his fingerprints left behind on anything that could incriminate him.

Brubaker looked at Rock like he was crazy, but inside he was smiling. Thanks to a deal that Joseph Barton had made with the Agency years ago, Brubaker's plan to get rid of Avon Tucker was going to work. No more bumps in the road for Brad Brubaker. He would finally get the career that Avon Tucker had denied him after the fatal shooting accident years ago.

Brubaker was almost giddy with excitement and could hardly contain himself. All he had to do now was sit back and wait for the chips to fall in place. All of his efforts and assignments that made Avon look like a crazy undercover rogue were coming together. He couldn't wait to be back in the good graces of the DEA and among the top brass again. He even thought he might get promoted to assistant special agent in charge.

Broady had been sitting at his brother's desk in the back office of Club Skyye, getting high for hours. He felt just as powerful as Junior now. He turned Junior's swivel chair around when he heard the footsteps behind him, his eyes low from the drugs in his system.

"What? You came to give me a lecture? I know, I know. I shouldn't fight with my girlfriend and bring attention to myself," he droned, chuckling.

He didn't get a response.

"Ain't nobody here but us now. How you know I was here, anyway?" He laughed again.

His comment was met with silence.

Broady tried to stand up, but instead staggered backwards.

Suddenly, there was a gun pointed in his face.

He flopped back into the chair. "What the fuck you gon' do with that?" He grinned lazily, too high to acknowledge the danger.

The gun came down on his skull, and his skin split open.

Broady squealed, lifting his hand to the side of his head. The gush of blood threatened to blow his high. Broady's vision blurred. "What the fuck is you doin'? I had a fight with her, that's all. I left her alone after that," he slurred, planting his hands on the table, trying to brace himself to stand upright.

Another blow from the handle of the handgun sent him reeling back into the chair, his monstrous weight tipping it backwards.

Broady landed on the floor, the back of his head cracking on the hard marble tiles. He lay there dazed for a few minutes before attempting to stand up, but his bulky body slipped back down each time he tried. The combination of drugs and hits to the head rendered him immobile. His entire body felt as if it were made of lead.

He screamed as a sharp pain shot through the top of his hand when a pair of hard-soled shoes pressed down on it.

Suddenly a black-gloved hand applied pressure to the center of his throat, finding his jugular notch.

Broady wheezed, his eyes bulging. His hand began to bleed as the sharp shoe heel pierced through his skin. "Pa—ple—as—e," he begged. Vomit crept up his esophagus with nowhere to go, since his airway was blocked.

Finally, the pressure on his neck relented.

Broady gagged, trying to fully catch his breath.

This time, the gun cut across his jawbone. *Wham!*

Broady slumped to the floor. Blood ran from his head, over his chin, and down his left arm.

"What did you say before you did it?" a muffled voice asked, the gun at Broady's temple.

Broady's eyes went wide. He grunted in pain as he received a kick in his thick side. "What? Whatchu talkin' about? It . . . it wa—wasn't me," he rasped.

"Liar!" the voice growled.

Broady coughed, his head feeling like it would explode. He had two large white-meat gashes in his head, and his jaw felt shattered in more than one place.

A heavy foot rose and fell on his windpipe.

"When you inflicted the torture, were there screams?"

Broady's body bucked. He tried to defend himself but was powerless against his aggressor.

Another stomp rendered him motionless before the handle of the .40-caliber weapon connected with his face again. Blood and small bits of flesh adhered to the end of the gun.

"You are a fucking monster that the world can do without! Your little girlfriend, yeah, she's dead," the person cackled.

"Noooo!" Broady gasped, not able to get enough air into his mouth to utter any other words. He didn't know Shana was dead. He had hit and choked her but left her as soon as he felt himself losing control. Tears leaked from the corners of his eyes.

"How should I kill you?"

The gun leveled over him now, Broady closed his eyes and resigned himself to death.

"Open your eyes, motherfucker! You need to feel the fear. You need to see it coming."

When Broady refused to open his eyes, he was hit again, this time on the bridge of his nose, and a gush of blood erupted from his nose like a volcano. He began coughing and gagging. Blood was leaking down into his inflamed esophagus.

"Shooting you would be too easy. I think I'll watch while you drown in your own blood." Broady's assailant smirked.

Broady felt a foot apply pressure to his chest. His head moved wildly as he tried to catch his breath. He gurgled blood, and his body convulsed.

Then two shots rang out, and Broady's body went completely still.

Gun in hand, Candice placed the back of her wrist up to her mouth. She felt the urge to dry heave. She hadn't seen anything so gruesome since she had found her family.

The sight of Broady's body made her rush back to that day. Anger welled up inside of her, threatening to boil over. She had the urge to pump more bullets into his body just to satisfy her need for justice.

With a dead body lying in the middle of the office, Candice scrambled to get out of Club Skyye before anybody else arrived on the scene. Although her mind told her to run, her legs wouldn't comply. Her heart galloped inside her chest, and her body burned. She was filled with so much anger. *I can't believe I'm late again!*

Candice snapped out of it when she heard voices just outside the office door. She was frantic; she needed to get out fast. The rush of adrenaline, combined with the smell of Broady's flesh, raw blood, and excrement splashed on the floor, was enough to send her stomach roiling.

"Fuck!" she whispered as the voices and footsteps grew closer. Looking for an escape route, she spotted a small door to the left of the office desk. She slipped her shoes off and twisted the doorknob, and the door popped open to a small bathroom.

Inside, Candice tried to get her breathing under control. She placed her hand over her mouth to keep any sound from coming out. There was no window in the bathroom, just a toilet and a sink. Not even a tub that she could lie down in and hide.

She gently placed her bag down on the floor and took her other gun out. She swallowed the lump of fear lodged at the base of her throat and placed her back flat against the wall opposite the door.

She looked into the small mirror to watch if the doorknob moved. She would start blasting before they even stepped through the door. Another lesson she'd learned from Uncle Rock.

Candice slid up against the wall closest to the office to listen to their conversation. Her life depended on it.

Tuck bent over and threw up the contents of his stomach. He tried to reach for his weapon, but the wave of nausea was too overpowering.

"Fuck!!" Junior growled. He couldn't stop the tears from coming. He kneeled down beside his brother's dead body. He lifted Broady's battered head into his hands and rocked. "It's my fault. I got you in this game. I shoulda left you alone with your dreams. I fucked up your life. I was angry, but I wasn't gonna kill you, son." Junior cried like a woman, his voice high and quivering.

Tuck was struck silent. All along he'd thought Junior himself wanted to off Broady. He was sure that business and keeping up his relationship with the uptown cats were more important to him than Broady's life ever was.

"This nigga Phil is a dead man," Junior growled, still holding Broady's head tightly to his chest. "That nigga crossed the line."

Tuck had just witnessed Junior on the hunt for Broady, talking a lot of shit about snapping his neck with his bare hands, yada yada. Now Junior wanted to kill Phil, even though he knew Broady's death was a revenge kill for Phil's little brother.

Tuck just shook his head. There was no use in fighting for a career that was completely slipping away now. He had no idea what to do now that his most important case had gone to shit, and his family now belonged to his traitor-ass coworker.

"C'mon, son. He is gone. We need to get going and call somebody," Tuck said softly, placing his hand on Junior's shoulder.

Junior looked up at Tuck.

"C'mon, you don't want the cops to get to your moms first. You gotta be the one to break the news to her," Tuck said, knowing that would get Junior to move.

Junior started pulling himself up off the floor, blood covering both of his arms and his hands.

"Stay right there, son. I'll get you something to get that cleaned off before we bounce." Tuck walked over to the small door next to where Broady's body lay. He twisted the doorknob and pushed the door in.

Tuck looked up into the mirror in front of him, and his heart jumped into his throat. His ebony skin turned ashen white as he stared through the mirror at two guns pointed at him by the one woman he truly cared about.

He slammed the door back and turned around like he'd seen a ghost. Still holding on to the doorknob, his heart raced painfully against his sternum.

"What happened, son?" Junior asked, noticing Tuck's facial expression.

"Too much blood in there, son," Tuck huffed, thinking quick on his feet. "Let's get the fuck outta here, nigga!"

"They worked a nigga over like that? Same shit they did to Razor. Maybe my baby brother was right. Maybe I been tricked. That nigga Phil probably did all this shit. He probably sent that little fuckin' blue card, talkin' shit."

"I don't know, son, but we need to get out of here." Tuck couldn't take a chance on Junior asking to look inside the bathroom. Tuck was kicking himself. He should've known when Candice just appeared out of nowhere that something wasn't right about her.

"A'ight, you right. I need to go see my moms." Junior smeared the blood from his hands and arms onto the front of his pants.

"We can grab you a change of clothes and shit," Tuck said, making small talk to keep Junior preoccupied. "You gonna have to get rid of that outfit, son."

Junior exited the office first, and Tuck walked backward out the door behind him, more sick to his stomach now that he knew the identity of the real killer.

Chapter 12

Junior and Tuck filed out of the doors of Club Skyye onto the street, both disturbed by the turn of events. Tuck held his phone up to his ear with a shaky hand. He dialed 9-1-1 to report finding Broady's body.

Junior pressed forward toward his parked car, preoccupied with thoughts of how he would give his mother the news. He didn't think it mattered that she didn't care for her youngest son, but he knew witnessing his mother's pain was going to kill him inside. Her guilt over the way she'd treated Broady over the years would probably hurt her more than the knowledge of his death.

Tuck grabbed the door handle of Junior's Benz and began to pull the door open. Suddenly, the sound of glass shattering cut through the air, and Junior's windshield glass rained into the car's interior.

Tuck sucked in his breath and snatched his hand back like he had touched fire. "What the fuck!"

Just then a bullet whizzed past his face. Instinctively, he dropped to the ground, taking cover behind the passenger side of the car. More bullets flew. This time one of the headlights popped.

"Oh shit! Junior, get down!" Tuck screamed, as the bullets flew overhead.

Junior ducked behind the open driver's side door, and more bullets slammed into the side of the car, barely missing his head.

"What the fuck!" Tuck belted, crouching down with his gun in his hands. He didn't know where the bullets were originating. It seemed to him like shots were being fired at both sides of the car.

"Yo, son, can you see where they're coming from?" Tuck asked as more bullets whizzed through the air.

"We gotta get the fuck outta here!" Junior screamed, taking a chance by lifting himself up and climbing into the car.

"Get down! Stay down!"

It was too late. Junior screamed out in agony. Then more bullets.

"Junior!"

Not knowing the source of the gunfire, Tuck decided he was going to just start shooting back. If he took care of his side of the car, that might stave off the shooters and buy them some time to get away. His mother would be devastated by another line-of-duty death, especially her only son's.

Tuck reverted to the mind-set of Avon Tucker, DEA agent. *Cover, cover, cover, scan, cover.* He wasn't trying to die in the middle of the street. He peered from behind the car's front bumper and let off five rounds. The shots cut through the Manhattan air with no immediate destination. He just needed a distraction for the shooters.

"Get the fuck in the car! I'm hit!" Junior ordered, feeling a fire erupt in his arm.

Tuck tried his luck with opening the passenger side door. He was able to get in, but as soon as he did, he heard bullets hitting the car's metal frame.

"Fuck! Drive, nigga!" he hollered at Junior.

"Agggh, son. I'm hit. I think it's my shoulder! I can't feel my hand!" Junior winced.

"Nigga, it's either drive, or we gonna die right here in this fuckin' car!" Tuck bellowed, the sound coming from some place deep.

Junior lifted his almost numb arm and cried out in excruciating pain.

"Drive!" Tuck screamed.

With bullets raining down on them, Junior gritted past the pain and wheeled the car out of the spot in front of the club. Both men were breathing so hard and fast, they threatened to steal all of the oxygen from the car.

The car's tires screeched down the street as the back windshield exploded.

Tuck ducked, and Junior swerved in response to the last couple of shots that pierced the car before they made it off the block. Tuck swallowed hard, and Junior moaned. Neither man said a word at first, but silent assumptions were made.

"That nigga Phil is going hard right now. He gotta die before he gets me," Junior proclaimed, his words laced with anger, fear, and hurt.

Tuck didn't believe Phil was responsible for any of the deaths related to Junior and his crew, but he knew there was nothing he could say to change Junior's mind. He was starting to believe they were all just simply casualties of war, that Candice had orchestrated this entire bloodbath. He just had to find out why.

When Candice saw Tuck in the bathroom mirror, her heart almost exploded. The feelings she had for him caused her to hesitate, something that might cost her her life. Tuck could've called her out or shot her. Candice couldn't help but think now that he had feelings for her, too. He was probably now convinced, from the looks of things, that she had killed Broady.

She was also the last person seen with Razor, and now she was hiding in the midst of a crime scene, holding two guns, with a dead body right outside the door.

Candice could only imagine what Tuck must be thinking. From what she'd overhead in the bathroom, Junior believed that Phil killed Razor, Broady, and Shana. She knew better and was starting to have her own suspicions about the identity of the killer.

Candice waited a few minutes after Tuck and Junior left the club's office to come out of hiding. Candice knew she'd have to give them a couple of seconds to get into the car and pull off before she got the fuck out of the club, just to be on the safe side. She couldn't chance Junior doubling back for anything.

When she thought the coast was clear, she tiptoed out of the bathroom and averted her eyes away from Broady's bludgeoned corpse. In the process, Candice ran dead into someone right as she reached the office door. She was infamous for this shit now. Panic struck her like a one-ton boulder. Instinctively, she raised her two guns, one in each hand.

"Whoa, little lady!" the man said, raising both hands in surrender.

Sweat ran down Candice's face now. She didn't recognize the man.

"We ain't got no beef with you, ma. We came here for a nigga." The man motioned for her to move out of the way. He was also holding a gun.

"Yo, Dray! Them niggas got away!" another man called out, his voice moving toward them.

In a knee-jerk reaction, she lifted her gun and slammed it into the head of the man in front of her. He crumpled to the floor like a deflated balloon, and his gun misfired.

The sound of the shot gave away their location, and she could hear someone running toward the office.

"Dray!" the man cried out from beyond the room.

Candice turned her full attention to the office door as a man ran into the office.

"What the fuck you did to Dray?"

The man held a gun at his side, but didn't have time to raise it before Candice charged into him. She hit his gun hand with a brachial stun, just like Uncle Rock had taught her. The man's hand went limp, and his gun skittered onto the floor. Candice hit him in the throat, a direct blow to his windpipe, and the man stumbled backward, his eyes wide with fear as he clutched at his neck.

Candice let off a warning round. The man dropped down to his knees. He didn't want any trouble with her. As the man cowered on the floor, Candice lifted her gun and knocked him on the back of the head.

"I—I wasn't gonna hur—hurt you." The man gurgled out his words.

Candice needed him to be completely unconscious. Biting her lip, she gave his head another solid crack, and he flopped down flat on his belly like a washed-up sea turtle.

Phil had sent his lieutenant and another one of his workers to get Broady, and they ended up in the wrong place at the wrong time.

Candice's legs felt like jelly. Her body was shaking all over. She had never really used her skills before. Although she felt a surge of power from overtaking all of these thugs, a feeling of dread washed over her all at once. Vomit crept up her throat as her stomach muscles seized repeatedly.

Candice could hear the faint sound of police sirens in the distance. The sound jolted her, and she pulled herself together. She ran for the club's back doors, where her car was parked. As soon as she made it out into the fresh air, Candice let it rip. She hunched over and threw up.

Shaking off the spooked feeling, she slid into her car and revved the engine. Police cars whizzed by as she pulled out of the back alley. Candice froze until the last car had gone. Then she eased out of the alley and onto the street, going in the opposite direction.

Candice was too preoccupied with her escape to notice that she was being watched. Tuck wasn't the only person to know she was at Club Skyye and suspect her of killing Broady.

Candice thought about Uncle Rock as she drove like a bat out of hell. Once again, he had been right. Cleaning should rid the world of bad people and not be used for selfish reasons like revenge. The bodies were piling up, and Candice still had not gotten the retribution she sought. She could only imagine the nightmares she was going to have now. She had seen too much death in her life already. Candice wasn't sure how much more she could take.

Candice might be as sweet as candy to her uncle Rock, but she was definitely "Hard Candy" on the streets. She still had one last important mark left, and she planned on getting to him before anyone else could beat her to it.

Uncle Rock rolled over onto his back, his chest rising and falling rapidly. His heart raced, and his chest burned. The tip of his gun was still hot from the shots he'd let off. The shoot-out was a necessary evil. Rock knew he was being watched by the Agency. They could have hired any number of their trained cleaners, but they'd chosen him. It was a form of control.

Rock's flying bullets had caused flesh wounds at best. If he'd wanted to take out his mark, he could have. He had several chances to take the perfect shot, but he just couldn't do it. He couldn't kill an innocent federal agent who had been used as an expendable pawn in a deadly government game. He had seen shit like this happen over and over again.

The government would paint Avon Tucker as a rogue agent who had lost his way while being undercover and gotten killed in the line of duty as a result. Unlike in the past, Rock couldn't complete the job this time. He knew there would be consequences for his failure to complete the mission. The

Agency would come after him, or they would come after those he cared about, Candice being one of them.

Rock pulled himself up off the concrete and leaned his back against the short ledge of the rooftop. He reached over with a trembling hand and dug his handgun out of his black bag. He put the gun up to his temple and slid his gloved index finger into the trigger guard. He squeezed his eyes shut and began pulling back the trigger. He pictured Candice's face. He pictured the wrinkled-face head of the CIA's assassin program. He pictured Junior's face. He pictured Tuck's face.

With a heavy sigh, he took his finger out of the trigger guard and dropped his arm down at his side. He punched the top of his bent knee with his other hand. Angry, Rock blamed himself for not keeping Candice out of this game. He had let her live with the lies that the government had fed to the media about her father's death. He had a responsibility to Candice. To Easy. He had to stop her from murdering an innocent man.

Rock knew, by process of elimination, where Candice was headed. He would just have to get there before she did. Candice needed to hear the truth once and for all. Whether she hated him or not, Rock had to tell her the truth about her family's murders.

He threw his supplies back into his black bag, and a slip of paper floated to the ground. It was a photograph of his newest mark.

"I can't kill you if I die first," he whispered to the crumpled picture.

Rock had a plan that would satisfy everyone, including the CIA. He rushed down the roof ladder, agile as a cat, but suffered from the burst of energy when a coughing fit assailed him as he reached the bottom rung. He doubled over, spat out the blood that came, and told himself that his days were numbered, either way he looked at it.

Rock was prepared to sacrifice his life to protect the ones he loved. For the first time in many years, he let go of his anger and resentment toward love and embraced what he experienced over the years with Candice.

Maybe he should have never stopped believing in love to begin with. Candy's love, over the years, had certainly healed many of his emotional wounds, yet the scars still remained.

***

The day after the government released Rock back onto the streets of New York, he had a green military bag, an old driver's license, and one thousand dollars in cash in his pockets. In his assessment, there was little else he needed. He was a free man, after all.

Rock stood outside of the train station on Thirty-fourth Street and Seventh Avenue, right outside of the largest Macy's in the United States. Things had changed since he'd left for the war. It was 1980, and although the war had been over for five years, he had remained with the CIA, carrying out missions and paying his dues.

Standing on the New York street corner, Rock looked out of place in his army fatigues and combat boots. As the city's residents whipped by him, he felt discombobulated by the frenetic pace of life. His mind was still a bit fuzzy from the drugs he'd been given, making it difficult to remember his way home.

Finally, with the assistance of passersby, he boarded the number 3 train and headed to Brooklyn. He needed to go home and reclaim what was his.

When Rock arrived at the Wortman Houses, he banged on the heavy metal door. Anxious, he shifted uncomfortably at the front door.

The door flung open, and a woman stared at him, dumbfounded. Rock stared back, his heart pounding in his chest. Neither of them spoke a word for at least thirty seconds.

When the shock wore off, she twisted her lips into a scowl and folded her arms across her chest.

Rock stared at the black eye she wore like a fashion accessory.

"What the fuck you want?"

"Betty, I—I—I . . . ," Rock stammered. The drugs still messed with his mind. He felt as if his brain was short-circuiting. Most days he had an entire sentence in his head, but today he couldn't get the words to come out of his mouth.

"You come back here after almost six years, and I'm supposed to greet you with open arms? You think I don't know the fuckin' war been over since seventy-five? Where you been?"

Just then a little boy ran to Betty's side and tugged on her
hand.

"Go back inside, Junior. This ain't nobody you know," Betty
said, scooting the little boy away from the door.

Rock stared at the boy until his little round head disappeared into a bedroom. He was stunned speechless.

"Who the fuck is that Betty?" a man's voice boomed from
somewhere inside of the apartment.

Rock clenched his fist. He was ready to kill, automatically
assuming the man was responsible for Betty's black eye.

"Yeah, I got a new man now," Betty spat, her hands now
resting on her ample hips. "So you better be leaving before he
comes to the door," she cautioned, starting to shut the door in
Rock's face.

Betty had definitely changed, but for the worse. When
Rock left to go to war, she was a beautiful young girl. They
had been courting for almost a year. Right before he left,
he had consummated the relationship by taking her virginity. Betty was the only woman he had ever loved.

Rock stuck his foot between the door and the frame so she
couldn't close it. She looked at him with sad eyes.

"The boy," Rock managed to say.

"You figure it out!"

Her words cut across Rock's heart like steel.

"Betty! Get ya ass from that door!" the man inside screamed.

"I gotta go, Rock. I don't love you no more."

Rock moved his foot and let her slam the door in his face.
He stood there for a good five minutes trying to deal with
the new situation. He could hear Betty screaming inside and
the little boy howling, probably in reaction to his mother's
distress. Although Rock wanted to plow down the door and
reclaim what he had lost, he remained solid and silent as a
rock. He stomped away from the door and never looked back.
He had written off love for good.

But, for some reason, Rock couldn't leave the neighborhood.
Instead, he watched the little boy grow up from a distance.
He had even convinced a local drug dealer to help the kid out.
He knew deep down inside that the boy was his son. A son
conceived out of love but raised to live in a world full of hate.

Chapter 13

Junior drove himself to Long Island College Hospital for treatment for the gunshot wound in his shoulder. Tuck left him at the hospital after convincing him that he had to get out of there before the police arrived because of his "parole" terms.

In New York, whether you were a gunshot victim or the perpetrator, the police showed up with a mouthful of questions. Tuck couldn't risk the local police questioning him and blowing his cover. He was under and alone. He hadn't heard from Brubaker since the incident with his wife back in Maryland. Tuck didn't know where his case or career status with the DEA stood, but after he got locked out of the system, he knew something wasn't right. Tuck was too preoccupied after Junior's call to gather his shit from his apartment, but now he needed it.

After much consideration, he took a huge risk and hailed a cab to take him to his undercover apartment. All of his amassed evidence against Junior and Broady was inside, along with his computer and equipment. He needed to get inside, get his shit, and try to get help from some of his DEA counterparts—without involving Brubaker.

When the cab arrived at his apartment building, he rushed up the steps and immediately noticed that the door to his apartment was open. Tuck slid his gun from his waistband and inched up to the door to listen for noise. There was no sound, so he peeked through the small crack between the door and the frame to see if anyone was still inside.

Satisfied that the coast was clear, Tuck kicked the door open. When it swung open wide, he put his back up against the wall, his gun held in front of him, his eyes darting around the ransacked apartment. The couch was over-turned, and all of the tables looked like they had been axed down the middle. The kitchen cabinets hung open, with their contents spilling out, and the drawers were open as well, the contents dumped out onto the floor as if someone was looking for something in particular.

Tuck ducked his head and quickly peered into the bedroom. It was empty too. He rushed into the bedroom, hoping the intruder didn't get into his safe. He moved the clothes in the closet, to check for the safe, scrambling around amid the piles of clothing that had been pulled off the hangers.

"Bastards! Shit!" Tuck cursed in a harsh whisper. The safe was gone, along with his computer and original undercover cell phone.

Tuck didn't trust calling anybody on the cell phone that Brubaker had given him. He had to get out of there before anyone came back. He rushed out of the apartment, thanking his lucky stars that he'd kept the keys to the Lexus with him when Junior offered to drive to Club Skyye. But first he had to return to Junior's house to retrieve the car.

Tuck stumbled out onto the street, paranoid. He rushed up the street and around the corner, looking desperately for a pay phone. He raced another block up until he spotted one. "Finally!" he huffed, exasperated.

He rushed into the pay phone booth, praying that the phone worked. His shoulders slumped in relief when he heard a dial tone. He pecked the buttons and said a silent prayer that the DEA agent he was trying to reach picked up.

"Operations. Carlisle speaking."

The voice filtering through the dirty pay phone receiver sounded like music to Tuck's ears. Dana Carlisle was the closest thing Avon had to a real friend inside the DEA. She was in his unit and had been on the scene when the accidental shooting took place years ago. Carlisle had always had Avon's back, even when it seemed like the entire agency had turned on him. After the incident, Avon's only friends on the inside were Carlisle and Brubaker. Now he was down to one.

"Carlisle, it's Tucker," he breathed into the receiver.

"Tucker!" she shouted, happy to hear from him after he'd been under so long. She was well aware of all the nasty rumors circulating about him at work.

"Shhhhh," Tuck whispered. "You can't let anybody know you're speaking to me. They're after me."

"Okay," she whispered back. "What's going on with you? They have your picture up everywhere in here."

"I'll explain that later. I need you to look something up in the system for me. They have my computer." Tuck was wary of every person that passed the phone booth. He could swear everybody was watching him. "Go into the case system. I need everything about Eric Hardaway. They called him Easy," Tuck said, his words coming out fast and jumbled.

"Okay," Carlisle said.

Tuck could hear her typing the information into her computer. "Don't let anybody see your screen," he cautioned.

"I got you. Okay, here goes. Eric Hardaway. Known drug kingpin in Brooklyn. Target of Operation Easy In. Born in Brooklyn, New York. Father was—"

"Just tell me how many children he had," Tuck said, wanting her to get to the point quickly. "I know about the one son . . . the murder and stuff."

"Okay, let's see. Hardaway children—Eric Junior, Errol, Candice, and Brianna. Wife is Corine. Affiliations—"

"Shit!" Tuck had finally figured it out. "Fuck! How could I be so stupid!" he cursed under his breath. He held the phone to his ear as his mind raced. *Candy is Candice Hardaway. She was the one killing off Junior's crew because she believed they killed her father. But what is her connection to Joseph Barton?*

"Go to the operations screen. Tell me more about Operation Easy In," Tuck instructed, his voice frantic.

"Okay, okay," Carlisle said, typing rapidly.

Tuck shifted his weight from one foot to the other and wiped beads of sweat from his head.

"It says here, Eric Hardaway had become a distributor for Rolando DeSosa. But wait. Wasn't DeSosa already working for the government as part of his immunity deal? Wasn't he one of the big kingpins back then that made a deal with the Reagan administration?" Carlisle asked, spewing facts like an encyclopedia.

"Keep reading. Anything about a Joseph Barton?" Tuck whispered, his voice barely audible.

"Says here, Hardaway was a distributor for DeSosa. Things going as planned. Barton enters the picture. Hardaway wants out. He reneges on his deal. He was talking to people. There are no notes after that."

"Who are the media suspects in the Hardaway murders?" Tuck asked, already knowing the answer to his question.

"Even I know that without looking at the file," Carlisle responded. "The suspects included a dealer named Junior Carson, his brother Broady Carson, a Corey 'Razor' Jackson, and Hardaway's own son, Eric Junior. All of the living suspects went free. You know the rest."

Tuck realized now that his case with Junior and Broady could've never been solved. He didn't know that Junior, Broady, and Razor were all viewed as possible suspects in Easy's murder. Junior was the replacement for Easy, but his connect was Easy's connect as well. *The fuckin' government!* Tuck screamed inside his head. He had been set up. They had all been set up. *But why?*

"You all right? What's going on, Tucker? They saying—"

Suddenly the phone line went dead.

"Hello? Carlisle?" Tuck breathed into the receiver. She was gone. Tuck knew they'd probably traced his call to the phone booth.

He took the phone Brubaker had given him with the tracer device in it, dialed Brubaker's cell number, and placed the phone on top of the booth.

Tuck knew that at any minute a sniper would be homing in on him or a swarm of DEA undercover recovery agents would be storming the scene. He raced away from the phone booth and hailed a cab. He needed to find Candice before she murdered an innocent man. He also needed to tell her that Junior didn't kill her father. Racing against time, he just prayed that he'd make it there before she did.

Candice followed Tuck's cab, being careful to stay a few cars back. She knew he'd lead her straight to Junior. Her mind was racing with a thousand thoughts. She wanted to call Uncle

Rock so badly, but there was no time. She needed to get to Junior before whoever was killing his crew did.

As Tuck's cab rounded the corner onto Junior's block, Candice fell back. She had to strategize. Getting caught inside the house would be deadly. She wanted to find a place to lay out her sniper gear.

Tuck jumped out of the cab and raced toward a Lexus. A black truck pulled up alongside the car. Candice watched as Tuck stopped to speak to the driver. He nodded his head, looked around, and got inside the truck.

"Fuck!" she cursed under her breath. "It must be Junior picking him up."

The truck sped up the block so fast, she had to frantically shift gears to catch up.

Candice was exhausted. She'd hardly slept in days. Uncle Rock would've told her to go home and rest because her skills would be diminished in her state.

But she refused to give in to exhaustion. After finding Broady, she was determined to be the one to put hot lead into Junior. At this point, she was willing to do it out in the open, witnesses and all. Hell-bent on revenge, she didn't care about being a trained cleaner.

Candice followed the black truck onto the Belt Parkway. Traffic was backed up. That was good. It would buy her some time to get her mind right.

As she inched along just a few cars away from her mark, she noticed the old beater out of her rearview mirror. A flash of heat came over her. *Uncle Rock, please stay out of this.*

There was nothing she could do now. She was sandwiched between cars, and the second lane was packed just as tightly.

"You better not try to stop me from doing this shit, Uncle Rock," Candice cursed out loud. She should have figured he would be following her.

She gnawed on her bottom lip now. Uncle Rock had been taking out her marks before she could get to them. He had always told her that although he was teaching her how to be a cleaner, he never expected her to use those skills unless she was in a life-or-death situation.

"How could I be so fuckin' dumb!" she scolded herself. Candice should have known from the years of living with Uncle Rock that there was no way she could have stolen shit out of his safe without him finding out about it. She felt like a stupid kid. Uncle Rock was always clipping her wings, trying to protect her from everything. From men to danger, he didn't trust her to take care of herself.

Candice noticed the black truck dip in and out of traffic, navigating its way forward in the heavy traffic. She waited for an opportunity and did the same, hoping they didn't notice.

She noticed in her rearview that Uncle Rock didn't dip with them. In fact, his car eased off the highway at the next exit. She crinkled her eyes in confusion. She knew her uncle too damn well. *Uncle Rock already knows where they are going!*

Candice's hands shook with a mixture of anxiety, anger, and fear. She didn't know if she was more worried about Uncle Rock killing Junior first or about her ability to carry out her plans.

The black truck took the next exit ramp, and Candice followed, a few cars behind, in hot pursuit.

Tuck kept dipping his head back to look into the rear window of the truck. He had a feeling they were being followed.

Junior had told Tuck that his mother didn't take the news of Broady's death well, and that he wanted to have one last meeting with his connect before getting the fuck out of New York.

Tuck held on to a small glimmer of hope that this meeting with the connect would somehow reinvigorate his case. That idea quickly vanished when he realized that the connect was probably DeSosa, a man who worked for the fucking government.

Junior, driving with his one good arm, drove the truck down a series of side streets. "This is where it all started, son," he pointed out. "Those right there is the projects I grew up in."

Tuck took in the dismal surroundings.

"That abandoned store right there is where I met Easy, where all this shit began. Good ol' East New York."

Tuck looked at the street sign as they drove toward what looked like a dead end—Fountain Avenue. The night he and

Junior had come to meet the connect, Tuck wasn't able to make out any of the landmarks.

Junior slowed the truck to a halt in an open lot with trash heaps just about everywhere and an old, abandoned warehouse in front.

Tuck remembered the building as the same one he had been taken to that night. "You sure he gon' show up this time?"

"Yeah. He knows all about the war on the streets. He gon' show up."

"So what's your plan, man?" Tuck made small talk, trying to keep his nerves at bay.

"I'm gon' make this one last quick lick, and I'm out of the game. I'm too old for this shit now, nigga. The power, the glory, the bitches, the money—you grow tired of it at some point." Junior grew solemn. "I done lost my brother to this shit. There ain't much else I'm willing to give up, feel me?"

Tuck had also given up a lot. Albeit for a different type of power and glory, in the end, the drug game claimed lives on both sides.

A car pulled up in front of the warehouse.

"A'ight, son," Junior told Tuck. "It's showtime. Once I introduce you, the game is all yours. I'm warning you, these Spanish cats don't play. Keep your mind right, and everything I built can be yours."

Tuck shook his head, clenching his ass cheeks together to keep himself from shitting his pants. The shit would hit the fan at any minute. He looked around the deserted lot.

"C'mon," Junior said, pulling open the door.

Tuck followed suit.

They walked side by side, both of them nervous for different reasons. As they approached the darkly tinted Cadillac, Tuck took a deep breath.

Junior tapped on the window, and they both stepped back.

Then Tuck heard it. The voice.

"Don't move, you fuckin' murderer!" Candice screeched, gripping her Glock 22. She placed the gun up against Junior's temple, her hands trembling.

"What the fuck!" Junior screamed.

Tuck whirled around and pulled his gun on her.

Candice was shaking all over.

"Drop your weapon!" Tuck ordered.

"Stay out of this! You don't have shit to do with this beef!" she yelled at him, her voice quivering.

"Look, baby girl, we can talk about this," Junior pleaded. "I didn't have nothing to do with Shana getting murked."

"And this ain't got nothing to do with Shana, either," Tuck interjected.

Candice's eyes stretched slightly.

"She thinks you're the one who killed her father. Eric Hardaway."

Junior was stuck on stupid at Tuck's revelation.

"Mind your fuckin' business!" Candice growled, the tears forming in her eyes. She tried to will them away. Getting emotional was a sure way to blunder the mission.

"Yo, shorty, you got the wrong man," Junior said calmly.

Candice shoved her gun harder into his head.

"He didn't kill your father, Candy," Tuck assured her.

"Yes, he did!" Candice screamed. "Broady was there! So was Razor!"

Junior looked at the tinted car windows and wondered why the fuck his connect's henchmen didn't get out and blast this little girl.

"I'm tellin' you, ma . . . it wasn't me!" Junior said in a placating tone.

"You motherfucker, don't you fuckin' stand in my face and lie! My father had just argued with you! You were jealous and wanted to take over his business. You set him up, and you and your little crew came in and killed him and my whole family!" Candice screeched. She racked the slide on her Glock just to make Junior flinch.

"Candy! Let me tell you the real story! You can't shoot him. He is innocent," Tuck exclaimed, his gun still trained on her.

"If you don't drop your fuckin' gun, his brains go flying now!" Candice growled. She didn't know why the fuck she just didn't blow Junior's brains out and then shoot Tuck. Now she realized why Uncle Rock told her that feelings fucked up everything.

Tuck placed his gun down and raised his hands above his head. "Candy, I put my shit down. Listen to me. I told you before I wouldn't hurt you. I'm not going to lie to you. I'm about to tell you everything. The whole truth."

"Just shut the fuck up!" Candice screamed. She was crying now.

"Listen to him, ma," Junior said, although he didn't know what the fuck Tuck was talking about.

"Your brother Eric Junior was the one who really shot your father, your brother, your mother, and your sister, and then killed himself. He was being used, brainwashed."

Tuck's words fell on Candice's ears like atomic bombs. She gripped the gun harder now. "You're a fuckin' liar! I found them! My sister was naked. They raped her! They raped my mother too!" Candice cried, her legs buckling a bit as she recalled the scene in her head. It wasn't her imagination. The dreams were real.

Tuck was at a loss for words. He didn't know anything about that.

"I came there after the fact," Junior filled in. "Your father had called me to come control your brother. He had gotten out of hand."

Candice yelped, "You are a fuckin' murderous liar! I watched the news. You were a suspect. Your fingerprints were in the house!"

"Yeah, I went in, but I ran back out," Junior explained.

"Your brother bragged about it. He was on the streets saying he shot my father and got off."

"That's just how Broady was," Tuck chimed in. "He talked a lot of shit. He was tryin'a make a name for himself."

"You just tryin' to fuckin' save your friend!" Candice screamed. "Well, it's too late." She pulled her trigger finger down from the side of the gun and placed it into the trigger guard.

"Candy, wait!" a voice wheezed.

Candice jumped.

"Let me tell you the truth once and for all," Uncle Rock gasped out.

Tuck bent down quickly and tried to pick up his gun. Within seconds, Rock had his face in the dirt.

"Who the fuck are you?" Tuck gasped, Uncle Rock's foot heavy on his back.

"Yo! What the fuck is going on here?" Junior barked.

Candice's demeanor softened. Uncle Rock had come to save the day. If she wasn't so angry, she would have laughed.

"Candy, let me tell you the truth about what happened to your father," Uncle Rock said softly, his voice raggedy and breathless.

"Stay out of this, Uncle Rock," Candice choked out. She was angry at herself for being so emotional.

"Your father made a deal with some very dangerous people, Candy," Uncle Rock began.

Easy held his head in his hands as he listened to the voice on the phone.

"Junior, don't you ever fuckin' question any of my executive decisions. I'm the boss. Remember that shit. If you don't want to be excommunicated and shut out of this hustle, you better do what the fuck I say to do. I am your fuckin' father. You don't run this operation!" Easy growled. He didn't know how he'd completely lost control of his own son. If he didn't know any better, he would've thought Eric Junior had been given a bad batch of PCP. The boy had seemingly changed overnight.

Easy hung up the phone on his son. He looked around and saw his oldest daughter in the doorway. He gave her an uneasy smile. Easy didn't like his kids to see him angry.

"C'mere, Candy Cane." He called her to his side. Easy hugged her tight. "Please be home on time from practice. Your mother will be beefing if you don't."

Candice sulked. "She gonna beef even if I get here on time."

"I'ma send a car to the gym for you," Easy told her.

"No!" Candice protested. "I'm gonna be on time," she assured, starting out the door.

"I'm trusting you, Candy Cane."

Just then Easy's phone rang again. He looked at the number displayed on the small screen and sighed. "Yeah," he answered.

"There is nothing you can do or say to change my mind. I'm gettin' outta the game. I'm an old man now. I've grown out of all of this shit," Easy said. "C'mon, DeSosa, ain't no reason to raise your voice. I should be the one pissed with you. I hear you been talkin' to my son. He is not going to go against me."

Easy listened some more.

"You can make all the threats you want. I'm out of the game," Easy said with finality. He disconnected the line.

Easy dialed Rock's number, but there was no answer. "I wish this dude would get a cell phone," he huffed. He couldn't reach Rock on the ancient landline he used.

"Eric!" Corine called out. Easy snapped out of his trance. He shook off the feeling of trepidation that lurked in his mind and walked out of his home office to see what his pain-in-the-butt, high-maintenance wife wanted.

"Whatchu wanna buy now for this party?" Easy yelled out as he moved toward the living room. He pushed the strings of a dozen helium balloons out of the way, just to see where he was going. "This woman would buy these kids the world for a damn party," he mumbled.

Easy stepped into his living room, and his heart almost stopped.

"What the fuck are you doing, Junior?"

Easy's son, his junior, his firstborn, was holding a gun to his own mother's head, and there were three other men of Hispanic descent with him. That much was obvious. They hadn't even bothered to cover their faces, even though ski masks lay on the floor near them. Easy knew what that meant. He wasn't going to make it out alive.

"Shut the fuck up!" Eric Junior screamed, his voice sounding deranged and off-kilter.

The other men started speaking in Spanish.

Eric Junior relinquished his trembling mother to the men. His baby sister and his brother had already been subdued.

"Junior, don't do this," Easy begged, a sharp pain stabbing him in the chest. His heart was breaking. His own son.

"Why?" Corine cried out as one of the men manhandled her.

The other two went about binding Easy up.

"There is only one way out of the game," Eric Junior said, his voice sounding harsh and unfamiliar.

"What did they give you, Junior? What kind of drugs?" Easy asked.

His son walked over to him and hit him across the face with the gun, and blood spurted from Easy's mouth.

The Hispanic men began laughing.

Easy bent his head. He had given up right then and there. There was no greater pain than to have your own flesh and blood betray you in such a way.

"Hold ya head up, nigga!" Eric Junior screamed as he hit his father again.

Easy refused to do as he was told. His neck was throbbing with an unbearable shooting pain. It had been snapped back, left and right. Another blow to the face caused something to crack at the base of his skull this time. It felt like a fire had erupted in his brain. Easy could not even open his mouth to let out a whimper, much less a scream.

"You thought you could leave the game just like that? I asked you to be boss, to let me take over. You didn't want that. Thought I wasn't ready. You think I'm crazy, and had those fuckin' people calling me a manic-depressive psycho," Eric Junior growled. He hit Easy again, this time even harder.

Easy didn't budge. His pride wouldn't allow it. It wasn't in him to fold and give in to another man, even his own son. Cut from a different cloth, he wasn't going to show weakness now.

"How does it feel to have your own son turn on you, motherfucker?" one of the Hispanic men taunted, getting so close to Easy's face, his breath hot on Easy's nose and lips.

Still, Easy continued to let his head hang, his blood dripping on the expensive Oriental rug that covered his living room floor.

"Rolando DeSosa says you can't leave the game alive. You still willing to die and sacrifice your family?" another of the assailants asked. He was trying his best to provoke Easy to relent, to say he would remain in the game.

Easy didn't say a word.

Eric Junior hit his father again and again.

Easy's body swayed from the constant blows, but he still didn't lift his head or give the men the satisfaction of knowing they were hurting him.

"Fuck this whole family!" one of the men called out.

Then Easy heard the high-pitched screams of his youngest daughter.

"Daddy!" Brianna wailed from someplace distant at first. "Daddy, help me!" she screamed again, this time more high-pitched and frantic.

Easy opened his battered eyelids and fought to lift his head, turning it painfully toward the sounds of his youngest daughter's voice. The sounds grew closer as the intruders dragged her by her hair to Easy's location.

"I want my daddy!" Brianna belted out again.

Her voice caused a sharp pain in Easy's chest. His breathing became labored as a surge of hot adrenaline suddenly coursed through his veins. It was the first time Easy had felt nervous since the entire ordeal had begun.

Easy had conditioned himself to believe that he would die in the game, so this wasn't totally unexpected. But he'd never thought that his own son would betray him like this. That Eric Junior would watch as his own flesh and blood suffered at the hands of men who didn't give a fuck about him or them.

Out of his severely swollen eyes, Easy could see his baby girl squirming and fighting with blood on her face.

"Now are you gonna change your mind? You gonna give DeSosa what he wants? This is your one last chance!" one of the men said.

Easy closed his eyes in anguish. He didn't want to see them kill his baby girl. At that moment, his heart felt like it would explode—a mixture of pain and pure anger. He envisioned himself killing all of the intruders slowly, torturing them unmercifully, even his own son.

"I always knew you was a fuckin' punk! You ain't none of my fuckin' father. You a pussy!" Eric Junior hollered in Easy's face.

Easy knew if he said he would stay in the game, they would kill them all, anyway.

"Eric, please! Give them whatever they want . . . please," Corine begged. "Eric, please! I'm begging you! Junior, why are you doing this?" Corine let out another bloodcurdling plea for help from her husband.

Even with his wife pleading with him and his daughter screaming, Easy didn't budge. He refused to open his mouth. It wasn't pride or selfishness; this moment was like living an art-of-war principle. The one rule he was going to live and die by was never to give in to the enemy when he knew they planned to kill him, anyway. In Easy's eyes, that would be giving them double satisfaction.

"Eric!" Corine screamed again frantically, her mouth full of blood and her eyes pleading.

Nothing. No response from Easy.

"Take off her clothes," one of the Hispanic men ordered.

Easy's eyes popped open. He looked directly at his son. Eric Junior looked horrified. He hadn't signed up for this.

Easy began fidgeting against the layers and layers of duct tape and rope that held him captive, his knees burning from the kneeling position they forced him in. He stared at his son, begging with his eyes. Easy remembered feeling this powerless when, as a child, he took beatings from his aunt's drunken husband.

"Daddy!" Brianna let out another throaty gurgle, her ponytail swinging as she tried to get away from her captors.

The first man slapped her with so much force, she hit the floor like a rag doll.

Easy watched as one of the three men stood over her and began unzipping his pants. He bit down into his jaw, drawing his own blood. His blood was boiling in his veins, but still he didn't say a word.

"You still playing hard-ass? Well, I'm about to show you real hard-ass," the same Hispanic said. "Do it," he ordered the other man in the room.

Eric Junior snapped out of his drug-induced haze. The drugs were wearing off a bit. "Hell naw! Y'all not gonna rape my fuckin' baby sister!" he screamed.

"What!" One of the men whirled around and leveled the gun at Brianna, who let out an ear-shattering scream.

Eric Junior let off one shot, but it missed the Hispanic man and hit his sister instead.

The other man lifted his gun menacingly. "Oh, you had a change of heart just like your punk-ass father?" He grabbed Eric Junior by the neck.

"Oh God!" Corine cried out. One of her kids was shot and lay bleeding to death, and she was about to watch the other die.

Easy rocked back and forth, his fist clenched so tight, he was sure the bones in his knuckles would burst through the skin.

The most evil of the Hispanic men dragged Eric Junior over to his mother. "Shoot her! Shoot her in the face!" the man demanded.

Eric Junior was crying, his mind muddled and his vision fuzzy.

The man grabbed his arm and hoisted it up. He pulled the hammer back on the gun that rested against Eric Junior's head. "Kill her now!" he whispered harshly in Eric Junior's ear.

Eric pulled the trigger without even thinking, and his mother's body slumped forward.

The other man used a knife and cut away the material of her dress, leaving her naked, to further degrade her. "Now you will kill your father," he said, dragging Eric Junior over to Easy.

Easy didn't look up. He hung his head.

Eric Junior was bawling now. "Dad, I'm sorry. I didn't mean for all of this to happen," he cried.

"Junior," Easy said softly.

Eric Junior blinked back tears.

Before he could open his eyes, in that split second, another of the Hispanic intruders emptied a magazine into the back of Easy's head.

Eric Junior began to scream.

"Now you will kill yourself," the man holding him hostage said.

With his heart racing, Eric Junior lifted the handgun he'd been given earlier to use against his family and shot his brains out. His blood splattered against one of the intruders' clothing; his body fell right at the entrance to the living room.

The men exited the living room via the hallway. One of the men reached back and pulled the door closed with a bloody hand. There was a car waiting out front for them.

Candice doubled over as if she had been punched in the stomach. Uncle Rock's story had shaken the very foundation of her life.

"But why?" she cried out. "Why?" She needed to rationalize the events of her past before she could move forward with her life.

"Your father made a deal with the government, and there was no turning back. Rolando DeSosa worked for the CIA, and so did I. They used your father, and they weren't finished with him when he decided he wanted out of the game. I found out about the government's plan and convinced him to leave the game. Easy trusted me. It was partly my fault that he and your family died," Uncle Rock lamented.

"But why would Eric Junior turn on him?" Candice asked.

"Because . . . they had taken him. Snatched him off the streets and gave him the same mind-altering drugs they gave us after 'Nam. Once they put that stuff in your system, your mind would be so fried, you would do anything, including kill your own flesh and blood," Uncle Rock explained, knowing from firsthand experience.

"You had pictures. . . . There were news reports," Candice cried, still refusing to move her gun from Junior's head.

"They were all media feeds. I only kept them because I thought it was so fucked up. I wanted to track and see if the government would eventually kill these supposed murder suspects. They would have to do it to cover up the fact that any DNA tests they ran at the crime scene would come up negative."

Uncle Rock's explanation made sense, but Candice still didn't want to believe it.

"So who the fuck killed Razor, Broady, and Shana?" Tuck grumbled. Rock had pulled Tuck up off the ground but still had a gorilla grip on his arm. He knew not to fuck with the old man.

Uncle Rock was silent.

"Phil killed them," Junior answered.

"All of you are fuckin' wrong, wrong, wrong," a voice called out.

They all turned their attention toward the entrance of the abandoned warehouse as Brad Brubaker stepped out of it. The black-tinted car was a prop. He'd set it up that way, using a remote control "bait car" with dummies inside. He knew Junior would be coming to meet the connect—the government's man.

Candice pulled her gun from Junior's head and pointed it at the unknown white man, and Uncle Rock did the same.

Junior finally managed with his one good hand to get his gun from his waistband.

Tuck was speechless, but he bent down and snatched his small handgun from his ankle rig. He squinted his eyes into tiny dashes. "You motherfucker!" he screamed. "You were working with them all along!"

Brubaker laughed. "All of you have been pitted against each other. Can't you see that?" he taunted.

"The story will be spun like this. Barton, you killed Corey Jackson so that little Hardaway here would keep her hands clean. Carson, you will look like you killed your own brother because of the war he started, and the girl, Broady's girlfriend . . . Well, it will just look like she was a revenge kill. Don't you see how we wanted it to look?" Brubaker laughed again, so pleased with himself.

"Now, none of you are leaving here alive. Not even you, Tucker," Brubaker said with a sneer.

Brubaker had set up a team to handle this crazy standoff. He didn't trust that Rock would take care of Tucker. When Brubaker had seen Rock's condition, the CIA director's plan didn't sit right with him. Brubaker wasn't going to take a chance and let his moment of triumph go up in smoke. Taking down all of them was the ideal scenario. Brad Brubaker could see his name etched in glass at DEA headquarters already.

"Take them down!" Brubaker screamed into a small black clip-on radio attached to the lapel of his suit jacket.

Everybody took cover.

Candice hit the dirt. Junior ducked behind the car. Tuck inched to the back of the car, staying low.

Rock, however, didn't budge. "You can't be that stupid," he said, walking toward Brubaker with his gun leveled at him.

Brubaker's face turned so white, it was almost transparent. "Take them out!" he screeched into the radio again.

"They're not coming. They hired me for one last cleaner job, but it wasn't for who you thought," Rock said, a cough starting to well up in his chest.

"What the fuck are you saying, old man?" Brubaker said, his voice quivering.

"Did you think the government would laud you for being a traitor? Did you think they would promote you and respect you after you threw your own partner to the wolves, betraying him, lying on him, committing murders and putting them on him? Did you really think they would kill another federal agent to get him out of your way? Couldn't you see, while you thought Tucker's case was all one big red herring, that you were being duped?" Uncle Rock rattled off.

Brubaker shook his head in disbelief. He hadn't even brought his weapon with him, because he was so confident that the DEA and CIA sniper teams would be ready to take down all of his pawns.

Rock advanced on him like an avenging angel.

"You—you can't kill me," Brubaker pleaded, his palms extended in supplication.

"I always complete a job when I'm paid to do it. I never renege on deals, especially with the government. Don't you see where that got my best friend, Easy Hardaway? Don't you see where that got you?" Rock asked, ready to unleash his full fury.

Rock placed both of his hands on his weapon, thumb over thumb, closed his weak eye, and let off a single shot that hit Brubaker in the center of his forehead. Brubaker's body remained standing for a few seconds then dropped like a heavy sack of potatoes. The back of his skull burst open like an overfilled water balloon.

Candice, Junior, and Tuck watched the scene unfold, speechless.

Uncle Rock turned around and began walking back toward them.

Tuck gripped his gun tightly. He couldn't be sure that Barton hadn't been hired to also take him out.

Rock, coughing fiercely as blood dribbled from his lips, walked right past Tucker.

"Uncle Rock!" Candice cried out, moving toward him.

"Stay there!" Uncle Rock screamed, halting her steps.

"Yo, this is some straight-out-a-movie shit! All I wanna do is take my fuckin' dough and get the fuck outta here! I can't have my moms burying two sons!"

"Wait!" Uncle Rock yelled at him.

"Candy, what you read in my last will and testament was true. I am dying. I have cancer. I did love someone at one time, and that love bore a son. His name is Joseph Carson, but his mother called him Junior," Uncle Rock said, leaning over to cough up more blood.

"What, nigga?" Junior barked, lifting his gun. Staring at Rock, Junior remembered him as the old dude hanging with Easy when Easy gave him a job. "You fuckin' punk-ass bitch nigga! You let me go years without a father? Suffering at the hands of Broady's fucked-up pops, watching my moms get her ass beat up. You watched me go fuckin' hungry and have to steal from the store, and you ain't do shit." Junior choked on his words. He was a man, and he wasn't going to let no tears fall, especially at no soap opera shit like this.

Uncle Rock spat up more blood.

Junior growled, "I should kill your fuckin' ass right here!"

Candice raised her gun. "I don't think so. He saved your fuckin' life today."

"Candy, let him do it," Uncle Rock rasped out. "Let him do it before they come for me."

"What are you talkin' about?" Candice asked.

"I'm dying anyway. Shoot me now. Don't let them have the satisfaction."

"No!" Candice screamed.

"All of you have to go. Get out of here! Run! It's never over when you have information about the government." Uncle Rock wheezed.

"You can go with me. I have the money, from, from Daddy." Candice couldn't stand losing her uncle Rock. Not now.

"Candy, you especially need to go. They will have a bounty on your head. You need to run."

Before any of them could blink, Uncle Rock looked at Candy and let his gun hand drop to his leg. Then he fired a single shot.

Candice opened her mouth to scream, but it happened too fast.

"Noooo!"

Uncle Rock's body dropped to the ground, but his eyes were still open. Blood leaked from his mouth, but he was still trying to talk.

Candice ran to him. She knew she had only ten seconds or less. Uncle Rock had taught her about this very moment. She bent down at his side and could see the blood soaking through his pant leg.

"Why!" Candice screamed, trying to apply pressure on uncle Rock's wound.

"Be—because I—I love you," Uncle Rock managed. Then his head lulled to the side, his eyes open and vacant.

"What the fuck!" Tuck huffed, bending down next to Candice.

She looked at him. Tears ran down her face in buckets. "He shot himself in the femoral artery," she cried.

Tuck grabbed her around the shoulders. "There's nothing you can do for him, Candy. He did it all for you."

Junior walked over and stood over the man who had just confessed to being his father. He wasn't going to shed a tear.

"Yo, Tuck, who the fuck are you?" Junior asked.

Tuck stood up, face-to-face with Junior. "I am Avon Tucker, a DEA agent that got set up by his own partner."

Candice looked at him strangely, too overwhelmed with a mixture of emotions to be mad. They had both operated under false pretenses.

"So you were tryin'a take me down?" Junior asked.

"That was my assignment, but it was all a fuckin' joke. You've been working for the government, anyway," Tuck told him.

A loud chopping sound could be heard overhead. The helicopters were hovering just above them.

"They're coming. Barton warned us. We need to get out of here," Tuck said urgently.

"What about Uncle Rock's body?" Candice asked.

"They will make this one big crime scene. Once they do their investigation, they will contact his next of kin," Tuck told her.

"Which is you," Candice said to Junior.

The sound of the helicopters was louder than ever, and sirens could be heard in the distance. They all started to disperse like rats in an alley.

Candice went left, Junior went straight ahead, but Tuck remained back. He was the only one who didn't have a ride. He watched Candice walk toward her car and disappear from the darkened street. Junior quickly got into his truck and peeled off.

Within five minutes Tuck was surrounded.

He lifted his hands in the air in surrender. "I am Avon Tucker, DEA agent," he screamed out.

One of the black Impala doors swung open.

"Are you still a DEA agent, Avon Tucker?" Dana Carlisle called out.

Tuck smiled and put his hands down. Thank God for honest DEA agents like Carlisle.

Chapter 14

The Aftermath

Candice pressed her foot lead heavy on the gas pedal and drove away from the crime scene like her life depended on it. Pulling up near her apartment building, Candice wiped the tears off her cheek. She had to focus on getting the hell out of the area, like Uncle Rock had instructed. *You're a big girl. . . . It's time to grow up. It's just you against them. C'mon, Candy, you can do this. Make Uncle Rock proud.* Candice gave herself a stern pep talk as she exhaled and put the gear into park. She rushed out of the car, whirling her head around in every direction, making sure she wasn't being watched. With her heart racing, Candice took the steps leading to her apartment two at a time. This was one of those times she had to heed Uncle Rock's lessons about being stealthy, accurate, focused and fast when on a mission.

Candice reached the floor where her apartment was located in the old high-rise building. The hallway was empty. Candice's hands were shaking badly; she could barely get the key into the lock. Finally the lock clicked and she pushed her way inside the familiar doorway. Before she could get her bearings, her jaw went slack with shock.

"These bastards!" Candice growled as she moved slowly. She took in the nightmarish scene and instinctively fumbled in her bag until she located her two favorite weapons, a .40-caliber Glock 22 and a .357 SIG Sauer. Her fingers instinctively chose the Glock.

Shaking her head from left to right, trying to make sense of what she was seeing, Candice slowly moved through the now-unfamiliar space filled with the debris of her ruined personal effects. Candice kicked a path clear and roved the rooms with her protection gripped tightly. Everything in her apartment had been turned upside down. Candice moved slowly toward the back of her apartment, where her bedroom was located. In there was a safe, which contained her life savings. Candice swallowed hard and forced her legs forward. Her survival instincts began to take over. She had to get that money, and get the hell out of there fast.

Moving with her back up against the walls, in case someone was still lurking about, Candice finally made it to the bedroom doorway. With her gun leading the way, she dipped her head inside quickly and backed out, just as fast. She said a quick, silent prayer and rushed through the entranceway. As she entered the room, glass crunched under her feet. Candice stopped breathing for a minute. She bent down and picked up the shattered photo frame, which contained a portrait of her slain family. Her heart jerked in her chest as she looked at the jagged lines from the broken glass running across her father's face. How ironic that his face was sliced in half by the glass, much like the double life he had led as a drug-dealing government mule. Quickly coming back to the reality of her situation, Candice whirled around in the middle of the floor, with her weapon pointed out in front of her. It appeared that whoever had been in her apartment was long gone.

Breathing a sigh of relief, Candy tried to unravel the mystery behind her trashed apartment.

What the fuck were they looking for? Candice wondered as she trod carefully around her once-immaculately-clean bedroom. The box spring lay exposed and her mattress was on the floor, sliced and diced, with the cotton spilling out as if someone had been digging in the middle of it. Her closet had been emptied of its contents, with her clothes, shoes and handbags tossed into a pile on the floor. Her desk had been turned over, and her laptop screen smashed. The cork message board that was usually above her desk, which had contained pictures of Junior and his crew, was also broken into three pieces. All of the pictures had been removed. Who would want to steal those pictures?

Maybe Uncle Rock was right. Maybe the government was after her because of the skills she possessed and the information she was privy to as a result of her association with Rock. Or maybe Junior was coming after her to avenge the death of his brother, Broady. The conspiracy theories abounded in Candice's mind, but she didn't have time to give them any real thought. Her first priority was locating the safe in the bottom of her closet. Frantically she tossed aside the pile of clothes and shoes that covered the closet floor. She blew out a cleansing breath; then she noticed that, strangely enough, the medium-sized gray fireproof safe was still there, seemingly untouched. Candice was no dummy. The safe wasn't still there because the intruders wanted her to have money to live. The whole thing reeked of a setup; whoever had wrecked her apartment wanted to make a statement, but they also wanted her to get away.

Candice entered the safe combination, but her hands were unsteady and she had to spin the wheel a couple of times before it opened. Once the lock clicked, Candice pulled the small metal door back. She let out a long sigh of relief when she noticed that the money her father had left her—what she hadn't spent keeping up with Junior and his hustling crew—was still there. All of the ammunition was still there as well. Money, guns and bullets—that was all she had left in the world. It was also all she had conditioned herself to believe she needed. The safe would be too cumbersome and heavy to try to carry out of the apartment, so she quickly emptied the contents into a duffel bag.

Fuck love. Fuck having a family. Candice told herself she was about to step out into the world alone. Before she left, Candice carefully placed the picture of her family on top of the stacks of money in the bag, picked up her loaded weapon, and raced for the front door. With a quick, last look around, Candice knew she would never again set eyes on this place. She was about to embark on a whole new life, and she was painfully aware that she was no longer the hunter, but the hunted.

After almost being killed by Candy and watching Rock take his life, Junior fled the scene and headed straight to his mother's house. He had rushed up the front steps of his mother's house, unable to get a handle on his feelings. How could his mother have so willfully deceived him about who the fuck his father was? He entered the brownstone furious like a gust of wind around a tornado.

"Ma!" Junior called out as he stalked through the hallway leading to his mother's kitchen. "Ma! Where you at?" Junior belted out, his voice a quaking baritone. No response. He finally found his mother sitting at the kitchen table, with her head down, clutching a wadded-up napkin.

"Ma, didn't you hear me calling you?" Junior huffed, his tone going higher with irritation. "We gotta talk! I need to ask you some questions right now, and I want the truth!" he boomed, slamming his fist on the table. He was ready to lay into his mother about who his father was, but his plan was quickly derailed.

Slowly raising her head, Betty Carson looked up at her eldest son. Fear was evident on her face. Junior halted in his tracks at the sight of his mother; he rushed to her side.

"Ma, what happened to you?" he barked incredulously. His mother sobbed even harder and quickly lowered her head. "Ma . . ." Junior's tone had softened; sympathy was tracing his words.

His legs felt weak and something deep in the center of his chest ached. He placed his hand under his mother's chin and lifted her face so he could get a better look. Junior let out an animalistic moan as he examined every inch of her paper bag–colored skin. Her left eye was swollen shut with dark purple and deep red rings forming around the outside of it. Her nose was red and swollen, with crusted blood rimming the inside of her nostrils; dark welts were rising on her cheeks.

"What happened to you?" Junior asked again, his heart thumping wildly at the idea of someone harming his mother.

"What did you do? What did you do to your brother? What did you do to me?" His mother suddenly came alive, her voice a high-pitched screech. The bitterness in her tone caused Junior to take a few steps backward.

"What are you talking about?" Junior replied, pleading ignorance.

"They told me what you did! They came here and did this to me!" Betty belted out, unable to control her wails now.

Junior swallowed and bit down so hard into his cheek that

he drew his own blood. The acrid taste seemingly fueled his homicidal feelings. He felt like wrecking shit around him. The heat of his anger rose from his toes and climbed up into his soul.

"Who was it?" he managed to croak out as his chest rose and fell rapidly. He balled his fists in an attempt to keep his rage at bay.

"He said his name was Phil and that you killed his baby brother, so he killed yours. Said you tortured that boy, a twelve-year-old boy, and then killed him!" Betty sobbed, accusing her son through her one good eye. "Oh, Junior . . . I saw that story on the news!" she wailed some more. "Are you out there killing people, Junior?" she asked in a low whisper, her eyes pleading for an explanation.

Junior stood mutely at her side.

"Oh, God!" his mother called on the Heavenly Father for understanding and comfort.

Junior suddenly felt too weak to stand. He flopped down onto one of the kitchen chairs. His mother took his disregard for her question as an admission of guilt, but there was no way that he would tell his mother that Broady was actually to blame for most of what had happened. Junior's body felt hot, and his healing gunshot wound began to throb from the adrenaline pulsing through his body. His head pounded with a migraine-caliber headache at the base of his skull. He squeezed his eyes shut and let the silence in the room settle around him—the calm before the storm.

Phil, the leader of the uptown crew of drug dealers, had crossed the line when he touched Junior's mother. Junior and Phil had called a truce years ago. It was agreed that Junior would run the Brooklyn street empire, and Phil would remain Uptown. They were supposed to be peers in the game, on the same level, but Phil had reached down too far. Junior would never have thought to touch any member of Phil's family. Junior had even told Phil that it was Junior's hotheaded brother, Broady, who had harmed Phil's little brother, Carmello. Junior thought Phil understood, but now he knew different.

Junior's eyes were ablaze, and his nostrils were flared. He felt the strong desire to grab his mother into his arms and comfort her with a hug. He hadn't hugged his mother since he was a small child. Betty was never real big on affection. It was a wall that her children simply acknowledged as insurmountable. Though she never told them with words or actions that she loved them, they knew she did in her own way. But perhaps this urge to comfort his mother was merely an excuse to receive it in return. Obviously, sorting out the truth with his mother about his real father was a conversation Junior would have to have another day and time. Right now, he had to get back to the streets.

"I've told you all that I know!" Avon Tucker screamed, clenching his fists so tight his knuckles paled. He looked around at all of the accusatory faces and bit down into his jaw. This was some bullshit. It had been two weeks since the shootings that had claimed his partner's life, and he was still being interrogated as if he were the bad guy.

The DEA, NYPD and, of course, the FBI had converged on the scene, each wanna-be-in-charge acronym vying for jurisdiction over the scene. Avon had raised his hands like a suspect, his street clothes, obligatory diamond Jesus piece and long chain not helping him make the case that he was actually an undercover Drug Enforcement Administration agent.

Immediately following the shooting, Avon was treated like a victim. At first, he was given time to "think things over." He was taken under the wing of the Employee Assistance Program. This was called the "get your story together" time among law enforcement officers—a week's worth of meetings with EAP shrinks, and strict isolation from the media and the U.S. Attorney's Office investigators. In fact, this was his first "on the record" interview regarding the incident, and everyone wanted a piece of it.

Avon's role as "victim" somehow blurred into "suspect" as probing, accusatory questions seemed to become the order of the day. Where was Tucker when Brubaker had been shot? Had he identified himself as a DEA agent? How long had he been undercover? Wasn't it true he had committed violations of the undercover rule, and only Brubaker had knowledge of this? Did he blame Brubaker for the shooting incident that involved the fifteen-year-old boy early in his career? It was a memory he couldn't shake anytime someone brought it up.

All of the people in the room now were supposed to be on his side; but the earlier shoot-the-shit atmosphere had been replaced by a harsher, more attack dog format. Now Avon sat in the hot seat and was forced to defend his honor and his actions. Had Avon set Brubaker up to die, after finding Brubaker having an affair with his wife? Did he know Joseph Barton personally? Did he want Brubaker dead because he would expose Avon for committing crimes while undercover? And finally, why didn't he try to save Brubaker?

Apparently "no" or "I don't know" were not satisfactory responses to the investigators. Instead, they would simply rephrase their questions to try to trip up Avon. It was a law enforcement philosophy—the more times someone had to tell the story, the more holes they might find. And, of course, these were holes that might be filled with lies.

Letting out a long sigh, Avon roughly rubbed his hands over his face in exasperation. It was going to be a very long day.

"Like I said, Joseph 'Rock' Barton was the shooter. He was the older guy on the scene. He said that he was working for some fuckin' body inside of this agency—the DEA!" Avon's voice rose an octave or two, startling his fresh-out-of-law-school Federal Law Enforcement Officer's Association–funded attorney.

Avon couldn't help it; his emotions were on a hair trigger. He had been shot at, betrayed and hunted while working undercover on a case that was never intended to go anywhere. And now he was suddenly a suspect in some fictional conspiracy.

Avon closed his eyes and placed his palms flat on the table. In an unnervingly calm voice, he recounted everything that happened between Rock and Brubaker for what felt like the tenth time in less than an hour. Avon looked up at the ceiling, as if recalling the entire scene from some distant place in his mind. He wanted to finish his recount of the events with his own personal opinion that the traitorous rat bastard deserved to have his head blown off, but he refrained himself from doing so, knowing those types of statements would make him look like he wanted his partner dead.

"Do you wanna take a break? Um . . . I think my client needs a break," Avon's pimply-faced Georgetown-graduate lawyer stammered, sounding just like one of those clichéd television series attorneys. No one in the room paid him any mind. "Okay . . . may-maybe not." The attorney shrank back down onto his seat.

The DEA interrogators who surrounded Avon turned quiet; it was a tactic Avon recognized. Silence usually unnerved guilty suspects, making them feel the need to fill up the silence with words, which would inevitably cause a slipup. Avon was silent too. He was trying to read them. Were they appeased? Were they still suspicious? The tension in the room was stifling. Some of the interrogators' faces had looked as if Avon had just announced that he had a terminal illness, while others looked less surprised and more suspicious.

A tall, square-shouldered white man broke from the group and walked over and placed one leg on the edge of the table, where Avon sat. The man leaned in so close—Avon could smell stale coffee on the man's breath. "And you didn't attempt to save your fellow agent's life?" the man asked again, his bulldog jaw shaking with emphasis as he spat the words in Avon's face.

Avon slammed his hand on the small, wobbly silver table, causing the man to quickly remove his leg and stand erect. Avon jutted his pointer finger toward the beefy man. He was tired of the accusatory tone of this whole circus.

"Are you listening to what I am saying? Brubaker tried to have me killed. He left me undercover with some of the most danger-ous drug dealers in New York, and then he went and fucked my wife—just for the hell of it! Somebody paid Barton to kill him, and then Barton turned the gun on himself! But it wasn't me! This entire fuckin' movie-like conspiracy is much bigger than me. I shouldn't be the one explaining it all. Somebody should be explaining to me why I was thrown in the thick of a fuckin' government cluster fuck, and why my case agent was a crooked motherfucker who was probably working for you! Not only could I have been killed, but a lot of innocent people died because of this little fucked-up game you're running here!" Avon barked back, the muscles cording in the chocolate skin of his neck. They had finally penetrated his resolve.

The interrogators eased back and softened their tones. Another tactic. Now they'd play nice guy and try to get some type of admission, if not a confession. They'd never seen any guilty person speak with so much conviction.

"Agent Tucker, we know this is hard. We just need the facts. Tell us one more time where you stood. What about the girl?" the lone female of the bunch chimed in, her eyes soft and placating.

Avon's face softened when he pictured Candy's face in his mind's eye. He had been thinking about her nonstop. He wondered where she had gone and if she was in any danger. Avon rested his elbows on the table and placed his bald head in his hands. He had to admit, as young as Candy was, she had done something to his heart. He had tried to tell himself that the night they shared together was purely a result of finding out his wife and partner were playing house during his absence, but Avon admitted to himself that he really had feelings for Candy. After the night they'd shared, he could not stop thinking about her. He felt sick, crazy even. Candy was a young girl, and he was a married man; yet she was a recurring thought.

Everyone in the room seemed to be suspended in time waiting for Tucker to answer the question. Avon opened his mouth to tell them the story again. He would pick and choose what he told them about Candy.

A loud knock, echoing through the door, interrupted his thoughts. Avon's shoulders went from tense to relaxed; the knocking was a welcome distraction from the line of questioning. Everyone else turned toward the thick metal door as well, unsure of what course of action to take. The female interrogator stood up in a law enforcement stance—her legs were shoulder width apart; her hands up and at the ready, like she needed to be prepared for Armageddon.

One of the DEA interrogators stalked over to the door and snatched it back like he was ready to chew out whoever was interrupting their show. The man standing behind the door walked into the room—it was like Moses parting the Red Sea to reach the Promised Land. Time seemed to stand still.

"There will be no more questions, unless we are the ones asking them," Grayson Stokes announced firmly, his voice raspy like his throat was covered with phlegm.

Avon's lawyer shot up from his seat; all of his papers flopped all over the floor, as he forgot they were on his lap. "Wait a minute, my client—" he interjected.

"Shut it!" Stokes snapped, pointing a curved finger at the attorney. The attorney snapped his mouth shut; it was as if the man had put him under some sort of spell. All of the agents in the room reacted as if they were a group of teens who had just gotten busted at an underage drinking party.

"If you ever want to earn a paycheck from the United States government again, I suggest you get the fuck out of here," the old man hissed, pointing a yellow fingernail. Immediately taking the man for an authority figure, the rank-and-file agents all began to scatter.

"Everybody leave," the man demanded, gazing at the attorney and the few brave investigators lingering in the room. They silently cleared out, though many of the faces looked none too pleased.

"Wait a minute here. He works for the DEA and we have the—" one of the bolder DEA agents dared to challenge. However, the icy stare and stone-faced grill he received from Stokes had him taking three steps backward toward the door.

Stokes's *Men in Black*–looking escorts waited for the attorney to gather his papers before ushering him out of the room. Talk about walking clichés.

"Are you going to be all right?" Avon's lawyer turned and asked from the doorway.

"Didn't I say get the fuck out of here!" the old man barked. His chest suddenly erupted and he exploded into a fit of coughing. His escorts each grabbed one of the attorney's arms and shoved him through the door.

Avon started to stand up too, but the man clapped one of his liver-spotted hands on Avon's shoulder.

"Not you, Agent Tucker . . . or should I just call you Avon?" the old man asked, forcing Avon back down onto the chair. The metal door slammed shut with a ring of finality.

"Look, I don't know where you're from, or what you want, but I know I have the right to an attorney," Avon demanded, starting to stand up again.

The dark shade–wearing escorts moved in closer.

Avon slumped back on the chair. "I am not under arrest . . . or am I? If I am, I need to hear my Miranda warnings, now," Avon snapped.

Stokes let out a sarcastic snort. With his hazy, silvery, medicine-dilated pupils trained on Avon's face, the man sized him up.

"You're right. You're not under arrest and you do have certain rights, under certain laws. But at what cost would you exercise your right to leave?" he grumbled, reaching into the left side of his suit.

Instinctively, Avon went to his waist. He found nothing there, of course. The old man chuckled, and then another fit of coughing.

"Did you think I was reaching for a gun, Agent Tucker?" the man asked. "I have something far more valuable to you," he corrected, flicking two glossy 8x10 photographs on the table in front of Avon.

The photographs floated onto the table and slid perfectly into place in front of Avon; it was like a special magic trick. Avon sucked in his breath. He felt like someone had kicked him in the chest. He stared down, unable to peel his eyes away from them. He was experiencing changes in his body chemistry that he couldn't explain—sweat seemed to pop up on his forehead, like unwanted dandelions on a fresh green lawn, and his breathing felt labored. His ears began ringing and he lifted his hand to his chest. He felt like someone had sucked all of the air out of the room. Avon snapped his head up from the pictures. It was as if someone had pulled it up abruptly with an invisible string. His eyes hooded over and he set his jaw squarely.

"Who the fuck are you? And what the fuck do you want?"

Avon gritted his teeth, eyeing Stokes evilly. The man remained silent as he placed another picture down on the table. It was a picture of Avon and Candy leaving Kings County

Hospital together on the night her friend Shana had died. Avon's heart jerked in his chest, and he couldn't stop staring at all of the pictures now. Obviously, this old bastard had been watching him very closely.

"I didn't think you'd be interested in leaving after you saw those. Listen, Special Agent Avon Tucker . . . Tuck, the drug dealer, or Tucker—or whatever the fuck you want to be called these days," the man said snidely. Moving close to Avon's ear, he leaned over Avon's shoulder so that Avon could smell his Ralph Lauren Safari cologne, cigar smoke on his clothes and his breath. "This should be easy. I am Grayson Stokes. I used to work with Joseph 'Rock' Barton. Sound familiar? I thought it would. Barton trained your little friend Candice Hardaway . . . or maybe you call her 'Candy.' See, Agent Tucker, we have a few friends in common and I need you to do something for me. It has to be you, or it wouldn't even be worth it," he said, moving away to see Avon's expression and reaction.

Avon's face was drawn into a scowl and his jaws rocked feverishly as he ground his molars together. He didn't like this old bastard mentioning Candy.

"You don't have to like it. I know you already know some things about Operation Easy In and Joseph Barton, but not nearly enough to think you know the entire story. You do what I say, and you get to see these little angel faces again," the man proposed.

"What do you want? I don't know shit," Avon said through gritted teeth, his nostrils flaring.

"The girl . . . Candy . . . I want her, and you're going to be the one to bring her to me," the old man said sternly, using his head to signal one of his men to surround Avon. "Are you in? Do we have a deal, Agent Tucker?" Grayson Stokes asked, reshuffling the pictures in front of him.

Avon Tucker was a captive audience now; and he knew no matter what his answer was, he would be making a deal with the devil.

Chapter 15

Going Ghost

Three Weeks Later

Tears drain from the corners of Candy's eyes and she is shivering all over. For some reason she is strangely aware of the cold, wet grass under her knees as she puts pressure on them in front of the tombstone. The feeling reminds her of the cold, empty feeling she had in her heart since the death of Uncle Rock. She can't believe he is dead. She also can't believe that she has returned to Brooklyn after she has been warned not to come back.

Candice doesn't care about the potential danger of her return. She has never had a chance to pay her respects to her family, but she feels an overwhelming need to come see the resting place of her uncle.

Now she kneels at Uncle Rock's grave, painfully aware that she is alone. She is left to fend for herself. Candice pulls off the little white plastic top from the steaming hot cup of green tea and pours it slowly on the green and brown grass in front of Uncle Rock's tombstone. "I know you must miss your daily cup of green tea," Candice whispers, her voice shaky.

Candice feels a rush of wind on the back of her neck, which causes the tiny hairs there to stand up. She is sure it was Uncle Rock giving her a hug. She isn't really religious, but she starts to say a silent prayer.

Just then she hears the faint sound of leaves crunching behind her. Alert, she places her hand into her bag and grips her Glock 22. Her heart begins to pound against her chest bone as the sound seems to get closer. Candice grips her gun more tightly.

It is them, she is sure.

Slowly she begins to stand up. She lets her bag stay on the ground and she lifts up her weapon out of it. With her chest heaving up and down, Candice is fully aware of the person's presence at her back. She attempts to turn around, but it is too late. More than one person rushes her at the same time.

She can hear a man's muffled voice: "We told you we would find you if you ever returned."

"Agh!" She lets out a short-lived scream.

Then blackness.

"Oh shit!" Candice jumped out of her sleep and out of the bed. She whirled around on the balls of her feet, trying to get her bearings. Her body was covered in sweat and her ears were ringing. Clutching her chest, Candice flopped down on the side of the bed. She exhaled and looked at her gun on the hotel's nightstand. The dreams were worse now than ever before. She didn't even realize she had dozed off in the middle of the day. It had been a long, exhausting day spent buying wigs and costumes, and perfecting her disguise. Candice shook off the nightmare and walked into the hotel's bathroom.

"Can't believe I have to sleep in this stuff too," she whispered to herself. She stared at her image in the large vanity mirror hanging over the hotel bathroom's sink. She hardly recognized herself anymore. The wet and wavy lace front wig she wore was cut into a short, high-low bob; it was also at least five shades lighter than her normal dark brown hair. She adjusted the wig a few times and secured it by applying the lace front glue, like the little Asian lady in the store had told her to do. Candice shook her head left to right to make sure her wig wouldn't go flying off at random. Candice was so accustomed to having long hair; the change seemed drastic. But that was exactly the look she was going for. She leaned in close to the mirror to examine her new eye color—gray. These new cat eyes were courtesy of a brand-new pair of light-reflecting colored contacts that accented her natural color with just rims of gray. Candice turned to the side to examine the most drastic change in her identity shift. She touched her midsection, lifting her new overhang gut. Candice had to laugh at the sixty extra pounds around her stomach and sides, thanks to the fat suit she'd purchased from a costume store. She looked like an overweight Spanish woman as she pulled up the thigh pads that made her usually long, slender legs look grossly misshapen and riddled with cellulite.

Walking back out into the hotel room, Candice couldn't help but take another look at the collage she had created on the far left wall. With her hands on her hips, she stood in front of what she considered her new target board. She had taped a bunch of photographs, names and maps together in perfect pattern—a masterpiece in her mind.

Moving her eyes across each face, she studied each name and each place, making sure she would not forget the real individuals responsible for the massacre of her family.

"Rolando DeSosa . . . sons Arellio and Guillermo," Candice read aloud, for probably the one hundredth time. "You, Guillermo, are not that bad-looking, still not my type," she said with a tsk. "I guess it really doesn't matter, though, now . . . does it?" she continued as if the man in the photo could somehow hear her. She rolled her new eyes and smiled. "We will meet soon; and when we do, your ass is mine," she murmured.

It had been easier than she'd thought to find information on the Internet about DeSosa and his family. Candice had to doubt what her Uncle Rock had told her before his suicide about DeSosa working for the CIA. In her assessment there was just way too much information out there about the supposedly notorious man. Candice had found information on several of DeSosa's past arrests, his current and past real estate listings, his legitimate business holdings, court documents from past indictments containing his whereabouts, his children's names and even some of the names of his many mistresses. The fact that this information was so readily available made her skeptical about Rock's claims—after all, the government was quite capable of planting information if it suited their needs.

Candice clicked on her laptop and inserted her Rosetta Stone CD. She needed to get her accent down pat. Uncle Rock had taught her basic Spanish while he had homeschooled her, but she wanted to be great before she set out on her new mission. Once she infiltrated DeSosa's circle, she needed to be able to keep up with every conversation within her earshot.

Picking up her laptop, Candice walked over to the bed and settled her back against the headboard, with the laptop on her thighs. As she focused on the computer screen, the photograph of her family on the nightstand fell silently to the floor. The air in the room seemed to become lead heavy. Keeping her emotions in check was no easy feat. Now that Rock was gone, the only link to her past was this solitary 3x5 family photo.

Candice flopped down on the side of the bed and picked up the portrait. On the one hand, she wanted to turn it on its face so that all of the smiling faces would stop taunting her; but on the other hand, she needed to see them like she had for the past four and a half years. She looked at each face and the anger she had previously felt in the years since their deaths finally eased into real sorrow—pure mourning. The photo had been her talisman for many years, keeping the kindling lit under her seething anger and need for revenge.

Candice didn't even realize she was gnawing on her bottom lip as her eyes carefully gazed upon each face. The picture had an entirely new look now. Everyone looked different in her eyes. Gone was the innocence of a family of victims. Now, with the information shared with Candy by Uncle Rock prior to his death, she saw them with fresh eyes. Each one, with the exception of her baby sister, harbored secrets that were now being uncovered.

"Your father made a deal with the government, and there was no turning back. Rolando DeSosa, the man who supplied your father with all of the drugs, worked for the CIA, and so did I." Those had been Uncle Rock's final words before he took his own life.

Candice's temples throbbed as she searched the recesses of her mind, digging into her memory for some clue, some inkling, that would help her understand her father's double life.

Why had her father treaded such dangerous territory, putting his own family into the fray? Tears fell on the shattered glass that covered the picture. Candice used her trembling thumb to swipe the glass clean. Her sweet baby sister stared back at her with a toothy grin. Candice's chest felt tight. She leaned her head back and closed her eyes, racking her brain for memories that would bring her sister back to life.

Hardaway Home, 1998

Candice was six when her baby sister, Brianna, came home from the hospital. She had waited patiently at the front window of their new home for what seemed like an eternity. Her knees burned and she had to pee, but she refused to move until she laid eyes on the newest member of the Hardaway clan.

It had only been two weeks since her father, Eric "Easy" Hardaway, had moved his family into a beautiful, new brownstone in the heart of Bed-Stuy, Brooklyn. Although their home address frequently changed, this was only the second move Candice could remember. The house was bigger and better than their last place. Even though Candice was young, she was fully aware that the new house and new car her father drove was more expensive than the last.

With her fists propped under her cheeks, Candice waited by the window until she spotted her father's sleek, large-bodied black Mercedes-Benz ease up to the curb in front of the house. Candice's mouth curled into a smile like someone had pulled up the corners with a crane—her dad affectionately referred to it as her "Joker" smile.

When her mother stepped out of the car, holding the tightly wrapped pink bundle in her arms, Candice felt her heart jerk in her chest. It was a mixture of excitement and fear. Until now, Candice had been the baby of the family, spoiled rotten by her father and overly protected by her brothers.

"Eric Junior! Errol! The baby is here!" Candice screeched, jumping off her knees, which were tattooed with an imprint of the couch's seams.

Her twin brothers were front and center in a matter of minutes.

The babysitter whom Easy had hired, a raven-haired girl named Lutisha, pulled back the door and Candice bolted outside.

"Let me see! Let me see the baby!" she panted, jumping into her father's arms so she could get a better look at the small body.

"Whoa, whoa, Candy Cane, let's get inside," Easy chuckled, his tone similar to a cowboy corralling an unruly horse.

Candice's mother, Corine, carried the baby up to the newly decorated nursery. Candice was hot on her heels.

"You're excited, huh?" Corine smiled softly at her daughter.

Candice nodded her head as she shifted her weight from one foot to the other.

Finally baby Brianna, who was wrapped up like a burrito, was unwrapped and introduced to Candice. Candice stood in awe. The baby's smell—a soft mixture of baby powder and Similac—made Candice want to never let her go. She loved the baby the minute she laid eyes on her. Brianna stared back, mutually infatuated.

The fanfare surrounding Brianna's birth didn't stop with Candice's obsessive attention, begging to hold her sister nearly every minute of the day. A week after coming home from the hospital, Easy and Corine planned the biggest welcome-to-the-world party for their newest addition. There was a huge pink-and-white cake, enough helium balloons to fill a small party hall and beautiful, poster-sized professional portraits of Brianna's first couple of days at home. Candice especially liked the picture with her holding Brianna alone.

Over seventy people attended the house party in honor of her baby sister. This made Candice feel somewhat envious; but even worse than that, there were no kids to play with. All of the attendees were adults and mostly friends of her father, along with their spouses or girlfriends. Candice found herself utterly bored.

Her father found her sitting in a corner with her arms folded. He walked over, his white teeth gleaming against his

Hershey's chocolate–colored skin. "What's the long face for, Candy Cane?"

Candice ignored the questions and continued to pout.

"C'mon, Candy Cane, tell your favorite guy what's going on." Her father smiled.

"I don't want these people to touch my baby," Candice huffed, pushing her lip farther out.

Her father threw back his head, laughing. "Aw, Candy Cane, when everybody leaves, she'll be all yours again. I tell you what, why don't you go count all of the gifts in the front and I will make sure you get double the number of gifts for your birthday." He smiled and rumpled the top of her head.

Candice's eyes lit up. She knew her father always kept his promises.

"Okay! I'm going to stay there all night and count every gift!" she exclaimed, and ran toward the front foyer.

The gifts stacked on the floor near the front door were both large and small. Some were wrapped in pink paper, and some in pale green and yellow. Candice was careful and diligent in her job of counting the gifts as they arrived. She planned to remind her father of the deal he had made when her birthday came around.

As she stood at the front door, collecting and counting the gifts like a hired hostess/butler would, she noticed a man enter through the door without ringing the bell. He was a tall man with skin that made him look like a figure from the wax museum. The man's eyes resembled two black lumps of coal, and his hair was so dark and shiny that she couldn't help but stare at it.

"Hola, mamasita. Are you the hostess?" the man sang, bending down in front of her face.

He smiled and the shiny gold front left tooth nearly blinded her. Candice stared, mesmerized by the sparkly diamond skull and crossbones that was encrusted on the man's gold tooth. He looked like a dark pirate. Her mouth hung open and was filled with unladylike saliva.

"Is your Papa home?" the man asked her.

Before Candice could get her brain to connect with her tongue, she heard her father's voice interrupt her thoughts.

"Ayyy! I didn't expect to see you, boss," Easy said, his voice snapping her out of her trance.

Easy rushed toward the man and extended his hand; his face was plastered with feigned enthusiasm. Candice took note that her father seemed nervous; his speech was quicker and higher-pitched than usual. His normally relaxed mannerisms appeared tense. And no one made her father nervous.

"Easy, I wouldn't miss this for the world. We always take care of our own, and now you are one of our own," the man replied, inviting himself into the party room.

The way he spoke told Candice that he was like the man who owned the bodega at the corner of her block. The man who her mother always said was "Spanish," when Candice and her brothers laughed at the funny way the man spoke.

"But how did you know where I lived?" Easy asked, letting out a nervous chuckle.

"I know everything, amigo. Not for you to worry, right? Now let me come in and see that new bundle of joy," the man replied, slapping Easy on the shoulder and shaking his hand roughly.

Three men followed him inside the house. Candice was struck by the fact that, despite the warm and muggy weather outside, the men wore long leather trench coats, which were shiny and black like their hair. They all shared similar skin tones and eyes—like they weren't black, but they weren't white either. Candice did not like the way they looked or the way they talked. And she definitely didn't want anyone with a black leather coat or shiny gold tooth looking at or talking to her baby sister.

Still, she warily collected the boss's gifts and added it to her count. Candice lost interest in counting gifts after the "bad men" arrived. Candice couldn't stop sneaking a peek at the man and his three shadows.

Her mother also seemed not to be thrilled with the new party guests.

"Eric, I thought you told me you didn't get into the deal with the Dominicans. I don't like him. . . . He seems . . . very dangerous. Why would they come to something like this?

To see a baby? How did they find where you live? They are trying to send a message, Eric. I don't like it." Her mother's tone was worried and on the verge of panic.

Candice watched as her father kissed her mother on the forehead.

"Corine, you worry too much. They just wanted to welcome the baby into the world," Easy said, but the creases in his forehead and the strain around his eyes told a different story.

Candice snapped out of her reverie and clicked play on her language CD. It was time to put things into motion. Step one was to embrace her new identity. The face of the man with the diamond-encrusted gold tooth was still plastered in her mind. Especially now, since the man seemed to be central to uncovering her father's secrets. Candice would never forget the man's face, but she just hoped he had forgotten hers.

Chapter 16

Untangling the Past

Junior sat on the leather couch in his upscale SoHo apartment as he stared across the small space at his mother. His mother slept peacefully on a custom-made circular bed, which Junior had imported from Italy a couple of years prior. Betty's Ambien-induced sleep was the norm for her lately.

Junior hadn't been to the apartment recently, but it was the only safe haven he had right now. When he originally rented the place, it served as his creep spot, a refuge from his boys and a place to take his women. Only a select few people knew about the apartment, and Junior was glad that he had heeded one of Easy's many street lessons: always keep a safe haven that nobody but you, and maybe your women, know about.

Junior thought about Easy a lot lately. Junior also wondered what Easy would do in his situation—the war with Phil and the uptown crew was far from over. Junior knew this, but it wasn't an ideal time to be thinking about killing people. Junior knew he couldn't just lie down and roll over—he had to fight and declare war, but it was all much easier said than done, especially given that his opponent was laying low and moving in silence and violence.

Junior had a lot of other things on his plate as well. He wondered what Easy would say about his daughter Candy trying to off him. Or if he told him that old dude Rock was, in fact, Junior's biological father.

As he rubbed his goatee, Junior sat and watched his mother sleep. His mind was racing with possibilities. His mind jumped from one thing to another. He was reminded of the many times he had come to his mother's rescue as a child. Junior was the one who helped his mother self-treat her wounds after her boyfriend would whip her ass, leaving her with busted lips and black eyes.

Seeing her hurting back then and now made Junior feel helpless and threatened and ready to kill.

Junior kept replaying scenes from his past in his mind, and he grew angrier each time he remembered. Junior thought back to the first murder he'd committed, and the irony that it was Easy who'd taken him under his wing and helped him out of that bad situation. Junior had suddenly been having a lot of memories of his life on the street with Easy.

Wortman Houses, 1988

Thirteen-year-old Junior stealthily walked up behind his mother's boyfriend like a quiet storm. Betty noticed him as she cowered in a corner, her body bent like a pretzel with her raised arms to shield off the next blow. Junior heard her suck in her breath at the sight of him. Sweat dripped down his brow and evil flashed in his eyes like he was of a demonic nature. Junior wore a wife beater, with his bony collarbone jutting out from the top, and a pair of jeans hung so low on his slim pelvis that the elastic band on his boxers was exposed. His eyes were hooded over with ill intent, and his mother could see fire flashing red in his wide pupils.

"Get ya hands off my mother, you punk-ass bitch!" Junior growled, baring his teeth like a hungry animal about to strike. His arms were extended out in front of him shaking fiercely, a combination of nerves and the weight of his newly acquired .22 special gripped tightly in his bony hands. "Slick! I said, get the fuck away from my mother!" Junior hissed again, his words firmer.

Slick was a tall, charcoal-colored man. He had a barrel chest and shoulders so wide that he resembled one of those ill-proportioned superhero action figures. He had been in and out of Betty's home for most of Junior's teenage years. Slick was his mother's current boyfriend who sometimes doubled as his baby brother Broady's father. Junior despised Slick from the first day he'd met him. When Slick started putting his hands on his mother, Junior's hate became palpable.

"Oh, you ain't hear me, bitch! I said, get ya fuckin' hands off my mother!" Junior barked again. This time he clicked his gun for emphasis.

Slick momentarily stopped beating his mother to peer at him, as one would a pestering insect.

"What, little punk? I know you ain't talkin' to me," Slick replied, turning to face Junior. His eyes went low at the sight of the gun in Junior's hands. "Whatchu gon' do with that?" Slick chortled incredulously. He faced Junior now, standing with his chest stuck out like a rooster about to go to battle over his hen.

"I'ma fuckin' shoot you, if you don't stop puttin' your hands on my mother!" Junior spat out, waving the gun in front of him.

"Oh yeah, go 'head and shoot me," Slick challenged, cracking the knuckles on his gorilla hands.

Betty scrambled to her feet and threw herself in front of Slick. "Stop it before somebody gets hurt! Junior, where did you get that thing? Put that gun down right now!" she demanded. Her voice had reached a high keening note.

"Move out the way, Ma. I'm not playin' with this bum-ass dude no more! I'm not sittin' in here, letting him punch on you no more!" Junior growled as sweat dripped into his left eye.

"I said put that thing down and get it out of my house!" Betty screeched unrelentingly.

"You gon' take up for him against your own son? I can't believe you! This no-good nigga be beating your ass! He don't give you no money! We starving around here! If I don't bring in food, we don't eat!" Junior screamed. His voice was cracking with hurt. The gun shook fiercely in his hands as his nerves got the better of him. Junior felt a sharp pain in his stomach; it was the gut punch of hurt feelings. His mother had chosen sides . . . again.

"Boy, you better listen to your mother before you end up in the Kings County morgue," Slick threatened, taking a stance behind Betty in case he needed a body shield.

"You' a punk-ass bastard hiding behind a woman," Junior spat. He looked at his mother with pure disdain and shook his head. "Stupid," he mumbled as he lowered his gun and turned on his heels and stomped into his room. Junior grabbed his newly purchased Polo leather-armed jacket and slid his feet into his newly purchased sneakers—all courtesy of his new job.

"Where you going?" Betty hollered at Junior's back, but all she heard in response was the slamming of a door.

Junior walked so fast down his block—he almost came out of his untied sneakers. His breath came out of his nose and mouth in strong, labored puffs, and his adrenaline coursed hot in his veins. Heading back to his spot on the block, Junior dared any crackhead or competing corner boy to try to test him today.

Just when he reached his usual post, he noticed Easy's car. "Shit," he cursed under his breath. Junior wasn't much in the mood for talking; and anytime he was around Easy, since the first day he'd started working for him, all Easy did was lecture Junior about the things he needed to be "smart" about.

Easy, of course, spotted him right away.

Easy was hanging with the old black dude again. "Ay! Why you lookin' like you wanna kill somebody?" Easy hollered out as he noticed Junior's high-yellow face flushed with anger.

The old dude eyed Junior up and down, sending an uncomfortable feeling over him.

"I almost just did!" Junior barked, sticking out his chicken chest like he was a big man.

"What? W'sup, kid?" Easy asked, placing his shoulder on Junior, steering him toward his car and away from the other corner boys in hearing distance.

Junior's chest was still rising and falling rapidly. He used his hand to swipe at the tears on his face and the snot running out of his nose.

"Who fucked with you kid?" Easy asked, his tone more serious. "You tell me if somebody is messing with you on these streets."

Junior looked into Easy's face and then over at the old dude, who was still standing a little ways away, acting like he wasn't listening. Something about the old dude seemed familiar to Junior, but he just couldn't place it.

"Nah, it's my mom's boyfriend. That dude be hittin' on her and I was gon' bust my piece in his ass just now, but she took up for his sorry ass, so I left," Junior explained.

Easy could relate. After all, he was Junior's age when he got fed up with an abusive male figure himself.

"What's his name?" Easy asked calmly, looking off into the distance.

"Slick, but his real name is Broady too, like my li'l brother."

"Where he be at?" Easy inquired, leaning back on the hood of his car, rubbing his hands together like a mad scientist concocting a diabolical plan.

"At that gambling spot behind Poppy's store. He be in there all day gambling away my mother's welfare check and his little piece of paycheck and any money we get in the house. That's why you seen me stealing the food that day you bought me the stuff from the store. . . . We don't have shit because of that nigga Slick. And my momz just keeps on taking him back in, like she dumb or sumthin'," Junior whined, jerking his head and shoulders with feeling.

Easy's gaze turned serious as he analyzed the situation.

"He's a fuckin' duck! I just wanna kill his ass!" Junior spat, shifting his weight from one foot to the other, itching for action.

"Calm down. Watch ya mouth! I'm still your elder. And stop letting all these jealous eyes out here on these streets see you upset and making threats. Niggas will turn state's witness on you in a New York minute," Easy warned. He nodded at the old dude, and the dude walked over.

"Seems like our little friend here got a problem he wanna take care of," Easy said to the old dude.

"This is my friend Rock . . . Mr. Rock to you, young'un," Easy introduced.

Junior remembered the man from the first day he met Easy, but he still didn't feel comfortable with the weird old dude, who always seemed to stare at him too long.

"Let's go pay your mom's boyfriend a visit in a bit." Easy assured.

Junior breathed a sigh of relief. Easy seemed to have all the answers to his problems. He felt powerful around Easy, and he wanted to be just like him when he grew up.

Easy found Slick playing deep at one of the back tables in the smoky, underground gambling hole. He effortlessly kicked the legs of the folding chair Slick occupied, sending him toppling to the ground.

"Say sorry to the kid," Easy hissed, his dark boot pressed against Slick's neck. Slick knew who Easy was, and he wasted no time bitching out to his fear.

"Junior, li'l man . . . you know I be messing up some-times, but—" Slick had started to speak, but his words were short-lived when the butt of Easy's gun landed on his skull, rendering him speechless.

"All I told you to say was sorry," Easy spat.

Slick's bladder involuntarily emptied on the floor of the basement gambling hole. The rest of the patrons of the illegal gambling spot had cleared out as soon as these intruders had arrived with their guns pointed and raised.

Junior felt powerful, like God right now. He was proud to be associated with Easy, and he loved seeing Slick humiliated.

"Now try it again," Easy instructed, forcing Slick's head up so he could look at Junior's face.

"Junior . . . little man," Slick said.

His words caused Mr. Rock to flinch.

"Don't call me that," Junior gritted. "I'm not none of your li'l man. You don't be acting all nice when you tryin'a kick my mom's ass, nigga!" Junior spat out.

"I—I'm sorry, man. I love Betty. You gotta believe me. I . . . can't control it sometimes," Slick pleaded.

Watching his grown ass start to cry like a bitch was a shameful sight to see.

"You a sorry-ass bitch. You always sayin' sorry, but you go right back to doing it," Junior accused. Mr. Rock whispered something to Easy.

"This is taking too long, Junior. It's time for you to get your feet wet. You always face your enemies and let them see your eyes before you engage in warfare," Easy told him.

Junior looked Slick in the eyes. He leveled his gun at his chest and pulled the trigger. Junior's body stumbled back-ward from the powerful shot. He dropped the gun like it was a piece of hot coal.

Slick's body slumped to the floor.

Junior stood stock-still; his eyes were as wide as saucers, and his body trembling.

Easy grabbed him by the shoulders before he collapsed to the floor.

"Let's go. You a man now," Easy declared as he led Junior away from the murder scene. Easy stopped him for a minute and looked at him seriously. "You only ever kill people that are a threat to you or your family, and you never get back at a man through his woman or children," Easy sternly lectured. Junior nodded his agreement. "I learned that from him," Easy said, nodding toward Rock.

Word on the street the next day was that Slick was killed in a gambling spot over a bad debt.

Junior was now reminded of just how powerful he felt the day he took a man's life. The thought compelled him into action. Junior picked up his cell phone and dialed a number.

"Hey, it's Junior. I need a meeting. This *is* fucking life or death," Junior spat. After hanging up the phone, he walked over and touched his mother's cheek. She moved slightly but was still knocked out.

"I didn't let anyone hurt you then, and I'm damn sure not going to let them do it now," he promised before leaving the apartment.

Chapter 17

Sorting Out The Truth

Avon took the long way to Dana Carlisle's house. As he pulled up, he could see Carlisle peeking through her front blinds. He smirked when she pulled the door back before he could even lift his fist to knock.

"Come in," Carlisle greeted. Tucker walked inside just like he had for the past three weeks of crashing at Dana's place.

"Look, Dana . . . about the way I acted . . ." he started to apologize. He had argued with her the day before. Tucker had grown frustrated when Carlisle insisted that she would help him find information on Candy and Easy Hardaway. Tucker had told her it was too risky, but she had insisted on helping him. She had never seen him so passionate about a case. He had also never seen her so hell-bent on getting involved in one.

"Shh. I understand. You were just trying to protect an old friend," Carlisle joked, winking at him. She gave him a thorough once-over. She stared at him, starstruck by all his sexiness.

"I can't stay long. I have a lot of things to get straight in my life," Tucker explained, taking a seat on Carlisle's futon, which had served as his bed when he stayed with her.

"I understand," she whispered. "Are you finally going to try to go home? You know . . . work things out with her?" she asked, trying to sound nonchalant. In reality, the green-eyed monster of jealousy was slowly crawling up her back.

"You said you had something important to show me, right?" Tucker got straight to the point. She had called him with an urgency to come by. He figured it would be something related to Candy.

"Yeah, I do." Carlisle conceded his abrupt shift in subject, knowing that she had struck a nerve. She rushed into her home office, talking over her shoulder. "So you must be glad to be in one piece after all you went through," Carlisle called out, her voice growing faint as she walked to the back of her house.

"Yeah. It's all been really crazy. Look . . . let's not . . ." Tucker replied evasively. He had already told her he couldn't involve her.

Carlisle shuffled back into the living room, dragging a large box behind her. Tucker offered his assistance by casually brushing her hands away and lifting the box onto the pub-style dinette set in her kitchen.

"Well, this is what I wanted to give you. Don't say I've never given you any gifts," Carlisle said flirtatiously.

"What exactly is all of this?" Tucker asked, surveying the large, dusty box.

"It's all the shit you need to know, all packaged up. It's also the thing that could get me fired from the DEA, and probably earn me the top spot on somebody's fuckin' hit list, so guard that stuff with your life. I don't really understand everything, even after I read through most of this stuff. But it seems like after the Hardaway family was killed, the DEA tossed the house and found what's in the box. I couldn't really believe it myself. Never thought I'd ever see the day when a drug dealer would be writing down his life story," Dana said, shaking her head.

Avon looked at her strangely.

"Yeah, that's the same reaction I had when I saw what was in those boxes," Dana told him. "I'm telling you, the shit reads just like a fiction novel, Tuck. Eric Hardaway was in deep. You have to read this shit for yourself," Carlisle huffed, placing her hands on her hips.

"Where'd you find—" Avon started to say.

"Don't ask me any questions. You didn't want me to ask you any, and I don't want you to ask me any. Just take it and make good use of it," she said, smiling wanly.

Tucker had no idea just how desperate she had been to help him get the information he sought. Or the depraved acts she had performed to gather these documents. She owed more than a few people in the classified archives a bunch of favors.

"Thanks for this and for everything else. I'm sorry I can't ... I never intended to ..." Tucker was stumbling, truly tongue-tied. He never meant to drag her into the mix. All he'd wanted to do in the first place was go undercover, make a big bust and then redeem himself.

Dana shifted her weight from one foot to the other and shoved her restless hands into the back pockets of her jeans. Avon was clearly having a difficult time saying the words that were in his mind, but not on his tongue: *I'm sorry I kind of used you, although I know I could never be attracted to you, because I am in love with someone else.*

Things between them had happened so fast. The revelations that Brubaker was trying to set him up to look like a rogue agent; watching Rock Barton shoot himself in the femoral artery. Watching Candy suffer as she learned that her own brother, under the government's direction, had killed her father. It was enough to make anyone go crazy.

Carlisle had been there at the end. Her smiling, loyal face was the only comfort in the face of death, destruction and betrayal. Dana had opened up her arms and her home to Avon, listening to him pour out his heart over his wife, over Candy and over his time on the street.

In the end her porcelain skin and the lemony smell of her shampoo had made him feel clean and whole. She'd rubbed his bald head and massaged the tension out of his neck. Her long, spindly fingers kneaded him, probing him.

Their first kiss was electric. It was hot, fast and furious. Animalistic.

He'd devoured her tongue like a starving refugee. She nearly ripped his shirt from his muscular chest. Her mouth moved over him so fast—he felt like she'd set his chest ablaze.

Carlisle had made the first move by removing her jeans and then her panties to expose her woman's core. Tuck felt flush; his body betrayed him. His emotions were on overload

*and he mindlessly took her: forcefully, brutally, clenching
his ass cheeks with every release of his hurt, frustrated
loneliness.*

*She had screamed out more than once—mostly from
pleasure, not pain—but she certainly could not have enjoyed
their coupling very much.*

*He had been brutal and selfish and completely insensitive
to her wants and needs. After ejaculating, he had collapsed on
the futon, spent.*

*The next day, neither spoke about the events that had
transpired in the dark. Instead, the focus had switched back
to Avon's impending task—finding Candy.*

Shaking away the memory—the mistake—Avon finally
decided he would just let the heavy silence that stood
between them remain intact, like the Great Wall of China.

"You okay?" Carlisle asked, noticing his glassy, blank stare.

"Oh . . . yeah. I'm—I'm just gonna go," he said, stumbling,
his palms sweaty. He leaned toward her awkwardly, giving
her a clumsy hug.

Carlisle felt light-headed and unsteady on her feet. She
lifted her arms uncomfortably and pat his back—a friendly
pat like what men would exchange. She fought the urge to kiss
him on the neck. She inhaled his scent and closed her eyes.
She was glad that she could help him unravel the Hardaway
case. In the meantime, she planned to keep a close eye on
him—whether he liked it or not.

Avon got into his car and stared over at the box he had placed
on the passenger seat. His first thought was to drive to a safe
place and look inside, but the anxious feeling in the pit of his
stomach prevented him from moving. The dark-tinted windows
on the car gave him a sense of security that no one would be able
to see inside. He finally gave in to his curiosity and pulled back
the thick gray duct tape sealing the box.

The first notebook on the pile was an old-school black-and-
white marble composition book. Tucker picked it up and read
the cover: MY LIFE, BY ERIC HARDAWAY. Pressed for answers
that might lead him to learn more about the young girl he'd

become so obsessed with, Avon placed the old dusty notebook against the steering wheel and began to read. Just like Carlisle had said, it was like reading a book.

Avon immediately escaped into the life of Easy Hardaway.

Brooklyn, New York, 1983

"You little bastard! Get ya ass over here!" Doobey screamed, his pale face turning crimson.

Eric stood rooted to the floor. His fists were balled at his side. His chest was rising and falling rapidly. He wasn't going that easily this time.

"Did you hear me?" Doobey barked, stepping closer to his nephew.

Eric squinted his eyes into little dashes and folded his face into a scowl.

"Oh, you gon' stand there like you that fuckin' man! You s'pose to scare me? I'ma show you who the man is in this muthafucka!" Doobey spat out. Small sprinkles of his Colt 45–scented spittle landed on Eric's face.

Still, Eric refused to move while his drunken uncle struggled to get his cowhide belt off his pants.

This type of commotion was commonplace in his Aunt Deena's house; so much so, that his cousins didn't even bother to intervene. They simply exited the room as soon as the altercation took place. Deena never intervened when her husband beat the shit out of her nephew; in fact, in Eric's assessment, his aunt encouraged it.

Deena was his mother's sister. She had seven children of her own—all cramped into a two-bedroom apartment—so she resented the fact that she had to care for her sister's orphaned child.

Easy's mother, Cynthia, was one of the first female drug dealers in Brooklyn. His father, Erv, had turned Cynthia on to the game. They were an unstoppable duo, until jealous rival dealers executed them both.

Immediately after their deaths, Easy went to live with his grandmother, who died of a broken heart, he believed, shortly after his mother's murder.

Then he moved in with his maternal aunt, where he was reminded daily that he was unwanted and unloved.

"Now! I said get the fuck over here, boy!" Doobey growled, finally getting his belt free.

Eric looked at him evilly. "Fuck you! You ain't my father!" Eric hissed, clenching his fists so tightly that his nails dug half-moon–shaped craters into his palms.

"After this ass whupping you gon' wish I was ya daddy!" Doobey slurred, raising the belt over his shoulder.

Eric felt a hot rush of adrenaline come over his body. Moved by some unknown force, he lifted his left fist. When Doobey went to plow into him, Eric punched his uncle in the balls with all of the strength he could muster.

Eric growled as his unsuspecting uncle doubled over in pain. It was a bold move; but like an animal trapped in a corner, Eric felt his only choice was to attack. He started swinging wildly, landing punches at will on Doobey's head, face and chest.

With his equilibrium off from drinking, Doobey tried to stop Eric's wild blows, but he couldn't see straight enough to grab the ferocious fists flying at him.

"I hate you!" Eric screamed, throwing more punches and kicks. He finally tackled his uncle to the floor; he sat on his chest and lit into him.

"Get him off me!" Doobey gasped, the combination of alcohol and head injuries making him feel nauseated and dizzy.

Eric was like a machine that could not be turned off. He thought about all of the nights his uncle had come home, stinking drunk, and beat him out of his sleep just because he could. All of the times his uncle took his dinner plate, forcing him to go to bed with his insides churning from hunger. He thought about all of the times his grandmother allowed his cousins to tease him about his raggedy sneakers and clothes.

As if possessed by the devil himself, Eric felt spit fly out of his mouth, and tears ran down his cheeks. For the first time in his life, he felt an overwhelming sense of power over his life. He felt invincible, strong enough to kill his uncle with his bare hands.

Blood leaked out of his uncle's nose by the time Deena shuffled her obese body into the cramped living room and tried to pull her lunatic nephew off her drunken husband.

"Boy! You ain't gon' be hittin' on my man! You need to get the hell out of my house!" Deena hollered as she tried in vain to pull Eric off Doobey. A crowd of cousins surrounded the two tangled bodies and moved in like vultures over a dead carcass.

"Get the fuck off me! I hate y'all! I hate all of y'all!" Eric screamed, kicking and flailing, as his eldest cousin, Poopie, finally pulled his arms behind his back. "I hate this house!" Eric screeched.

Turning to Deena, he eyed his aunt with all of the hate he'd augmented over the years. "This is all your fault! You evil bitch! You just jealous because my mother had everything and you ain't got shit!" he growled, pushing his aunt in the chest.

"Oh, God!" she implored, clutching her chest as she stumbled backward into a beat-up armchair. She had just narrowly missed hitting the floor.

"Uh-nuh! No, he didn't!" Screams erupted all around Eric and the entire house reacted, thirsty for his blood.

"You ain't gon' be hitting my mother!" one of his less courageous cousins barked from a distance.

There was no telling what Eric would do next. In a matter of seconds, the group converged as one large avenging angel. Blows started to land on Eric's body. Somebody dragged him down to the floor and kicked him sharply in his kidneys. His breath escaped painfully, but he refused to show any other signs of weakness. Another blow to the top of his head made him see small streams of squirming lights behind his eye sockets.

There was no way he could win against all of his cousins. Scrambling on the floor, trying to protect his head, Eric finally made it to the door.

"Let him up! He wanna leave. Let the bastard leave!" Deena shouted, her face filling with blood and her double chin jiggling.

Eric snatched the door open and ran out of the apartment. His nose was bleeding; his left eye was nearly swollen shut. His knuckles were raw, and he felt like he had broken a few ribs.

Slamming the door shut behind him, Eric realized that he was walking away from the only family he had ever known. But not all families, in his estimation, were worth holding on to. He had survived all these years, and he would survive many more. At just thirteen years old, he may have been homeless, but he wasn't hopeless.

The first night his aunt kicked him out, Eric sat in a dark, dank space behind the stairs of the apartment building, nodding in and out of sleep. When he emerged from his hiding spot the next morning, his insides were churning from hunger. His body ached and his left eye was black and swollen shut.

Eric walked three blocks to the corner store, praying that he wouldn't run into any of his cousins. His plan was to sneak in the back of the store, grab a few bags of chips, to kill the hunger pains tearing out his insides, and then dip back out, unseen. He had been psyching himself up all the way to the store. He had never stolen anything in his life. As he turned the corner, he heard shouting and screaming. He remained hidden behind a large dumpster, silently watching two men punch, kick and stomp on the body of a man who lay on the ground, screaming and squirming.

Eric had never heard a man scream like a woman before. He kept his eyes glued to the scene, but something in his peripheral vision caught his attention.

A long, darkly tinted 1975 black Cadillac Sedan Deville, with whitewash wheels, sat parked in front of the store. The back window was halfway down and Eric could see the face of a man watching the brawl. The man wore a dark brown suede fedora with a red feather attached at the side. His face was the color of molasses, and a mustache covered his top lip with thick, coarse black hair.

Eric turned his eyes from the man in the car back to the victim, who had stopped squirming and screaming. Judging from the amount of blood pooling on the ground around the man's head, Eric decided that the man was probably dead.

"That's enough!" the man in the Cadillac yelled out the window, snapping his fingers. Like well-trained dogs in obedience school, the men stopped beating the limp, lifeless man.

"You, kid! C'mere," the fedora-clad man called out to Eric.

Eric's mouth hung open, and he frantically looked around, hoping that there was another kid nearby whom he was beckoning. When the man pointed his finger directly at him, Eric nearly peed his pants.

"Me?" he croaked in fear.

"Listen, little brotha, don't play with me. You don't see nobody else out here at six o'clock in the damn morning, do you? Now, I said, c'mere," the man snapped.

Eric walked over like a man on his way to the gas chamber. His legs felt like lead pipes, and the hunger pangs in his stomach were replaced by doom-filled cramps.

The man who had summoned him reached his hand out the window toward Eric. Eric immediately took notice of the huge yellow-gold and diamond ring on the man's pinkie. The man grabbed the collar of Eric's shirt and pulled him up to the side of the car so that the metal door frame pushed into his chest.

The man moved his face a mere two inches from Eric's. "You see that jive-ass bitch over there on the ground?" the man asked.

With his one good eye stretched wide to its limit, Eric moved his head up and down in concurrence.

"Well, he got what he deserved for being a bitch. Ain't nothin' worse than a man who acts like a bitch. Don't you agree?"

Eric nodded his head up and down rapidly.

"All right, then. If you tell anybody who you saw giving that bitch what he deserved, that same thing gon' happen to you. 'Cause if you tell, that would make you a rat bitch, now wouldn't it? You feel me? Look like somebody done worked yo' ass over, anyhow," the man ground out, looking at Eric with squinted eyes.

Eric moved his head up and down. The man finally released his grip on Eric's collar.

"What's your name, boy?" he asked, softening his tone. There was something about Eric that he liked—an innocence he could fuck with.

"Er . . . um . . . Eric."

"Well, I'm Early. Ask anybody roun' here about me if you don't believe what I'm telling you 'bout what can happen to you," the man warned. "Now, if the police ask you what you saw here, what you gon' say?" Early asked.

"I'ma say I ain't s—see nothin'," Eric stammered. His tongue felt thick and heavy in his mouth.

"See . . . you wrong already. Whatcha gonna say is that you saw some young boys robbing that dude right there and they beat him up till he stopped movin'."

Eric nodded in agreement. "Yeah . . . that's what I'ma say."

"Good," Early replied with a half smile, half sneer. He was going to have fun with this young man.

He gave Eric a once-over. "Why you out here so early in the damn morning, anyway? School don't be starting till another two hours or so." Early chuckled. He hadn't been in a school building in nearly two decades.

"Um . . . I . . . I . . ." Eric was scared to tell the man the true reason for his vagrancy.

"Don't think about lying to me, boy. I can find out anything I wanna know about these streets. Now I see somebody don' kicked yo ass around, and you look hungry and thirsty with those crusty white-ass lips. You best tell me what's goin' on," Early demanded.

Eric hung his head low; he didn't even know where to start. Instead of coming up with a good story, Eric decided that the truth would be easier to tell.

When he had finished his tale, he was surprised to find Early in deep thought. The man twirled one end of his mustache, as if contemplating the meaning of the universe itself. Suddenly he stopped, looked at Eric, opened his Cadillac door and said, "Get in. I think you need a job, young'un. And a good street name to go with it. You seem real easygoing kid, so I'm gon' call you Easy."

Eric cracked a nervous smile. "Easy . . . I like that name."

Early took his young new protégé to McDonald's to fill his empty belly and then to the shopping mall to buy some new clothes. After a shower and a few hours of sleep, Eric felt like a new person. Early took Easy under his tutelage and they formed a quick bond. Easy didn't really have a choice in the matter. Early promised to protect him, and he did just that.

"Punch this punk bitch one more time," Early instructed, twirling the end of his mustache nonchalantly. Easy did as he was told. He pulled back his fist and laid it into his uncle Doobey's lower abdomen one more time.

"Aggh," Doobey coughed. Early laughed.

"You ain't so tough now, are you?" Early hawked up a mucus-filled wad of spit and spewed it into the center of Doobey's face. "I ain't got no respect for a bitch-ass man who puts his hands on a helpless kid," Early observed as his follow-up.

Easy looked on as one of Early's henchmen kicked Doobey square in the balls. His aunt would definitely not be producing any more children in the years to come. Watching Doobey double over in excruciating pain gave Easy a sense of satisfaction that he'd never felt before. Revenge felt like a drug he could indulge in often.

The beating continued for what seemed like an eternity. "I'm sick of looking at this chump-ass pussy. Take his ass outta my sight," Early instructed.

His workers hoisted Doobey's badly battered body from the floor. They stopped in front of Easy. Early walked over and grabbed a handful of Doobey's Afro and lifted up his head.

"Say sorry to this fuckin' kid," Early instructed.

Doobey moaned. His lips were so swollen that Easy couldn't even understand his words.

"Did you hear him say 'sorry'?" Early asked Easy.

Easy nodded his head up and down. He didn't think he was ready to watch someone he knew die.

Easy never saw Doobey or any of his family members after that day. He worked for Early, and in his Brooklyn neighborhood that meant something. Nobody fucked with him anymore; in fact, he was gaining a lot of respect around his way.

Easy's job was to pick up packages from a Spanish dude in the Bronx and bring the goods back to Early. Early paid Easy $100 for each delivery, which was more money than Easy had ever seen in his life. He grew to love the feel and the smell of money, and the freedom it could buy him. With Early's generous paychecks, Easy bought his own clothes, his own food and anything else that he desired. Early even provided a roof over Easy's head by offering him a cot to sleep on in the small living space in the back of his pool hall.

Easy quickly became known at the hangout spot and all around the neighborhood as "Early's kid." Easy liked being claimed by someone; it made him feel wanted. He looked up to Early, and he wanted to be just like him.

Easy would stand in the tiny pool hall bathroom and practice walking, talking and looking like Early. Over the years Early would kick little jewels of knowledge to Easy, like telling him to never, ever trust a man who couldn't look him in the eye.

"If a man can't look you straight in the eye," Early lectured, "the man is hiding his real self."

Early had even gotten Easy his first piece of ass. The advice that followed was invaluable.

"Never fall in love with your first," Early had lectured. "If you do, you'll never have shit to compare it with, so you'll never know what you're missing out on."

Tuck wondered how much Candy knew about her father's upbringing. There was so much more to Eric Hardaway than met the eye, and so many loose ends that needed tying up.

Chapter 18

Deal with the Devil

Candice followed the small Hispanic woman with her eyes. The petite, raven-haired woman balanced a chubby-faced baby on one hip and held the hand of a little boy who looked to be preschool age. The woman released the little boy's hand for a quick second while she struggled to open the door of the sleek black hybrid vehicle. As soon as she released the boy's hand, he took off running like a prison escapee.

Candice was able to see his face clearly now. The family resemblance was stark, with classic olive-toned skin and slanted dark eyes. The boy's shiny black hair bounced around his perfectly round face as his arms pumped with each stride of his run. The woman looked frantic as she took off after the little rascal, the weight of the baby on her hip slowing her down. Candice held her breath as she watched the show unfold.

"Rolando! Come back! Rolando, please!" the woman called out, clearly exasperated.

Candice slid farther down into her seat as the boy, named after his grandfather, ran straight in the direction of her car.

"Rolando! *Por favor!*" the woman huffed pleadingly; the baby was bouncing precariously in her arms. With an out-stretched arm the nanny caught a handful of fabric from the back of his shirt and twisted him around. She spoke rapidly in Spanish; her raised eyebrows, twisted lips and tight hold on the boy indicated a severe scolding was ensuing.

Candice let out a long sigh of relief that the woman had caught the boy just before he neared her vehicle. It might not have gone over so well if the woman had noticed Candice sitting in a car with dark shades covering her eyes, watching them. This was the second week Candice had spent observing them.

Every Thursday, at eleven-thirty in the morning, the nanny took the children to the park. Candice was surprised that such a notorious family as the DeSosas would allow their nanny or any member of the family, for that matter, to be in such a strict routine. Didn't they worry that their enemies could be watching?

Candice thought the DeSosa grandchildren would be chauffeured around in grand limousines by huge, strapping bodyguards with dark shades covering their eyes.

Some notorious drug kingpin, she thought. *Maybe my father was the only paranoid drug kingpin to ever live?*

Either way, DeSosa's slipup worked in her favor.

Once the woman secured the kids into their respective car seats, Candice started her ignition. She had to be at the ready. Keeping a safe distance behind, Candice followed the vehicle to the beautiful Saddlebrook, New Jersey, home.

Just last week Candice had followed the nanny inside Starbucks to study her target at closer range.

"Hey, Flora . . . you want your usual light caramel macchiato?" The barista smiled.

Flora.

It was amazing how much she could find out about a person, even by something as simple as following her into a coffee shop. Candice knew she could take Flora out with no problem. One pressure point stun and the little woman could be easily incapacitated. Candice had kept that in mind.

Lucky for Flora and DeSosa, Candice lived by her father's creed—no women and children. The lesson had obviously been lost on DeSosa when he decided that her mother and eight-year-old sister were fair game.

However, a little manipulation and deception were needed to accomplish what Candy envisioned, and that entailed using women and children as a means to an end. So long as no women or children were physically harmed, Candy felt she could live with the consequences.

The following day, Candice took a different route to the city. She already knew the nanny was heading to the petting zoo at

Central Park, but not before she would pull up to the Starbucks just outside of the park to grab her light caramel macchiato. She consistently left both children in the idling car.

Candice was already parked across the street from the Starbucks when the familiar black hybrid pulled up. "Like clockwork," Candice whispered, an involuntary smirk spreading across her lips. She watched Flora get out, run around the back of the car and rush into the Starbucks.

Go! Candice prompted herself. She scrambled out of her car, raced across the street, crouched down on the side of the car that was facing the street, and used a gloved hand to open the vehicle's back door.

Little Rolando sat up and looked at her, his little head tilted curiously. His baby sister was sound asleep.

"Shh," Candice whispered, placing her finger up to her lips. "Rolando, you wanna see a doggy?" Candice reached inside and unfastened his car seat strap. The boy still looked at her strangely; then he smiled and nodded his agreement.

Rolando wasted no time showing that he was a big boy, happy to be free from the captivity of his car seat. He hopped out of the seat and took Candy's proffered hand. She closed the door, careful not to wake the baby.

"C'mon, let's go see the doggy," she announced. She lifted him between two parked cars and put him on the sidewalk. "Go, look at the doggy over there," she said, pointing to a dog-grooming service two doors down that had their latest customers on display in the window. "Go ahead, big boy," Candice urged when he hesitated. She patted him on the bottom; then she looked around, making sure she didn't draw too much attention to herself or to the boy.

As expected, Rolando took off running.

Candice watched him for a few seconds, keeping her body low. She peeped at the Starbucks and saw that Flora was already coming toward the door with her drink. A flash of heat engulfed Candice's chest. She was spurred into action. She turned quickly, but she couldn't dart across the street just yet. The Manhattan traffic was whizzing by.

"Shit!" Candice huffed, jumping back. Breathing hard and tapping her foot, Candice waited, eyeing the car. Flora was inside now.

Finally there was a break in traffic. With her heart hammering wildly, Candice sprinted back across the street, hoping the woman hadn't noticed her next to the car. With her chest rising and falling rapidly, and her nostrils wide, Candice slumped back into her car. Once inside, she let out a long sigh of relief.

Candice glanced at the black hybrid and noticed Flora standing beside it with a look of terror etched on her face. Her hands were up in the air, swaying wildly, and her head whipped left and right in a frantic motion. She looked to be on the verge of screaming or fainting.

Candice lowered her window slowly so she could hear the commotion more clearly.

"Help! *Por favor!* Help!" Flora screamed, her voice a grating, high-pitched call of distress. Flora yanked open the backseat door and snatched the crying infant to her side as if afraid that she would disappear as well. "Help me!" she screamed again at the top of her lungs. People began to stop and look. Some Good Samaritans offered to dial 911, while others tried to calm her down. Flora continued to whirl around; hysteria was setting in now.

Sirens blared in the distance. Candice knew the boy's exact whereabouts. He had done more than just look at the dogs in the shop's window. When a dog owner had exited, he quickly slipped into the grooming store, which fit beautifully into Candice's plans. A warm sense of satisfaction rose from her stomach into her heart.

Flora was sitting down in the driver's seat of the vehicle; her feet and legs were hanging out the door. The baby was perched on her lap, and the crowd of Good Samaritans was around her, anxious for the authorities to arrive. A few of them volunteered to look for the little boy and they spread out across the block, calling out "Rolando."

Candice knew that it was only a matter of time before the boy was found in the pet shop.

Four police cars, with flashing blue and red lights, arrived at the scene, parking haphazardly around the vehicle. Two officers questioned Flora; two spoke to the bystanders; the rest of the officers began a methodical grid search.

Candice had to chuckle a bit. The boy was right under their noses. The police began checking the stores almost immediately, just as Candice predicted. The officers who would find the boy would be dubbed heroes back at the station for reuniting the lost child with his nanny.

This incident would be the first of many tragedies that would befall the DeSosa family in the coming weeks, if Candy had anything to do with it.

Shortly after the cops arrived, a white Range Rover came to screeching halt near the police cars. Arellio DeSosa, whom Candice recognized from her photo collage, was out of his car before it even came to a full stop. Rolando DeSosa's eldest son burst through the throngs of onlookers and officers and headed straight for Flora. His body language was rigid and menacing.

Before Arellio could even utter a harsh word, a petite blonde, with a lithe build, rushed from behind him. Her hands were extended in front of her as if ready to scratch Flora's eyes out.

"You bitch! Where is my son?" the blonde screamed.

Candice slouched down even farther in her seat and smiled. She'd finally gotten to see Arellio's wife. A police officer grabbed the woman's arms behind her back and directed her toward the Range Rover before she could do any real harm to the nanny. The woman's hands and mouth were moving a mile a minute.

Arellio scolded Flora, his finger wagging accusatorily in her face. Snatching his daughter from her arms, he headed back toward his wife.

"You're fuckin' fired!" the blonde screeched, trying to outmaneuver the officer. "Where is my son?" The woman broke down, her shoulders shaking, as she covered her face with her hands.

Flora was sobbing as well. She had always been careful. There was no way the boy could've unfastened his own car seat straps. The thought caused Flora's knees to give out. She almost hit the ground before an officer caught her in his arms.

Candice watched intently as Arellio handed his daughter to his wife and engaged in an intense conversation with the police officers. Candice watched him still trying to be the cool kingpin as the pressure mounted. Candice hated him more and more by the minute. She made her hand into a fake gun. Closing her weak eye, she aimed it at Arellio's head.

"Boom!" she whispered as she pulled back her pointer finger in a mock trigger pull.

Arellio went over and embraced his wife; their baby daughter was snuggled between them.

Such a loving family, Candice noted sarcastically.

Alas, the play was nearing its final scene. Heads turned simultaneously to the left as shouting could be heard in the distance.

"Found him! We found him!" a police officer belted out as he walked with a child in his arms toward the crowd. Cheers erupted from the worried onlookers.

Arellio and wife rushed toward their child. "Thank God!" the woman cried as she scooped her son up into her arms and squeezed him tightly. Arellio was right on her heels. He kissed his son on the top of his head and held on to his wife and children for dear life.

The scene sent sparks of white-hot anger over Candice's body. Her cheeks were aflame and she bit down so hard into the side of her mouth that she broke the skin.

"Now I know how to locate your Achilles' heel," Candice vowed aloud as she followed Arellio DeSosa with her eyes. Family clearly mattered to him, as much as it did to her. If that was his point of weakness, then that was where she planned to strike first.

Standing nearly six and a half feet tall, Arellio DeSosa was a hard-to-miss target. He was nearly the spitting image of his father—olive-colored skin, shiny black hair, strong broad shoulders, large flat nose and long prominent chin. He joined his father's business when he was just seventeen years old and was groomed to be just as ruthless. Unlike most teenage boys, however, Arellio's rite of passage into manhood was murder.

Harlem, New York 1991

As a .357 Magnum shook in Arellio's hand, his father and his goons waited for the young protégé to find the cojones to finish the job.

"There is no hesitation, Arellio!" Rolando DeSosa barked.

Arellio jumped at the sound of his father's voice. He had always been scared of his father, who was very much an authoritative figure in his life.

"When a man betrays you, your family, everything you stand for, you have no choice but to kill him—no matter who he is. There is no coming back for a man who has no dignity and no pride," DeSosa lectured his son.

"This man stole from me. He lied to my face! He threatened our family by talking to the police. He is a snake . . . no, more like a fuckin' rat," DeSosa hissed, his accent strengthening.

Arellio looked down at the bloodied man whom he'd once called Uncle. The man squirmed on the floor in a last-ditch effort to edge toward the door and save his life; he really did look like a slithering snake.

Arellio followed him now, leveling his gun at his chest. He couldn't breathe. His heart beat so fast—he thought he'd go into cardiac arrest.

"What are you waiting for? He is no longer part of our family. He betrayed me, our family name and everything we stand for." DeSosa was urging his son to finish the job. He needed to know that Arellio had the heart to kill. It was the only way he could guarantee his family's reputation as cold-blooded businessmen.

"This is your chance to live up to the DeSosa name. You must not feel anything for a rat bastard like this. Now, prove to me, and everyone here, that you're worthy of this family's name," DeSosa growled. He was growing frustrated with his son's apparent hesitation.

With his body covered in a cold sweat, Arellio lifted his gun hand and aimed it at the man's head. His uncle flipped onto his back. He looked into his nephew's eyes, pleading for a small measure of compassion.

"Please, please . . ." the man's voice quavered. "Your mother is my sister. What will she think when she finds out I'm dead at your hands? You can't devastate her like this. You're just a young boy. You don't understand what is going on here," the man cried out, his words barely audible through swollen lips.

Arellio gazed at the men gathered in the room to witness his first kill. He couldn't disappoint his father in front of all of his workers. Arellio had to prove that he was worthy of the family business and of his father's love. This was his chance.

"Shut up! Don't talk about my mother!" Arellio shouted. "You are a fuckin' rat bastard, just like my father said!" Arellio could nearly feel the testosterone flowing in his veins. He got closer to the man and put the gun to the man's temple.

"You must die," he announced to his uncle. He closed his eyes and pulled the trigger before he could have any second thoughts.

The gun blast reverberated up Arellio's arm and caused his body to rock backward. When he opened his eyes, he saw part of the man's brains lying on the floor. There was so much blood. Arellio felt his knees go weak. Blood and brain matter had splattered all over his shoes and the bottom of his pants.

Taking the man's life made him feel as powerful as God Himself. He gripped the gun more tightly now. He looked around wildly. His eyes darted from face to face. He locked eyes with his father. Arellio bit down into his jaw and tried not to crack a smile. Instead, he adjusted his features into a scowl, as was appropriate for a murdering man.

"Good job, my son. I knew you could do it," DeSosa said proudly as he clapped his son on the shoulder.

Arellio could not stop staring at his handiwork. The smell of the blood, like raw meat gone bad, made him feel like an animal in the jungle prowling for his next meal. Only Arellio didn't think this particular appetite could ever be truly satisfied.

Junior sat across from Rolando DeSosa Sr. Their eyes were locked on each other. DeSosa lifted a Cuban cigar to his lips slowly, sucking in, and blew a smoke ring in Junior's direction. His infamous diamond skull and crossbones gleamed on his front tooth. Junior bit down into his jaw and adjusted his neck.

"Junior," DeSosa drawled, rolling the *R* at the end of his name.

Junior didn't break eye contact.

"You come here for my help, no?" DeSosa said in an unnervingly calm tone of voice.

Junior nodded slightly.

"But you question me also?" DeSosa followed up. He didn't appreciate the way Junior had accused him with fingers pointed.

"Look, DeSosa, I'm sorry for the way I busted in here. I'm just telling you what this dude said. First he said you worked for the government, and then he said he was a fuckin' DEA agent," Junior confessed as he recalled the nightmarish scene that had unfolded weeks earlier.

"I had no idea. I feel like my ass had been set up by you, by him. . . . I just want some answers, man. I also want help with this problem," Junior continued, humbly now. He was very careful with his tone as he warily eyed DeSosa's goons positioned on either corner of the room. Another was stationed on the other side of the closed door.

DeSosa moved his shoulders back uncomfortably. "You came here for my help? You say Phil harmed your family? Is that right?" DeSosa asked, blowing out more smoke rings. He completely ignored Junior's concerns about him being down with the government.

Junior nodded, rocking in his chair now. His frustration was mounting.

"And what about his brother? His family?" DeSosa asked.

"I told that nigga I didn't have nothing to do with the shit that happened to his brother. It was all Broady. He thought Phil killed his best friend, Razor, so he took revenge. I didn't have nothing to do with that," Junior explained. "But Phil hit my moms," Junior finished with venom. Nothing more needed to be said.

DeSosa seemed to contemplate what he was being told.

"Yes, I know everything, including the fact that you allowed a narco into my midst. Into my business!" DeSosa snapped, finally acknowledging Junior's confession.

"I didn't know Tuck was an undercover rat. It doesn't matter, anyway, does it? Aren't you untouchable?" Junior replied snidely. He was tired of the DeSosa bullshit.

DeSosa eyed him evilly. "You think Easy would've ever brought a rat into his company? You think he would've been that weak? You never were as good as he was at this business," DeSosa said cruelly, chuckling.

Junior swiped his hands down his thighs and shifted in his seat. He could feel heat rising in his chest. His eyes darted across the room at the two men standing around, trying to look casual, their weapons making visible bumps under their suit jackets. Junior knew better than to express his outrage. He was here to ask for help, after all.

"Do you remember the day Easy brought you to me, Junior?" DeSosa asked. The rolling *R* sent a cold chill down Junior's spine. "You were so poor, so pathetic. Coming from nothing," DeSosa said, curling his lip to show his disgust.

Junior swallowed hard. DeSosa liked to antagonize, and he knew just what to say to crush his opponent.

"You could never be Easy, eh, Junior, because you always make things so difficult for yourself." DeSosa laughed at his play on words.

Junior rolled his eyes to the ceiling. He couldn't escape Easy's shadow for the life of him. His lips formed a hard, straight line as DeSosa ripped into him.

"You were a skinny kid. Hungry to be a part of something. Easy was proud of the job he wanted you to do. He had given you the responsibility of taking the package . . . the same way he started out. Easy was always loyal when he trusted someone," DeSosa recounted, puffing on his cigar.

It was all too much: the words, the disrespectful smoke, the memories. Junior sat uncomfortably erect, uneasy. His hands were curled into fists; the veins in his wrists were bulging with restraint.

"Ah, yes, Easy Hardaway, the consummate humanitarian. He fed you. He taught you. He trusted you. *You* wanted to be *him*. I remember the day I met you. You stunk of envy. You reeked of animosity. I could see it in your eyes. You secretly hated the man who had fed and clothed you. From that day forward, I never trusted you. I knew when Easy wanted out, you would be the one I could count on to keep up the deal I had made with the devils, but I still didn't trust you. I knew you were so hungry for power that you would kill any man who stood in your way. You were born a snake. It is in your blood . . . a fucking cold-blooded killer like your father," DeSosa hissed cruelly.

Junior's temple throbbed and sweat beads lined up on his hairline like ready soldiers. His chest heaved at hearing the truth. If he hadn't been so outgunned, he would've slapped the shit out of the old man for speaking to him so disrespect-fully. But DeSosa was no real threat to Junior. Junior saw him for what he was: a shell of his younger self, a feeble old man racked by Multiple Sclerosis.

"Easy was not a saint. He killed one of my best friends, and he was a power hound. You know this. He only got out of the game because of Rock. A fuckin' hypocrite hit man acting as Easy's gotdamn moral compass," Junior denounced.

DeSosa stubbed his cigar out and dropped his hands at his sides. He pushed on the wheels of his wheelchair until his entire body emerged from around the table.

Junior looked at him without sympathy. He secretly wished he had been the one who'd put the bullet years ago into DeSosa that had taken away his ability to walk.

The "sniper's bullet" had been a hiccup in DeSosa's career, but it had not taken him out of the game. Now, though, the disease had done what a bullet couldn't do; it made him weak and vulnerable. Seeing his time on earth as limited, DeSosa was forced to tie up some loose ends from the past.

"Junior, I can help you with your problem with Phil, but I want you to find the girl. Easy's daughter. I want her," DeSosa said, close enough for both the sweet and pungent smell of his cigar to lodge in the back of Junior's throat.

"I don't know where to find her," Junior replied in all honesty. He didn't want to make a two-sided deal. If he had to, he'd take care of Phil alone.

"Well, then, our business is done here," DeSosa said with finality.

Junior swallowed his pride. He knew he needed DeSosa, and he wanted to feel like DeSosa needed him.

"All right, man, tell me what you want me to do. But I want guarantees that I will be the fuckin' one to put a bullet in Phil's head. He hit my moms in her face," Junior growled.

"Good. Then we have a deal," DeSosa said ominously.

Avon drove to his home in Bowie, Maryland, for the first time since his meeting with the DEA and Grayson Stokes. He had to make sure his kids were safe. Stokes had scared the shit out of him. Now, as Avon pulled into the housing subdivision, he couldn't help but remember the last time he went home.

As Avon recalled the entire nightmarish scene, he felt the same sharp tug in his heart. Avon blinked back tears. All he could do now was hope that his kids had forgiven him for making such a nasty scene. In the meantime, he would focus all of his efforts on seeing them to safety. He walked into his home to a hero's welcome. It was as if the kids had forgotten about the things that had happened. It had made Avon's heart smile to get a neck hug from his little girl—a hug that nearly choked him with its strength. Things with Elaina were strained. Avon didn't let that deter his focus.

Once the pleasantries and hellos were over, Avon wasted no time demanding that Elaina and the kids pack up and go some place until he felt it was safe to come home again. Although there were few places they could go undetected, he felt fairly comfortable leaving his wife and kids under the watchful eyes of Elaina's parents.

So they headed there together.

Paranoid, Avon spent the first two nights at his in-laws', staying there until he felt certain that his family was in good hands. Avon sat up all night like a guard dog, watching and waiting.

Avon hugged his kids and gave his mother-in-law a dry kiss on her cheek before leaving his family.

"Thanks for doing this, Helen. It won't be that long," Avon assured her.

Helen raised her eyebrows and crossed her arms over her chest; her displeasure was evident. Helen didn't appreciate the fact that his job had placed her daughter and grandchildren in jeopardy.

Avon picked up his daughter and gave her a big kiss. She laid her head on his shoulders and asked him not to leave. Although Avon and Elaina had tried to pretend that their visit was casual.

"I promise to come back soon. Mommy is going to be here with you, okay?" Avon assured. With his heart heavy, he placed his daughter back down on the floor and turned toward Elaina.

The tension that settled between them made him feel queasy. An awkward silence ensued. They hadn't said anything of substance to one another since he had returned and ordered them to pack their belongings in haste. After the first day, all of the pleasantries had dissipated between the two.

"How long are you going to be gone this time?" Elaina asked. Her voice was laced with resignation and irritation.

Elaina hugged herself in an attempt to quell the trembling that racked her body. She hung her head, unable to hold eye contact with her husband. He was a stranger to her now. His being gone so long without so much as a call or an occasional visit, then the affair—and now his frantic plea that she and the kids relocate—was simply taking its toll on her body and soul. Elaina felt Avon always put his need to succeed above all else in his life, including her and the children.

Avon let out a long, frustrated sigh. Though their relationship was strained, her safety was still important to him. And she had some nerve being angry with him, he silently groused.

"I don't know how long I'll be gone, but I want you and the kids to stay here until you hear from me." Avon needed to know that his wife and kids were out of harm's way.

Elaina shook her head from left to right and gnawed on her bottom lip. The pain and burden of it all was evident on both of their faces.

Elaina stepped closer to him, shifting her weight from one foot to the other. She reached out a trembling hand. "Look, Avon, for what it's worth . . . it didn't mean anything to me. It was the closest thing I had to you," Elaina confessed, her voice cracking and tears rimming her eyes.

He flinched and moved a safe distance from her grasp. Her words sent a sharp pang of hurt through Avon's chest.

Elaina had been the first woman Avon truly loved. But she had also hurt him in the worst possible way. He knew his pride would never allow him to be with Elaina again, but divorce proceedings were the furthest thing from his mind right now.

Avon shoved his hands deep into his pockets to keep himself from reaching out and touching her. He wanted to embrace her, hold her face in his hands and tell her he was sorry for leaving and not calling. He wished he could explain that it had all been part of his job; it had all been for her safety. But he knew that wasn't entirely true, and they didn't need any more lies between them.

Her eyes begged him to understand, to love her again.

"I gotta go. I want you to stay inside the house as much as possible. Call me if you have to leave for longer than a few minutes," he finally said in an all-business tone.

Elaina had hoped to hear a glimmer of love or affection in his parting words. Instead, his parting words had been cold and formal. Without a glance backward, he turned his back on her and walked out of her life once again.

Avon pinched the bridge of his nose, hoping to release some of the tension in his head. He looked down at the box he had just hefted from his trunk. Digging inside, he pulled out the next notebook and began to lose himself in the story unfolding before his eyes. It was a necessary and welcome distraction.

He was starting to feel like he knew Easy. He could only imagine what a man who'd grown up like Easy must've gone through to protect his own family.

Avon Tucker was even more compelled to find Candy now.

Brooklyn, New York, 1986

"You see that bitch-ass right there?" Early asked.

Easy looked over and stared out the window on the side of the car Early sat on.

"You gon' jump out, blow that weasel's head off and get right back in here. You gotta earn ya wings. Ya dig?" Early said, still staring out the darkly tinted window.

Easy watched as the man walked out of the club with a woman on each arm.

"He's a fake-ass pimp, ya dig. He owes me more than a little bit of bread, and I'm tired of waiting. He been in that club all night spreading my bread around like he Jesus feeding the hungry," Early told Easy.

"You just gon' kill him over some money?" Easy asked incredulously.

Early stared at the sixteen-year-old boy as if he were speaking a foreign language.

"Li'l nigga is you dumb, deaf or blind? Which one? I ain't gon' kill the muthafucka in the first place. You gon' kill this jive-ass weasel over my bread. And for the record, I'll kill a nigga just to prove a point, so what is you sayin'? I mean, if you scared, I can go find me a real soldier," Early demeaned. He didn't like to be questioned or second-guessed.

Easy had seen Early's wrath more than a few times in the three years he'd been living under the older man's tutelage.

"Um . . . no. I can do it. I—I ain't scared of n-nothing," Easy stammered. He didn't really have a choice.

Early had given him a home and a job since he had found him homeless and hungry. Early had offered him protection and introduced him to everybody who worked the streets. This task was simply part of the job. Easy owed him that much. If he refused the order, life as he knew it would be over.

"I thought you would come around," Early said, smirking. "Here. This baby will do the trick and ain't got a lot of recoil either. Nothing more reliable than this baby here." Early handed Easy a silver Colt revolver.

The gun felt as cold as ice in Easy's trembling bony hand.

"Now go on over there and return the favor I did for you when I got rid of your auntie's no-good husband."

Easy's heart hammered intensely; he felt like he was going to be bruised from the inside. Inhaling deeply, trying to calm his nerves, he grabbed the car door handle. His sweaty fingers slipped off the metal.

Early grabbed Easy's arm. "Calm down, li'l nigga. This is part of being a man on these streets," Early said.

Easy nodded his head up and down rapidly. He didn't even realize his eyes were blinking faster than a humming-bird's wings. Taking a deep breath, Easy finally got the car door open.

His target was bigger than he had appeared from the car. At six feet three inches tall, the man looked intimidating. The giant laughed; his voice was deep and guttural. Two women flanked him as they huddled together, sharing a white reefer joint.

Easy was walking fast now; his legs were seemingly moving on their own. His mind was adrift, blank. One of the women noticed Easy first.

"Aw, look at this little cutie-pie. You came to pay for some pussy, didn't you, baby bo—" Her words halted, and the smile plastered on her face crumbled into a look of abject horror.

Easy raised his hand and let off three shots into the man's face before the woman could shriek.

The man let out a scream that was nothing less than primordial. He staggered for a few seconds; his face seemed to break off and explode with each subsequent shot. His large body crumpled to the ground like a wall of bricks. The man's fedora lay under his head and served as a makeshift bucket for the blood leaking from his head.

Easy stood frozen with fear. His mind told him to run, but his body wouldn't cooperate. It was Early's booming baritone that finally spurned Easy into action.

"Get yo' ass over here!" Early barked.

Easy raced into the car. He was hyperventilating; his chest rose and fell so hard. He tried to swallow back the vomit. As the car sped down the streets, making hairpin turns, he lost all hope for keeping his cool. Easy placed his head between his legs and threw up the contents of his stomach.

"Damn, boy! I can tell this was your first time offing a nigga. Well, you can bet that it ain't gon' be your last. You gotta be that ruthless, nigga, on these here streets, baby boy. You gon' have to get used to this shit without losing your lunch."

Early laughed unsympathetically as Easy retched.

Chapter 19

The Insider

Candice pressed the doorbell and waited, tapping her left foot rapidly on the concrete step. She could feel sweat beads running a drag race down her back.

"Can I help you?" asked the woman who had snatched open the door.

Up close, her icy blue eyes and lemony blond hair had Candice stuck on stupid. Arellio DeSosa's wife looked as though she had just stepped out of the pages of *Vogue* magazine.

"Who are you and what do you want?" the beautiful Caucasian woman snapped, her forehead furrowed.

"I'm sorry. I am here from the agency . . . the nanny job." Candice stumbled over her words, her fake accent making her tongue feel foreign in her mouth.

She had been watching Flora long enough to know which agency she worked for and was finally able to get up the nerve to go inside and apply for the job.

The woman gave Candice the once-over and her face softened. At least they hadn't sent a beautiful young girl, like they usually did. Cyndi DeSosa wouldn't have to watch her husband around this little, fat, frumpy girl. There was an awkward pause as both women took measure of the other.

"Come in," the woman finally said, stepping aside from the door. "I hope you have your act together . . . not like that last one," Cyndi grumbled.

Candice felt slightly weak in the knees as she crossed the threshold of the DeSosa home. A funny feeling came over body; her nerve endings felt alive. She was inside! She was so close that she could hear the DeSosa woman breathing and smell her rich perfume.

Uncle Rock would've warned against this method. He liked to be the furtive hit man who took his targets by surprise. Candice was the opposite. She wanted to be near her victims, to witness their pain up close as she picked their lives apart, piece by piece.

"Did they tell you there were two children . . . little ones, very active," the woman explained.

Candice just nodded. Her brain was having trouble sending the right signals to her tongue. The room swayed around Candice and her ears rang. Her stomach had huge bat-sized butterflies bouncing around in it. The excitement and nervousness was overwhelming Candice.

"What's your name?" the woman asked as she noticed the glazed-over look in her eyes.

"Um . . . I—I am Dulce," Candice stammered, her horrible attempt at an accent coming and going like the uneven slopes of a mountain.

"Hmm, Dulce, like candy, is Spanish? Interesting," Cyndi commented.

Mrs. DeSosa wore slim-cut jeans, a pair of black patent leather stilettos and a close-fitting Lycra shirt that hugged her ample breasts. Simple but elegant—both at the same time. She had the body of a Victoria's Secret model.

"I'm Cyndi DeSosa . . . Mrs. DeSosa to you," the woman introduced rudely, not bothering to offer her hand. She needed to establish a strict employer-employee relationship early on. No more little bitches close to her kids, close to her husband.

"You have the papers from the agency?" Cyndi asked suspiciously.

Dumb ass. You should've asked before you let me in. I could've killed you and your family by now. Candice put on a fake smile and dug into her oversized purse, careful not to let the woman see her two best friends—Glock and SIG Sauer—lying snugly inside. Candice retrieved the paperwork and Cyndi snatched it from her hands. She looked at Candice and then back down to the paperwork.

"I only deal with people that Ms. Sanchez sends. Did she send you?" Cyndi looked at Candice with one raised, speculative eyebrow.

Candice thought about how she had put a gun to Flora's head, threatened her life and took all of Flora's agency paperwork. She'd then put the barrel of the same gun into Ms. Sanchez's mouth and told her that if she ever contacted the DeSosa family about her little visit, she would die. Both women had readily agreed, but Candice still left them with a nice gun butt scar to prove she meant business.

"Yes, she did. Ms. Sanchez sent me because Flora was fired for losing your son in the city or something like that," Candice relayed mendaciously.

Cyndi's facial expression grew dark; her eyes went into slits at the mere mention of Flora's name.

"That bitch is lucky to be alive," she said menacingly. "Let me show you around. I am very particular about my house, my children . . . and my husband," Cyndi said sternly, summoning Candice to follow her like a true subordinate.

Candice's knowledge of the incident had sealed the deal. She was officially in. She followed Cyndi through the beautiful house. Gold and cream seemed to be the theme colors throughout. A bit opulent for Candice's taste, but definitely rich. Candice took mental notes of doors, windows and things that could be obstacles to a fast break, if she ever needed to get out fast.

"Your sleeping quarters are upstairs, right next to the children," Cyndi continued.

As Candice followed Cyndi up the winding staircase, she looked intently at the gallery of family portraits on the long wall leading up the steps. She could probably name everyone in the pictures by now, and that made her smile inside.

When she got to the last step at the top, there it was: a larger-than-life portrait of their patriarch, symbolizing his position as head of the family. Candice's pulse quickened as she stared at the picture. He was older now; a jagged line of silver ran through his thinning dark hair. He was sitting in a wheelchair, flanked by his family.

Candice had read all about Rolando DeSosa getting shot. Behind them, a huge neon sign blazed in red letters: BAILE CALIENTE. Candice squinted her eyes into dashes. She couldn't peel her eyes away. *No emotions, Candy. No emotions right now.* Suddenly her right contact lens began to itch as her eyes started to well up with angry tears.

"That's my father-in-law. And that's my husband's and my club. He cut the ribbon that day," Cyndi explained after noticing her interest in the painting.

Candice nodded her head and smiled nervously. She wondered how long she'd been staring at the picture.

"You've seen him before?" Cyndi asked suspiciously, trying to see how much Candice knew about their family.

"Um . . . no. It's a nice picture, ma'am," Candice fabricated on the spot.

Cyndi gave her a sideways glance.

"Well, he used to be a very important and very dangerous man . . . not so much these days. He lives with us now and is winding down his life to be a grandfather and, finally, a father. I hope Ms. Sanchez told you the requirements of working here in this family. . . ." Cyndi looked at her expectantly.

Candice nodded.

They were both on the same page.

Mrs. DeSosa took Candice on a tour of the remainder of the 12,000-square-foot home.

"My father-in-law lives on that side of the house. He is a very sick man, and the kids only see him when he comes over here. He loves them, but they can sometimes be too much for a man in his condition," Cyndi explained as they passed through a long hallway leading to the off-limits wing of the house.

Candice knew she'd be venturing over there at some point. Cyndi told Candice she'd expect her to stay some nights because she often traveled with her husband or worked at the club late into the early-morning hours.

Candice met the children for the second time that week. The baby screamed as soon as Candice touched her soft, round cheeks, and little Rolando remained hidden behind his mother's legs. Candice wondered if the kids could tell that her hair, eyes, fat stomach and legs were all phony, just like her résumé. Children, in Candice's experience, were much more discerning about people's intentions than adults.

Cyndi didn't appear too concerned with her children's reluctance to meet their new nanny, however.

"They'll get used to you," Cyndi told her, only slightly embarrassed by her children's reactions.

Candice smiled and nodded in agreement. She'd have to get used to them too.

The most important thing for Candice was that she was within striking range of her targets, and close to bringing justice to her family.

Junior wrestled with the key in the old rusted door lock. His hands were sweaty and his heart was pumping hard and fast. He didn't know why he was so nervous to find out the truth, but he was. Junior told himself the only reason he had even come to Rock's apartment after all of this time was to get clues on Candy's whereabouts so he could turn her over to DeSosa like they'd agreed.

After Rock killed himself, Junior received the keys and a letter from Rock in the mail. Rock's punk ass had apologized for being an absentee father who had stood by and watched his son grow up rough. The note had informed him cryptically that there were things inside the apartment that would explain everything, but that he needed to be careful because enemies on both sides of the law would be watching him. Junior didn't give a fuck about any of that shit in Rock's final note. His sole purpose right now was hunting down Candy.

Junior entered the apartment and scrunched up his face in disgust. "How was this nigga living?" Junior whispered as he looked around at the shabby décor: old moth-eaten curtains, scratched and chipped wood furniture, mismatched table chairs, worn-out couch and holey chair.

He walked over to the coffee table; there was a box in the center. Junior peered inside and his heart leaped in his chest.

He had found what he was looking for.

After leaving the apartment, Junior rushed into Rolando DeSosa's office in a huff.

"I have an address for you," he blurted out. He wasn't going to tell DeSosa about the other things he'd found inside Rock's home.

"Very good, Junior. You work very fast," DeSosa commented.

"I really want this nigga Phil badly. He is hiding out, but I'm sure you have the power to find him," Junior cajoled.

DeSosa started laughing. "How about we take baby steps first. One man at a time," he said, extending his hand for the information Junior gripped to his chest.

Junior handed it over somewhat reluctantly.

"Go with them," DeSosa instructed, pointing toward his shadow men.

Without much of a choice, Junior did as he was told.

"Which one of y'all bitch niggas hit my moms?" Junior growled. His face was so close to Dray's that he could see the perspiration beads above the other man's clean lip.

"I don't know, man! I wasn't there!" Dray's arms burned as they were extended unnaturally far over his head. The metal chains dug into his wrists and his fingers had no feeling. They were already turning blue and purple from the lack of circulation.

One of DeSosa's goons walked in front of Dray's naked chest and laid his fist into Dray's sternum.

"Agh!" Dray screamed. His body bucked, which caused more pressure on the chains, and thus more pain.

"You still gon' act like you don't know shit about this? Phil is supposed to be your man, and you see what that shit got you?" Junior spat out. A large green vein was pulsing at his temple.

"Fuck you," Dray managed in a low growl, spitting up a mouthful of blood in Junior's direction. Dray wasn't going to let no Brooklyn cat make him into a pussy. If he was going to die, it was going to be on his feet and not on his knees.

"A'ight," Junior said, stepping back for a minute, swiping his hand roughly over his face. He nodded to the broad-shouldered Hispanic man whom DeSosa had assigned to assist him. The man rushed over and grabbed a gorilla fistful of Dray's balls.

"Agghh! Agghh!" Dray let out a bloodcurdling scream as the man exerted pressure on his man sac.

"You still don't wanna tell me who hit my moms, and where the fuck Phil is hiding?" Junior barked, extremely agitated. The area behind his eyes was throbbing.

Dray's head was hanging low; his chin was damn near touching the middle of his chest. He was too exhausted to scream anymore. Junior walked over to him, grabbed a handful of his hair and yanked his head upward.

"I said fuck you and your mom's nigga," Dray rasped.

Junior bit down on his bottom lip. He released Dray's head and pulled out his weapon.

"No, fuck you and your whole crew. They'll meet you in hell, bitch nigga!"

Junior leveled his gun at Dray's head and squeezed the trigger. He didn't stop shooting until the entire twelve-round magazine had been emptied into Dray's body.

"Get rid of him," Junior whispered harshly as he exited the room. "One down. One to go."

"In breaking news today, a mysterious shooting outside of Baile Caliente, a popular Latino salsa club, left two men dead. Police officials report that the shots seemed to have come from a distance, indicative of a sniper shooting," the newscaster said. "Police say that surveillance video in front of the club did not show any cars driving by or any shooters on foot. The two victims are rumored to work for Arellio DeSosa, the owner of the club and the son of the alleged former head of the Sindicato drug cartel. Arellio DeSosa's whereabouts at the time of the shootings were unknown. Police officials are combing the area looking for clues as to where the shots came from. We will continue to bring you live coverage as we receive updates."

Avon's head snapped up from the file he was reading when he heard the name "DeSosa" mentioned on the hotel television. "Shit!" he gasped, turning up the volume.

The shootings had Candy's signature written all over them. That was her modus operandi—take out her targets like falling dominoes. It was her way of building up to the big fish.

A lightbulb went off in Avon's mind. Candice was going after the most dangerous kingpin in the tristate area: Rolando DeSosa.

No wonder the fuckin' government was trying to find her—to keep her from assassinating their man.

Avon began pacing the floor. Candy was way out of her league. This was way different than fucking with a few street punks. She was playing a dangerous game now. Even more dangerous than the first time.

Avon had to contemplate his next move. He had been so immersed in the Easy Hardaway files that he'd lost sight of what he really needed to do . . . find Candy before the government or DeSosa did.

His cell phone rang, almost causing him to jump out of his own skin. Avon rushed over to the small desk in the far corner of the hotel room and looked at his phone. The number came up "unknown." It could be Elaina and the kids, he reasoned. He picked it up, with his nerves on edge.

"More people might die if you don't reconsider the deal I offered. That could've easily been Elaina or your son or your daughter. . . . Who knows who could go next?" Grayson Stokes threatened on the other end of the line.

Stokes's words coldly echoed in Avon's brain. He tightened his grip on the mobile device. His rushing breath was the only response Stokes received. His message had clearly hit home.

"Seems like our little friend is a trained assassin. I happen to know she's been trained by the best. I also happen to know where your family is, Agent Tucker," he rasped into the phone.

Avon closed his eyes. Why was he being put in the middle of this shit again? All he'd ever wanted was to be like his father—a good law enforcement officer who dedicated his life wholeheartedly to the job of bringing criminals to justice. Avon had made some mistakes along the way, yes, but nothing to warrant this sort of harassment.

"Let me find her on my own. I will bring her in," Avon finally spoke up. The only choice he had right now was to get down or lay down.

"Don't cross me, Agent Tucker. I don't like to be crossed. You should take example from Brad Brubaker. I hate liars and traitors," Stokes warned before hanging up the phone.

Avon looked at the phone for a long, hard minute. It had now become a matter of saving innocent lives. He snatched up the file he had been reading. He needed to know more.

Brooklyn, New York, 1988

Easy stood over Early's casket. He wanted to cry, scream, fight, spit and jump up and down—all at the same time. Early didn't look like himself. His face was extremely swollen and his lips looked like fish lips. The undertaker had told Easy that the shots Early had taken to his head made it hard for them to work with his natural face. They added a fair amount of wax and makeup for the open-casket service. Easy had protested against the casket being open, but he'd lost to Early's old lady, Syrita.

In fact, it was Syrita's ear-shattering screams that brought Easy out of his stupor in front of the casket. Syrita was making her way to the front of the funeral parlor in the most dramatic fashion possible.

Easy moved backward and took a seat in the front pew. He watched as one person after another came up to Early's casket to pay respects. Without a doubt, many of them simply wanted to assess the damage the bullet holes had done to his body.

Easy grew angrier by the minute. He was angry with himself for not being around when Early took the shots that sealed his fate.

Easy had been on his run, picking up an important package. The story went that Early was leaving the pool hall with Bosco, his right-hand man, when someone called his name real loud.

The street reporters said Early turned around; but before he could even blink, seven shots entered his head.

The story unsettled Easy, causing him severe stomach cramps. The method by which Early was murdered was nearly identical to the one he'd used two years earlier when he'd killed a man at Early's request. Easy felt in some degree responsible for Early's premature death, like it was Karma coming back to bite him in the ass.

Easy also felt more alone than he ever had in his life. So many street dudes hated Easy because of his association with Early. Now there was no one left to shelter or protect him. He must be his own man on the street. After the years he spent following Early like his shadow, he knew he could think, walk and talk like Early. And, most important, when need be, he could be as ruthless as Early as well.

Once Early was buried, Easy set out to make his mark. He had to stand on his own two feet now.

The first thing he did was move his belongings out of his makeshift room in the back of the pool hall. Easy got a room inside of an old rooming house in East New York. He had a little money saved, so he decided to take a chance and go see the big man from whom he regularly picked up packages. Easy planned on convincing the man he could take over Early's operations on the street.

Easy stood in his spot on the corner, his hands shoved down into his pockets. It had been a year since he'd earned enough trust to get his own package. Though he was surrounded by loudmouthed wannabe gangsters, he never fed into their ways. He was always quiet and unassuming while conducting his hand-to-hand sales.

Easy had been out hustling all day and had almost finished his bundle when he was approached by a basehead named Charlotte.

"Easy, lemme get something on credit," Charlotte begged.

"Nah," Easy said in a low tone.

"C'mon . . . don't be like that. You usually hook a sista up," she pleaded.

"I said nah," Easy said firmly.

"You muthafucka! I'm one of your best customers and you just gon' put me off like that? You can't hook me up 'til check day?" Charlotte spat out, getting too close and too loud for Easy's comfort.

"Why don't you go ask one of them dudes," Easy said calmly, nodding toward his noisy counterparts. They were making fun of an older dude whom Easy had seen going into the store.

"*You know your shit is the best out here. Stop playing!*" *Charlotte screeched. She nervously scratched against her arms.*

"*Yo, go 'head, man. I'm not giving you anything on credit.*" *Easy dismissed her with a look of utter disgust.*

"*Fuck you! You ain't shit, anyway. I know a couple of niggas who will beat ya ass and take all ya shit.*" *Charlotte wagged a skeletal finger close to Easy's face. She hawked up a mucus-filled wad of spit and spewed it into Easy's face. Loud roars erupted from the rowdy corner boys. Easy had been played.*

Easy quickly grabbed the bag-of-bones girl around her neck, lifting her off her feet. She dangled like a choked chicken. He scowled as he squeezed her neck without the least bit of conscience.

"*Yo, kill that bitch!*" *one of the boys screamed out.*

Easy was in a blind rage. He was about to catch a case.

"*Yo, nigga, she about dead. That bitch turning purple!*" *someone yelled out.*

It was the only thing that snapped Easy out of his rage; he couldn't commit murder in plain sight like this. He quickly came to his senses and dropped Charlotte back to her feet. She was coughing and rolling around wildly trying to catch her breath.

Easy lifted his foot and gave her a swift kick in the ass. "*Don't let me see your fuckin' ass around here ever again!*" *Easy spat out.*

Charlotte scrambled up off the ground, finally able to catch her breath enough to argue back.

"*You gon' get yours, you bastard!*" *she rasped, still holding her bruised neck.*

"*Get the fuck outta here, you dirty bitch!*" *Easy called after her.*

A man exited the bodega behind him, and the next thing Easy knew he felt a rush of wind and a pair of hands pushing him out of the way. The old black dude from the bodega was taking down a man in a black leather trench coat who held a gun in his hand. Easy's heart began to pound as he watched the older gentleman clamp down on the gunman's wrist.

The gunman cried out in pain and the gun skittered to the ground.

When the guys on the corner noticed the commotion, they all began to scatter. "Oh shit, a gun!" they yelled. The last thing they needed was for the cops to come around.

Easy couldn't move; he was in shock.

The stranger calmly picked up the gun, dropped the magazine out of it, dismantled the slide and threw the bottom half of it at the guy on the ground.

"Oh shit! That bitch tried to set me up!" Easy finally found his voice, his heart racing as he realized what had just happened.

The old dude nodded in agreement.

"Fuck! Thank God you were here. That nigga woulda shot me right in the back of my fuckin' head," Easy concluded.

The old dude nodded again, but still did not speak a word.

"I'ma fuckin' kill him!" Easy screamed, his blood boiling.

The old dude put his hand up to Easy's chest to stop him.

"Not here. Not now." The old dude finally spoke.

Easy backed down. Something about the stranger's calm, fatherly words struck him as soothing. In some ways the man reminded him a lot of Early.

"I'm Eric. But everybody calls me Easy," he said, introducing himself.

"Rock," the old dude said, taking Easy's extended hand and shaking it firmly.

"Yo, man, how can I repay you for that shit?" Easy asked earnestly.

"No need," Rock said, handing Easy the magazine full of .40-caliber rounds and the slide of his would-be assassin's gun.

"Nah, there has got to be something. Some money, some food, clothes, something," Easy offered. He didn't like feeling indebted to any man.

"Just go inside and get my BC Powder. I have the worst headache," Rock said calmly.

Easy scrambled to do as Rock had asked.

***

What had started out as a chance encounter quickly blossomed into a friendship.

Easy and Rock had only been friends for four months when Easy went to Rock for advice about an offer he thought he couldn't refuse.

"This dude Rolando DeSosa is the man up in Spanish Harlem. He came looking for me the other day," Easy told Rock.

Rock rubbed his chin, digesting the information. "If he is 'the man,' like you say, why would he come looking for a corner boy like you?" Rock asked logically.

"Because he heard I was 'the man' out here in Brooklyn. I guess Chulo, the dude I was getting my package from, told him about me. How I'm moving my shit like no other cat out here," Easy boasted with excitement.

"It just doesn't sound right. Be careful," Rock said ominously.

"Nah, man, this is my come up. Besides, I got you to protect me, right?" Easy laughed.

Rock nodded in all seriousness. He had heard the name DeSosa before, but he couldn't for the life of him remember in what context. He'd definitely be keeping a close eye on young Easy in the meantime.

Chapter 20

Learning Lessons

Candice grips the down pillow tightly in her hands. Her forehead drips with sweat. She stands ominously over the sleeping form, watching the sheet move gently with each slow breath. Candice's chest rises and falls rapidly—part excitement, part fear.

She will have to be strong enough to withstand the fight. The bucking and thrashing will probably be severe at first. The human body can become quite powerful when fighting to stay alive; this was one of Uncle Rock's many lessons.

She has been waiting a long time for this. Her arms jerk involuntarily toward her victim. Candice closes her eyes and lowers the pillow over the nose and mouth. She applies the pressure of her entire body weight on top of the pillow. She feels the figure come alive.

A short, muffled scream splits the air; then frantic, louder screams ensue.

Candice pushes down harder. Her victim's hands valiantly fight, grasping at the pillow material in an attempt to propel the assailant off his body.

Candice exerts all of her body weight over the thrashing form. The head attempts to turn sideways, but Candice bunches her forearms and strengthens her hold. The muscles in her arm cord against her skin.

The thrashing is worse than she'd anticipated. The torso bucks just before the screams fade against the material. Candice is being scratched and slapped by the hands now.

She takes it.

She gnashes her teeth and wills the force of gravity to aid her in her endeavor. The abuse Candice endures is short-lived. She feels the arms go weak and drop down to the side of the limp body.

One last body jerk and it is all over.

Candice stands proudly above the victim, congratulating herself on a job well done. She picks up the pillow to take a look at her handiwork. She wants to see the lifeless face and feel the satisfaction of knowing she can at last be at peace.

Candice's heart comes to a stop.

Her father's face gazes back at her with wide, vacant eyes.

"No!" Candice woke up, screaming out loud. Her nightgown clung to her chest, soaked in sweat. Candice blinked her eyes rapidly, trying to collect her thoughts. A round of loud knocks on her door forced her to get her bearings quickly.

"Dulce! Are you awake?" Cyndi called out from the other side of the door.

Candice looked around the room. *Shit!* She jumped up and wrapped a thick robe around her fat suit.

"Dulce!" Cyndi impatiently called out again.

Candice quickly padded over to the door and pulled it back. A fine sheen of sweat still covered her head.

Cyndi looked at her suspiciously.

Candice was immediately concerned that her wig was twisted or maybe her fat suit was hanging the wrong way.

"Are you all right?" Cyndi asked.

Candice hugged herself, still visibly shaken from her too vivid dream.

"I'm fine. Just stayed up late with the baby—that's all," she said, almost forgetting to add her accent.

Cyndi eyed her up and down. She didn't have time to deal with Dulce's odd behavior right now.

"We are heading to the funerals. Everyone is going, so it'll just be you and the kids today," Cyndi said solemnly.

Just a week ago Cyndi had been crying and upset when she'd come home from work.

"What's the matter, Mrs. DeSosa?" Candice had asked innocently, her forehead furrowed for good measure.

Cyndi took one look at Dulce, her nanny, and collapsed onto her chest with racking sobs.

Candice didn't know what to do. So she stood stock-still, hoping that Cyndi would be so caught up in her grief that she wouldn't feel the fakeness of her ample stomach and breasts, or smell the caked-on makeup coating her face, or notice her contact lenses.

Candice pried Cyndi's arms from her body and moved her to the cream leather sofa, which was rarely sat upon. In the end Cyndi had just wanted someone who would listen to her and feel her pain.

"There was a shooting at Baile Caliente," Cyndi sobbed, swiping at her eyes with an overused, crushed tissue.

"Oh no," Candice commiserated, giving her Academy Award–worthy performance.

"Yes . . . and my brother . . . my brother . . ." Cyndi was crying, barely able to get the words out.

"Did something happen to your brother, Mrs. DeSosa?" Candice asked softly, trying very hard to keep her excitement at bay.

"He is dead! They killed him!" Cyndi wailed.

Her words had sent a surge of satisfaction over Candice's body that felt better than an orgasm. She sat silent and relaxed as Cyndi DeSosa continued to pour her heart out to the hired help.

"I hope you'll be okay today," Candice said, snapping out of her reverie. She was sure to lay the accent on thick this time.

"I don't know how I'm going to stand watching my mother mourn for her only son," Cyndi replied, tears welling up in her eyes.

Candice looked at the pain in her eyes and actually felt some sympathy for the woman. She wondered if Uncle Rock had seen that same pain in her own eyes when she'd lost her family.

"I understand your pain. I lost two brothers myself," Candice said without thinking. It was a slipup, but she didn't regret the words at all. She was witnessing a pain she had already experienced.

Cyndi seemed slightly caught off guard by Candice's admission, but her face quickly softened. "Oh, Dulce, I'm very sorry. I can only imagine what you must've gone through. I never want to think about anyone experiencing the pain that I feel right now," Cyndi lamented.

Candice looked at her and tried hard to feign sympathy.

"Cyndi, let's go!" a man's voice boomed from the bottom of the stairs.

Candice and Cyndi both jumped, but for different reasons.

Cyndi closed her eyes tightly and exhaled a windstorm of exasperated breath.

"Dulce, I have to go. Please kiss the kids for me when they wake," Cyndi said softly. She cracked a small smile, satisfied that she'd chosen the right nanny this time around. Cyndi turned to walk away and Candice followed her with her eyes.

When she'd disappeared down the steps, Candice walked to the edge of the staircase balcony, watching the DeSosa family. They were like one solid unit, comforting each other. Arellio placed his hand on the small of Cyndi's back, ushering her forward, while his brother, Guillermo, navigated his father's wheelchair.

It was the first time Candice had seen all three men gathered together. Heat rose from her feet and settled in her chest. She gripped the railing to keep herself from screaming out. Watching DeSosa with his sons reminded Candice of her own father and brothers.

Hardaway Household, 2005

Errol and Eric Jr. were Easy's two eldest children. They were twins, but polar opposites. Even as little kids, Errol was always quiet and reserved; he was the one who thought all of his actions through before making a move. Eric Jr., whom everyone called Junior, had always been the one to act first and think later.

Easy had a close relationship with both of his sons. As soon as they were potty trained, Eric had the boys play every Little League sport imaginable—soccer, basketball, baseball, football—you name it; they played it. He also did typical father-son activities like watching professional sports together and going camping with their Boy Scout troops.

As the boys got older, though, things started to change.

"Get the fuck off me! I hate you!" Eric Jr. screamed as he fought against Easy's death grip.

"Calm the fuck down, boy! What has gotten into you?" Easy tried to restrain his son, using his arms as a human straitjacket.

Eric Jr. gnashed his teeth and thrashed his body wildly, bucking like a wild animal. It was like some unknown force had taken over him.

Easy was seriously struggling to maintain his grip. The gangly sixteen-year-old was almost as big as his father now. It wasn't as simple anymore as holding him down until the fight left his body. Easy's arms were aching and his back stinging. His son seemed to gain strength by the minute.

"I'ma kill you! I'ma kill you!" Eric Junior threatened now; his lip was bleeding from his own teeth biting down into it.

The entire house was awake now.

"Oh my God! What is going on?" Corine cried out as she raced to the scene. She had been worried about her son lately. His violent outbursts had become more and more frequent. It was like she didn't even know her own child.

"I said, get the fuck off me! I'ma fuckin' blow your brains out!" Junior screeched.

Easy was so shocked that he loosened his grip for just a minute. His son broke free, like a caged animal turned loose. He turned on his father and stood toe-to-toe with him. Junior's eyes were wild; mucus ran out of his nose, sweat covered his face, and his chest was swollen like someone had inserted a balloon under his shirt.

"They told me to kill you! You are the enemy!" Eric Junior hissed. The fire was visible in his eyes.

Lately Junior's behavior had become increasingly erratic; he continued to threaten his father with bodily harm and violence. His behavior was characteristic of a schizophrenic.

Easy sighed with deep regret and sadness. The "voices" were obviously telling him to kill his father.

"You better sit the fuck down," Easy barked. Sometimes the easiest way to handle his son was to take a no-nonsense approach. He took a few steps away from his crazed son in the event that Junior decided to strike him.

"Eric Junior, please! Stop it!" Corine screamed now.

Junior looked at his mother for a minute with a fiery glare. The look in his eyes chilled Corine to the bone.

"What is the matter, baby?" she whined. Her head was tilted in dismay and confusion. Corine had never come to terms with the fact that her oldest son had serious psychological issues. "Please, baby, just listen to your daddy" she pleaded, trying to reach the innocent baby boy she knew lurked inside. Her words appeared to fall on deaf ears.

Eric Jr. growled like a lion in heat and charged into his father like a wrecking ball crashing into an old landmark. The demons inside him had full control of his limbs.

"Oh my God! No!" Corine screeched as her husband went crashing to the floor. The back of his head slammed into the hardwood floor. He lay still for a few seconds; Corine feared that Easy had been knocked unconscious.

Junior was on top of his father immediately after the fall, pummeling his dad's face and head with punches.

"They told me to kill you!" Eric Jr. growled again. "I have to kill you!"

"Who are you talking about? Who told you to kill your father?" Corine cried out. She hoped her son wasn't hearing voices in his head again. They had taken him to several psychiatrists. However, each time they wanted to put him on medication, Corine had refused. She was regretting her decision now.

The entire house was awake now; the commotion had roused them all from their sleep.

Candice rushed down the steps toward the noise.

"Daddy!" she screamed, her mouth and eyes wide at the sight.

Easy groggily regained his bearings. He put his hands up in defense and grabbed his son around the neck. Easy picked his throbbing head up off the floor slightly and applied pressure to his son's neck. He squeezed and squeezed and squeezed. Junior's body began to go limp; saliva dribbled from his lips and his face turned a garish shade of purple.

"Eric, you're gonna kill him! Stop it!" Corine screeched at an ear-shattering pitch.

Errol nearly barreled over the heap of tangled body parts. This was not the first time he pried his father loose from his brother's deranged grip. This time, however, it was his brother's neck that needed to be rescued from his father's brutal clutch.

"Daddy!" Candice screamed, jumping up and down. She was crying hysterically.

It was her voice that snapped Easy out of his murderous trance. Easy's grip relaxed; Errol managed to pull his brother's limp body away from his father.

Easy stood up; the room swayed around him. He looked at his son, who lay on the ground, coughing and rolling around, gasping for air. Easy had come so close to taking his own son's life. He couldn't understand what was going on with the kid.

"Are you all right, baby?" Corine bent down at her son's side. "What's the matter with him? It's like he's on something!" she cried out, looking to Easy for some explanation.

Easy couldn't call it. His son's behavior had grown more and more erratic lately. Easy had never put two and two together that his son's behavior had gone off the chart right around the time Easy had started grooming his boys to join the family business. He was too preoccupied with his feelings of failure that one of them was clearly mentally unstable. He'd lost a lot of sleep over the matter lately. He was beginning to think that Junior needed medication to keep his moods in check.

"Daddy" Candice whispered as her father stormed out of the room, disappearing in his office. Candice approached the closed door and debated whether or not to knock before she entered. She could hear her father talking on the phone.

"Rock! I need to see you right away. This shit is a matter of life and death," Easy had rasped into the phone.

Why did her brother and father have to fight all of the time? And what was her father planning with Uncle Rock? Candice slid down the wall, onto the floor, and began sobbing. She just wished her family could all get along with each other. She felt totally helpless, caught between a deep love for her father and sympathetic feelings for her brother, whom she'd watch spiraling out of control.

Candice crept around Rolando DeSosa's living space. It smelled of liniment and hospital disinfectant—not exactly a smell she would expect to find in the lodgings of a self-proclaimed "Scarface" type of kingpin.

Candice felt anxious as she walked through the man's private rooms. She glanced at the bed and wished she could just place a poisonous snake under DeSosa's covers and be done with it. But she had some digging to do first. She quickly headed to the small makeshift office. A cherry wood desk with pictures of his sons and grandkids sat atop the desk. The bookshelves were also sprinkled with family photos, much like Candice's father's own office. She rifled through the drawers of the desk, looking for any important documents. What she came across was mostly hospital bills, utility bills and random notes. Frustrated, Candice tossed the papers back into the drawer.

In the long drawer in the center of the desk, where one usually stored pens, pencils and other small desk essentials, she found a single photograph. Candice felt a chill come over her, like someone had pumped ice water into her veins. She swallowed the golf ball–sized lump of fear at the back of her throat and willed herself to calm down. Reaching out tentatively, she picked up the photograph. She clapped her hand over her mouth to keep herself from screaming at the image of herself. DeSosa had some handwritten notes on the top: *Easy Hardaway's living daughter. Find and turn over to Stokes for reward.*

Candice gripped her chest, trying to keep her heart from beating too fast. Uncle Rock had told her the government would be looking for her, but she didn't realize how close she was to being found. Candice dropped the picture back into the drawer. She decided it was time for her to step up her game; it was do or die for her. She rushed blindly out of DeSosa's living quarters and headed back to her room.

A lone figure stood at the end of the hall and watched the new nanny furtively exit DeSosa's private quarters.

"Tucker, you can't just assume that these people are bluffing," Dana Carlisle said as she watched Tuck pace the floor of her apartment for the fifteenth time.

"They're not going to fuck with my family," he huffed, hoping that his speaking the words would make them somehow true. The truth was he didn't know what to expect from Grayson Stokes or the DEA for that matter. They were all corrupt in his eyes.

"Well, now she's out there killing off their people. Getting closer and closer to DeSosa," Carlisle recounted.

He had told Carlisle all about his call with Grayson Stokes after the Baile Caliente shootings. Everyone just assumed it was Candy; that had been Tucker's first assumption as well. But now he was plagued with doubt. He had come back to Carlisle's house because he needed help reading through the Hardaway books. If they worked together, the puzzle pieces would start falling into place a lot faster, and they could finally see the big picture. At this point Carlisle was his best and only option.

"You really think it's her? I'm not sure I believe that anymore," Tuck countered. He knew Candy. He had spent almost two months with her. Though she was trained well, he didn't think she was capable of cold-blooded murder.

"That's exactly what she wants you to think . . . that she isn't capable of killing. She wants everyone to think that. But the government ain't buying it," Carlisle said pointedly.

Tucker roughly wiped his hands over his face and let out a deep breath. He walked over to the piles of books scattered on the floor and dining table.

"I guess we better keep reading for now. We don't have that much time, and I need to be armed with the truth this time," he said in a resigned voice. He lifted the cover of the next set of books and flopped down on the couch. Dana Carlisle perched herself on the back of the couch and began reading over his shoulder.

"Yeah, I'm hoping somewhere beneath all of this conspiracy theory bullshit is the truth," she said, scanning the paper for relevant information.

Brooklyn, New York, 2006

Easy and Rock sat across from each other, gauging the other's thoughts.

"I don't know if I can do what you're asking me to do, Rock," Easy said, breaking the tense silence that had settled in the room.

It wasn't what Rock wanted to hear.

Rock closed his eyes and tilted his head to the side. Easy's words stung like a swarm of angry yellow jackets. Already a man of few words, this topic left his stomach reeling. He planned his words very carefully, not letting on too much. It had been a hard decision to ask Easy to leave the game. Especially now, when Easy was at the top, riding high.

Easy had graduated from pushing packs of heroin to running the entire crack cocaine game in Brooklyn. That was what made Rock so sick to his gut.

Rock cleared his throat roughly; the grating sound causing Easy to jump a bit. The tension in the room was palpable now. Easy had always taken Rock's advice; in turn, Rock had served as Easy's loyal "cleaner." But perhaps he was asking too much of Easy.

"I can't tell you what to do. I can only advise you to get out of the game now. I've heard that DeSosa is working with some very dangerous people," Rock said, his tone ominous.

"How do you know anything about DeSosa? I know you never liked him, but you've never told me why," Easy said, frustration mounting in his voice. He respected Rock, but right now Rock was overstepping his boundaries.

Rock looked at Easy, square in the face. "I know more than you think."

"Here you go with the conspiracy shit, Rock. C'mon, man, all that crap is TV bullshit. I've listened to your stories, but I'm not about to make an important life decision based on your crazy-ass thoughts." Easy was trying to keep his composure now.

Rock was quiet. He looked different, like he had been up all night in a fight and had barely come out of it alive.

Easy eyed him closely. He appreciated everything Rock had done for him over the years. He didn't want a beef with his old mentor.

"I have been in the game almost twenty years now, Rock. I moved up. I'm finally at the top. You have to understand that," Easy said, softening his tone while trying to level with Rock. "I can't say no to DeSosa just cuz you telling me I should quit because you got a bad feeling about my connect." He needed Rock to understand where he was coming from.

"Look here!" Rock barked, coming alive. He looked crazier than Easy had ever imagined.

"What's up with you, man?" Easy asked, alarmed at his friend's angry demeanor.

Rock took a deep breath. "Easy, this is something you have to do. Don't ask any more questions. Call up DeSosa and tell him you're leaving the game. You have to trust me on this," Rock said, his voice full of concern.

Rock stood up. His large body cast a dark shadow over Easy. Easy gazed up at Rock. He had trusted this man with his life—literally—from day one.

"I'll think about it," Easy said, trying to hide his frustration.

"You better not think about it too long," Rock warned before rushing out of the room.

Easy contemplated the consequences of actually carrying out Rock's order, but he needed to discuss a few things with DeSosa first. Easy dialed DeSosa's number, but he quickly hung up when it started to ring.

He needed to think this out a bit. Telling DeSosa he was leaving the game would be no easy task. He needed to talk to Rock first and figure out a plan for disengaging himself. Extricating himself from DeSosa's network certainly would not be as simple as a phone call.

Chapter 21

Dangerous Encounters

Junior pulled up to the DeSosa home, like he'd done every three days for the past several weeks. He rushed inside and was frisked at the door—the normal routine. Junior was nervous for some reason; he had a strong premonition that today wasn't going to be a good day.

DeSosa was sitting with his back turned toward the door, but he felt Junior's presence. A long, awkward silence ensued.

Junior opened his mouth to fill the choking silence, but he wasn't able to get a word out.

"So what do you have for me?" DeSosa asked without turning around. Cigar smoke danced around his head and colored the air a hazy gray.

Junior cleared his throat. He had been dreading this meeting, since he had nothing substantive to report. He balled up his toes in his shoes, rocking on the balls of his feet.

"DeSosa, man . . . I'm—I'm . . . sorry," Junior stammered. He cleared his throat again. He wondered if DeSosa, like Junior's mother, would be able to tell he was lying just from the shaking in his voice. "No new updates. I been to the apartment she used to stay in and it was trashed, but she wasn't there. I don't know where else to look . . . I mean . . ." Junior continued, glad to have gotten his lie out without pause.

He had no intention of trying to find Candy; and if he did, it wouldn't be to turn her over to DeSosa. Junior needed DeSosa's help getting at Phil.

"For some reason, Junior, I don't believe you," DeSosa snapped. His face was drawn into a scowl; the look sent chills down Junior's spine.

"Well, I'm telling you the truth. I have no idea where she is or where to find her," Junior said, false frustration lacing his words. He had to make it look and sound believable. His sheer frustration with trying to find Candy, the gotdamn assassin, had consumed his days and nights.

"Well, then, Junior, our business is finished. We have no more to discuss until you bring me what I want. I can't give you Phil without assurance that I will get what I want. Looks like our deal is off. You can go," DeSosa rasped dismissively.

Junior felt like a kid who'd just been suspended from school. He looked around the room, then back at DeSosa. He knew DeSosa too well; it would never be over that easily.

"C'mon, DeSosa! I'm sayin', how the fuck do you expect me to find this bitch? I don't know where she is! I hardly even know her! I find out this punk-ass old man who raised her is my own fuckin' father, but that don't mean I know where to find this bitch! I told you everything. . . . I gave you every fuckin' thing I could!" Junior forcefully detailed. He was on the brink of tears. "You, of all people, should understand why I want Phil! If somebody did something to your family, you would be the first one out for blood!" Junior whined now, pleading his case.

DeSosa's henchmen closed in on him, but he didn't care. He was coming apart right now. His business had dried up. DeSosa was no longer supplying him because he thought he might still be a target of the DEA. And now he'd never be able to get his hands on Phil.

"DeSosa! You can't do this to me now!" Junior pleaded.

DeSosa didn't flinch or blink. He didn't have any respect for a man who couldn't stand his ground. That was the one thing that had set Easy apart in DeSosa's mind. Although he ultimately viewed Easy as a traitor, which was the most detestable form of human being, at least he could respect Easy for sticking to his decision about turning his back on the game.

"You can leave now. When you find out any information, you are welcome to come back. Maybe by then you'll grow some balls and find some loyalty," DeSosa spat out in Junior's direction. His words cut like small carving knives.

"Fuck you, DeSosa! Fuck you and your little game!" Junior boomed. His newfound courage wrapped around him like a dark cloak.

DeSosa let out a snort, followed by a maniacal laugh. His goons surrounded Junior now. Junior wrestled his arm away from the big gorilla-shaped goon who roughly helped him to the door.

He straightened out his rumpled jacket sleeve and followed their lead to the door. Before he got there, he stopped in his tracks to address DeSosa. His action garnered glares from the goons.

"You really fucked up for this one. You just gonna leave me out there like that after I murked Phil's right-hand man at your request? Those niggas are looking for me and you just gonna leave me open out there with no help and no protection? I'm tellin' you, what goes around comes around. . . . You better sleep with one eye open." Junior issued his warning; his voice was quaking—filled with one part anger, one part fear.

His words got him grabbed by the neck by a goon.

"You are weak! You can't find one girl who tried to fuckin' kill you! I have nothing to say to you! Get the fuck out of my presence!" DeSosa barked at Junior's back.

Junior was tossed outside the house like yesterday's trash. His ego was bruised, and so were both of his knees.

"I want him followed. I think he knows something and he is just not letting on." DeSosa snapped his orders, flicking his hand in the direction of the door. He needed some time to regroup and rethink this whole situation with the girl.

Outside, Junior picked himself up off the concrete ground and shouted for DeSosa and the world to hear. "Y'all ain't seen the last of me! You muthafuckas fucked with the wrong nigga!"

He stepped backward out of the gate, when he spotted a woman out of the corner of his eye. She was herding two little kids in the opposite direction of the commotion. He was angry, but for some reason he took particular notice of her. Maybe it was because she watched the scene a bit too closely.

"Mind yo' fuckin' business, bitch!" Junior yelled at the unsuspecting nanny.

The woman scampered into the house with the children in tow like he was a pedophile on the sex offender registry. Something about the fat, frumpy nanny made Junior pissed. She had the nerve to be watching *him* get embarrassed.

Junior waited outside the gate for DeSosa's thugs to bring his car around. He needed to get far away from this place and come up with a new strategy for finding Phil and catching that cunt, Candy.

***

Tuck slumped down farther into his seat as he watched Junior get tossed out of DeSosa's estate. Then Tuck noticed the woman who watched from the sidelines, much like himself. Something inside his chest jumped; her face was disguised but familiar.

"Candy," he whispered, his breath catching. Tuck forgot everything: the danger, his cover, her cover, everything. He was up in his seat now, with his dark glasses far down on his nose. He needed to see her in natural light. He needed to know if it was really Candy or if his mind had conjured up her image.

Candice glanced in his direction as she hefted a baby girl onto her hip and grabbed the little boy's hand. Tuck watched her rush away—her body not the same, but her eyes telling a different story.

Tuck was brought back to reality when Junior revved his car engine. With his heart sitting in the back of his throat, Tuck shrank back down into his seat. He would sit outside all night if he had to until Candy emerged.

Tuck's mind was too preoccupied to realize that he was being followed as well.

One of DeSosa's henchmen picked up his cell phone to call in his report. "*Sí*, tell the boss he was right. Junior is being followed by the DEA agent. I have my eye on him right now. He is watching the house." The man relayed his visuals into the phone.

He could hear DeSosa's booming voice in the background. He cursed Junior's name and condemned him to hell for being a traitor. The man listened, knowing that Junior had sealed his fate.

The one thing DeSosa couldn't stand was a traitor. He viewed them as low-down, dirty scum of the earth. It was the same reason Easy Hardaway had suffered the fate that he did. DeSosa finished his tirade with specific instructions.

Neither Junior, Tuck nor Candy was safe.

Candice rushed the children back into the house. Her head was spinning. She'd seen Tuck and she knew that he'd seen her.

What the fuck is he doing there? How did he find me?

He'd definitely recognized her; she was sure of it. She didn't want to believe Tuck was part of the government bastards who were after her. But now he appeared to be spying on her, and she had to reconsider. Could it be that he was just another hired gun after her head?

Candice felt sick to her stomach. His betrayal burned badly. Candice's hand shook and her body was covered with a fine sheen of sweat. The fat suit felt extremely heavy on her body and her legs felt wobbly. Stumbling around like a cow, she could barely carry the baby up the stairs. Candice reached to the wall for support and caused one of the pictures to crash to the floor. Candice jumped, her nerves on edge. She looked down at the shattered glass frame that held a picture of Guillermo. Candice stared at the picture like it was a bad omen. She felt like throwing up.

Cyndi rounded the corner like a bat out of hell in response to the loud noise.

"Dulce, are you all right?" she asked, noticing Candice's pained expression. Cyndi looked down at the shattered frame, then back up at Candice.

"Um . . . I—I'm not feeling good. I need to leave early, if you don't m-mind," Candice stammered, using the wall to hold herself up now. She couldn't even be bothered with the accent, and she didn't even care if Cyndi noticed.

Cyndi eyed her suspiciously and grabbed her baby before Dulce dropped her.

"I have to go," Candice panted; her chest felt tight. She was afraid that if she stood in front of Cyndi another minute, she would definitely blow her disguise.

Candice slid down the steps and out of Cyndi's line of vision.

"Okay. Okay, you go ahead. I'll keep the kids tonight," Cyndi called out from the balcony landing.

All Candice wanted to do was get out of the house and take in a deep gulp of fresh air. She moved fast now, ignoring everyone and everything.

As Candice moved away from her, Cyndi noticed that her nanny's shirt was hiked up slightly in the back. Cyndi squinted; Dulce's skin looked wrinkled and rubbery. Perhaps she had been burned in a fire as a child? Cyndi shook her head. Maybe her eyes were deceiving her, or the lighting was bad, but a nagging, suspicious feeling invaded her mind.

Something about Dulce just didn't sit right with her, and she couldn't put her finger on it. She had a funny feeling about her from day one, but she'd ignored it. With everything that had happened, she had been preoccupied, but the feeling was back. Cyndi hurried up the stairs and put her baby down in the crib. She rushed to her bedroom and retrieved her cell phone.

"Hello, Ms. Sanchez? I need to ask you some questions about the nanny you sent to replace Flora. Yes, I want to know everything," Cyndi demanded.

Tuck watched the chubby Hispanic woman rush through the gates of the DeSosa home. He started up his engine as soon as she got in her car; in a matter of seconds he was on her tail.

"You are a bold bitch, Candy," he said out loud to himself. He could not believe she was inside DeSosa's home, playing with his grandkids. He thought Candy had been bold when she infiltrated Junior's crew to get closer to them, but this took the cake. She was one bad bitch, and he knew he'd have to tread lightly with her.

He followed Candice with every dip, turn and U-turn she made. He had to give it to her—she was slippery as a snake. Rock Barton had obviously trained her well.

Candice pulled her car over abruptly. Tuck had to stop short to keep from rear-ending her.

"Fuck!" Tuck cursed, slamming his palms on the steering wheel. He had been made.

Candy rushed toward his car, digging into her bag at the same time. Tuck went to his waistband as well. She yanked open his passenger door and plopped into the seat. Her gun was under his chin, and his was at her temple.

"Why the fuck are you following me?" Candice growled. Her finger was in the trigger guard, ready to blow Tuck's head off.

"I'm not following you! I was following Junior!" Tuck panted, his nerves on a hair trigger.

"You're a fucking liar! How did you know it was me?"

"I recognized you, even with all of that padding, makeup and fake-ass eyes! What made you think you could disguise your eyes?" Tuck's voice cracked. He still seemed to have a soft spot for her.

"Tell me who the fuck sent you, or you die right here and right now." Candice couldn't care less about the gun that rested on her temple.

"Put your gun down and I'll put mine down. We need to talk," Tuck said calmly.

"No! I don't trust you!" she barked, working her jaw and readjusting her grip on her weapon.

"You have no fuckin' choice right now! There are some very dangerous people hunting for your ass, and I'm the only person who can tell you who they are and why they want you dead or alive," Tuck said seriously. "Now put your fuckin' gun down and I'll put mine down," he said firmly.

"You first," Candice said, not buying it. If Tuck tried anything funny, she would take Tuck the fuck apart, limb by limb.

He reluctantly lowered his gun from her head. She took a deep breath and did the same, but she kept it at the ready. Tuck placed his gun back into his waistband as a symbol of trust. He wanted her to know he had no ill intentions toward her.

Candice didn't give a shit what he did. She kept her gun ready, willing and able to blow his skullcap back.

"Now let me explain everything to you," Tuck began with a sigh.

"You already said that bullshit. Start talking . . . and fast. The way I see it right now is you were working for the bastards who killed my family the entire time."

"Candy . . . I was never working for anyone who had anything to do with your family's murders, but I have a lot of information that may be of use to you. I have your father's books—all of his secrets, his life story," Tuck said, his words coming out slowly and deliberately. Candice seemed to soften a bit.

"Where would you get my father's books from if you don't work for the fuckers who killed him?" she asked, her eyebrow raised.

"It's a long story. We don't have time now. I want to show you some of the books and give you a different perspective on your family's past. I want to help you get away from here before you get hurt."

"I can't get sidetracked right now. I will meet you at the Monte Carlo later tonight. You better come alone, or else you die," Candice growled.

"Candy . . . you need to be careful. They are probably watching us right now," Tuck cautioned.

"I'm a big girl. I can handle myself," she said pointedly, reaching for the door handle. Before Tuck could take his next breath, Candice was out of the car and up the street.

Tuck picked up his cell phone to call Carlisle. He needed to gather up all of the files so he could hand them over to Candice.

The phone vibrated in his hand. "Shit!" He jumped, putting his hand over his heart.

"Hello," Tuck barked into the phone.

Ear-shattering screams filtered through the receiver, threatening to burst his eardrums.

"Elaina! What's the matter? What?" Tuck felt his chest heave with effort. He dropped his phone and screeched away from the curb.

"Fuck!" Tuck screamed, taking off like a madman.

They were fucking with the wrong man's family. The game was about to change . . . drastically.

Candice, meanwhile, didn't bother to pull out until she saw Tuck leave, along with his tails. She got out of her car and disappeared down a side street. She dipped into a building before her followers could even get out of their cars.

She watched two men turn down the block, their ties flapping in the wind as they ran from building to building, peeking their heads inside doorways.

After a few minutes the men threw their hands up in exasperation. They were not very diligent in their efforts.

"So fucking impatient and predictable." She smiled.

It was time for her to ramp up the heat on her marks. Candy knew she should have murked all of them as soon as she gained access to the house. Uncle Rock had told her about becoming personal with her marks; now she had to turn things up. She was back in her hard candy mode.

No man, woman or child would be safe from her wrath.

Chapter 22

Secret Assignations

Guillermo DeSosa took a long pull off his cigarette. His hands shook involuntarily. He paced outside, near the spot he'd agreed on. He looked at his watch impatiently and blew out a thick cloud of smoke. He plucked his cigarette to the ground and began to walk away; his shoulders were slumped in disappointment.

"Did I keep you waiting long?" an effeminate male voice filtered through the crisp night air. The man seemed to materialize from thin air. That shit unnerved Guillermo; he reached for his waistband, jumpy and anxious. He was always on edge with these meetings, especially when he dealt with someone new.

Guillermo kicked himself for answering the Craigslist advertisement. Why didn't he just go his usual route?

"Shit! Don't you know better than to sneak up on a gangster's son?" he huffed, moving his jacket aside so the man could see his shiny piece. He wanted this man to know who would be in charge this evening. He avoided the man's direct gaze; it would be easier this way. They had already discussed through e-mail how things would work. Guillermo wanted to stay low-key, but he disclosed his father's status—just in case the man was thinking about setting him up.

"Pay me first, like we agreed, then tell me where to meet you," the mysterious man said.

"It's all in the envelope," Guillermo said, his voice quavering. He was taking a chance, and he knew it. When his desires took over, all logical thinking evaporated. Walking toward his car, Guillermo quickly placed a small white envelope on top of a black car that was parked three cars away from his.

Guillermo quickly picked up his pace and rushed to his car as if the Furies were on his heels. The man walked swiftly by, swiped the envelope from the car hood, then headed in the opposite direction of Guillermo's car. Guillermo was panting now as blood and adrenaline rushed to his brain. Once inside, he took a deep breath, looked around and pulled away from the curb. After all of these years, the heat of embarrassment still climbed from his chest and settled on his face when he set up these rendezvous. And each time, he felt dirty and ashamed. If his brother and his father knew about his secret lifestyle, he would definitely be excommunicated from the family or—worse—put to sleep like a horse with four broken legs.

The urges had started when Guillermo was just twelve years old; he had felt an overwhelming level of attraction, which he couldn't explain, for members of the same sex. The first time he remembered having a physical response to another boy was in the locker room after gym class. The physical education teacher had entered the locker room and instructed them all to disrobe and jump in the showers after a grueling day of climbing ropes. His friend had dropped his drawers right next to him and casually walked to the showers. As soon as he spied his friend's flaccid penis, he felt himself grow hard.

Guillermo had felt like reaching out and grabbing his friend in his most private area and even kissing him. His friend caught him staring and sent him a look that spoke volumes. Guillermo smiled nervously before running into the bathroom stalls and hiding.

Inside the stall he vomited into the toilet from the shame he felt. He sobbed uncontrollably and wondered what was wrong with him. Why couldn't he be like the other boys, interested in staring at women's breasts and butts? He smacked himself in the head, trying to beat the sordid thoughts out of his own brain.

It hadn't worked, of course. Every day afterward, Guillermo struggled with his identity and unnatural desires, learning to satisfy them in the most discreet ways possible.

When Guillermo spent time with his father and older brother, he acted the consummate ladies' man, even going as far as slapping women's asses in public. He was a wonderful actor and an accomplished liar. Though he often felt like a fraud, he felt these were necessary evils he must carry out to remain a part of the DeSosa family.

Guillermo was Rolando DeSosa's youngest son. He was also DeSosa's illegitimate son; he was the product of his father's well-known philandering. Guillermo's mother was a beautiful young girl who had newly arrived in America from Colombia; then she met Rolando DeSosa. Although he was married, DeSosa just couldn't resist her beautiful dark hair, butter-soft skin and sparkling green eyes. He was twenty-five years her senior when she discovered she was pregnant with his son.

She was the ultimate mistress and played her position well. When she was with DeSosa, she made him feel like he was the only man in the world. When she couldn't be with him due to his family obligations, she held her head high and waited for him to return. She never forced the issue of being number one in DeSosa's life; in turn, he respected her and always took care of her and her son.

DeSosa made sure Guillermo was well cared for as a child, although circumstances didn't allow him to spend as much time with Guillermo as with his legitimate son, Arellio. DeSosa had made sure Guillermo and his mother lived well in a posh New York City condo. He paid tuition for Guillermo's private schools and made sure he had the best of everything.

DeSosa didn't want Guillermo to be in the family business; he had been brutally honest with his son that he didn't believe he had the "heart" to carry out certain business matters. Guillermo had been livid with his father's proclamation and stormed out of his office. He'd gone on a rampage for an entire week. He needed to prove a point to his father.

Guillermo had broken out several windows in his school and set a fire in the school's gymnasium; then he took his rampage to the streets. He'd gotten on a city bus without paying his fare and once inside slapped an innocent woman in the face just for "looking" at him. His wannabe-gangster rampage came to a halt after he stabbed one of his classmates during an altercation, just barely missing the boy's lung.

When DeSosa picked Guillermo up from juvenile hall, he'd calmly asked his son, "You want in so badly, you do all this? Well, you got in. Not because of your stupidity, but because you would go through all of this to be with me . . . to be a part of this family. But you keep doing stupid shit and it will get you killed. Never draw attention to yourself unless it's absolutely necessary."

Everyone in the DeSosa organization knew that Guillermo was soft, so they gave him all of the easy lifting. He sold weight to low-level drug dealers; he attended meetings with his father as a "second gun"; sometimes he rode shotgun with his brother when something slightly dangerous was going down. It suited him just fine. He was probably the most well-paid second-string gangster in New York City.

Guillermo pulled up to the Blake, a small hotel situated on a side street, out of the glaring New York City lights. He'd already picked up his room keys earlier in the day; the second key lay in the hands of his new prospect, nestled carefully in the envelope.

Inside the hotel lobby Guillermo looked around suspiciously. He nodded at the front-desk clerk, who stared at him a bit too long and hard. Guillermo always wondered if people recognized him as readily as they did his father and his brother.

The elevator seemed to take forever to get to the sixth floor. The familiar *ding* as the doors eased open was like music to his ears. Guillermo rushed out, but then he slowed his pace, not wanting to appear too eager. The hallway was a like a ghost town. He exhaled a sigh of relief; he hated seeing people milling about the halls. He always felt paranoid about running into one of his father's acquaintances, or meeting a set of judgmental eyes.

With trembling hands Guillermo used his key to enter the room. No matter how many times he did this, he was nervous all over again. It was dark inside. The only light came from a small candle, which was on the nightstand. He smirked to himself.

"You trying to be romantic?" he called out as he shrugged out of his leather jacket. There was no answer. Guillermo tossed his jacket aside and moved farther into the room.

"C'mon, I don't like playing games," he called out.

Frustration and anxiety could be heard in his voice. He felt spooked by the dim lighting, so he reached over and flicked on a light. His boy toy must be getting ready in the bathroom. Guillermo didn't like waiting for anyone or anything, especially not after he'd been so long without a man.

"I'm taking off my clothes, which means get your ass out here and give me what the fuck I paid for," he barked as he unbuckled his pants and stepped out of them. He figured his little plaything was playing hide the dick in the bathroom. Guillermo wasn't much for games. He planned to bust in that damn bathroom and shock the little punk-ass guy with a stiff dick in the ass. Guillermo stomped over to the bathroom door.

"You like to play these kinky games? Well, I'm going to show you who can do it best," he called out, using one hand to rub his flaccid dick. He wanted to be ready to pound into that ass.

Guillermo snatched the bathroom door open, intending to surprise his date with his rock hard dick. Guillermo's mouth dropped open and his eyes threatened to pop out of their socket. His dick instantly went limp and his bladder released itself.

"What the—" Guillermo had started to speak, but then put his hands up in front of him defensively. It was too late. He had nowhere to run, nowhere to hide. He was half naked and completely defenseless without his weapon.

"P—please," he managed to stammer out, but his words died in the air. He screamed like a bitch as he came face-to-face with the devil. He fell to the ground, feeling the cold porcelain tiles on his back. He could taste his own blood pooling in his mouth. Suddenly Guillermo's vision faded and his world went completely black.

Elaina barreled into Avon's chest like a bulldozer as he walked through the front door of her mother's house. He let out a puff of air and stumbled backward, caught off guard. She was sobbing, her body shaking uncontrollably.

"Shh," he comforted, wrapping his arms around her protectively. He held her tightly for a few minutes and stroked the top of her head. Her body eased into his embrace and she seemed to calm down significantly in his arms.

Avon pulled her away from his chest so he could look at her face to make sure she wasn't hurt. Her face was blotchy and red from crying, but beautiful nonetheless. He felt his heart thump in his chest. At that moment he didn't care about the past, about her betrayal or the affair. Despite all that they had been through, he still loved his wife.

"Elaina, tell me what happened," Avon said softly, gazing into her eyes.

"They—they . . . shot . . . Pfeiffer and the car. We had just gotten out. . . . They just missed me, the kids . . . oh my God!" she cried, collapsing back onto her husband's chest.

"What! Who?" Avon gasped. He felt like the air had been squeezed out of his lungs. They had come after his family, after all. He was livid, beyond rage.

"I don't know who! The gunshots were so loud! They hit the car like hail pellets. I screamed and grabbed the kids. We had just pulled into the driveway. Then . . . then Pfeiffer fell. He was bleeding all over the place. We pulled him inside the garage . . . but . . . he—he's dead!" She cried some more, her body quaking all over.

Avon flexed his jaw and hugged her even tighter now. His world was spinning off its axis. He couldn't believe Stokes actually came after his family like he'd threatened. This shit meant war.

Avon let Elaina go and started for the garage. His nostrils flared so hard that he thought he'd hyperventilate. He gritted his teeth and lifted his forearm over his nose at the unbecoming smell in the air. The metallic raw meat smell of blood threatened to make him hurl. He stepped over the dead dog and looked at the car. He surveyed the damage and surmised that the holes were made with a high-powered semiautomatic weapon.

Avon slammed his fists on the hood of his wife's car. He could feel adrenaline pulsing through his veins, fast and hot.

"We need to call the police," Elaina said from the doorway. She interrupted Avon's murderous thoughts.

He looked at her, with fire flashing in his eyes. His hands were balled into knuckle-paling fists. "No, we are not going to call the local police. They won't do shit but bring more attention to the house. I will find out what happened. I will protect you and my kids, Elaina," he assured her, pinching the bridge of his nose.

"Where are the kids?" he asked, noticing the unusual silence in the house for the first time. "Where did you send my kids?" he persisted, stalking toward his trembling wife.

Elaina threw her hands up in the air. Her mouth was open, but no words were coming out. She seemed to be melting down before his eyes. Her mother in the backdrop scowling did not help the situation.

"Elaina! Where are my fuckin' kids?" Avon snapped, shaking her shoulders roughly. Panic was choking him around the throat.

"Oh God!" she cried, knocking his hands away, as if she were a victim of domestic violence.

Avon removed his hands from her person as if she were a hot stove that had just burned him.

"Elaina, I'm sorry. Please . . . tell me where the kids are." He softened his tone, moving a few steps away from her. His heart hammered against his chest bone.

Avon grabbed his bald head and squeezed it, trying to calm himself down. He took a deep breath and put his hands out in front of his chest. He would be calm and reasonable with his wife.

"Baby, I'm not going to be angry. Just tell me where they are so I can protect all of you." He steadied his voice, letting his anger subside like a flame smothered in dirt.

"I have them hiding in a closet downstairs," she finally admitted, hanging her head as if she were the worst mother in the world. Relief washed over Avon; at least she hadn't done anything drastic or stupid. "Avon, I was scared. That's why I put them there." She seemed to be stumbling in explanation.

He placed his finger against her lips. "Hush, you don't need to explain, I understand," he whispered, the words catching in his throat.

Elaina lifted her head; her eyes pleaded with him for answers. "Avon, tell me what is going on? Who is after you? Who would do this to us?" She searched his eyes, his face, for answers from her estranged husband.

Avon didn't respond. He didn't have the words. His own mind raced. He brushed past her and rushed from the garage back into the house. He ran over to the basement door and yanked it open; he rushed down the dark stairwell to free his children from their confinement.

He found his kids huddled together in the corner of the closet. The sight of them cowering in fear sent a pang of hurt through Avon's stomach. His daughter was crying as she held her brother in a death grip, like he was her life raft. His son sat in urine-soaked pants. The sight broke Avon's heart. Tears burned at the back of his eyes as he knelt down and scooped them both up into his strong arms. He needed them to know he would never let anything happen to them . . . ever.

"C'mere. Daddy is here now," Avon whispered, the heat of his breath on his daughter's face, a soothing balm to her tears.

She immediately buried her face in her father's neck and sobbed, just like her mother had done a few minutes earlier. His son was another story. The boy's sweat-and-piss-drenched body hung in Avon's arms, stiff and stoic. He didn't bend or respond to his father's soft words. Instead, the boy stared right past his father's face and looked off into the distance, at nothing. The boy was scared shitless. One tear streaked, unchecked, down his cheek.

"You guys okay?" Avon whispered, kissing both of them on the forehead. He had to make sure his children didn't see how angry or terrified he truly felt.

"Daddy, somebody shot Pfeiffer!" his daughter wailed. Her little voice quavered with fear. "Oh, baby, I know. I know. I'm so sorry Daddy wasn't here. I'll never let anything like this happen again. I promise," he comforted, meaning every word. His son didn't say a word and still had not responded to his presence. He just stared blankly above his head. Avon shook him and tried to get him to talk. The boy was still in shock.

"Fuck," Avon huffed under his breath. There would be fucking hell to pay when he found the bastards who had shot at his family. Avon was taking off the kid gloves and going full-metal jacket with these pricks.

He took the kids back upstairs to their rooms. There was no way he would allow them to stay in a closet like scared puppies.

When his mother-in-law came home, her face was dark and her body stiffened at the sight of Avon. Helen held on to her daughter like she was a treasure beyond worth.

When he moved closer to Elaina, she tightened her grip, turning her face up at him as if he were a smelly skunk. There was really nothing he could say to comfort a woman who had come so close to losing her daughter and grandkids within the blink of an eye. Despite her resistance, Avon needed to make some quick and hard decisions that involved Helen's acquiescence.

"We all have to leave here," Avon announced seriously.

Elaina looked up in surprise and fear. Helen looked at him like he'd lost his damn mind. She stared at him with coldly hooded eyes.

"No! We need to call the police and get to the bottom of this! You can't keep coming here with all of your secrets and spy games, putting my daughter and grandkids in danger!" His mother-in-law lit into him. She was on her feet now, standing toe-to-toe with Avon like a lioness protecting her pride.

He felt her pain, but he also felt his cheeks go flush with anger. It didn't matter how long he'd been gone in the past and what mistakes he'd made, he was the head of his family. Avon ground his back teeth together and composed himself. He jutted his finger toward his mother-in-law and squinted his eyes.

"You can stay here, but my wife and kids are coming with me!" Avon countered. He looked at his wife expectantly; when she didn't follow his lead, he grabbed both of his kids by their hands and ushered them toward the front door.

Elaina got up reluctantly and looked at her mother with tear-filled eyes. She was so torn; it was all too much to process.

"You have to come with us, Mama. It's not safe here," she begged. Her mother pursed her lips and wrangled her arm away from her daughter's desperate grasp.

"It's not safe where he is either," her mother replied, folding her arms across her chest, refusing to leave her home.

Elaina gave her mother a desperate look, but she knew it was useless. In the end, like a dutiful wife and mother, she followed her husband and kids out of the house.

All she could do now was pray that her mother would be safe. That's all she could do for all of them—pray that they would be safe.

"Ma! Ma!" Junior called out in a state of panic as he rushed back into his SoHo apartment. He was sweating profusely and his legs shook. The apartment was not big; so when Betty didn't answer, Junior's stomach began to cramp.

"Ma?" he belted out again, his voice cracking with desperation. Then he heard the water running from behind the bathroom door. He rushed to the door and knocked, hoping that his mother simply hadn't heard him over the rush of the running faucet.

"Ma!" he called out again, twisting the doorknob. Now was not the time for him to worry about invading her privacy. The door gave easily. The shower was running, but the curtain was pulled closed. Junior reached out and snatched back the curtain.

"Oh shit!" he huffed. Those were the last words he spoke before his world went black.

A black hood had been forcefully placed over his head, snatching his breath away. A sharp pain invaded his spine and his legs buckled. His body went limp; his legs betrayed him as he fought against his own body to stay standing. Junior knew falling was the kiss of death; yet it was the inevitable. His back hit the marble tile floor, sending a spine-crushing pain through his back and down his legs. Junior opened his mouth to scream, but the sound was stuck in the back of his throat. Instead, he took in a mouthful of black fibers from the hood, which scratched the back of his throat. He was being dragged now; his legs flip-flopping like a fish out of water.

Something crashed into his diaphragm. Vomit involuntarily spewed up from his stomach and into the black sackcloth. His hands clawed at the edges of the material, which threatened to cut off his air supply. His esophagus was being crushed; he felt tiny needles creeping up his body from his feet. Junior knew that meant he was drifting away, losing consciousness. The thought caused him to fight harder.

His assailant's communications sounded like muffled, hushed whispers in his obstructed ears. A crushing blow to the face caused something to explode behind Junior's eyes. He could feel the moisture seeping into his death hood from his busted face. A kick in the nuts sent a shock wave of pain through his entire body. He reacted as if someone had put him in an electric chair, his body seizing and jerking violently.

Junior couldn't hold on for much longer. He could see Broady's face like a painting on his eyelids. Then his mother's face—the last vision of it, contorted, stiff, came into focus. Another hit to the body brought Junior back momentarily.

"You fucked with the wrong ones, nigga!" he heard, barely making out the choppy voices. He didn't know if it was the hood or the fact that his ears were ringing. He was dragged to a new spot on the floor; the carpet was burning his back. More punches, kicks and boot stomps rained down on his body.

"Don't kill him! The boss wants him alive," one of his assailants said before he laid his fist into Junior's gut for good measure.

Junior was transported from one black world into another.

Chapter 23

Upping the Ante

Candice rushed through the familiar doors of the shooting range. Her heart immediately sank. She missed her uncle at times like these. In fact, she had been thinking about him a lot lately. Candice wondered what he'd think about her current predicament.

"Candy, you can't be a cleaner and be so emotional," he'd tell her.

The range was a place of solace for her. The smell of lead, the sound of bullets flying and the power she felt when she shot her weapons helped alleviate much of her stress. Also, she needed to sharpen her skills a bit.

She looked down at the other range stalls; three were occupied by men. None of them were paying her any attention. *Good.* She rolled the bright orange foam earplugs between her fingers until they were small enough to fit into her ear canals. She smiled as she remembered Uncle Rock's voice instructing her to "always double bag your ears or you'll be like me, a deaf and dumb old man."

It was a cheesy joke, but it always made her giggle. Occasionally he would even crack a rare smile over the comment.

She plugged her ears with hard ear protection and slid her specialized clear plastic protective eye goggles over her eyes. The black gloves were the last step. She worked her fingers into the leather gloves; she hated shooting with gloves because it made getting her rounds on target and in the five rings a bit more of a challenge. But Uncle Rock warned her hundreds of times about the dangers of lead particles getting all over her hands, contaminating her skin and blood.

Candice set her jaw and stomped her left foot, angry at herself for getting all mushy. Candice swiveled her neck and cracked her knuckles. She needed to toughen up for this war. "This is all for you, Daddy. Uncle Rock, I'm going to make you proud. I'm going to do everything right this time," she whispered to herself.

The sound of rounds being fired from the adjacent shooting lanes gave Candice the push that she needed. She pulled down the gun rest and placed her perfect plastic case on it. The handmade case had been created by Uncle Rock to house what Candice considered the best gift she had ever received. Candice slowly unlatched the case and pulled up the top in a dramatic fashion, as if unveiling the Hope Diamond. When the case flapped open, Candice's eyes sparkled and she smiled down at her uncle's gift. The feeling of excitement that Uncle Rock's beautiful AR-15 had given her many years ago was even stronger today.

Candice moved to the left and put the weapon on her support-side shoulder. She blew out a cleansing breath and tried to relax. She closed her eyes for a few seconds and imagined Uncle Rock guiding her movements. She placed her support-side ear on her shoulder.

"Candy, you gotta get your head down behind the sights or else this will jump back and hit you in the face. Grip it here, like your life depended on it. C'mon, Candy, now take this. Get your head behind those sights. Get a firm grasp and learn how to treat this baby like it's your own." Uncle Rock's voice guided her from the grave and beyond.

Candice let her legs go soft and bent her knees slightly, with her back straight. She got into the correct stance and positioned the gun properly. Closing her weak eye and keeping her dominant eye open, Candice tugged on the trigger. When the first couple of rounds exited the end of the gun in rapid fire, Candice looked down range at the ripped-up target. She carefully pulled the trigger back again and again. Finally she was satisfied as she called in the obliterated target.

"Well, DeSosa, you better be fuckin' ready because your time has run out." Candice didn't care who heard her or who watched her. She was completely in her element, and single-minded in her objective.

***

Arellio DeSosa opened the strange manila envelope left on his car windshield. He read the strange writing on the front. It was his name spelled out in letters that were cut out from magazines and newspapers. Curious, he turned the envelope over and dumped out its contents.

Arellio doubled over like he'd taken a powerful gut punch. His heartbeat sped up; his hands were racked with tremors. He looked at graphic 8x10 glossy photographs. He frantically flipped through them; each one was worse than the previous one. Finally he arrived at the last picture.

"No!" Arellio let out a guttural scream, dropping all of the pictures to the ground. Cyndi came rushing out the front door and down the long, circular driveway. She found her husband sitting on the ground next to his car, sobbing like a woman. He shouted "No! No! No!" over and over again. A cold chill shook Cyndi to the core. Something very bad had gone down.

"Arellio? What is it?" she asked, touching him on the head. She quickly discovered his source of distress. Cyndi went to her knees to retrieve the scattered photographs. Her chest tightened and tears burned behind her eyes. She picked up the photographs and was overcome with a mixture of grief and disbelief.

The first photo depicted her brother-in-law, Guillermo, with his head thrown back and eyes closed as another man took in a mouthful of his manhood. Cyndi felt sick as vomit crept up her throat.

With her eyes wide she shuffled to the next picture. "Oh God!" she gasped. It was a frontal shot of Guillermo, his face clear as day. He was on his knees, a man mounting him from behind. Guillermo's face seemed contorted—whether in pain or pleasure, Cyndi could not tell. She felt light-headed. How could she comfort her husband through this disgrace?

The next picture showed Guillermo picking up a man and handing him money on a dark street corner.

The following picture felled her completely. Guillermo had a look of pure shock and terror on his face. His eyes bulged almost out of his head, and his mouth hung open in a terrified *O* shape. A severed penis was shoved between his lips.

Cyndi let out a loud screech. If this had been some kind of nightmare, she would have hoped she'd wake up soon. With trembling hands she flipped to the last picture in the stack. Cyndi twisted her body away from her husband and vomited on the driveway. The eviscerated remains of her brother-in-law were too much for herself and her husband to handle. How could they offer comfort to one another when they both were in so much pain?

"You motherfucker!" Tucker boomed, rushing toward the old man, spit flying from his mouth. "You fucked with my family? I'm going to rip your fucking head off and shit down your neck, you old bastard!"

Three black suits stepped in Tucker's path, forming a wall around their charge. Grayson Stokes didn't even flinch, his icy eyes remaining steady and calm. He folded his wrinkled hands on the table in front of him like he was watching a boring variety show rerun.

Avon struggled against a wall of muscles. "I'm gonna kill you! Fuckin' white devil!" he barked. The walls of the room felt like they were closing in on him. "Face me like a man!" Avon challenged.

"Is that why you asked to meet me, Agent Tucker? So you could curse at me? So you could make yourself look like a total fool?" Stokes said calmly in his throaty, phlegm-coated voice.

"No, I asked to meet you so I could fucking kill you, you piece of shit! What type of fucking games are you playing?" Tucker could barely contain his anger. Veins throbbed at his temple and in his neck. He felt like he was having an "Incredible Hulk" moment.

"What makes you think it was me that tried to harm your family, Agent Tucker?" Stokes asked, peering around the broad backs of his protectors. "Do you really think you are that important to me?"

"Who else would do it? Who else would have a reason to do it?" Tucker contorted his jaw so hard he gave himself a headache.

"Did you ever think that DeSosa would do something like that? He is a fucking criminal, Agent Tucker. He knows you were undercover, infiltrating his top drug-dealing thug. Don't you think he has a reason to go after your family?" Stokes painted these scenarios for him to make him think twice about his current conspiracy theory.

"DeSosa wouldn't even know where to find my family!" Tucker boomed, jutting a trembling finger at Stokes. Stokes chortled and then was overcome with a fit of coughing.

Tucker felt like he'd been bitch slapped by Stokes. His patience snapped. Tucker bulldozed into the three Stokes protectors. "You think it's funny, you half-dead motherfucker!" he screamed as he dived across the table with his hands outstretched.

He wasn't fast enough. He was roughhoused by the suits and put into an arm bar, his arms raised over his head and locked behind his neck. The pain that rushed down his spine as a result rendered Tucker helpless. He had no choice but to calm down. Breathing like a captured animal, he finally stopped flailing and fighting.

With a deadpan expression Stokes watched Tucker's face; the old man's demeanor was as calm as a placid river. Finally he waved his right hand in the air like it was a magic wand. "That's enough," he called out, snapping his fingers as though calling off well-trained attack dogs.

Tucker was released. He collapsed onto a chair and waited for the feeling to come back into his arms.

"Another hotheaded Tucker." Stokes shook his head in disappointment, as though Tucker was simply a lazy student who didn't do his homework.

Tucker was back on alert; his eyes were hooded over with ill intent.

"You think I didn't know about your hero daddy? Agent Tucker, I know everything. But do you? I bet you didn't know your father *wasn't really* the undercover narcotics detective shot dead in a buy and bust," Stokes said cruelly.

"You shut the fuck up!" Tucker growled. His teeth were clenched together tightly; his words were barely audible.

"Your father was no more than a dirty drug cop who was taking payments from drug dealers. He got shot because he wanted out—just like Easy Hardaway. He wanted to get into a game he knew nothing about, and there was no turning back. There's never a way out, only a fucking way in, A-gent Tu-cker!" Stokes spoke like a preacher in the pulpit; his eyes were dilated and flashing with malice.

Tucker shot up out of the chair. He was faster this time and managed to catch Stokes around his frail turkey neck. Tucker squeezed as hard as he could from across the table. "You're a fuckin' liar! I'm gonna kill you, once and for all!" Tucker howled, snot pouring from his nose. His brain felt as if it would burst through his skull with all of the pressure building inside his head.

The men in black were on him in a matter of seconds. He held on as if his life depended on it. Stokes was making a horrible rasping noise, like a grating car engine that wouldn't turn over.

"Die!" Tucker hissed.

Finally the men were able to pry him off Stokes. His body shook with angry tremors. Tucker was forced back down onto his chair. He held his head in his hands, while his chest rose and fell rapidly.

Stokes was ruining his life and tainting the memory of his father. Nothing in his life was off-limits. Everything that was holy and sacred had been desecrated by this bastard.

Stokes coughed through his maniacal laughter. "Now, Agent Tucker, are you ready to hear everything? Are you ready to talk so we can work together to find the girl and protect your family?" Stokes asked.

They appeared to be back at square one.

With his chest heaving and nostrils flaring, Tucker narrowed his eyes and glared at Stokes. He would at least hear him out. If it involved his family, there was nothing he wouldn't do to protect them.

"All right, then. Now that I have your full attention, let me start from the very beginning," Stokes said, sliding a file in Tucker's direction. "I know you've already seen these, but you only have the Hardaway files. I don't think you know much about Joseph Barton or Rolando DeSosa . . . or the government for that matter," Stokes said.

"I don't wanna read any more of your fuckin' lies! Be a man. Tell me the truth, eye to fucking eye! Tell me how you manipulated a man into selling drugs that poisoned his own fuckin' people. Tell me how the fuckin' government sells drugs to buy weapons for fuckin' militants in other countries. . . . Yeah, tell me!" Tucker growled. He wanted Grayson Stokes to know he was not on his side now, and he never would be a part of his fucking games.

"All right, then, Agent Tucker, I can do that. But you have to be able to handle the truth," Stokes replied. The old man then steepled his fingers together, allowing the pad of each digit to match with its counterpart on the opposite hand. Stokes began to narrate, cleansing himself of it all and taking Tucker on a journey through the past.

He might hate Stokes's guts, but this was exactly the kind of information Tucker needed to help Candy.

Chapter 24

Players and Traitors

New York 1984

"Hit him again," Grayson Stokes growled, circling the victim like a buzzard over a dead body.

Stokes possessed the body of a U.S. Marine and the face of a Calvin Klein model; yet he was as ruthless as a black widow spider. His new mission had come directly from the director of the Central Intelligence Agency—an honor for an agent as high as being knighted by the queen of England.

At his direction a huge gorilla-shaped man approached. The man's meaty hands held the opposing ends of two battery cables; the clamps squeezed open like the hungry mouth of a shark. Stokes nodded at the man, giving him the signal.

Without any facial emotion the man roughly clipped the menacing metal clamps onto the victim's exposed nipples.

The other man fiddled with a box; soon there was a crackling electric sound, like an old transistor radio. Guttural screams emerged from the victim's diaphragm and echoed off the walls. Stokes rubbed his chin, contemplating his next move.

"Rolando DeSosa . . . the Dominican kingpin of New York City," Stokes said sarcastically, circling again. "Are you going to tell me to go fuck myself again, or are you going to get with the program?" Stokes pushed DeSosa's suspended body, causing it to swing like he was a slab of meat in a butcher shop.

DeSosa's body was racked with tremors; he was a far cry from the cocky, slick-talking Tony Montana–wannabe who had strode into the room earlier.

"*Fuck you,*" DeSosa rasped, his throat feeling like he'd swallowed acid.

Stokes's eyebrows arched high at DeSosa's bravado. "*Fuck me, huh?*" Stokes laughed. Then his smile faded as fast as it had formed. Stokes quickly nodded to his henchmen. One of the suited thugs came forward with a scalpel.

DeSosa moaned. There was only so much pain a man could tolerate in his lifetime. "*No, no, no,*" he mumbled, his battered eyes assessed the torture tool. His mind was barely able to comprehend the cruel trick that fate had played on him, for surely he would suffer dearly for his sins before he died.

The thugs made several small incisions on DeSosa's chest, like tribal initiation markings. Then they poured salt and alcohol onto it. DeSosa didn't have any sound left in his voice box; his mouth just hung open in sheer terror.

Stokes turned his back, anxiously rubbing his fingernails on the breast of his suit. He closed his eyes as DeSosa finally got enough wind in his lungs to let out a bloodcurdling scream.

"*Now, Rolando. Again, let me tell you who I am. Maybe your English is not too good, so you didn't understand me the first time. I work for President Ronald Reagan. You do know who that is, right? He's the man who allowed scum like you to enter our country, only to find out that you came here to get rich by selling drugs,*" Stokes said condescendingly, addressing the top of DeSosa's downturned head.

DeSosa couldn't and wouldn't dare answer. He'd had enough.

With the flick of his hand, Stokes's people were pulling DeSosa down from the chains and relocating him to a cold metal chair. His head was fighting a major battle with his neck; eventually it lobbed forward until his chin hit his chest. Stokes stood menacingly in front of him.

"*You feel better sitting on the chair?*" Stokes continued, not giving DeSosa a chance to even respond. "*So, now, this little thing we want you to agree to. It's sort of like an immunity deal. We take you out of prison. We give you access to the newest spin on cocaine, and you do our good president a favor by finding the right people in the worst neighborhoods to distribute this new phenomenal wonder drug—which we call crack cocaine—to. You following me, DeSosa?"*

Stokes grabbed a handful of DeSosa's thick, dark hair so that he could look him directly in the eye. DeSosa could barely keep his battered eyelids open long enough to stare back.

"Rolando, I have about twelve more ways to make you say yes. Why don't we avoid using those methods? All you need to do is just open your mouth and repeat after me: 'I, Rolando DeSosa, will agree to help this great country of the United States, which allowed my cockroach spic ass to come here and make money off its people,'" Stokes dictated. "Or should we start with that machine right there? I believe it does something permanent. Tell me, how much do you value your eyesight, Rolando?" Stokes threatened in a maddeningly calm tone.

DeSosa still did not acquiesce right away; instead, it took four more methods of torture before he finally cracked. In the end he agreed to the CIA's program to distribute crack cocaine in low-income neighborhoods in New York City and Los Angeles.

At the time no one, not even the CIA, knew the distribution was being used to fund Reagan's Contras. Stokes had only agreed to the program because he was told that controlling the distribution of this new and cheap spin on regular cocaine would help the government rid its country of the worst ghettos, like a self-inflicted genocide.

Stokes had signed on because he was a loyal employee of the government. He had thrown his moral compass in the trash compartment many years ago, and had no intention of retrieving it anytime soon.

Easy Hardaway was recruited into Operation Easy In, after his name had been passed to DeSosa by an NYPD detective named Francis Moore. Francis Moore was a decorated police hero; he was a rising rank-and-file detective, street legend and hard-nosed narc, who had put the worst of the worst behind bars for life.

Rolando DeSosa knew Moore differently. He knew Moore as the dirty detective he had kept on his payroll for years. Their relationship had proved very beneficial to DeSosa. Each and every time he had a run-in with the NYPD, his name would be cleared; then he'd be back on the street in a matter of days, and sometimes hours, thanks to Moore's diligent work.

Until Moore's only daughter, Corine, had begun dating a scraggly street kid known to every cop and detective as Easy, his life had been pretty uncomplicated. As the protégé of Early, a longtime criminal, Moore naturally had concerns about the safety of Corine in the presence of Easy.

One night Moore stormed into DeSosa's hangout spot in Harlem, sweating and visibly upset. He had been searching for DeSosa for days. He needed DeSosa to take care of his little "problem." But clearly, DeSosa had problems of his own.

"What the hell happened to you?" Moore asked, noticing the healing cuts and bruises on DeSosa's face, neck and hands.

DeSosa had waved off the questions. "What is it that you want from me, Detective Moore? I haven't been out there, so I don't have anything for you."

"What makes you think I want something?" Moore asked defensively.

DeSosa raised an arrogant eyebrow. "Because dirty cops only come around when they want something."

Moore explained the situation with his daughter. He believed Eric Hardaway to be a no-good street thug who had stolen his daughter away from him and his wife.

DeSosa dismissed Moore's paternal concerns, at first. "I'm not doing jur fuckin' dirty work. You have a personal vendetta against the kid, ju handle it," DeSosa said dismissively.

Moore was his employee, not the other way around. DeSosa didn't fucking have time for this personal bullshit— what with the government breathing down his back.

Moore, however, persisted like a bulldog with a bone. He simply knew that if Easy Hardaway stayed romantically involved with his daughter, Corine would end up dead in a back alley. It simply wasn't a risk he was willing to take.

Exasperated, DeSosa heard Moore out, but he considered a different course of action. Why kill a perfectly good drug dealer? The instruction Stokes provided to DeSosa was to recruit specific types of people for the program—poor people, illiterates, high-school dropouts. These recruits also needed to be hungry for fast money and posses a work ethic strong enough to generate a decent cash flow.

Easy, in many ways, was a highly qualified candidate for the program. Easy was like a wrapped Christmas gift that had been left under the tree for DeSosa.

Moore gave DeSosa information about Easy's last whereabouts, as well as his street affiliations, daily routine, known accomplices, etc. He had done all of the legwork, which meant all DeSosa had to do was track him down and make him an offer he couldn't refuse.

Easy was a kid coming up on the street, making a name for himself; he was known to many for being the quiet kid who ran in silence and violence. Easy was always hungry for his next dollar. He beat the block, day in and day out. He worked tirelessly at his job and was very smart at evading the police radar. No matter how many times they tried to snag him, Easy had strategically avoided detention and arrest. If the cops thought they had enough probable cause to do a "stop and frisk" of Easy's car, they never found what they were looking for, because there was never enough evidence to haul his ass off to jail.

Easy was smart about his hustle; he knew Early would have been proud of the name he had worked hard building for himself. Easy became especially careful in his dealings, however, after falling in love with and impregnating the daughter of a cop. He didn't want to jeopardize his newfound family by making rookie mistakes. Now his main responsibility was feeding the unborn children who grew in his girl's belly and protecting them all from harm.

DeSosa sent a man with a message for Easy. "Rolando DeSosa, the biggest kingpin in New York, wants to see you. He heard about how hard you work out here on these streets, and he wants you to come and talk to him. He wants you to move fuckin' weight for him."

Always the skeptic, Easy didn't take the guy very seriously. In fact, Easy looked the little Hispanic dude up and down, scowling, and said, "Get the fuck outta here with that fantasy bullshit. Y'all niggas always tryin'a set a nigga up. A nigga like me been on these streets for a minute. I was born at night, nigga, not last night!" The small man scampered away like a dog with his tail caught between his legs.

After that encounter Easy stepped up his arsenal of weapons, strategically placing them at home, in his car and on his person. He didn't trust a damn soul anymore.

It wasn't until DeSosa sent his own men, and not a street flunky, to deliver the message personally to Easy that he even considered the possibility of working for DeSosa.

He had spotted them walking feverishly toward him from a heavily tinted car. Easy was on the high ready, reaching for his waistband, but they responded by opening their trench coats and showing their bare waistbands. With hands raised in peace, one guapo boomed, "We bring a message from our boss."

Still wary of their presence in his territory, Easy kept a safe distance from them. DeSosa really wanted to see him; this was the general song the honchos were singing.

Easy had some questions that needed answering first. "Little ol' me? Why me? Of all the hustlin' dudes in BK . . . why me?"

The men assured him that all of his questions would be answered when he met with their boss.

Though Easy was flattered by the offer, he worried that he was being set up. Perhaps DeSosa wanted to get rid of all the competition and expand his own enterprise. Everyone knew DeSosa—he was the man pushing the fast-moving cocaine, which not only cost less than other street drugs, but brought in more profit by sheer volume of sales than heroin or weed could ever net.

After two sleepless nights of weighing the pros and cons of doing business with DeSosa, Easy finally had decided he would strap up and at least meet the man in person. He would hear the man out; and if DeSosa even hinted at taking over Easy's spots, the meeting would be over before the shit even started.

In the meantime, Easy remained cautious with whom he shared his news. He knew better than to blab his mouth to any of the jealous dudes he worked around on the streets. In fact, there was only one person Easy trusted, aside from Corine, and that was Rock Barton.

Easy appeared in DeSosa's Spanish Harlem club office. His baby face was clear of blemishes, wrinkles or worry. The budding goatee he grew was the only indication that he was even old enough to drive. Easy stood a gangly six foot two inches; his rail-thin frame was covered in his best digs. He was decked out in a butter-soft leather blazer, cashmere mock neck sweater, Potenza slacks and his first pair of suede Salvatore Ferragamo loafers. A lone gold crucifix with a ruby crown at the top sat in the middle of Easy's chest, a diamond pinkie ring graced his left pinkie. His gaudy way of dressing screamed drug dealer *or* pimp. *This was something his friend Rock had been lecturing him to change lately.*

"Sit down, Easy," DeSosa instructed in his thick accent.

Easy nodded respectfully and took a seat. Easy's heart hammered and his palms were soaking wet. He splayed them open, flat on his pants legs, and rubbed them dry.

DeSosa's style was simple. No jewelry, no flashy clothes, just a very regal presence that said, I'm in charge. *DeSosa stubbed out his customary cigar and leveled Easy with a look.*

"I selected you for my own reasons," DeSosa began. He bombarded Easy with a series of questions; within an hour they were speaking fluidly and comfortably.

Easy felt a great amount of respect for DeSosa. He felt like DeSosa was a kindred spirit, someone whom Easy had known his entire life. Easy and DeSosa built their relationship on mutual respect and on a common goal—getting rich fast.

DeSosa educated Easy on the business of marketing mass quantities of crack cocaine at prices that would guarantee sales at lightning speed. In weeks Easy became the man to see in Brooklyn. Everybody knew he was pushing weight and he was offering a fair price for his product. Soon Easy's drug operation grew, and he became one of the biggest crack cocaine distributors in New York City.

Rolando DeSosa was his lone supplier. It was like a match made in heaven. At first, Easy was just getting eight ounces or so at a time, worth about $15,000. But as Easy's drug empire expanded, he began putting in orders for kilos' worth of crack cocaine, worth tens of millions of dollars. Easy never asked DeSosa any questions about his access to such vast quantities of product. That was one of the reasons his relationship with DeSosa worked so well. DeSosa did the supplying and Easy met the demands on the street—no questions asked.

Before long, Easy became a certified kingpin, with over a dozen crack houses in Brooklyn, churning out $30,000 to $50,000 a day in profits. His network of drug dealers sold so many crack rocks daily that Easy gained as many enemies as he did loyal customers.

Easy was making money hand over fist. Little did he know that the millions he made could be directly attributed to the CIA and DEA operatives who supplied DeSosa with unlimited amounts of cocaine. Easy was a boy from the hood—a squirrel trying to get a nut; DeSosa was fulfilling his agreement with the government and the Reagan administration. It all worked like a well-oiled machine.

Their business relationship soon evolved into a personal one. DeSosa often invited Easy to break bread with him and his family, and sometimes DeSosa even dropped by the Hardaway house for a social call.

Detective Moore had been watching Easy and DeSosa's relationship progress. He was waiting for the day he could shake DeSosa's hand and thank him for blowing off the head of the man who'd destroyed his daughter's life. He was furious with DeSosa for falling back on his word.

"You fucking lied to me! We had a deal!" Moore had screamed when he stormed into DeSosa's new club, Baile Caliente, gun in hand, badge in the other. He was a man possessed. He didn't get very far before he was hemmed up by DeSosa's henchmen.

"You're a fucking liar, DeSosa . . . after all I did for you! All of the times I saved your ass!" Moore strained against the stronghold he was placed in, his veins cording against his skin.

DeSosa was very calm; his smug demeanor infuriated the detective even more.

"Detective, I think you have your son-in-law all wrong. You should try to get to know him. He is a good, loyal kid," DeSosa said, blowing a smoke ring in Moore's direction. "As for what you've done for me? I don't think you would want me to tell your chief what I've done for you over the years. I'm sure you didn't claim those bags of cash on your taxes," DeSosa countered, following up.

Moore's frustration mounted. He had watched his daughter run off with a known drug dealer, get herself pregnant and then marry the bastard. He hadn't even seen or held his own grandchildren. DeSosa had promised he would take Easy out. But what had he done but empower the man by supplying him with endless amounts of product? Now Easy was not only rich, but impossibly powerful, which placed his daughter and grandchild in even greater danger.

Detective Moore cursed DeSosa out and vowed that this wouldn't be the last time DeSosa or Easy heard from him.

"I will get my daughter out of this lifestyle if it's the last thing that I fucking do! Even if it means bringing you to your knees too," Moore threatened.

DeSosa had laughed at the peon detective. He wielded no power compared to the people DeSosa was involved with.

Shortly after Detective Moore's tirade and threats, the local police suddenly became very interested in one Eric "Easy" Hardaway and his associates. In a task force led by Moore, the NYPD became dedicated to putting Easy and his counterparts out of the crack cocaine business.

The first time they attempted to arrest Easy, they didn't have enough evidence to keep him detained. Following that, prosecutors from New York approached Easy and tried to get him to become a government informant. Easy had scoffed at their offer. He had laughed uproariously and told them to kiss his ass and speak to his lawyer; he was no snitch, he'd told them.

Those fucks actually thought he would talk to them about where the loads of cocaine they saw hitting the streets was coming from. Easy immediately reported this run-in with the

NYPD to DeSosa. Needless to say, the NYPD's operation was short-lived. The locals had unwittingly stumbled into CIA territory, jeopardizing Operation Easy In, but not for long.

When Grayson Stokes swept through the NYPD Brooklyn South Task Force Office, he left captains shuddering in his wake. Detective Moore was forced to turn in his badge and shield; he became known throughout the law enforcement community as the detective who'd made the biggest drug fuckup in New York's history. He went home that night, placed his personal weapon between his lips and blew off his head.

Corine heard the report of her father's suicide from the eleven o'clock news. She never realized that her father's quest to destroy her husband, and to get his baby girl back, was ultimately the cause of his own demise.

Easy comforted Corine for the days and weeks that followed her father's suicide. Easy had held her, telling her it would be all right and that it was not her fault. But something about Moore's death had unsettled Easy. He'd known the man to be a very proud and religious person; he was a man who would never have taken his own life.

Rock immediately set out to discover as much information as possible about the circumstances surrounding Moore's suicide. Rock briefed Easy in person about the information he came across. Only once had they spoken over the phone about the information Rock had learned about the CIA's involvement with DeSosa.

Rock regretted this slipup until the day he died.

The CIA had been tapping all of Easy's phones. Rock's revelation about the CIA's plans to distribute crack cocaine in poor neighborhoods had raised red flags.

Rock, of course, had tried talking Easy out of the game. Unwittingly, Easy had been a pawn of the government, helping to kill off his own people. Rock thought the decision would be a no-brainer.

Easy had been very unsettled with the information Rock had provided him with, but there was no easy and quick way out. To Rock's great dismay, he continued with the farce. After all, they both were aware that the only quick and *sure way out of the game was through death. Neither was prepared for that inevitability. Nevertheless, Rock vowed to protect Easy, no matter what.*

Naturally, Grayson Stokes was not pleased to hear that Rock Barton, one of his debriefed cleaners, was smack-dab in the middle of Operation Easy In. Rock served as the catalyst for the CIA's decision to turn Rolando DeSosa against Easy Hardaway. They needed a scapegoat for the mayhem that would ensue when DeSosa turned against his protégé.

Stokes set about planting seeds of doubt in DeSosa's head about Hardaway's allegiance to him. When Stokes presented DeSosa with pictures that he'd taken of the NYPD hauling Easy into the precinct, DeSosa quickly wrote Easy off as a traitor. Stokes convinced DeSosa that Easy had turned government informant.

Easy's latest discussions with DeSosa about leaving the game was the final nail in his coffin. Easy Hardaway had reneged on his deal, and for that he must be *eliminated.*

DeSosa sentenced Hardaway to the worst sort of death— death by the hands of his oldest son, his namesake Eric Junior. Where DeSosa was from, a man killed by his own offspring let people know he was the lowest of the low, the scum of the earth. In DeSosa's mind traitors like Easy were deserving of such a fate.

Chapter 25

Sins of a Father

Rolando DeSosa slammed his fists down on his desk until the sides of his hands went numb. He made an animalistic moaning sound, like he'd been mortally wounded. Pain was etched in every worry line on his face. His rage was palpable, and everybody in the room felt like it was alive—a big ugly monster standing in the middle of the room.

Arellio stood up to remove the pictures from his father's desk. He was kicking himself now for giving them to his father, but he didn't know what else to do, whom he should turn to. He reached out to grab the photos, but DeSosa came down on his hand, hard. He gave Arellio a look that would have felled a small creature. Arellio snatched his hand back and sighed. He thought it morbid that his ailing father wanted to stare at the disfigured and depraved photographs of his brother.

"*Papi*, let me take them away," Arellio whispered, trying to reach out to his father. "We will get whoever is responsible for this," Arellio consoled, stepping around the desk and clapping his hand on his father's shoulder.

DeSosa let his head hang low. Arellio could hear a cry bubbling up from deep inside his father's chest. He had never seen his father so broken down; it was killing him to see his father in this condition.

Rolando DeSosa hadn't cried since he was a boy in the Dominican Republic and his mother had been shot during an uprising in the small, poor ghetto where he had grown up.

DeSosa had become hardened by the event and had never shed tears for anybody since. But today the tears came and they could not be stopped. He wailed for his second-born child. Family meant the world to DeSosa. Someone would pay for his son's death. Revenge was high on DeSosa's list of rules to live by. If people went around committing evils without any consequences for their actions, the world would be an inhospitable place for everyone.

"It had to be Junior," Arellio said, breaking the silence, squeezing his father's shoulder in commiseration. "He was the only person . . . the only one who you recently had a problem with. We have to find him and fuckin' destroy him." He hoped that by steering his father toward avenging his brother's untimely death, he could bring him out of his melancholy state.

"No," DeSosa whispered, his voice cracking like a woman's.

Arellio stepped from behind his father and looked at him oddly. "*Papi*, don't tell me no. You can't protect these fuckin' bastards. I know Junior was the one who did this shit. . . . There's nobody else. . . ." Arellio was decisively protesting his father's dismissal; his eyes were ablaze with rage.

"No!" DeSosa snapped once more; his aching hands were clenched tightly in front of him. The veins in his neck pulsed dangerously close to the surface.

Arellio visibly shuddered at his father's grating, high-pitched shout.

"I took care of Junior," DeSosa whispered regretfully. "But it wasn't him. I knew it wasn't him. I thought he was lying to me, so I put Phil on him. Junior is taken care of, but this—this was not his doing. He didn't have the heart or the balls," DeSosa was saying, shaking his head as if he had all the regrets in the world sitting on his shoulders.

Arellio fell back onto an empty chair like the wind had been knocked out of him. "But who else could it have been? Who would do that to him, *Papi*?" Arellio asked. He could not fathom who would commit such a heinous act on his brother, who everyone knew was harmless, soft even.

"It was somebody who knew him, *Papi*. Whoever it was, they followed him," Arellio started, his voice cracking. He could not believe his poor, unsuspecting younger brother had gotten caught out there like that. The story would be all over the news. Their family would be humiliated.

DeSosa was rocking now; it was a habit he'd picked up since he'd been confined to a wheelchair. He heard his son rambling on about the possible suspects, but DeSosa wasn't really listening. There was one possible suspect that neither of them had discussed.

"It is her," DeSosa admitted in an almost inaudible whisper. "She came back for us, once and for all. She was here. . . . I can feel it," he wailed, inhaling a shaky breath.

One of his men had reported that the nanny had been spotted snooping around in his office. DeSosa had waved it off. He had met the nanny and believed her to be a harmless presence in his home. But now he saw the nanny in a new light—as a skillful, crafty and dangerous individual. She had infiltrated his home under false pretenses. She'd been right under his nose the entire time, laughing at them and plotting their downfall.

"Who, *Papi*? What are you talking about? You're talking crazy. . . . You think a woman killed Guillermo?" Arellio asked in rapid succession. In his mind there was no way a woman could have inflicted that degree of damage on his brother. "*Papi* . . . answer me. What are you talking about?" he pressed.

DeSosa couldn't even look at his son. His father never hung his head for anything; he had too much pride for that. Arellio could feel his blood pressure rising with every minute that passed. He wanted to shake the answers out of his father, but he knew his emotional and physical state was already on very shaky ground.

"*Papi*, what did you do? What do you know?" Arellio raised his voice and placed both of his hands flat on the front of DeSosa's desk.

DeSosa could hear his son's labored breaths exit his flaring nostrils. He had no choice but to come clean and tell Arellio everything.

"Everybody out!" DeSosa came to life with renewed vigor. All of his men looked at him strangely. He hadn't been left without bodyguards in years, even when he visited with his own children. "I said get the fuck out! Everybody out!" he barked again, a feral look in his eyes. "I need to speak with my son," DeSosa whispered. His voice went high, then lowered like a wave at high tide.

His bodyguards and other workers filed out of the room.

"Sit down, Arellio," DeSosa said gravely, nodding toward the chair.

Arellio's chest felt heavy with dread as he sat on the chair.

"I have to tell you everything. It may mean the difference between your life and your death. I've already lost one son because of my sins. I don't want to lose you as well," DeSosa revealed. That was the closest DeSosa had ever come to saying "I love you" to his son.

DeSosa closed his eyes and started at the beginning. Confession was good for the soul, or so they said. He needed to prepare his son for what was surely to come. He needed to give him as much information about the lady assassin as he had. The more he knew, the better chance he had of coming out alive in the end.

New York, 2006

Grayson Stokes dropped the envelope on DeSosa's lap. He was flustered that his word wasn't enough.

"I guess I have to make you a believer, huh, DeSosa?" Stokes chuckled while he waited for DeSosa to spill out the contents.

DeSosa jutted his jaw. He didn't care for Stokes. In fact, he hated the ground Stokes walked on. But DeSosa realized that Stokes and the CIA owned him now. It was either get down or lay down, when it came to the government spooks. DeSosa shook out the contents of the package. It only took him a few seconds to realize what he was looking at. His eyebrows shot up involuntarily at the sight. It was too late to try to put on a poker face; Stokes had already taken notice of his reaction.

"Now do you believe it?" Stokes asked, watching DeSosa's breathing pick up speed. "I don't have to lie to you . . . ever," Stokes said triumphantly, smirking.

DeSosa shuffled the pictures; he studied each one separately, hoping his eyes were deceiving him. His hopes were dashed. DeSosa's eyes bugged out when he examined a close-up photo of Easy, standing with his hands shoved into his pockets and talking to two detectives. The next shot was of Easy looking around suspiciously, like he was afraid he was being watched. All of these poses were the signs of a police informant. The sight sent a wave of stabbing cramps through DeSosa's lower abdomen.

Maricon, cabron! DeSosa screamed in his head. He positioned his lips into a straight line and rolled his eyes. He looked up at Stokes. "I would have never believed it. He was always loyal . . . so driven," DeSosa said disappointedly, trying very hard to keep a straight face. He didn't want Stokes to see how betrayed he felt.

"Well, DeSosa, the old saying goes, 'There's no honor among thieves.' I guess there's no honor among drug king-pins either," Stokes posited, chortling.

"So what now?" DeSosa asked, although he already knew the answer. He wanted to find Easy Hardaway and person-ally cut his balls off. He hated being deceived, especially by one of his own men. To think that Easy was trying to set him up made DeSosa's fucking blood boil.

"I want you to have your men get his son . . . the son with all of the problems. Who is going to notice if one schizo kid acts a bit crazier?" Stokes asked matter-of-factly. He spoke as if he were asking DeSosa to pick up a loaf of bread from the store. The man was ruthless and cold-blooded, always looking to get a man in his Achilles' heel.

"A couple of days of this stuff, and we'll have Hardaway's kid working for us," Stokes stated confidently. He pushed a small metal case toward DeSosa nonchalantly, like he was offering him a drink.

DeSosa looked down at the silver case and then back up at Stokes. This bastard is crazy! His face must've betrayed his thoughts because Stokes started laughing.

"Open it," Stokes urged him, smiling like a Cheshire cat. DeSosa did as he was asked. Inside were five small unlabeled bottles of liquid that resembled immunization shots. There were also five injection syringes in sealed packages. DeSosa raised one eyebrow. This was all too much.

"This is what you'll give the boy, once you pick him up. It's what we like to call our truth serum, mind control. Trust me, he will work like a robot for us," Stokes explained.

DeSosa's face was drawn into a scowl as he glared at the sick piece of shit standing before him.

"Ah, Rolando, you're too nice. It won't kill him. Just makes him do what we say. And Easy and his wife . . . well, with the boy's behavior they won't know the difference. You know the boy already has a lot of mental issues," Stokes continued, laying out his depraved plan.

DeSosa was astonished that Stokes had already had this plan all mapped out. It sent a shudder down DeSosa's spine. If he didn't know any better, he would have thought that he was dealing with el diablo himself.

Stokes read doubt and hesitation in DeSosa's face, so he toughened up his stance.

"Do as you are told, Rolando, and we'll always be on the same page," Stokes threatened vaguely. With a grave snap of his fingers, he and his men were gone.

DeSosa lost sleep over the task at hand. However, when he looked at the faces of his own sons and thought about his line of work, he decided that he had no choice. It was do or die.

DeSosa wasted no time carrying out the dastardly deed of his puppet master. His men coaxed Eric Junior off the streets as he left his session with his psychiatrist. It was much like the way DeSosa had coaxed Easy into his trap in the beginning—using his reputation and his men to ask for an exclusive meeting. Eric Junior had been excited that his father's boss, the only man ranked higher than Easy, had asked to see him.

Eric Junior had been stable on his medication for a few months when DeSosa asked to see him. Things had even been going well at home. His father had started grooming him for the business, showing him things about the streets and dropping little jewels of street knowledge on the boy. Though he still had the occasional outburst, they were on a much smaller scale than before he was diagnosed with psychosis.

When he was brought to DeSosa the first time, Eric Junior was smiling, all goofy and childlike. DeSosa took one look at the overzealous kid and didn't have the heart to fuck with his head—not yet, anyway. So he had the boy come back a few times, and told Eric Junior to keep it between them. He made it crystal clear that if Eric Junior told Easy about their meetings, it would jeopardize Eric Junior's chance at moving up without his father.

Eric Junior bought the story and kept the information from his father, but there was no way he could keep it from his brother. He wanted to make sure his brother knew he was no peon, and so he boasted to him one day about his meetings with DeSosa. His brother didn't pay him any mind, thinking that his medications were causing him to hallucinate.

DeSosa thought he could work on the boy's head, brainwash him without giving him any CIA poison, but the process was taking too long for Stokes. When Stokes found out that he wasn't giving the boy the serum, he threatened DeSosa's family with bodily harm. That quickly put DeSosa back on track with the plan, with little room for deviation.

Eric Junior showed up for a meeting with DeSosa, hoping to talk to the kingpin about giving him his own slice of the business. He needed to get out from under his father's thumb and make a name for himself. As soon as he got to the front door, he was ambushed, knocked out, blindfolded and driven to a remote location.

When Eric Junior regained consciousness, he found himself on a gurney, tied down with restraints. He fought futilely against the ties. His face was etched with terror as he looked around at all of the frightening faces. He fought long and hard, but his body betrayed him and finally gave out.

The first injection of the drug had burned going in.

"Aggh! What the fuck!" he'd screamed. Eric Junior's body had bucked and seizured.

DeSosa thought the boy looked like a lab rat on the experiment table. The boy's eyes had bugged out of his head; his jaws started flexing involuntarily and veins all over his body were cording against his skin. Eric Junior's eyes were glazed over; his mouth hung slack and saliva dripped down his chin. The boy looked like he was going to convulse until he was dead.

DeSosa's men had been scared to death at his reaction to the drug. After all, it wasn't intended to kill him. They were all a bit relieved when the boy's body went limp.

Then the brainwashing session began. He was told his father was the enemy. He needed to kill Easy because his father was going to try to kill him, or, worse, would try to send him to live in a mental institution. He was told that the only person he could trust was Rolando DeSosa.

The boy was dropped off a block away from his home. It had taken him hours to find his way home on that first day. He'd felt so disoriented and couldn't remember where he was going and why he was on the street.

DeSosa repeated the process five more times, as instructed by Stokes. The boy's mind deteriorated faster than Stokes had expected. Stokes was a happy camper. He'd even paid DeSosa a rare compliment.

"Maybe I should hire you as a CIA mind control expert," Stokes had joked.

DeSosa hadn't cracked a smile.

After what he'd done to Easy's son, DeSosa avoided Easy Hardaway like the plague. DeSosa also didn't trust that Easy wasn't trying to set him up; he was a police informant, after all.

Each time Easy asked for a meeting with DeSosa, the older man refused. Whenever Easy called, DeSosa was real short with him. Easy had always received his kilos directly from DeSosa, but suddenly there was a middleman.

DeSosa's sketchy behavior did nothing for Easy's already growing suspicions about DeSosa. With Rock buzzing in his ear, Easy started to see things differently. He'd been stressed beyond the norm. His home life had grown chaotic.

Eric Junior had begun acting erratically again. Easy had been trying to reel Eric Junior in, but the boy had other ideas. He wanted his own business, to do things his own way. This posed a major problem for Easy. Had he been one of Easy's other workers, he might've found himself going ghost a long time ago, but this was his son.

Then there was Easy's worker Junior, who had been giving Easy a lot of push-back and resistance lately. Junior was still mad that Easy had commissioned Rock to make Junior's best friend disappear. The man had been a liability from day one, but it was hard to convince Junior to see it from his perspective.

The reality of Easy's world had caught up with him—the distrust, the danger, the family matters—and he simply wanted out. He'd stacked some paper and was ready to quit the game. There were just too many dangers, too many signs to ignore. He needed to cut his losses and move on. He realized it wasn't going to be that simple, and so he'd requested a meeting with DeSosa to tell him face-to-face that he was leaving the game once and for all.

DeSosa again refused to meet with Easy. That was all the confirmation Easy needed. Rock was right; Easy needed to get out of the game.

"Rolando . . . it's Easy. Nah, I asked for a meeting and you refused. I'm letting you know I'm out. I'm done," Easy had announced, his voice wavering, just like his emotions.

Rock had sat stock-still as Easy made his announcement. He realized that the decision would come with consequences. When Easy hung up the line, Rock could see the trepidation on his face. Rock was struck with a bout of chest pains. What had he done?

"Yo, Rock, something about this just doesn't feel right, man. DeSosa was way too calm," Easy said, falling back on his chair.

Rock was quiet as he contemplated this.

Just then, Easy's phone rang again. He looked at the number displayed on the small screen and sighed. He pointed at the phone, signaling to Rock that the call wasn't good.

Easy inhaled, then exhaled loudly before picking up the line.

"Yeah," he answered.

"There is nothing you can do or say to change my mind. I'm gettin' outta the game. I'm an old man now. I've grown out of all of this shit," Easy lied. The truth was, he didn't trust DeSosa one bit—not after all that had transpired with his wife and his son.

"C'mon, DeSosa . . . ain't no reason to raise your voice. I should be the one pissed with you. I hear you been talkin' to my son. He is not going to go against me," Easy assured the man.

DeSosa stumbled over his words. He couldn't believe Easy knew that he'd been speaking to Eric Junior.

"You can make all of the threats you want. I'm out of the game," Easy said with finality before he disconnected the line.

That call had sealed his fate in more ways than one. Easy knew there would be consequences for his action; he just hoped he'd be able to live through them.

Arellio DeSosa was hanging on his father's every word. He knew his father was ruthless, but using a man's son to do his dirty work seemed beneath the DeSosa name.

"So you killed him?" Arellio asked. He knew the story of Easy Hardaway's death and the massacre of his entire family. He never knew his father was involved in it.

DeSosa nodded. "I sent them back with the boy. Easy suffered at the hands of his own son," DeSosa whispered.

Arellio still looked at him, confused. His father had gone over the entire long story, but still there was no mention of a girl. DeSosa could read the questions in his son's eyes.

"There was one girl left alive. When Stokes gave us the green light, he told us the whole family was home. He lied. He knew the girl would run to Barton. He knew Barton would train her. He had altered Barton's mind, like a robot. Stokes allowed Barton to train the girl to be an assassin so he could get rid of me when the time came. So he could bury his secrets—the government's secrets—with me and my entire family," DeSosa revealed.

"So he was the one who led her right to us," Arellio replied, like the pieces of the puzzle were finally coming together.

His father nodded his agreement. "She was here," DeSosa announced.

Arellio's eyebrows shot up. "The fucking nanny!" Arellio belted out, scrambling up from his chair and snatching the door open with a fury.

"Cyndi! Cyndi!" he screamed, his panicked voice echoing throughout the house.

***

The sun was shining down on the quiet neighborhood. The sounds of kids going off to school and fathers, with legitimate jobs, kissing their wives before heading off to work had already ceased. This was the time of day no one would be expecting anything. It was also the time of day that the DeSosas were beginning to stir, crawling awake after their previous night of criminal activities.

Candice knew all of their schedules by heart. She knew what time the eldest son went to confer with the father; what time Cyndi went to the nail salon; even what time DeSosa was given a sponge bath. But today would be different; today they would be grieving together and coming up with a strategy to avenge Guillermo's death.

How dare someone fuck with a DeSosa, right? Candice scoffed at their bullshit family pride. *How dare someone fuck with the Hardaways is more like it.*

She watched and waited for the right time to strike.

Crouching down, with her back rounded, she rested her elbows on her knees; her feet were planted flat so she could steady herself. *Crouching Tiger, Hidden Dragon,* she thought with a smirk. Her legs were spread, and her feet were lined up with each hip, just like Uncle Rock had taught her. *A sound base that can absorb gunshot recoil.*

She placed her dominant eye into the space on the round scope connected to the AR-15 and closed the other eye. Things came into focus real fast. Her ears filled with the rushing sound of her own labored breaths. Huge eagle-sized butterflies banged around inside her stomach now. She felt a sickening rush of anxious energy that made her feel powerful.

She spotted movement in the scope and adjusted it to focus in on her target. The eye of the scope was so precise and powerful; it was like the target was standing right in front of her. *Bam. Never know what hit you.*

There would be no more fucking target practice for Candice. No more getting beat to the punch. No more punking out or getting too emotional to stay on task. Nothing else mattered to her anymore.

Keeping her body as stiff and still as she could, Candice moved the pad of her trigger finger. She tested herself to see how steady she could be. A fine bead of sweat cleared a path down the side of her face. It tickled as it ran over the edge of her mouth and sneaked into her partially parted lips. Candice tasted the salt of her own sweat; it was a sign of things to come.

The anticipation inside her had built to a crescendo. She wanted to scream, to let out some of the tension. She blew out a cleansing breath, instead. There were only a few more targets left and she'd be done. Justice would be served for her family and for Uncle Rock, and she would finally have the peace she craved in her life.

Trigger. Trigger. Trigger, she chanted in her head.

Her legs were starting to burn as the newly formed sweat beads dripped into her eye; still, she didn't dare to move. Her arms trembled from the position she was in, but she kept her poise. This was her last chance, and she felt like she needed to take the opportunity before she lost it. Suddenly her heart jerked.

Right now. Clear shot. No hesitation. Focus. Trigger. Trigger. Trigger.

The target had been on the move a few minutes before but now stood still. There was nothing in her way.

Trigger. Trigger. Trigger. Now! Candice screamed inside her head. Her body tensed, but her hands did what they had been trained to do.

Candice was surprised by the sound of the click; the slack was out of the trigger. The trigger was all the way back one second and clicking to return to position the next second.

Again. Again. Until the threat is eliminated. Candice's head swirled with instruction. *One more time. Trigger. Trigger. Trigger.*

The sound of crashing glass brought things into focus for Candice now. It was done. Then the silent air was split in half by the shrill screams of a female voice. *Confirmation.* Instinctively, her shoulders slumped and she let out a long sigh. The hard part was over.

Loud screams and the eruption of pandemonium brought her back to reality. She wasn't at the range practicing with Uncle Rock's AR-15 anymore. Her muscles ached with tension and she was burning hot from the sun beating down on her in the hours spent lying in wait.

Panic struck her like a 1,000-pound boulder. She had to get away from here. Her breath came out in short, sharp pants. Candice's hands shook as she unhooked the legs from the weapon and folded them down. Then she handled the weapon like it was a crown jewel. She placed it in the case Uncle Rock had made especially for it and then slung the leather strap of the case around her chest and let it hang down her back. She was on the move within seconds.

Sirens could be heard in the distance now. This wasn't like the last time. . . . There would be no delayed reactions from the police and ambulances. Candice knew that hitting the victim in the home was risky business. There would be many more potential witnesses, for instance. But she'd practiced so many times, and she felt there was little room for error on her part. She employed every rule and tool Uncle Rock had provided her with to execute the job with expert precision. Candice thought Uncle Rock would probably give her an A+ on her work today.

With the confidence of an Olympic triathlete, she moved her body with great agility and speed. "Twenty seconds after kill shot. Damn, Candy, you are good," she complimented herself softly.

This time she didn't worry about who might be watching her. She wanted them to know she was coming for them too. If Candy got any harder, she would turn into cement.

Chapter 26

A Battle with Darkness

Dana Carlisle raised her arms above her head and arched her back. "Mmm," she moaned, then let her arms flop down at her sides. A huge yawn followed her feline-like stretch. Boredom was the order of the night. There was nothing on television that she hadn't already seen or was even remotely interested in watching.

Blowing out an exasperated breath, she got up from the couch and padded over to the window of the cabin. She clipped her fingers through the espresso-colored faux wood blinds and peeked out the window. Darkness. She called it her security sweep for the night.

When she first arrived at the cabin, she performed full gun-in-hand security sweeps of the entire house and area around it. Now she just made sure she sat tight and waited to be rescued. Something about the peace of the darkness actually made her feel whole and comforted. The sound of footsteps behind her startled her out of her reverie. It could only be one of three people, anyway. Carlisle wished that person had just stayed her ass in bed. Slowly she turned to see who was intruding on her alone time.

Carlisle's mood blackened at the sight of Elaina on the staircase. She rolled her eyes and turned her back to the window, hoping the darkness would wrap its arms around her to make her blend into the night. She really didn't feel like playing houseguest with Elaina right now.

Elaina shuffled her feet and moved into the kitchen. Carlisle was sure she had been seen; yet no words were exchanged. Carlisle was used to Elaina's cold, silent treatment. Lucky for her, the kids loved her and she was able to spend the daytime playing board games and singing along with the karaoke machine.

Carlisle didn't care too much for Elaina's prissy attitude. She was pretty fucking ungrateful, seeing that Carlisle had picked up and agreed to protect Elaina's unfaithful ass. Frankly, the only reason Carlisle had agreed to come out to Deep Creek Lake and stand guard over Tucker's family was because of her deep feelings for him and concern for the well-being of his children. Either way, Carlisle didn't like Elaina; she prayed that when all of the danger had subsided, Tucker would drop the bitch like a hot potato.

Carlisle could hear Elaina fussing around with the teakettle and rummaging through the cabinets. For the most part they avoided each other whenever possible. They were like polar opposites, circling around one another. Both were hyperaware of the other, but neither made the effort to initiate any kind of personal relationship.

There were so many days that Carlisle had been tempted to break the wall of silence that had settled between the two women—to tell her exactly what was going on. Or maybe talk about Tucker as a family man and as a professional. However, Elaina's stony demeanor kept her at a very formal distance.

Carlisle walked back over to the little end table next to the patchwork, paisley-decorated couch and picked up her pack of cigarettes. She examined the pack. Only three more left. Shit! She'd have to go into town tomorrow.

She stepped outside to light a smoke, and the cold, bitter air hit her arms. She cursed to herself when she realized her jacket hung over the back of one of the dinette chairs in the kitchen, where Elaina was playing house. Carlisle let out a long sigh. It was either go into the lion's den to get her jacket or stand out on the blustery porch and smoke in peace. A little cold never killed anyone, right?

The crisp night air blowing off the lake immediately whipped around her face and slapped at her bare arms. Springtime up at the lake didn't feel quite as nice as it sounded. Carlisle lit her cigarette and stepped down the three steps of the cabin porch. She took a toke and shivered. Aside from the small porch light, there was nothing but blackness in front of her.

Good thing she never left without her Glock. A few more drags off the cigarette and she felt like it wasn't even worth it anymore. She dropped her cigarette and mashed the lit end out with her sneaker tip. Her nerves were settled, but her teeth were chattering.

Turning around swiftly, Carlisle took the three steps in one long stretch of her legs. Just as she passed the two Adirondack chairs on the porch, a sound startled her. Carlisle whipped her head to the left, toward the noise. It must be that raccoon again trying to rummage through their trash. She still went to her gun; it could also be a damn big-ass papa black bear. She listened again for the sound and heard a strange knocking noise. Carlisle crumpled her face, part aggravation, part confusion.

With a two-handed grip on her gun, she moved toward the noise. This time the sound came from her right. Something wasn't right. Squinting her eyes against the dark, Carlisle lifted her gun and extended it out in front of her.

"Who's out there?" she called out. There was no answer.

She moved from the other side of the porch now. Fuck it. Carlisle was going to go inside, bolt down the door and hunker down like Tucker had told her to do. Just as she reached for the doorknob, she heard the loud screams of the teakettle inside the house. She jumped, nearly peeing on herself.

Fuck Elaina and her gotdamn late-night tea sessions.

Carlisle grabbed hold of the doorknob, ready to cuss Elaina out, when she saw something out of her peripheral vision. A scream lodged in the back of her throat as the shadowy figure placed a gloved hand over her nose and mouth and kicked her legs from under her. Her gun dropped with a clang. Her body went limp.

Unfortunately, with the teakettle whistling loudly on the stove, Elaina never heard the commotion. Nor did she hear the stranger's footsteps enter the cabin.

Tuck sat outside of the Monte Carlo, drumming his fingers on his steering wheel. He checked his watch again and let out a long sigh. Candice had told him to meet her there, but she was nowhere to be found. Tuck went back out to his car and waited.

Candy had to know he would come. They'd shared a night together; they had a deep connection, or so he thought. In his mind's eye he could still see the silhouette of her flat stomach, round hips and athletic legs. He remembered the tightness of her holding him captive; the possessiveness he had felt toward her when he realized no other man had touched her in such a way.

Suddenly Tuck shuddered as he thought about that night. It had been a mistake. He realized that now. He was an adult—a married man, the father of two children. Candy had been an eighteen-year-old virgin girl on a revenge mission. He had been seduced by her brains and body, but there was no real basis to their relationship. Candy was a fleeting fancy; his wife, on the other hand, was the real deal.

Tuck looked at his watch again and swore that if she didn't show up soon, he would leave. She had already stood him up yesterday, but today he felt like he'd be able to catch her unaware. So like a crackhead who needed one last hit, he waited.

Tuck practiced what he would say to her when she arrived. "I don't want anything from you. I don't even want to try to stop you from killing your enemies. I just want to give you these." That's what he'd say; then he'd hand over Easy's files for her safekeeping.

Tuck knew that getting Candice to trust him was a long shot, but he would still make the effort. Regardless of a one-night stand or not, Candice had serious trust issues. He told himself he was there for one thing, and one thing only: to give her the files so she would have insight into her father's life. He owed her that much at least.

But that wasn't entirely the whole truth, though. Candy did have good reason to suspect Tuck of ulterior motives.

At the end of his meeting with Stokes, Tuck had promised to hand Candy over to him to ensure the safety of his family and himself. He'd convinced Stokes that sending in a tail or setting a trap wouldn't work with someone like Candy.

"Trust me. Let me get her on my side and then I'll bring her right to you," Tuck had assured.

Being in the business of subterfuge, Stokes was highly skeptical of Tucker's plan. Tucker reminded him that if they knew
where Candy was all along, they could have easily picked her
up a long time ago. But the problem was that Candy could
change colors quicker than a chameleon.

"Remember, you thought you were God . . . but Rock Barton
and Candy Hardaway might be the bane of your existence. She
trusts me already," Tuck had argued.

Stokes had finally given in to his demands. He had few
options to begin with.

"She trusts you, Agent Tucker . . . but can I trust you?"
Stokes asked doubtfully.

Tucker never answered his question. Instead, he took the
additional Hardaway files and exited the room. It was all
a guessing game, anyway; no one really knew the other's
intentions.

But actions always spoke louder than words.

Candice silently watched Tuck from a distance. What was
she even doing here?

Tuck had promised her information about her father, but
he could have also been setting her up. Her heart was at war
with her mind. She didn't really trust anyone from her past.
The only people whom she trusted implicitly were dead.

Lately she could not stop thinking about that night. She
could almost feel the same hot rush that had suffused her
body when she had accepted him into her mouth, their
tongues intertwining in a sensual dance.

Candice closed her eyes for a split second, picturing him
as he moved his hot mouth from her lips and licked his way
down her neck and then to her breasts.

She still couldn't, she'd lost her virginity that night. And
now she couldn't stop thinking about it.

Candice wanted to slap herself when she realized she had let
her mind drift to the past. Shaking her head from left to right,
she rubbed her arms roughly and shook off those distracting
thoughts.

The first day Tuck had come to the Monte Carlo, Candice
watched him, amused at his bewilderment. Did he really think
she would be dumb enough to meet up with him in such a

public place? She watched Tuck get frustrated at being stood up, getting in and out of his car repeatedly with the look of defeat on his face. When he left, Candice watched closely for any tails or any sign that he had brought his crooked law enforcement friends with him. To her surprise, Candice had not noticed anyone following or watching him. No red taillights, no ghosts on foot and no other people materializing from the surrounding buildings when he'd left.

Still not convinced of his claims of innocence, Candice decided to watch Tuck for one more day. Shit, if he could be undercover for so long, pretending to be a common street dude, there was no telling what type of stunt he was capable of pulling off. Candice figured there was no such thing as being too careful. So she watched for a second day. And again there was no one mysteriously buzzing around. He hadn't met with anyone; he hadn't spoken to anybody on the street.

Perhaps Tuck was on the up-and-up, Candice concluded. Seeing him again that day, at the DeSosa home, had flustered her so much that it had almost taken her out of her game. She wanted to be sure she could handle things emotionally before she showed herself to him again.

When Tuck's car gurgled to life, she rushed from her hiding spot across the street from the Monte Carlo. She couldn't be sure he'd come back for a third day looking like a desperate asshole waiting for her. He didn't even see her coming.

The taps on the window nearly gave Tuck a heart attack. He jumped so hard that he hit his bald head on the roof of his car.

"Gotdamn!" he cried out, placing his hand over his chest in a clutch-the-pearls manner.

Candice ran around the front of the car and Tuck popped the door locks. Candice bustled into the passenger seat and hurriedly slammed the door. She shivered. Her nerves were screaming.

"You scared the shit out of me, Candy," Tuck gasped. He was still struggling to find his breath.

She wasn't the only one with hair trigger nerves. The fact that he seemed jumpy too made her feel superior in a silly, childish kind of way.

"Big, bad DEA agent scared of little ol' me." She chuckled sarcastically. Then her face got serious, and her lips twisted to the side. Tuck gave her a look that said *touché*. She'd scored a point for that one.

"Now, Agent Tuck, or whatever your name is, why do you want to see me so badly?" she asked. The undertone of her question was one part sassy, one part curious.

"Look, Candy, there are a lot of people looking for you right now. I am trying—"

"I don't give a fuck who is looking for me! I am looking for them too!" Candice boomed defensively, clipping off his conversation.

"Whoa, whoa . . . I'm here to help you, Candy. Everybody in the world is *not* out to hurt you."

Candy's vehemence had caught him completely off guard.

"Oh yeah? Says who? You? A fuckin' DEA agent who lies for a living? What the fuck do you know about who is trying to hurt me? Did you lose your entire family at the hands of these motherfuckers for absolutely nothing? Because they wanted to play government war games with the lives of innocent kids?" Candy screamed.

The incredible hurt was evident behind her words. Tuck was dumbfounded.

"I'm sorry about your loss, Candy. Trust me, this is not easy for me either. I know all about being betrayed by the government . . . and I was very fuckin' loyal to them. But I need to let you know there are people after you. You should've listened to Barton and gotten far away from here. Forget avenging your family's deaths. Getting away with your life is much more important," he retorted in all honesty.

"This was a mistake," she said, starting for the door handle. Her Glock dug into her side as she turned to make her escape.

"Wait!" he grabbed her arm.

"Don't ever put your hands on me again!" she shot back; her gun was in her hand just as quickly.

Tuck snatched his hand back like he'd just been stung by a bee. They were back to square one.

"Candy, I just want to help you. I swear. I put my entire family in danger just to help you. Let me," he pleaded.

Something about the pleading in his voice made her insides hot. Candice was angry with herself; she felt tears burning at the backs of her eyes. She was too fucking emotional these days.

"What did you really call me here for?" she asked, her voice cracking.

"I wanted to give you these," Tuck told her, reaching behind him into his backseat. He pulled up a thick packet. She furrowed her forehead at the stack of papers.

"Everything you need to know is right in here. Candy, your father was in a lot of shit. I want to warn you, some of this shit is very deep. Deeper than anything Barton could've even imagined," Tuck said in a foreboding tone.

Candice accepted the package, but she hesitated to look inside. She didn't want to learn anything about her father that would change her last view of him. In her eyes he was, and always would be, a stand-up family man who commanded respect and loved her more than anything in the world.

"Where did you get this, if you weren't working with them?" Candice asked, squinting her eyes.

"Let's just say I have friends in high places," Tuck replied.

"Yeah, that's just what I was afraid of. Thanks," she said in a low whisper.

Tuck nodded.

Before she left the car, Candice gave Tuck her cell phone number, though she didn't plan on having it for much longer. She knew all about the government's GPS tracking technology.

Tuck watched her disappear into the night. Now all he needed to do was get in touch with Carlisle and get his family the fuck out of Dodge.

Candice opened the notebooks as soon as she was alone. The curiosity was burning her up inside. She would read through her father's stories, but she wouldn't let it change her mind about what she had to do. There was still one more mission to carry out before she went ghost, once and for all.

"My Life," she read aloud, already captivated.

***

Hardaway Household, 2006

Easy walked into his bedroom and found his wife sitting on the side of the bed. She had obviously heard him arguing on the telephone. The vibe in the entire house was tense, to say the least. Easy glanced at Corine and knew that this conversation would not go over well.

Corine sat stiffly upright, her body language completely closed off to him. Deep worry etched extra lines around her eyes and mouth; she seemed to have aged lately. When Corine wasn't angry with him, she was detached and aloof in her interactions with Easy. This shit was harder than he thought it could ever be.

Getting out of the business was much harder than getting in.

"Corine, we need to talk," Easy told her. His voice was heavy with resignation.

She shuddered a little bit and looked down at her nails, anything to distract her mind. She knew they would be having this conversation sooner or later. Corine had expressed her dislike and distrust of the Dominicans on numerous occasions. Easy never listened to her; he always brushed off her concerns.

Easy sat down on his side of the bed; she stayed on her side; neither looked at the other.

"Listen, I want you to hear me out before you react crazy," Easy warned. He knew how hotheaded his wife could be at times.

She cleared her throat. Corine was ready for him; she had been preparing what she would say ever since she'd overheard his phone conversation with his regular confidant.

Easy continued talking. "We might have to leave Brooklyn, Corine. I think it's going to be best for us and for the kids to just take what we got and get far away from here. I'll find a new hustle," Easy announced gravely.

Her eyes went wide. She didn't even understand her shock. She should have felt relieved that he was getting out of the game. But uprooting the kids? Taking apart their lives? All of the sacrifices she'd made to build this life with him would be for nothing. Her insides grew hot.

"I told the Dominicans I wanted out. They ain't happy about this shit, Corine. It might mean war," Easy said, pinching the bridge of his nose. "I know I promised you that things would always be all right. I know you never wanted me to get down with them, but you have to trust me. I did all of this for us," he said, almost whispering.

It was always about Easy, never about Corine or the kids. He made all of the decisions—Corine and the kids were always an afterthought. His arrogance, even when trying to be humble, sent her over the top. Corine was on her feet like a demon had taken possession of her body and mind.

"I hate you! It was all for nothing! I hate you! You're a selfish piece of shit! I should have never married you, just like my daddy said!" she screamed.

Easy whirled around so fast—he almost gave himself whiplash. Her words hurt him deeper than a knife wound. Her reaction shook him to his core and totally caught him off guard. "Corine, I'm sorry." What else could he say to make up for the years of suffering she had experienced because of his poor life choices?

"You have no idea how you've ruined our lives! What about the sacrifices I've made? Huh? What about me—your wife? What real sacrifices have you made for this family, Eric? All you've ever cared about is making money!" Her caramel face turned almost burgundy with anger.

Easy worked his jaw. What the fuck was wrong with this woman? He could feel heat rising from his feet and climbing up. He put his hands out in a conciliatory fashion, trying to level with her.

"We've both made sacrifices, Corine. I have worked my ass off to give you this life. So you wouldn't have to work or do shit but sit around, shop and look fuckin' pretty!" Easy retorted.

The words hit her like a cold slap in the face.

He immediately regretted the words after they'd left his lips. His wife's face crumpled and her eyes turned dark, like a storm was brewing inside.

Corine doubled over at the waist, her body quaking with emotion.

"*Yeah, all I ever did was fuck you, stay barefoot and pregnant, and spend your money, right, Eric? That's all I ever did for you, right? I should be kissing your feet with appreciation, huh? Fuck you, Easy Hardaway! You don't know what I've done for you—you have no fucking idea!*" Corine erupted, propelled by her rage.

Easy was pissed now too. He was under enough stress without these dramatic outbursts from his wife.

"*Did you ever think about me? How I walked away from my own family to be with you? How I lost myself to this lifestyle? What about my sacrifices!*" Corine was screeching like a fishwife.

"*Corine, I don't have time for this shit right now. I have shit to handle that you know nothing about,*" he grumbled.

Corine shoved an accusatory finger into his chest.

"*Your little sacrifices don't mean shit in the scheme of things, Corine. And don't make your father into some kind of saint. He was a fuckin' crooked-ass cop who thought you were a prize to be won. Your mother always hated you, jealous of your relationship with your own father, so fuck your sacrifices. You don't even understand the meaning of the word,*" Easy boomed cruelly.

Corine had pushed him into a corner, and the only thing he could do was attack. In a knee-jerk reaction to his vituperative words, Corine reached out and slapped him across the face with all of her might. She'd hit him so hard that the palm of her hand stung. Corine didn't know what had come over her, but it felt good to get her aggression out. She lifted her hand to slap him again, but her fingers curled involuntarily into a fist. She flew at him like an avenging angel.

"*I hate you!*" she growled, going wild on him.

Instinctively, Easy grabbed her wrists in defense. He held them tightly until he felt the tenseness leave her body.

"*C'mon, we not gonna do this,*" he whispered. The last thing they needed to do was turn against one another.

Corine's knees suddenly buckled and she collapsed to the floor. She didn't have the fight in her anymore. She felt drained. She sobbed like a woman burying her dead baby.

Easy had no idea she would react to his news so violently. He got down on the floor with his wife, but she was beyond consoling.

"Corine, I'm sorry. It's going to be okay. I promise, just like from day one, I'm going to make it all okay," Easy lied. He didn't know how things would turn out. The truth was, he was scared to death for himself, for her and for their kids.

"No! It won't! They told me they wanted to get back at you! They said you were talking to the cops!" Corine wailed.

Easy's face folded into a frown. He looked at her like she'd lost her mind. What the hell was she talking about?

"Who? What? What are you talking about, Corine?" he asked incredulously.

"I didn't want to tell you! They wanted to hurt you. I didn't want to tell you," she rambled incoherently. Her voice was a shrill cacophony of pain. She rubbed her arms up and down, as if she had goose bumps.

"Tell me what?" Easy's voice boomed as he shook her shoulders. "What are you talking about?" he asked frantically.

"They—they hurt me, Eric. They violated me. They wanted to get back at you. They took turns hurting me!" Corine screeched, rolling around in pain.

The entire scene smacked of melodrama; Easy felt like he had been thrown into a bad soap opera. His ears began ringing. The room began to spin around him. He jumped up like his wife was a contagious disease. How could she have hidden something like this from him? She clearly didn't trust him enough to share the information with him.

"Eric . . . please!" she cried out, stretching out her hand for him. She knew this would be his reaction. She knew he wouldn't be able to handle it. "Please!" she begged again.

Easy began stalking the room like a caged animal overdue for a feeding.

"When?" he asked harshly. His eyes were closed in agony. He hadn't stopped moving.

She didn't answer.

"When did it happen, gotdamn it?" he boomed.

Corine jumped. Her body trembled with trepidation.

"*The day I had you pick me up from the hospital, when I told you someone had snatched my purse and made me fall. Remember my supposed mugging? My black eye and busted lip? I concocted that whole story. I didn't want you to find out the truth.*"

Easy furiously stalked over to the dresser and swiped everything onto the floor. He was panting and growling now. He felt like someone was choking the very air out of his body. He wanted to throw up. Corine cried out even louder.

"*Tell me everything!*" Easy barked. His palms were splayed flat on the emptied dresser top; his head was slung low between his shoulders.

"*Don't make me, Eric. Please.*" She regretted that she'd ever gotten so emotional that she had broken her silence. She never wanted him to experience this sort of betrayal and hurt.

"*Tell me now!*" he barked, slamming his hands down on the dresser.

Corine closed her eyes and hugged herself. She opened her mouth and told Easy the whole truth. She recalled how she had left Macy's and had headed to her car, happy as a lark because she had just picked up two nice shirts for him. Corine loved nothing more than to surprise Easy with gifts, since he was always giving her beautiful tokens. When she got to her car, she placed her purse on top of the trunk and fished around in her pocketbook for her car keys.

While she was distracted with this task, a Hispanic man materialized out of nowhere. So did a van. She should've noticed when the van pulled too close to her car. When the man approached her, she felt a chill as his black eyes gazed at her a bit too long. A chill went up her spine. The man spoke in Spanish to her and appeared to be asking for her help. He was pointing to a car a few spots back.

Corine looked at him, confused. She couldn't understand anything he was saying. She was about to tell him she couldn't speak Spanish; but before she could get the words out, she felt a rush of wind behind her and felt a pointed pressure in her back.

She stumbled forward and the Hispanic man grabbed her. Another man had bum rushed her from behind. Within seconds, the two men, working together, had thrown her in that black van. She fought them off at first, scratching at skin, kicking, spitting and biting when she could.

All of her efforts were in vain. A black blindfold was securely tied over her eyes. She opened her mouth wide to scream and she smelled something strong. Not quite like alcohol, but more like hospital disinfectant. It burned her nostrils. Her brain felt blank and then her world went black.

When Corine regained consciousness, she cracked her eyes open but could only see little slivers of light through the blindfold. Her neck throbbed as she tried to move her head. She finally became aware of her entire body and the pain that permeated it. She moaned out loud. She felt a burning sensation between her legs and severe cramps in her abdomen. The pain was almost unbearable, but at least she wasn't dead. She tried again to lift her head, but she felt a pair of strong hands bearing down on her chest, forcing her back down.

Deep-voiced cackles sent chills down her aching spine. She squinted through the black material trying to make out shapes and faces, but it was nearly impossible. The shadows moved in front of her. This time she tried to move her arms, but they wouldn't budge; they had obviously tied them down. There was more Spanish being spoken. Foreign words filtered into her ringing ears. She felt hands on her legs. She jumped to kick the offending hands away, but they pulled her legs apart like a wishbone. She tried to scream, but the material from the gag cut into the corners of her mouth.

She might not be able to see them, but she could smell them clearly. A mixture of sweat, alcohol and hair grease assailed her nose. She wanted to vomit. She gagged but somehow managed to control her stomach. If she didn't get a hold on herself, she would choke on her own vomit and die. And then her children would be without a mother, and her husband without a wife.

She tried to scream as a man straddled her broken body. A hard slap to the face shut her up real quick. She knew one of them had gotten between her stretched legs. She prayed that

God would watch over her children, for surely she would die today in the most humiliating fashion. Pain rocked through her abdomen like an earthquake as she felt him pounding into her body. Her vagina was raw with burning. She bit down into the gag as tears leaked from the corners of her eyes.

One after the other, they each took their turns with her. They performed sordid acts, violating her in the most sickening ways. After an eternity the violence on her body came to an end. By then, Corine had wrapped herself in a cocoon of disbelief and denial. Oddly enough, she thought of her father and how much she missed him.

In broken English a new voice cautioned, "Not too much'a bruises."

Why this man was saving her from bruises, when the men clearly planned to kill her, was beyond her understanding. The man called an end to their sick little party; for that, she was grateful. His voice was raspy, and his cologne smelled familiar, but she couldn't place the fragrance.

"Tell your husband what we did to you. Tell him, we know he is talking to the police and he'd better stop. Tell him, we said there's only one way out," the older gentleman had whispered, close to her face. She tried to turn her head toward him, but they pushed her face away.

Her attackers had been instructed to clean her up and drop her off back at her car.

When Corine was deposited back in the parking garage, she tried to make out their faces. But this time they were smart enough to wear disguises. Corine didn't know whether to start screaming for help or thank them for not killing her. Her head was all messed up.

When she put the key in the ignition, she didn't know what to do or where to go. Every car that drove by made her jump. She'd sat there for almost an hour, crying off and on. Her body ached so bad; she didn't think she could grip her steering wheel.

Corine wanted to call somebody, but they hadn't returned her pocketbook or her cell phone—she was given just a lone car key.

She couldn't ask for help from strangers. She didn't trust anyone right now. Worst of all, she didn't know how she could possibly tell Easy about what had happened to her during these last few hours. The news would devastate her husband, giving her attackers twice the satisfaction.

Corine decided she would take her lumps on this one. She would be strong and come up with a plausible story to explain the bruises that were already darkening her face.

She planned to put the trauma behind her and move forward with her life. She would hold her head up high and never let those bastards see her falling apart. Corine knew the risks she'd accepted when she agreed to become a hustler's wife. She knew that one day she would have to make the ultimate sacrifice; today, unfortunately, was that day.

Corine pulled her car over to the side of the road about five times before she arrived at the hospital. She stumbled into the emergency room and requested a female doctor. Corine was examined by the doctor. The doctor immediately ordered a rape kit and told Corine she'd have to wait for the results of the STD tests. That had unnerved Corine. She hadn't even considered the consequences of her rape. Aside from the STD, the men could have impregnated her as well. Her womb shuddered in revulsion. She snatched the Plan B pill from the doctor and swallowed it in a single gulp.

"Please . . . you can't tell my husband about this. You can't mention it around him," Corine pleaded, holding on tightly to the white lab coat.

The doctor looked at her like she had lost her mind.

"He won't ever look at me the same. I couldn't handle that on top of this," Corine half lied.

The doctor consented to her wishes, although very reluctantly. She recommended that if Corine was not going to share the truth with her husband that she at least join a support group for victims of rape. Corine agreed to give it careful consideration.

When Corine finally called Easy from the hospital, he sounded very close to near panic. He told her he had been worried sick about her and had about a hundred dudes scouring the streets looking for his wife.

Easy made it to Long Island College Hospital in record time. When he saw Corine's face, his anger erupted like Mount Vesuvius. He seemed to buy the robbery story; for that, Corine was deeply relieved.

Easy knew that a nigga in Brooklyn bold enough to touch his wife had to be on a suicide mission. He had to find the fuckers responsible for robbing his wife. He had his workers all over the streets, fanned out looking for a ghost. After a while the manhunt died down.

Easy remained calm but cautious. Corine was practically under house arrest for the next two months after the incident occurred. She had new locks put on the house, and a more enhanced security system installed. She was paranoid that the men who had hurt her would return. Corine fought through her nightmares and continued to put on a brave face in front of her husband and children.

Corine didn't know what had finally compelled her to tell Easy the truth about the events that had transpired so long ago. Perhaps he had pushed her too far by his selfish claims or by his dismissive attitude about the sacrifices she'd made for her family over the years.

Nonetheless, Corine was relieved to have cleared the air between herself and Easy. Lately they had been growing apart, and a large part of the distance was a result of the dark secrets they had kept from each other.

Easy felt like he had been in a twelve-round boxing match by the time Corine finished reliving her ordeal. Easy had collapsed on the floor with his wife and held her close to him, wishing he could squeeze all of the pain out of her. They had both cried together into the night.

Corine could not explain what had come over her, but the confession felt good for her soul, and good for their marriage. If they wanted to make their relationship work, they had to start trusting each other again.

The next morning Corine woke up and felt better than she had in a long time. She didn't want Eric's sympathy, just his love. She was going to keep it together for her family. What she had confessed would never leave the confines of their bedroom walls; Easy had promised her that much.

"*Brianna's birthday party still needs to be planned,*" *Corine announced in a rather husky tone. Her voice was still raw from all of the crying she had done the night before.*

Easy gazed at his wife in true amazement; he could not believe that his wife was thinking about throwing a birthday party after all she had been through. She was truly a treasure above all treasures. He walked over to his wife and held her closely.

"*I love you, baby. Have I told you that lately?*" *Eric said in a husky tone.*

"*No, you haven't, but I won't hold it against you. I'm done with holding grudges, especially against my own husband,*" *Corine teased.*

Eric rewarded her with a passionate kiss that nearly stole her breath away.

"*Promise me that whatever you do to get revenge, you'll wait until after Brianna has her party. I know we may have to leave Brooklyn, but we need to make life as normal for our kids as possible,*" *she said calmly.*

Easy had been struck silent. He couldn't make that promise to his wife now.

"*You know me so well, baby,*" *Eric said. "I promise I won't do anything to ruin Brianna's party.*" *That was the best he could offer her right now.*

"*I want this party to be huge,*" *Corine said, too busy with party planning to pick up on the nuances of his promise.*

While Corine planned her big celebration, Easy planned his revenge. There was no way he could honor his wife's wishes on this one. He needed to see Rock right away.

Somebody needed to pay for what had happened to his wife. And he was pretty sure he knew exactly who that someone was.

Chapter 27

Justice

Tuck picked up his phone in a huff. He was so annoyed that he almost ran off the road.

"Carlisle, where the hell have you been? Where are Elaina and the kids?" he belted out before he could even stop to listen. He had been trying to reach her all night.

"You lied, Agent Tucker," a strange male voice filtered through the phone.

"Who is this?" Tuck yelled. His voice surged up a few octaves. He was all over the road again. "Shit!" he cursed as he nearly sideswiped an SUV.

"Who is this?" he screamed as he threw on his hazards and pulled his car over. He looked at his phone screen one more time, just to make sure he had seen it right. CARLISLE, the screen flashed. He was right; it had been her phone that had called him.

"We had a deal, Agent Tucker, but you lied. Did you think we wouldn't be watching you? You said you would bring her to us, but then your lovesick, pussy-whipped ass just let her go."

Tuck shut his eyes tightly. Regret filled up inside him. He clenched his fists.

"Stokes! Where is Carlisle?" Tuck was out of the car, pacing now. Cars whizzed past him. He looked like a stranded motorist, walking the side of the highway in the rain.

There was laughter on the other end of the phone. "You have the nerve to ask me questions," the voice said snidely.

"Answer me! Where the fuck is Carlisle? My kids?" Tuck asked, his voice cracking as he nearly lost his grip on his cell phone. He was soaking wet from the pounding rain. He didn't even care.

"I guess you didn't really want to protect your family, Agent Tucker," the man continued.

It wasn't Stokes. Tuck would've recognized Stokes's voice by now. This man was younger; his voice was stronger.

"Where is my family?" Tuck screeched, feeling like someone had punched him in the solar plexus.

"Daddy! Help us!" Tuck heard his baby girl shout in the background of the call.

"No!" he screamed, falling to his knees. He looked up into the angry sky and pleaded for mercy from above. Only divine intervention could save his family right now.

The throngs of news reporters and policemen lining the outside of the Ponce Funeral. They swarmed like angry bees, waiting to grill the former reputed drug kingpin, who was now burying two sons. The reports on the news had varied: Some said his sons had been killed as a result of an ongoing drug war with another borough; others said the crimes were revenge killings for DeSosa's past indiscretions. Police investigators were examining these incidents closely to see if the two murders were related. On the surface the MOs did not match at all.

Candy laughed at the circus that DeSosa was now forced to be a part of. She certainly enjoyed her role as the ringmaster.

The large crowd made the perfect cover and distraction. Candice made up her mind; she'd get in and out like the Grim Reaper. One fast sweep of blackness to finish the deed—the thought made her feel powerful, yet sad. What would she do when she no longer had revenge to fill her days?

Candice hadn't given that much thought to the future; she was still so consumed with the past and the present. She shook her head. No time to get fucking emotional right now.

Candice checked herself in the small driver's-side visor mirror one last time. An assassin in pink lip gloss; she had to giggle at that. The black wide brim hat, black oyster shell oval shades, black elbow-length gloves and nice fitted black sheath dress made her look very much the part of a high-class mourner. It was a look that suited her well.

Candice thought this funeral get-up might be her signature look. Going to these funerals was starting to give her a rise. She knew it was sick, but it was satisfying, all the same.

Candice picked up the oversized black purse, checked for her weapon of choice and stepped out of the rental car. Her heels clicking on the pavement sounded off like gunshots. She liked that too. *Power. Power. Power.*

Candice looked down the street at the burgeoning crowd. They had no idea that in a few more minutes they'd all be in harm's way; she planned to come at them with a fury. A no-holds-barred display. Her last hit. She checked her little timer.

Hmph, only a few minutes left.

If she had timed everything correctly, DeSosa, Cyndi and the kids would be arriving soon. Candice couldn't miss that now, could she?

As soon as she reached the funeral home entrance, she felt her damn cell phone ringing inside. Only one person had her cell phone number, and that was Tuck. She really wasn't in the mood to speak with him right now. The phone stopped ringing and started back up, almost immediately. She didn't need to draw any extra attention to herself right now. She fished the phone out of her bag and hit the ignore button. Nothing could interrupt this moment.

Candice hadn't even made it to the edge of the crowd when the phone started to vibrate. Fuck! This time she felt a thunderbolt of anger spark in her chest. Candice stopped midstride and whirled around angrily. She was going to pick up that fucking phone and curse out Tuck.

"What do you want?" Candice said gruffly, but low enough as not to attract any undue attention.

"Candy! I need you!" Tuck cried out in pain.

Candice was struck dumb for a second; her body went stiff. Was he really crying?

"Tuck?" she whispered. Her eyebrows folded down onto the bridge of her nose.

"They have my family! They're going to kill my family!" he screamed at the top of his lungs.

His words snatched away Candice's breath. She made a hic-cup noise and swallowed hard. A cold feeling shot through her body like somebody had pumped ice water into her veins. She gripped the phone tight and whirled around, her emotions on a collision course. She looked around wildly.

It was time.

Tuck was talking incoherently. He needed her to meet him right away. His family was in danger. His words were a confusing jumble in her ears.

Pandemonium broke out near the funeral home. Candice turned toward the commotion. Reporters started rushing in all directions; loud voices erupted from the crowd. Candice felt like someone had kicked her in the chest.

No! No! No!

Rolando DeSosa had arrived at his sons' funeral and Candice had missed her shot.

A bloodcurdling scream bounced off the walls of the long hotel hallway.

"Help! Help! Help!" the housekeeper screeched, running down the hall, her arms flailing.

Several nosy hotel patrons emerged from their rooms to investigate the noise. Within ten minutes the police were swarming the hotel.

The first uniformed officer to arrive on the scene had called in what he had observed: "Two DOAs, one white female, one black male, causes of death unknown. Both appear to have been dead for some time." Then he rushed into the bathroom and threw up. He knew he had probably contaminated something at the crime scene, but he couldn't help it. His stomach couldn't hold up to the smell of death that permeated the room.

When Candice prepared to turn onto the block of her hotel, she was stopped by a uniformed police officer. Confused, she rolled down her window like a dutiful citizen.

"Oh my goodness, Officer, what's going on?" She let her eyes dart to the police tape and all of the patrol cars and emergency service unit trucks that were parked haphazardly down the street.

"Ma'am, this street is blocked off. . . . Crime scene investigation is going on. You're going to have to come back later or use another route," the officer said perfunctorily.

"May I ask what happened?" She used her throatiest sex kitten voice. She could see the officer's face soften a bit. He looked like he knew better, but he was going to give the beautiful woman with the expensive sunglasses and voluptuous body the information, anyway.

"Two dead bodies in a hotel room is all I know," he answered, tapping the door of her car. Candice's surprise was genuine. She pushed her glasses back up to cover her wide-stretched eyes.

"I better get out of here then," she replied.

"Yes, ma'am, I'd say that's a good idea," the officer agreed.

She skidded away from the crime scene as quickly as possible. Her phone began to vibrate. Tuck was calling her again. "Shit!" she cursed under her breath. Her fucking nerves were really rattled now.

She reached over with one hand and snatched up the phone from the cup holder. He was supposed to meet her downtown, someplace crowded. BBQ's he had offered up as a meeting location. Candice had to change that now. She didn't have time to change her clothes or put on a new disguise. They'd have to come up with someplace that afforded a little more privacy.

"We need a different place to meet. Police are swarming all over my hotel. Your call," she announced. "Text me the address," she instructed before hanging up the call.

Candice busted a U-turn and headed in the opposite direction.

"Police are investigating the discovery of two dead bodies in a Brooklyn hotel room. A hotel housekeeper found the bodies when she went to clean the room earlier today. She reportedly told police, the person renting the room never asked for housekeeping services, and today was the first day the door was missing the Do Not Disturb sign," the anchorman stated.

"When the housekeeper went inside, she found the body of a black male, mid to late thirties, and that of a white female in her early thirties. A police source that has asked not to be identified reported that the woman was wearing some sort of federal law enforcement badge around her neck. Police are not releasing information about the person who rented the room, but they say they have a lead in the case. In other news, the double funeral for the sons of reputed drug kingpin Rolando DeSosa was held in Brooklyn today. DeSosa, who arrived under a shroud of security, is the reported ruthless operator of a drug business that brings tens of millions of dollars' worth of crack cocaine to the streets of New York and L.A. Both of DeSosa's sons were murdered in separate incidents just in the last week. Police would not comment on whether they believe the family was being targeted."

Tuck sat in his old booth at the back of the small hole-in-the-wall, pub-style greasy spoon restaurant.

He waited anxiously in the cramped booth for Candy to arrive.

Candy entered the small eatery and slid in across from him in a flurry. Candy looked beautiful, but he could see fear in her eyes.

Tuck looked tired. His eyes were still red-rimmed and puffy from crying. For some reason this did not make Tuck look weak in her eyes; a man who felt that passionate about saving his family was actually a trait worthy of admiration.

"Candy, you're the only person who can help me now. They've got my family, and they killed the DEA agent who tried to help me," Tuck confessed, his voice cracking again.

"Who are 'they,' Tuck?" Candice whispered.

Tuck hung his head. He knew if he confessed the truth, she might tell him to fuck off and then he'd be screwed.

"The CIA," he croaked out. He couldn't even look at her.

Candice curled her hands into fists. She leaned into the table. "Why the fuck does the CIA want to hurt your family, Tuck?" she whispered harshly. The wheels of her mind were already turning with ideas.

"Look, I made them believe I would help them find you so that they would leave my family alone. But I never had any intention of helping them. If I did, I would've led them to you yesterday when I gave you the file. I would've turned you over and walked away if I didn't care. I was trying to protect everyone involved, including you. You have to believe me, Candy." Tuck laid it all out there, not even taking a breath between his words. He didn't want to give her a chance to walk out on him.

Candice leaned back, feeling the busted-up leather of the booth digging into her shoulder. "You made a deal with the CIA, even after you knew what they did to my family?" Candice asked with all the condescension she could muster. How could he be *that* stupid?

"I told them to fuck off until they shot at my wife and kids," Tuck confessed. The words "wife and kids" rang in Candice's ear like a shrill alarm. She swallowed hard. Her sexual fantasies involving Tuck evaporated into thin air.

Fuckin' bastard.

"So you were going to hand me over to them until you realized you needed me more than they did? Fuck you, Tuck," Candice said as she moved to scoot out of the booth.

Tuck was out of his seat in a flash. He grabbed her arm. Candice whirled on him so fast—he didn't even have time to react. Her gun pressed into his chest bone.

"Fuckin' dare me," she taunted.

Tuck lifted his hands. He could see some of the patrons looking at them uneasily; though Candice was pretty careful not to brandish her weapon quite as openly.

"C'mon, Candy. You're not going to shoot me in the back of a fuckin' greasy spoon with eyewitnesses. Rock taught you better than that. Hear me out. I'm on your side. Right now, I bet those two dead bodies were found in your hotel room, which means, even if you used a fake name, the surveillance cameras will pick you up in that same outfit. There are cops fanned out all over the city looking for you right now," Tuck pleaded his case.

Candice inhaled and exhaled. She lowered her gun back under her hat, where she had hidden it on the seat next to her when she arrived.

"Sit down and let me tell you what I know. We have to work together. We can save my family, give you the man you really want to get, and then we all can get the fuck out of here." Tuck was trying to get her cooperation. He took her silence to mean consent.

"First things first—do you ever remember seeing anything in Barton's house containing the name Grayson Stokes? Anything?" Tuck asked seriously.

Candice had studied many things that she'd stolen from Uncle Rock's safe, but she couldn't be too sure.

"I—I . . . can't," she started.

Tuck leaned in; there was a look of panic on his face. "Please, Candy . . . you have to think. Please! My kids will be dead if we wait too long," he said solemnly. Tears were rimming his eyes. Candice looked across the table and bugged out as she saw the face of her father staring back at her. She had to shake off the hallucination. Tuck's passion about his kids reminded her so much of her father.

"I remember. I do remember that Uncle Rock had been studying Stokes as one of his marks," Candice confessed in a near whisper.

Tuck leaned back and clapped his hands together. Now they were getting somewhere.

"That man was one of the people who had tortured Uncle Rock when he was in the military back in the day. I read his stuff. . . . Uncle Rock wanted to kill Stokes, but something had him afraid," Candice told Tuck. "I have all of the information. It's a good fuckin' thing I never kept all my shit in that hotel room," Candice announced, digging her safe-deposit box key from her purse.

"Let's go, Candy! He has my family!" Tuck exclaimed, hopelessly optimistic. He wanted to hug and kiss her, but that could wait until after he found his wife and children. One thing Stokes had gotten right was that Candy was a force to be reckoned with. Candice and Tuck both shot up from the booth, ready for action. The greasy spoon owner had just started over to their table with Tuck's usual dish in hand. Tuck also noticed the man held Brubaker's favorite in his other hand.

"Not today. I can't stay." Tuck put his hand up, halting the man's ungainly stride. The man looked confused and crushed. "But here . . . remember what we talked about." Tuck dug into his pocket and placed a wad of cash in the man's dirty apron pocket. The money would more than cover the cost of the food and ensure the owner's silence when it came to other matters.

Cyndi DeSosa walked the long hallway that separated her and Arellio's wing of the home from her father-in-law's living quarters. Her heels clacked against the marble floors and she wrapped her arms around her body, fighting off the chills. Her face was still swollen from her ordeal; no amount of makeup could hide the fact that she was still grieving.

Cyndi hadn't even processed the heinous acts that had been carried out on her brother-in-law before she witnessed her own husband's death. It had all happened so fast. Cyndi didn't think she would ever get over the fact that her husband was standing in front of her one minute, and then dead the next. His brains had spewed out the front of his head and splattered onto her face, neck and clothing.

Cyndi had screamed until her throat was raw and bleeding. It had taken her two days of scrubbing her skin raw until she no longer saw or smelled his blood on her skin.

Cyndi was a shell of a person now. She felt cold down to her bones; and each time she closed her eyes, she replayed the scene in her mind like a movie. Cyndi took a daily cocktail of Valium, Zoloft and Ambien to try to stay sane, but she barely got an hour of sleep if she was lucky. She couldn't stand to be inside her house. Her husband had died in their living room; the room had been roped off like a quarantine area. No one was allowed in or out. Her house felt like a mausoleum.

Her bedroom reminded her that she was now a widow. Although she knew her husband was dead, she couldn't bear to pack away his belongings. Cyndi slept in the kids' room. She was always crying; and when she wasn't upset, it was only because she was so high from the drugs she took.

Little Rolando kept asking for his daddy. Each time he did, Cyndi would run to the bathroom to cry until she threw up.

The baby was too young to understand; but each time Cyndi thought about her daughter growing up without a father, it made her double over in pain.

Cyndi arrived at DeSosa's quarters and folded her arms across her ample breasts. She cracked a halfhearted smile at DeSosa's guard, who stood in front of his bedroom door. The guard nodded in return, looking at her strangely.

"Is he okay?" she rasped, widening her red-rimmed eyes to look up at the hulk of a man. The man answered her in Spanish, stating he hadn't seen DeSosa all day.

"I'm going in to check on him. This is hard for all of us," Cyndi said softly; her throat was raw from all of the crying and screaming. The guard didn't dare resist her request for entrance. He stepped aside and opened the door for her.

Although DeSosa had said no visitors, he hadn't specified if his live-in daughter-in-law was considered a "visitor."

Cyndi stepped inside the darkened room and chills rushed over her body. There were three men inside. They were all sitting around a small table huddled together, whispering. The lights were dim and it was obvious Rolando had already gotten into bed.

Cyndi approached the men. *"Hola,"* she whispered.

They all looked at her in surprise.

"I want to have some time alone with him. Please give us a few minutes," she whispered.

The men looked at her and then at each other. No one was ready to say no to a grieving widow.

Cyndi immediately read their hesitation. "I just buried my fuckin' husband, and he just buried both of his sons. We are all we have left. . . . Surely, you fuckin' understand. Now get the fuck out," she commanded with all of the authority she could muster.

Stunned, the men scrambled up from their card game and hustled out of the room.

Cyndi watched and waited until she was alone with DeSosa. She walked to the back of the suite and pulled DeSosa's wheelchair away from his bedside. She tiptoed over to where he lay and watched him closely for a few minutes.

He was sleeping peacefully, probably because he'd been given a sedative cocktail to help him rest. Cyndi watched his slow breathing for a few minutes. She could definitely see her husband's face in her father-in-law's. Tears welled up in her eyes. She cupped her hand over her mouth to muffle her whimpers.

She couldn't understand how one man could cause so much death and destruction. Yes, she knew he sold drugs, but she had never wanted to admit until lately just how deep her father-in-law played in the drug game.

When she'd called Dulce's cell phone to tell her that she was going to call the cops on her, Dulce had told her everything. Cyndi didn't believe it at first, but how would Dulce know such details about her family if she were concocting a story out of the blue?

Cyndi never had a chance to tell Arellio what she'd learned about his father. As far as Cyndi was concerned, Rolando DeSosa was scum of the earth. He was responsible for her husband's death too; there was no doubt in Cyndi's mind about that. She swallowed the golf ball–sized lump in the back of her throat and approached his sleeping form.

"*Papi* DeSosa," she whispered, shaking his arm softly with one of her trembling hands.

DeSosa lay stock-still.

"*Papi*," she said a bit louder, shaking him a bit more vigorously.

He let out a long sigh. At least she knew he was still breathing.

"*Papi* DeSosa," she called, moving her face lower, within his line of vision.

He finally stirred. His medication-dilated pupils rolled open; his eyelids slowly inched upward as if they were lead heavy. Cyndi felt a flash of relief.

"Are you awake now?" she asked, tapping his arm. He grunted. She could tell he was fighting against the drugs to wake up. She tapped him a few more times. He grunted again, but this time his eyes came all the way open.

"Cyndi?" DeSosa croaked out. His voice sounded like sandpaper against a wall. "Cyndi, is that you?" he asked, lifting his head slightly to look at her. He looked so weak, so feeble now. Cyndi had a hard time keeping the image of him as a cold-blooded murderer in her mind's eye.

"Yes, it's me," she said. Her voice cracked, and her eyes filled with tears. She watched him through blurry eyes, tilting her head to the side as if she were a child asking for a favor.

"What is it?" he asked. His eyes and brain were fully alert now. He reached out to touch her hand.

Cyndi snatched her hand back. She folded her arms across her chest. She didn't want his evil to rub off on her.

"What's the matter, Cyndi?" DeSosa asked more urgently this time.

"Why? Why? Why'd you do it?" she cried. Her shoulders shuddered as she was overcome with pain. "How could you? How . . ." she wailed now, beyond words.

"What, Cyndi? What is it?" DeSosa asked, with raised eyebrows. He was growing worried about her. He looked down to the foot of his large bed. Then his eyes darted across the suite; he quickly noticed that his security detail was missing. He looked back at his daughter-in-law, and an uneasy feeling came over him. "Where is everybody, Cyndi?" he rasped.

"Was it worth it—losing your sons? How can you live with yourself?" Cyndi's voice was as hard and as sharp as steel.

DeSosa didn't have to ask her what she was talking about; she had discovered the sort of monster he'd become and was horrified to be living under the same roof. He didn't blame her. Tears ran out of the corners of his eyes. He was powerless. He couldn't even get himself out of bed. His head flopped back down on the pillow, defeated.

"You ruined a lot of lives! You killed women and children! You dragged your children into this! They only wanted to make you proud, so they joined you. They wanted to be like you! What kind of man are you?" Her voice was accusing. Her sobs changed to pure anger. "My kids don't have a father! I don't have a husband! All because of your selfish, evil ass!" she boomed through tears.

DeSosa didn't respond. He had made a lot of mistakes in his life and was paying for them now.

"Answer me!" Cyndi demanded. "Answer me, you fuckin' devil!" She could hear the security men at the door, trying to get inside. Cyndi's hand shook as she dug into her shirtfront. She pulled the small .22-caliber Smith & Wesson revolver from between her breasts and leveled it at her father-in-law. "You ruined too many lives. You ruined my life! You have to pay for your sins!" she belted out.

She could hear the footsteps rushing toward her. It was too late. With a rush of panic engulfing her, Cyndi fired off two shots.

DeSosa's eyes stared blankly at the ceiling. Her point-blank shots left two great gaping holes in his forehead.

DeSosa's security detail stormed the room and sounded off four shots. Cyndi's body dropped to the floor like a deflated balloon.

The men had arrived too late; their employer was dead and now so was his killer daughter-in-law.

Chapter 28

Day of Reckoning

Candice and Tuck both looked surprised when they arrived at their destination. The ranch-style 1960s-era house, located off a dirt road, and in the middle of a damn near forest, was not the place that one would expect the head honcho of the CIA to call home.

Candice peered out the car window. Tuck ducked his head and did the same.

"You sure you got this right?" Tuck asked doubtfully.

"Yeah," she mumbled, equally astonished.

"I guess that's why you should never judge a book by its position in the government, huh?" Tuck said lamely.

"Yeah, I was thinking it would be a mini-mansion for Stokes. Instead, we're looking at something one step above a fuckin' trailer home."

"Hey, it's your intel . . . not mine," Tuck clarified.

They went over their plan one more time. Tuck was shocked to learn that Candice knew so many techniques—slicing the pie, stacking up, fatal funnel and so on. In fact, she had ended up schooling him on a few techniques he'd never even learned in his numerous training classes.

"Remember, our main goal is to get him to say where my family is, and then he's all yours," Tuck told her.

Candice exhaled. Her gut was jumping and her heart was pounding. "You ready?" she asked Tuck.

"As ready as I'm ever gonna be," he responded.

She went for her door handle. He stopped her by placing his hand on her arm.

"Candy, no matter what happens in here, just know I was always on the side of good," Tuck said in all seriousness. His words sounded like parting words.

She cringed and mentally scolded herself for still having those feelings. "Same here. It was always just about justice for my family," she offered in return.

They exited the car at the same time.

"Down," Tuck whispered harshly. Her head was too high. He could see the black-clad men from Stokes's detail roving inside.

The simple ranch-style house had a very nondescript exterior. The grass was brown and looked like hay. What was left of the shrubbery barely resembled greenery at all. There were two small trees on either side of the front door, which surprised Tuck. As a spook he expected Stokes to know that those trees made for a great hiding spot for enemies lying in wait for an ambush.

Candice took her place behind the tree at the left of the door, and Tuck went to the one on the right. Candice popped her head up and peeked in the window. The blinds were drawn, but she could see through the small slits. There was only one man in black in the front foyer of the house. He was drinking a Coke, taking a break. Perfect.

Candice signaled to Tuck to move forward. He reached his long arm out and banged on the door. They both took cover behind their respective trees. Candice saw the man inside put the Coke down on the table. She lifted her hand up to tell Tuck that the man was coming.

Tuck stood upright, still out of sight. When the man pulled back the door, Tuck went into action. He put his gun to the man's head from the side. Candice did the same from the other side. "Shh," Tuck instructed the man. Candice dug in his shoulder holster and took his gun. She threw it in her bag. Then she took his handcuffs.

Tuck tackled the man down to the ground on his stomach, knocking the wind out of him. Before the man could even cough, Candice applied a few pressure points; in a matter of seconds, the man was knocked out. Tuck handcuffed the man's hands behind his back and flipped him over. Candice rushed to loosen his tie. Her hands were shaking fiercely with excitement.

"Hurry up before they miss him," Tuck whispered harshly. Finally the tie came free of the man's neck. Candice was able to double the material and made a gag.

Tuck dragged the man behind the bush he'd been hiding behind and propped him up against the house. Out of sight. Out of mind.

"C'mon," Candice said nervously. Tuck was taking too damn long; even she knew that. Tuck finally emerged. He waved his hands silently, signaling their next move.

Candice slipped inside the front door and went left, while Tuck went right. Backs up against the walls, they began the process of clearing the rooms until they found what they were looking for.

Candice's back hit up against a frame and it swayed precariously on the wall. *Shit!* She turned just a second to steady the picture. Tuck had made it to the doorway. He was waving and pointing, signaling to her that the other two bodyguards were nearby. He needed her to take one; he'd take the other.

Within seconds Candice was right up on his back; the hairs on his neck stood up in response to her rapid breaths behind his ear.

Now they both heard voices.

Candice's heart rate sped up.

The voices were getting closer.

"Where is this guy?" one of the men asked as his voice got louder and louder.

"Now!" Tuck whispered in her ear.

They both rushed through the opening to the hallway; Tuck's gun led the way. The unsuspecting bodyguard turned a sickening shade of white when he came face-to-face with the end of Tuck's gun. Tuck placed his fingers up to the man's lips, ordering his silence.

Tuck dragged the man down and Candice went to work. They handcuffed him, but they didn't bother with the tie this time.

Tuck put up his pointer finger to make the number one. He turned the same finger toward a doorway on the left. He was letting Candice know there was one more threat ahead. But there was still another door to the right, nearly diagonal from them.

Candice knew this meant they'd have to split up. Somebody had to keep their eyeball on the other door to watch for any unaccounted-for and unknown threats. Tuck waved her on to the other door. Then he dipped into the door on the left.

Candice heard the man inside say, "What the . . ." but his words were clipped short. Obviously, the result of a quick blow to the back of his neck.

Candice was in front of the last door. She swallowed hard and tried to slow her rapid breathing. She reached down with her nonshooting hand and twisted the doorknob. The door clicked and it creaked open. With a two-handed grip, she slipped inside the room.

"I'm not ready to eat yet," the man inside scolded; his back was turned to the door. When he didn't get a response, he prepared his tongue to lambaste his shit-for-brains henchmen. He swiveled around in his chair with a scowl on his face. The man's eyes widened at the unexpected sight of the girl with the barrel of a gun aimed at his chest.

"Grayson Stokes? I'm Candice Hardaway. . . . I hear you been looking for me," she announced with the calm of Hannibal Lecter. He followed the gun with his eyes as it went up and came down with a *thwack* on his skull. Stokes growled before he slumped over like a sad heap of bones.

Candice was on the move. She dumped her bag out and retrieved the duct tape to make quick work with Stokes. With her gun tucked under her chin, she stepped behind his chair so he wouldn't have a visual of her. The tip of the tape was finally pulled up from the roll and she taped him to the chair.

"You don't have to do this," Stokes told her. She hit his ass in the shoulder with the end of her gun. His body involuntarily struggled against the restraints; his muscles pushed against his skin. Stokes had been caught off guard; he was attacked in his own home. He couldn't believe he was tied up and rendered helpless by a mere slip of a girl. With all of the things he had done in his life—the murders, the lies, the deceit—he would most likely not die of old age.

"You better start talking. Where are the kids?" Candice growled. Another blow sent a wavering shock over him. He could feel his teeth click in his mouth from the force of the blow. He wouldn't speak.

"Agggh!"

He let out a guttural scream as the end of her gun was driven into his testicles. He didn't know how much more of this he could take. Now he wished he couldn't feel anything . . . anywhere on his body. Another hit drew blood. A fit of coughing followed. The man whirled his head around, trying to will his lungs to fill back up with air. He was angry at his condition; his body had given out years ago, defying him over and over.

If Candice was anything like Barton, she had done her homework well and knew all about his weaknesses. The thought made him angry enough to kill. He gripped the handles of his own chair now. The large green veins in his hands bulged against his liver-spotted skin.

"Where the fuck are the kids?" Candice asked him, but he couldn't answer. He couldn't find the words.

His head—the pain trampling through it.

His ears—the shrill ringing.

It was all too much and rendered him speechless.

Blood leaked down the side of his face and into his left eye. The skin that was his eyebrow had parted wide, exposing pink flesh and white bone.

"Who are you?" he asked, sounding confused.

"Don't fuckin' act like you don't know who I am, you muthafucka!" Candice bellowed.

A maniacal laugh filled his ears.

"You don't know who I am? I thought you were like God. I thought you knew everything and controlled everyone." Her anger was as potent as the venom that dripped off each word.

"You're here to avenge your father? He deserved to die," Stokes said cruelly.

Candice walked over to her bag and retrieved something. Then she walked over to him and turned a box of salt upside down over his open wound. Tuck's Greek friend had hooked her up with a large bag of cooking salt, perfect for just this purpose.

"Agggh!"

Stokes was panting as the stinging from the salt sent a million tiny needles all over his body. Another hit from the gun rocked through his cranium. This time Stokes barely held on to his consciousness.

"I will ask you again for the truth. Where the fuck is Tucker's family?" Candice continued to pour more salt over his open wounds.

The man opened his lips and began to speak, but his tone was a weak whisper.

"I knew you would come. I had been expecting you," Stokes barely managed.

Candice's hands shook now; anticipation was making her antsy. She wanted to blow his fucking brains out, but she had to find out where Tuck's kids were first.

"I knew all of this time you would come," Stokes whispered again. Then his head dropped forward, and his chin hit his chest.

"Good. Then you should've been expecting this," Candice said in an even tone as she lifted her weapon. The man looked up at her out of battered eyes. He locked gazes with Candice. Stokes tried to hold back a coughing fit, but he lost that battle.

"How did you find me?" he asked weakly.

"Don't worry about that!" Candice responded. She was enraged. "Where the fuck are the kids?" She hit him again across the face.

Stokes's mouth filled with blood, making him look like a *Twilight* film extra.

Candice could swear the man was smiling. This angered her even further.

"Wh—why . . . don't you . . . as-ask Agent Tucker where his family is?" Stokes wheezed.

Candice swung her body around. Tuck was standing in the doorway; sweat was dripping down his face.

"He's not telling me anything. Our salt trick didn't work." Candice turned to Tuck.

Stokes began laughing; then another fit of that same cough that Candice recognized from Uncle Rock. Tuck moved into the room but didn't speak. Three goons in black were behind him.

Candice lifted her gun and leveled it at all of them.

Stokes started laughing again. "Can't you see what's going on here, Candy girl?" Stokes asked weakly, true merriment in his voice.

"Shut the fuck up and tell me where the kids are," Candice barked. Her voice was cracking. Things were going downhill fast.

"Ask Tucker," Stokes demanded. His voice was getting stronger now.

Tuck just stood there, silent as a church mouse.

No, not again.

"What is he talking about, Tuck?" Her gun was aimed straight for his head now.

Tuck let out a long breath.

"Don't you know that Agent Tucker would do anything to save his job? From day one he sold his soul to the very devil to make a name for himself. He used you, his wife and even his kids as pawns," Stokes rasped out. He was coughing and wheezing for breath between nearly every word.

Candice's body became engulfed in heat as the gravity of the situation sank in.

"We used you, Candy. All of the people who knew about Operation Easy In are now gone. We couldn't afford for that kind of information to get out," Stokes continued.

Candice looked at Tuck; hurt was evident in her eyes. She readjusted the grip on her gun.

"You better start fuckin' talking, Tuck. You better tell me that muthafucka is lying just to save his own ass!" she screamed. Candice was still holding out hope that this conspiracy theory was just a fluke—that Tuck hadn't sold her out to Stokes to save his own ass.

Tuck didn't say a word. Candice swallowed hard. His silence was louder than any verbal confirmation of the truth.

"You fuckin' traitor bitch!" she screeched. Hot tears were running down her cheeks. "I can't believe I let myself fall for your lies! I should've known a bastard that would go undercover for a year and not care to check on his family was a piece of shit!" Candice screamed. Her gun hand was shaking now, wavering dangerously between Stokes and Tucker. She didn't know which one she wanted to take out first.

"Agent Tucker agreed to lure you here. He knew he could get you here with a story about saving his family. He really did have to save his family from us. You're a Hardaway through and through," Stokes said cruelly. "I guess he sacrificed more than some fling with a revenge-filled little girl," Stokes cackled.

"Shut the fuck up!" Candice screamed, and with one motion she turned and shot Stokes in the head. Blood splattered everywhere. Her gun was back on Tuck within two seconds.

"That's what I came here for. Nothing else matters now," Candice cried, leveling her gun at Tuck's head. He lifted his gun and leveled it at her head in return.

"You know your father was down with the motherfucker who killed my father in the line of fucking duty," Tuck gritted out. "I found that out by reading over your father's fucking books. You're not the only one who craves justice." Tuck's weak eye closed instinctively. *Shoot until the threat is eliminated. Eliminated. Eliminated.* Tuck chanted this mantra in his head.

Candice moved the pad of her finger. *Trigger. Trigger. Trigger.* She was chanting her coda inside her head.

Bang! Bang!

Candice and Tucker lay in a pool of shared blood, like a modern-day version of *Romeo and Juliet,* waiting for their last breaths to leave their bodies. Revenge had not been nearly as sweet and satisfying as they had imagined it to be.

The darkness that engulfed them was cold and unwelcoming. The aftertaste of regret in one's mouth was always bitter.